T0034506

TRACE
OF EVIL

TRACE
OF EVIL

Alice Blanchard

MINOTAUR BOOKS
NEW YORK

This is a work of fiction. All of the characters, organizations, and events portrayed in this novel are either products of the author's imagination or are used fictitiously.

Published in the United States by Minotaur Books, an imprint of St. Martin's Publishing Group

www.minotaurbooks.com

THE LIBRARY OF CONGRESS HAS CATALOGED THE HARDCOVER EDITION AS FOLLOWS:

Names: Blanchard, Alice, author.
Title: Trace of evil / Alice Blanchard.
Description: First Edition. | New York : Minotaur Books, 2019. | Series: Natalie lockhart; 1
Identifiers: LCCN 2019032234 | ISBN 9781250205711 (hardcover) | ISBN 9781250205728 (ebook)
Subjects: LCSH: Murder—Investigation—Fiction. | GSAFD: Mystery fiction.
Classification: LCC PS3552.L36512 T73 2019 | DDC 813/.54—dc23
LC record available at https://lccn.loc.gov/2019032234

ISBN 9781250753052

Our books may be purchased in bulk for promotional, educational, or business use. Please contact your local bookseller or the Macmillan Corporate and Premium Sales Department at 1-800-221-7945, extension 5442, or by email at MacmillanSpecialMarkets@ macmillan.com.

First Trade Paperback Edition: 2020

For Doug, forever

TRACE
OF EVIL

1

Detective Natalie Lockhart pulled into the cemetery and parked in front of a run-down church covered in ivy and twining vines, her hands tightening on the steering wheel. This part of the weed-choked graveyard was isolated and neglected. She sat for a moment, scanning the grounds, chiseled engravings of skull-and-crossbones staring back at her with their hollowed-out eyes. Haunting stuff. The weeds grew tallest around the old slate stones from a cholera outbreak in 1825, obscuring the names of the dead. *Here lyeth Ezekiel Young. God Shelters Goodwife Palmer.*

Natalie shivered and glanced at her watch. Five o'clock. The sky was overcast. The Weather Channel kept predicting rain. Time to do this thing before the downpour ruined everything.

She got out of her smoke-gray Honda Pilot, popped the trunk, and gathered up her supplies—spritzer bottles full of harsh chemicals, a soft-bristle brush, trash bags, a plastic scraper, and her grass clippers. The air smelled of balsam and pitch pine. It was mid-April in Upstate New York, a time of renewal. A time for shedding the past and moving on. Except not today—not for Natalie.

Today was her sister's twentieth deathiversary.

She slammed the trunk and, juggling everything in her arms, proceeded along the overgrown path toward the newer part of the cemetery. At the top of the incline she paused to catch her breath and locate her sister's grave. *Willow Mercy Lockhart.* Fingers of fog curled around the granite slab, creating the impression of a damp loneliness. Willow would have been thirty-eight years old. Natalie was thirty, and her sister, Grace, was thirty-six. Their parents were gone.

Natalie's father, Officer Joseph "Joey" Lockhart, had been blue through and through until the day he died, a proud member of the Burning Lake Police Department for thirty-five years. He spent his career directing traffic, rescuing kittens, breaking up bar fights, and arresting drunk drivers. He was a fitness buff with scruffy brown hair and warm hazel eyes, and his favorite saying was, "Put a fork in us, we're done." As the father of three daughters, he'd always wanted a son, but after his wife put her foot down and said, "No more kids," Joey scooped up his youngest daughter—the one who adored him, the one he'd named after Natalie Wood—and taught her everything he knew about being a cop. Natalie was born with a knack for solving mysteries, Joey claimed. By the age of eight, she'd read all of Agatha Christie's and Sir Arthur Conan Doyle's novels, and she beat everyone at Clue and Trivial Pursuit.

Now Natalie turned up the collar of her cheap jacket. Wow. It got worse every year. She surveyed the graffitied headstones—pentagrams, 666, upside-down crosses, *Redrum.* The grass was littered with crushed beer cans, melted candles, and half-burned incense sticks—evidence of hard-partying kids who were into the occult. The local teenagers liked to speculate about life and hunt for spirits in the town cemeteries, hoping to communicate with the dead. Dabbling in witchcraft was something of a rite of passage in Burning Lake, New York, and Natalie sympathized, since she'd gone through a witchy phase herself—conducting séances, wishing for a boyfriend, hexing her rivals with an acne flare-up or two. *I wanna be a teen witch, fuck you.* The dark side had a powerful appeal in this town.

Natalie got down on the ground and started to clip the weeds around the base of Willow's headstone. She hacked away at the stubborn thistle stems, then sat back and glanced at the swollen sky, which was making ominous rumbling sounds. With a renewed sense of purpose, she picked up the plastic scraper and removed thin shavings of moss from the pink granite. A scrub brush and pump sprayer cleaned it up good. Now for the graffiti—pentacles, horns, hexagrams. The worst one was a resurrection spell calling Willow back to the world of the living. *Come through this Mortal door.* It disgusted Natalie. "Come on," she muttered angrily. "Let her rest in peace."

For centuries, Burning Lake had buried its most shameful secret. In 1712, three innocent women were executed as witches. It all began when two little sisters accused their village neighbors of bewitching them. Panic ensued. Accusations flew. In the end, three "scurrilous, wicked creatures" were convicted of witchcraft—Abigail Stuart, Sarah Hutchins, and Victoriana Forsyth. Many years later, their accusers admitted they'd made it all up.

The town fathers had tried to bury Burning Lake's sordid history for centuries. The city's rebirth began in the 1960s with the completion of the Adirondack Northway, which connected the idyllic beauty of upstate New York with Manhattan. In the 1970s, a book about the witch trials was published to critical acclaim, drawing hundreds of tourists to Burning Lake. By the 1980s, the town realized its potential and went full-bore Salem. A cottage industry blossomed around Abigail, Sarah, and Victoriana. Today, downtown Burning Lake was full of occult gift shops and New Age boutiques selling everything from spell kits to magic crystals. For those residents who were "into the Craft," you could find whatever you needed at the local 7-Eleven—Ouija boards, tarot cards, even a tiny cauldron. Fall was their season. Halloween was huge. There were guided tours, a witch museum, and a monument on Abby's Hex Peninsula, where the executions had taken place. In October, the trees blazed a spectacular orange color, and thousands of tourists came from all over to see the world on fire.

Now Natalie selected a chemical recommended to her by the paint store guy, a shy man with deep-set eyes who had a thing for her, and spritzed the headstone with it, then scrubbed off the offending graffiti until her arms grew tired. Willow had taught her how to hold herself erect and twirl around like a ballerina. She taught Natalie how to make a boat out of newspapers and float it in the lake, how to identify fish in the water. Her favorite was the darting sunfish, small as a hand, flickering in the early summer light.

Willow had woven herself into Natalie and was part of her now, and Natalie couldn't take a step without . . . somehow, somewhere inside her body, feeling Willow's faint presence, like a glimmer of life going on inside a house that was no longer yours. Just a glimpse of a tiny figure dancing back and forth, so tall and slender, so light on her feet.

Ten minutes later, only a "girly skull" sticker remained on the granite slab—an ironic skull-and-crossbones cartoon with a bright pink bow. Natalie used the scraper to chisel away as much of the sticker as she could, then dabbed on paint remover to get rid of the gummy residue.

Finally. Done. She stood up and brushed the grass clippings off her hands. Next she gathered up the beer cans and fast-food wrappers, filling two heavy-duty trash bags. Okay. Best she could do. It was closing in on six o'clock.

On her way downhill, heading back to her car, something caught Natalie's eye—a defaced gravestone with chalk marks covering the speckled granite. The handwriting was nearly impossible to decipher, but she recognized a few shocking words: *fuck, cunt, dead.*

She paused between rows four and five, feeling a stab of anxiety. The name on the headstone—Teresa McCarthy—was one of the nine cold cases she'd been assigned as a rookie detective in the Criminal Investigations Unit. Twenty-one-year-old Teresa was last seen one April morning more than two decades ago, hitching a ride out of town. Teresa had led a troubled life. She was a tweaker, a meth head who scratched her skin so much it was covered in sores. Her sunken eyes conveyed her shrunken dreams. Last year, her parents finally gave up hope of ever finding her alive and had Teresa declared legally dead. There was no body buried here. Just a stone slab to remember her by.

Now the wind stirred Natalie's hair. The graffiti on the grave was not the usual occult bombast—it was scarier than that. The handwriting was mostly illegible, but the ten percent she could make out displayed a unique brand of nastiness and bile—absolute hatred for the deceased. Who would do such a thing? Nobody in town remembered Teresa McCarthy anymore, except for her parents and the detectives who were keeping her cold case alive.

Natalie glanced warily around. None of the other graves in this part of the cemetery had been defiled. During her first year as the designated newbie of the unit, her assigned task was reinvestigating "the Missing Nine"— nine beat-to-hell plastic binders, battered around the edges, their dog-eared pages full of old leads, inconsistent witness testimonies, and dried-up lines of inquiry. All the other detectives in the unit had taken a shot at the Missing Nine and failed. It was tradition to pass the burden along to the newbie, since what was needed was a fresh pair of eyes.

In the past twenty-five years, nine transients had gone missing from Burning Lake, and it was Natalie's turn to find out why. Nine people had vanished off the face of the earth since the mid-1990s—drifters, drug addicts, indigents, alcoholics, the lowest rung of the ladder. The FBI field office briefly got involved back in the mid-2000s, but since the victims were all drifters by nature, it was assumed that they'd drifted on, passing through Burning Lake on their way to warmer destinations. It was difficult at best to keep track of the transient homeless population and freight hoppers who rode the rails.

In the end, the Missing Nine were Burning Lake's problem. These pitiful victims were mostly unloved and forgotten—people whose families had given up on them. With the exception of Teresa McCarthy, there were no graves for them. No deathiversaries. No wilting bouquets of remembrance.

Natalie studied the defiled headstone, every inch of dark granite covered in hastily scribbled words, placed too close together, most of it illegible— and yet the message was clear. *Teresa, shit, pussy, fuck, cunt, dead.* Deeply troubled, she took out her cell phone and snapped as many pictures as she could, while the sky made guttural rumblings in the distance. She leaned down to rub off one of the letters and validate her suspicion—yes, it was chalk. White chalk. Which meant the message would vanish in the oncoming storm. Natalie documented the scene as best she could, then checked her watch again. She didn't want to be late.

2

Natalie put everything away in the trunk of her SUV, used a hand sanitizer, brushed her fingers through her hair, and grabbed the bouquet of marigolds from the backseat. Just in time.

Grace Lockhart drove her Mini Cooper through the cemetery gates, while Grace's fifteen-year-old daughter, Ellie, waved at her aunt through the windshield.

Natalie smiled and waved back.

They got out of the Mini Cooper with their bouquets and silver helium balloons, and Natalie opened her arms wide. Hugs and kisses all around.

"Hi, Aunt Natalie."

"How's it going, kiddo?"

"Pretty good, thanks."

"Hey, sis." Grace was an exceptionally pretty divorcée who hadn't aged a day since high school. She had luminous blue eyes and a halo of golden Botticelli hair. She came across as placid, almost complacent, as if nothing fazed her, but Natalie knew a deeper truth. Grace was a natural-born worrier, the type of person who couldn't prevent everyday problems from weighing heavily on her. She was sensitive to a fault, although you wouldn't know it to look at her. She was a biology teacher at the local high school, and she'd divorced her hedge-fund-manager husband six years ago, when Ellie was nine. Ellie bore the scars of the divorce on her sweet, sad face.

"Sorry we're late," Grace said absently, checking her phone. "Ellie had a thing after school."

"I was with my friends," Ellie clarified.

"Sorry . . . what I meant."

"Mom, where's your head today? Put that thing away."

"Pot. Kettle." Grace smiled and finished checking her text messages.

"You told me to put *my* phone away," Ellie reminded her.

"Just a second."

"Sheesh. Pot. Kettle." Ellie was a stunner, an avid book-reader and the world's biggest cynic. Her lovely, skeptical eyes were a waxy blue. She'd dyed her naturally blond hair raven black in order to distance herself from her mother, but otherwise she was the spitting image of Grace. Ellie was born during a hurricane. The gale-force winds had swept in from the southwest, shaking the traffic lights and fanning the suffocating rains. Lately, she reminded Natalie of a hurricane, with her escalating moods and fiery defiance of her mother's rules.

"Are we all set?" Natalie asked.

"Yeah," Grace said, putting her phone away. "Let's go."

They found Willow's grave and placed their flowers at the base of the headstone, while Ellie handed out the balloons—one each. Every year, they performed the same simple yet heartfelt ceremony. First, they took turns telling Willow what had transpired since her last deathiversary; then they said a silent prayer; finally they released their balloons.

"Ellie, you go first," Grace said. "I'll go next, and Natalie, you're last."

"Wow, you're like a well-mannered bulldozer," Natalie joked.

Ellie giggled. "Mom's used to ordering her students around."

"I don't order anyone around," Grace protested.

"Then why are you rushing us?"

"Because I hate graveyards," Grace admitted with a shudder.

"You always do this," Ellie protested softly. "Every year, you come up with some excuse to leave early."

"No, I don't." Grace blushed. "Do I?"

Ellie turned to Natalie and asked, "Was she always this superstitious?"

"Grace is the most superstitious person I know."

"It's like . . . if I spill a grain of salt," Ellie said with a derisive snort, "she'll toss a pinch over her shoulder. If we come across a ladder or a black cat, she'll walk in the other direction. It's crazy."

"Go ahead and mock your mother. I can take it." Grace rolled her eyes. "Honey, you're up," she coached her daughter.

Ellie shuffled her feet. She was rail-thin, with an upturned nose, and today she was dressed all in black—black nail polish, black boots, a black lace blouse, black jeans. She was growing out her bangs, and you could see her sly eyes through a curtain of hair, the suggestion of mischief in her adolescent mouth. "Okay, well, um . . . Aunt Willow, I've been wondering lately . . . what it must feel like to lie underground, year after year, while everyone who visits your grave is so sad . . . all that negative karma must drive you nuts. And so I want you to know I'm feeling happy for you today, instead of sad, because you're beyond all the bogus BS."

"Ellie," Grace said.

"Well, she is," she insisted. "She's moved on, and we haven't. We're still wallowing in the past. Meanwhile, she's out there, flowing free with the wind and the water and . . ."

Grace put a hand on Ellie's shoulder. "Honey, just tell your poor aunt what happened since her last deathiversary," she pleaded. "C'mon, you know the drill. You've had all year to think about this."

Ellie glanced at Natalie, who refused to take sides. With a sigh, she said, "All right. I got straight As again this year, just like last year. Probably because I'm so good at regurgitating whatever my teachers tell me and sitting quietly for hours, like a good little conformist. I'm an upstanding member of the Honor Society who does what she's told . . . basically I'm Pavlov's dog. Mom thinks I'm a genius. She's my helicopter mommy."

Grace gasped. "Good grief. Where on earth did you come up with that?"

"What?" Ellie said.

Grace turned to Natalie. "Am I a *helicopter mommy*?"

Natalie felt the surprise in the pit of her stomach. This child knew herself. She seemed so utterly self-possessed, so very much her own person, that Natalie felt a little lost by comparison.

"Well, it's the truth," Ellie said obstinately. "School is mostly bogus. Anyone can get straight As. It's all about obedience and rote memory."

Grace grew disheartened. Her posture wilted. She lived off Burke Guzman's alimony payments, but teaching was her passion. "Can we talk about this later, honey?"

Ellie nodded and said, "Anyway, I've never met you, Aunt Willow, but I hope you've found peace. Perfect peace." She smiled softly. "Okay, Mom. Your turn."

Grace didn't bat an eye, she just launched into a recitation of last year's activities, hitting all the highlights—two weeks in Martha's Vineyard; a weekend in Boston to check out Harvard and MIT; Christmas in Bermuda. They were thinking of Harvard or Yale, maybe Columbia or Princeton. Ellie was in the top one percent of her class and doing great. Everything was great. Great, great, great. It was seven minutes and counting before she ran out of brag.

Then came Natalie's turn. She never knew exactly what to say in these situations, since she preferred to grieve in private, like her father, Joey.

"Well, let's see," she said. "Zack got a job offer, and I didn't feel like moving to Seattle, so we decided to separate. Test the waters." That wasn't the whole truth. Zack Stadler, Natalie's boyfriend of three years, had left her after a bitter fight during which unforgivable things were said. Zack hated that there was a gun in the house, whereas Natalie had grown up with a gun in the house. Zack hated the autopsy photos she occasionally left out on her desk, whereas Natalie had grown up with autopsy photos on her father's desk. Zack really didn't want a cop for a girlfriend, although he'd initially been fascinated by her uniform, her bulletproof vest, her duty belt, her handcuffs, her police baton, her tactical boots, and of course the gun and extra magazines. But once the sex got old, their relationship died. During their final year together, Zack seemed to be fuming underneath the surface, repressing his resentment, which he took out on Natalie by fucking her from behind, always turning her over so he wouldn't have to look at her indifferent face. Zack wanted prestige, he wanted status, he wanted much more than a town like Burning Lake could offer. And so, eight months ago, he'd packed his belongings and relocated to Seattle, where he went to work for a promising e-zine that covered the art scene. Natalie didn't feel bitter or heartsick about it, so much as empty. They used to mock other cardboard couples. In the end, they began to mock each other.

Now Grace and Ellie were watching her closely. She ignored the looks of sympathy and talked about her job, some of the domestic abuse cases she'd solved, some of the brutal men she'd put away.

When she was done, they all held hands, said a silent prayer, and released the balloons, which slithered into the fog like jellyfish.

"Mom, I'm going to take pictures of the graves," Ellie said.

"Sure, go ahead." Once the sisters were alone together, Grace said, "Wow. Twenty years."

Natalie nodded. "Hard to believe."

Twenty years ago, Willow Lockhart had been savagely murdered by a jealous boyfriend behind the Hadleys' old barn. Stabbed twenty-seven times. When Natalie's mother heard the news, she screamed until her voice wore out. Sixteen-year-old Grace ran upstairs and vomited in the bathtub. Joey collapsed on the sofa, tears streaming down his face and dripping off his chin, like a drooling baby's. Ten-year-old Natalie punched her fist through the mesh screen door and sprained her wrist. Days of mourning followed brutal loneliness. Her parents' fights late at night. Phone calls from the media.

Now Natalie couldn't help but feel that their grief had diminished over time, like a fading newspaper obituary. Every year, they stood in this same spot, summoning up the old heartbreak, but the loss wasn't half as sharp or bitter as it had once been. Today felt more like an obligation. Like something to check off the to-do list.

"She's growing up so fast," Grace said of her daughter, who was traipsing among the weathered fieldstones, snapping pictures. "It's a little scary."

"She's a good kid," Natalie reassured her. "You raised her right."

"One minute she's my adorable little girl, and the next thing I know, she's screaming at me like a banshee. Everything's always my fault. She wants to get as far away from me as humanly possible." Grace kept a careful eye on Ellie, who was taking pictures of a half-melted candle in front of a particularly decrepit grave. "Last night, for instance, she texted me IN ALL CAPS from the other room. And I told her—you need to come in here and talk to me face-to-face. I need to see you in real life."

"She's just testing the limits."

"Fifteen, right? I guess it's normal," Grace said with a tired, proud smile. "She reminds me of you at that age."

"Yeah?"

"Totally."

Not really, Natalie thought. Grace couldn't have remembered, because she had been six years older and living away from home by the time Natalie turned fifteen. Everything about being a teenager was difficult. Fifteen was a confusing, in-between age for a girl. You weren't a child anymore, but you weren't a full-grown woman yet. Life wasn't rainbows-and-kittens anymore. The clouds weren't made of cotton candy, other kids could be cruel, boys were suddenly interested, and it was up to you to navigate your way through this mess called adolescence, where your hormones kept pushing you toward spontaneous combustion.

"Anyway, she's acing all her classes. Blowing away the competition. My little brainiac." A damp gust made a play for Grace's golden hair. She patted it down and said, "Did you check out that dating app I sent you?"

"God, no." Natalie laughed. "Lol."

Her sister's pale forehead crimped with worry. "Eight months is a long enough time to waste on a broken relationship, Natalie. You should go out there and mix it up."

"Mix things up?" Natalie winced. "What is this, the nineties?"

"I'm serious. I started dating a few months after the divorce."

"Grace, you've been dating your entire life."

She smiled and shrugged. "I can't help it if I'm not as picky as you."

To the left of Willow's grave were Joey's and Deborah's plots. To the right of Willow's grave were two empty plots reserved for Natalie and Grace. Neither one of them wanted to be buried here. Grace rubbed her shivering arms and said, "We should really sell those stupid plots, don't you think?"

Natalie nodded. "Yeah, it's probably time."

"Just scatter my ashes somewhere pretty," Grace said. "Better for the planet that way. Less creepy than being buried here for all eternity. No offense, Mom and Dad." Her phone buzzed. She checked the number. "It's Burke," she said anxiously. "I have to take this. He wants to increase visitation rights, but then he shouldn't have signed the divorce agreement, right?" Grace's ex-husband, Burke Guzman, lived in Manhattan and was never around, so it fell on Grace's shoulders to raise their only child. "I don't want Ellie to overhear this. I'll wait for you in the car, okay?"

"Sure. It's going to rain soon anyway. We'll be down shortly."

Grace headed down the hill. "Burke?"

After a moment, Ellie looked up and noticed her mother was gone. She pocketed her phone, walked over to Natalie, and said, "You were in a coven once, weren't you, Aunt Natalie?"

"Yeah, sure. We all were, for a short period of time."

She tilted her head. "Why'd you quit?"

"The coven?" Natalie hesitated. "It got pretty dark."

"How dark?" Ellie asked, her face tensing with interest.

"My friends and I decided to stop. We moved on to other things."

"Your friends . . . including the girl who disappeared?"

"Bella. Yes. Only she didn't disappear," Natalie explained. "She ran off to California on the eve of our high school graduation."

Ellie tugged on her earlobe. "Did you ever see her again?"

"No. In fact, I never heard from her again."

"Oh." She frowned. "Then how do you know she's alive?"

"She sent a bunch of postcards to her parents. No return address. I don't think she wanted to be found."

"Why not?"

"Long story," Natalie said. Because her father was sexually abusing her, she thought, the old anger simmering just underneath the surface. "How did you find out about that?"

"Mom mentioned it once or twice," Ellie explained. "How dark did it get? In the coven?"

Natalie smiled warmly at her. "Where are these questions coming from, Ellie?"

"I'm just curious," the girl replied with deeper interest than mere curiosity.

Natalie nodded and said, "Bella and I thought it would be fun to explore Wicca, so we chose our witch names and slept under a full moon, you know . . . the whole nine yards. Black lipstick, astrology, Elvira streaks in our black hair. It was scary fun . . . until it wasn't. I'm guessing you're asking me about this now because you're in a coven?"

Ellie's pretty blue eyes widened. "How'd you guess?"

"Gee, I dunno." Natalie smiled warmly at her. "Maybe it's the hair that clued me in. Or the all-black outfit. Or the reference to wind, water, earth, and fire."

Storm clouds were rolling in. Ellie kicked at the grass clippings. "Mom hates anything witchy. She says she saw a ghost once during a séance, and it scared the bejeezus out of her. She says that's how she became so superstitious, because of the coven. She won't even let me get a tattoo. All my friends have them. It's no big deal."

Natalie shook her head. "Are you kidding me? It's a huge deal."

"India has one. Why can't I?"

Sixteen-year-old India Cochran was Ellie's best friend—a natural beauty with almond-shaped eyes and raven black hair, and just like the rest of Ellie's friends, a high achiever. Honor Society, debating team, class secretary two years in a row. "Since when did India get a tattoo?"

"Last summer. Besides," Ellie stubbornly went on, "Mom's got a tat over her left boob, which makes her a hypocrite."

"When you're young, all adults seem like hypocrites."

"*Seem* like?"

Natalie smiled indulgently. "Does Grace know you're in a coven?"

Ellie's face flushed. "No. And please don't tell her, Aunt Natalie."

"I won't. But you should talk to her about it. She might surprise you."

"Trust me." Ellie rolled her eyes. "She'll be furious."

"Look, your mom hasn't had an easy life. It may appear easy on the surface, but Grace is very sensitive. She cares a lot. Maybe too much. She only wants what's best for you."

Ellie glanced skyward. "Can I ask you something else?"

"Shoot."

"What happened to you and Zack?"

Natalie heaved a sigh—her niece was all over the place tonight. "A relationship can swallow you up. At first it was exhilarating, but after a while, it felt claustrophobic."

"Why?"

"Zack had to have an explanation for everything. He knew everything there was to know. He had to win every argument. And I let him, because it was too exhausting not to. After a while, we stopped communicating. And that's death to coupledom."

"What a horse's ass," Ellie muttered, the color rising in her cheeks.

Natalie tucked her hands in the pockets of her jacket. "We were just wrong for each other, Ellie. It took us both a while to figure that out. But I'm much happier now."

"How come?"

"Dodged a bullet."

With a loud clap of thunder, the sky opened up, and it began to pour. A flat-out torrent. They'd forgotten their umbrellas, so they ran down the access road together.

Grace waved at them from inside the Mini Cooper while Ellie hugged her aunt good-bye and hopped in the car, little loops of hair sticking to her pale face.

Grace rolled down her window and said, "Next time, Natalie, I promise, we'll have dinner afterwards. Like a *pro-pah* deathiversary."

"Sounds like a plan," Natalie said, knowing next time would be no different. She watched as the Mini Cooper backed down the crumbling road toward the cemetery gates. Soon the taillights disappeared into the fog.

Drenched to the skin, Natalie got in her car, started the engine, and turned on the wipers. The rain made ever-changing streaks of amethyst on the glass. She could feel the fury of the storm as it approached from the south, could feel it booming through the hills and darkening the air, stirring the trees and driving the birds to seek shelter—how did they hang on?

She switched on her high beams and studied the fractal intricacy of the yellow foxtail growing by the side of the road. Twenty years ago today, Willow was stabbed to death by a self-proclaimed rebel who liked to dress all in black—black T-shirt, black denim jeans, black Chucks, jet-black hair. Natalie used to think Justin Fowler was cool. Now he wore prison orange and was serving a life sentence for first-degree murder.

You never got over it.

Rest in peace, Willow. Same time next year.

3

In a midsize town like Burning Lake, New York—population 50,000—there were slow days down at the police station, and then there were crazy days. As a general rule, their call volume held fairly steady and wasn't as high as the typical caseloads you'd find in Albany or Syracuse, but the BLPD was busier than most of the sleepier burgs south of the Adirondack Mountains. They popped a lot of DUIs and had their share of domestic disturbances. This idyllic rural American town wasn't supposed to have a drug problem, but in the past decade or so, methamphetamines and opioids had flooded into the upstate market. Black tar—a low-grade form of heroin that was cheap to buy and came in little balloons you could hide in your mouth while cruising around—was taking over the west side of town, where the residents had been hardest hit by the economic downturn.

Downtown Burning Lake was clean and safe for the most part, and the business community worked hard to keep it that way. Main Street with its Victorian-era brick buildings and tree-lined sidewalks featured plenty of jazz clubs, bookshops, cafés, and art galleries. There was a summer music festival, a historical museum, and a performing arts center that headlined off-Broadway plays. Besides a myriad of cultural events, Burning Lake also boasted an enormous state park where you could go hiking, rock climbing, bike riding, skiing, and fishing. Not that the town was perfect. Far from it. The winters were bitterly cold. Heating bills could be a burden. Sometimes there was nothing to do. One of the main activities for the locals, especially during those long winter months, was drinking. Finding a bar wasn't difficult in upstate New York, where it could dip to twenty below in the winter and the waterfalls could freeze solid.

Tonight, Natalie found a convenient parking spot—a rare occurrence during happy hour in the commercial district—got out, and dashed through the rain, splashing through the puddles. She ducked into the Barkin' Dawg Saloon, very popular with law enforcement officers. Every Wednesday night, the lieutenant would get together with his staff over chili dogs and Rolling Rocks at the Barkin' Dawg to discuss any unresolved issues they might be having in the unit, a tight-knit group of seven detectives on rotating shifts who shared one week of "on-call duty" per month.

This week was Natalie's turn, lucky her. She checked her pager to make sure it was working and ordered a mineral water at the bar instead of her usual pinot grigio. No wine, no sleeping pills. You had to be alert and available twenty-four/seven.

The balding bartender didn't acknowledge her right away. Windom Petrowski had a ruddy, pocked face and huge strong arms from lugging around kegs and crates. He made no secret of the fact that he didn't think Natalie deserved the rank of detective and resented her promotion over his cousin, Officer Ronnie Petrowski.

"I'm on-call tonight, Windom," she said. "Just a mineral water, thanks."

He took his sweet time, serving another customer first, wiping down glasses, and counting out cash. Natalie leaned against the polished mahogany and decided to wait him out. The Criminal Investigations Unit consisted of six male detectives, one male technical expert, and the BLPD's first female detective—Natalie. In Windom's eyes, she was a diversity hire, but everybody knew that wasn't true. She'd come up in the ranks with the rest of the recruits—working foot patrol, directing traffic, volunteering for overtime, taking any shit detail she could. In fact, out of a desire to prove herself beyond reproach, Natalie had worked twice as hard as everyone else. Fortunately, the guys in the unit were cool with it. Only Windom and a few others weren't.

A few minutes passed before Windom strolled over and handed her a sparkling mineral water with a wedge of lime. She was tempted to give him lip for the lousy attitude. The BLPD was a high-testosterone zone. The language could get pretty coarse. Fortunately for Natalie, she had quite a mouth on her from all those years of hanging out with her father's cop buddies. When in Rome.

She took the high road instead and thanked him, asked about his wife and kids, asked about his job and how things were going, softened him up a little, left a modest tip, and wished him a good evening. Then she made her way through the bar, which was packed tonight. The flickering red candles on all the round tables gave the place its special glow. The waitresses were known for their sarcastic, ballbusting wit. Natalie spotted Lieutenant Luke Pittman in one of the back booths—he was alone, which was odd, because it was only seven thirty, and these bullshit sessions of theirs typically dragged on until eight or nine o'clock. So where were the guys?

"Hey," she said, approaching the booth with her Perrier and lime. "Sorry I'm late."

"Natalie. We weren't expecting you tonight," Luke said.

She shrugged. "It started to rain, so we ended it early."

"How'd it go?" he asked with a sympathetic smile.

"Feels like the past is fading away. And that makes me sad."

Thirty-eight-year-old Luke had the kind of handsome, weathered face that suited his chipped, rugged personality. He and Natalie had known each other since he was thirteen and she was five. Luke's father had abandoned him, and his mother had to work two jobs to keep them afloat. It wasn't long before Luke was hanging out with the Lockhart girls in their backyard. He'd been there during the most crucial events in Natalie's life. They shared such a rich history together that their current situation felt a little awkward at times, as if they were forever stepping over the line, and then retreating. She used to have a dreamy-eyed crush on Luke Pittman, but their timing was always off due to the eight-year age difference. By the time

Natalie hit puberty, Luke was in college. By the time she'd kissed a boy, Luke was getting married and having a baby. By the time she entered college, he was divorced and in the army, being deployed overseas. By the time she joined the BLPD, Luke was a rock-star detective and Natalie was dating Zack.

Now she pointed out the empty beer mugs on the table. "Okay, I give up. Where'd everybody go?"

He shrugged laconically. "I guess things have been pretty smooth sailing down at the station lately."

"Yeah, right. I work with six prima donnas, and I know that's a load of crap."

"Oh, you wanted the truthful answer. My bad." He grinned. "You didn't miss a thing, Natalie. I fielded a bunch of complaints and gave my usual spiel about budget cuts. They grumbled a lot. Brandon's still here. He's taking a leak."

"What kind of complaints?" she asked.

"Legit stuff. Nothing I can do anything about."

"Let me guess. Overworked, underpaid, lack of equipment?"

"Hey, you're good," he said with a warm grin. "I told them I'd bring it up at the next meeting with the chief, but I can't promise anything."

"There's my girl!" Detective Buckner came tumbling out of the men's room with all the galloping enthusiasm of a puppy. At thirty-six, Brandon was a big guy, with a round face and twinkly brown eyes, but hyperactive and enthusiastic about everything. "Shove over," he said, and Natalie made room for him in the booth. "How did it go tonight? The deathiversary?"

"Sad but healing," she said.

"Here's to Willow." Brandon raised his shot glass.

"To Willow, may she rest in peace," Luke said, and they all clinked glasses.

Brandon Buckner hadn't been Luke's first choice for detective, second grade, but Brandon's rich-as-Midas father and the mayor were good friends, and Chief Snyder had a long-standing alliance with both men. Fortunately for everyone, Brandon turned out to be an okay guy. Not the sharpest knife in the drawer, but funny. Quick on his feet. Loyal. Sincere. Now he knocked back his drink and said, "Christ, I'm thirsty." He signaled the waitress, who was way ahead of them.

Anorexic Teena swung by with another round. "A Rolling Rock for the lieu, a Perrier for the lady detective, and a whiskey double-neat for the biggest dick in town."

"Hey, I resemble that remark," Brandon said with a hearty laugh, and when Teena didn't reciprocate, he said, "You should eat something, Teena. You're a stick figure."

"Brandon," Luke groaned.

"Don't you make fun of my girl," Natalie scolded him.

"Go ahead. Keep spewing your diarrhea, frat boy," Teena said and walked away.

"Did she call me fat?" He looked down at his belly.

"Does Daisy approve of you being such an asshole?" Luke demanded to know.

"Daisy loves me. The whole beautiful package."

"Pfft. You and your fairy-tale marriage," Luke muttered.

"Speaking of which . . . big news." Brandon downed his shot and clapped the empty glass on the table. "We're pregnant. Ta-da."

"Hey, that's great news," Natalie said, genuinely happy for them. "Congratulations, Brandon."

"Right?" He grinned. "Drumroll, please."

It wasn't a secret that the Buckners had been trying to get pregnant for years now. Daisy Buckner, Grace's best friend since kindergarten, had suffered through two previous miscarriages.

"Daisy wouldn't let me spill the beans until after the first trimester," Brandon explained. "She couldn't face losing another one in front of the whole town, but the doc says three months is a good enough milestone."

"I'm thrilled for you guys," Natalie told him.

"Believe that? I'm gonna be a daddy." He shook his head, dumbstruck.

Luke's eyes softened with a faraway look. "Skye used to listen to Motown when she was little. 'Dancing in the Street' was her favorite song."

"Yeah, huh?" Brandon said encouragingly, since Luke rarely mentioned his daughter. Sixteen-year-old Skye Pittman lived in California with her mother, Luke's ex-wife, and it pained him to talk about it.

"I helped her make cookies shaped like bees once," Luke said, stroking his chin.

"Bees? Why bees?" Natalie asked.

"Why not?" He laughed, his eyes straying from the beer label to look at her. Luke's eyes had a gorgeous laziness about them tonight. He had a rangy, predatory grace, and she could picture his cynical, hip boyhood face superimposed over his no-nonsense, grown-up face. It made her smile. He was still there, underneath the professional veneer. Mocking authority and dreaming about his future.

"That's sweet," Natalie said.

"Hey, Teena! Over here!" Brandon signaled the waitress for another round. "Is she on strike or something? She keeps ignoring me. Hey, Teena!" He made another drunken swipe at the air, and Luke batted his hand away. "Ow."

"I'd stay out of the deep end of the bar if I were you, Brandon."

"Yeah, this is not a good look for you," Natalie agreed.

"You have to cut this shit out. You're going to be a father."

"C'mon, Lieutenant. I'm buying."

"You've celebrated enough." Luke scooped up Brandon's car keys from the table.

"Hey!" Brandon reached for his keys, but Luke held them out of reach.

"I'll take him home," Natalie volunteered.

"You sure?" Luke said.

"Yeah, no problem."

He handed Natalie the keys, then fished out his wallet and dropped a couple of twenties on the table.

"You leaving already, Lieutenant?" Brandon said with disappointment.

"Got to split."

"Party pooper," he said, sulking.

Luke stood up. "See you tomorrow, Natalie."

"Same bat-time, same bat-station," she said, keeping it light.

The way he studied her made her nervous. But he looked at everyone that way—dead ahead, like a cougar, sizing you up. Measuring your worth. "Don't keep my best detective too long, Brandon. She's on-call this week."

"Yes, sir." Brandon winked at Natalie.

Luke walked away, and they watched him tip the waitresses on his way out of the bar. As soon as he was gone, Natalie pocketed Brandon's keys.

His eyes narrowed to stubborn slits. "Jesus, I'm not that drunk."

"Are you kidding me? You're drunk enough to make a DUI stick. Drunk enough to make our stupid-busts list. Drunk enough to get your wife thoroughly pissed at you. Do you want me to call Daisy? Because I will."

"Daisy doesn't get mad at me. I told you, she loves me. . . ."

"Right, the whole sorry package." Natalie stood up. "C'mon, let's go."

The bar walls, like a pair of lungs, had absorbed decades of secondhand smoke. The lizard-skinned bouncer, Mickey, sat on his leather-padded stool watching ESPN. A bunch of locals were taking potshots at one another. Brandon grabbed a bottle of bourbon on his way out, and Natalie had to pry it from his sweaty hands.

"Quit embarrassing yourself," she said with exasperation.

He laughed. "I sincerely enjoy messing with your head."

They walked out of the bar together, sidestepping big puddles. Neon-blue lettering blinked on and off in the dusty plate-glass windows. Outside, the rain had blown away, and the evening mist slowly swirled up into the atmosphere.

"Seriously, Brandon. It's time to cut back on the drinking."

He stopped walking and just looked at her, his gaze slightly mocking.

"What?" she said, irritated.

"You and Luke."

"Shut up." She laughed dismissively but could feel the familiar tightening of her facial muscles, a physical reaction that occurred whenever Brandon—who prided himself on his candor—got too personal for comfort.

"Come on," he said, studying her with excruciating honesty. "Ain't no big thang. This is a small town, Natalie. Everybody knows everyone else's dirty laundry. Besides, I can see the way he looks at you. Especially since you dumped that loser boyfriend of yours . . ."

She cringed. "Keep digging yourself a deeper hole. Go ahead."

"Relax. I'm busting your chops."

"Well, cut it out! Quit trolling me."

"Sorry." He threw up his hands in surrender. "You know I love you, Nat."

"Love you, too, you big dope." She opened the passenger door for him. "Now get in, before I arrest you for loitering."

4

The distant mountains stole moisture from the clouds and soaked the county in forty inches of rain per year. Dense woods of jack pine, red maple, and yellow birch tumbled across the landscape, cloaking the valley in a lush green growth. Driving with the windows down, Natalie breathed in the chilly April air and felt an invigorating rush. As they crested the next hill, she could see the glittery lights of downtown in her rearview mirror. The frozen months of winter had left big potholes in the road, and one of these bumps woke Brandon up.

"Uh," he hiccupped, producing a beer bottle from his jacket like a magician.

She glanced over at him disapprovingly. "Where'd you get that?"

"Ain't sayin'."

"Seriously, Brandon. What's up with the drinking lately?"

"Nothing's up. Dickwise, that is."

She shot him a look. "What's that supposed to mean?"

"Nothing. We're fine. Everything's fine," he muttered.

"Who's fine?" she asked suspiciously.

This was a small community, surrounded by thick woods like a fairy-tale kingdom, and it was true—everybody knew everyone else's business, or at least people assumed they did. Brandon wasn't a problem drinker, but he'd been getting drunk after work lately—twice this week, three times last week, a worrisome trend. Natalie wanted to know why.

"I just felt like getting staggeringly wasted tonight, okay? So shoot me." He took a defiant swig of beer, rolled down his window, and chucked the bottle into the night. "There. Happy now?"

"Jerk. You just littered."

"I'm a deeply flawed human being," he admitted, raking his fingers through his brown, medium-length hair until it jutted out all over. "Stay for dinner, Nat? I'll let Daisy know you're coming."

"Sorry, Brandon. I can't tonight."

He ignored her and called home. "Huh," he said after a moment. "She's not picking up."

"That's okay. I can't stay for dinner."

Brushing her off, Brandon tried again. "Come on, babe. Pick up."

The car rolled toward its destination through an endless expanse of woods—there weren't many streetlights out this way. It got pretty dark and eerie out in the countryside, where the brambled trees reached for the moon. The wind blew year-round in Burning Lake, sweeping in from the southwest and deforming the hemlocks and sycamores over time, until they became as gnarled as old crones. At the heart of autumn, the constant winds made a haunting, ghostlike lamentation.

"Hey, did I show you my new barbecue yet?" Brandon asked, fumbling with his iPhone and swiping through the images. "Check this out. Thirty-six-inch grill, stainless-steel hood, rear-mounted rotisserie . . . she's a beaut, huh?"

"Awesome."

"And look at this," he said excitedly, still swiping. "I got so sick of my front yard looking like crap every Christmas, I decided to plant some evergreen trees, you know? Spruce things up a bit. Ha-ha. But then I found out there's more to it than that."

"More to it than what?" she asked, glancing at digital pictures of Brandon's torn-up front yard.

"It's called winter landscaping. You plant a bunch of colorful berries, like red-twig dogwood and Christmas holly," Brandon explained, showing her the results. "See? Yew bushes will catch the snow in their branches, and bayberry smells like the holidays. My house is gonna look like a fucking Christmas card this year." He put his phone away and sighed. "Okay, so my marriage isn't perfect."

She looked at him, startled by this admission.

"They say it's only natural. We've been married for twelve fucking years."

"Things are good enough, though, right?" she hedged. "With the baby coming?"

He shrugged it off, which disturbed her.

The clouds parted, and a frost of moonlight dappled the surface of the lake. Natalie took a left onto Lost Pines Road, which snaked through the gorgeous wooded countryside that used to belong to the Native Americans, then to the French fur traders, then to the Jesuit missionaries, then the pork farmers, and finally the apple farmers. Now it was a booming tourist destination with a budding technology sector. At least, that was what the town website wanted you to believe.

"I fell in love with Daisy in the fifth grade," Brandon said quietly. "She wrote this poem about shoes . . . how a person's footwear can tell you everything you need to know about them. God, she was cute. She said my sneakers looked comfortable enough to curl up in. That cracked me up. Anyway, life goes on, and then one day, you wake up, and suddenly you aren't on the same page anymore." He wore a look of frustration. "Daisy's satisfied with what we've got—a house, a car, a barbecue. Life's simple for her. It's a series of goals."

She glanced at his sweaty face in the moonlight. "But not for you?"

"Hell, no."

Natalie didn't know how to respond to any of this. Brandon had done nothing but brag about his marriage for as long as she'd known him.

"My wife's smart. Book-smart. She likes to read and think about stuff intellectually, whereas I prefer to get my hands dirty. Dig around in the dirt, you know? Like with the winter landscaping. I'm a spiritual person, and whenever I look at the sky and the stars . . . it moves me. But Daisy will spout a bunch of facts and figures, very cut and dry. Anyway, our sex life . . ." He shook his head.

"I'm sorry to hear it." She winced.

"Too much information, huh? Maybe the lieutenant is right. Me and my fairy-tale marriage. Pfft." He put the phone to his ear. "Still not picking up," he grumbled. "Funny, I told her I'd be home by eight."

Wolf Pass Road was home to generations of hardworking families and boasted some of the most beautiful Victorians and Gothics in town, painted all colors of the rainbow to highlight the original trim work. By midsummer, these historic residences would be swimming in oceans of black-eyed Susans and tangerine touch-me-nots.

"Listen," Brandon clarified, "my marriage isn't in trouble or anything. I love Daisy, and she loves me. We've been through some bad patches before. Maybe it's just the stress of being pregnant again, having all our hopes and dreams wrapped up in this baby . . . I don't know."

Natalie pulled into the driveway and parked next to Daisy's green minivan. Strange. The house lights were off. The property was completely dark—no porch or yard lights. The gabled house was bathed in moonlight.

Brandon got out and stood swaying in the front yard as if he were standing at the helm of a ship. The lawn was freshly seeded, and there were newly planted shrubs around the foundation with the price tags still attached—part of his winter landscaping scheme, she figured.

"Daisy?" Brandon shouted at the house.

Natalie left her keys in the ignition and followed him across the yard. On the wide front porch was a wrought-iron table and chairs with a floral centerpiece straight out of *Better Homes & Gardens*.

Brandon opened the door and banged his way inside. "Daisy? I'm home!"

Natalie prevented the screen door from slamming shut in her face and followed him inside. The first floor was open concept, with a long cherrywood bar dividing the living room from the kitchen area. Brandon brushed the light switch with his hand, and several designer spots cast a pale hue over the handsome built-ins crowded with sports memorabilia—football trophies and team letters.

"Babe?" Brandon said as he headed for the kitchen.

Natalie tensed. The air smelled vaguely familiar—earthy, coppery. A stiffness invaded her limbs as she followed him into the kitchen, then froze in the doorway. Daisy Buckner lay in a puddle of blood at the base of the refrigerator. She wore faded Levi's, a pullover top, and a pair of Marc Jacobs low tops. Her glassy eyes were open. Her arms and legs were sprawled across the floor. There was an ugly gash on the right side of her head, and her short red hair was matted with blood.

Brandon dropped to his knees as he tried to suck some relief out of the air. He crawled across the tiled floor toward his wife, and before Natalie could secure the scene, he was cradling her limp body in his arms. His mouth moved fishlike as he tried to produce a sound, but nothing came out. He sat there rocking his dead wife back and forth, silenced by grief, while Natalie stared at the bright spatter of blood arcing across the refrigerator and kitchen cabinets. A single can of soda had rolled against the base of the dishwasher, and there was a greasy cast-iron skillet on the floor not far from the body, and a smattering of cooked ground beef on the Mexican tiles. A blue-checkered dish towel lay crumpled nearby.

"Brandon?" She gently plied his shoulder. "You're contaminating the scene."

His eyes were frosted with shock. "What?"

"We need to protect the evidence. Put her down."

He shook his head viciously. "Back off!"

Her mind spun like a compass needle. They were wasting precious seconds. It felt like an eternity. She radioed Dispatch to report the crime, then pried Brandon away from the body. After propping him in the doorway, she checked for a pulse on Daisy's neck. Of course she was dead, but you had to make sure.

"I can't breathe," Brandon gasped, his eyes jerking in all directions.

"Stay there," Natalie commanded. "Don't touch anything."

She tested Daisy's skin for lividity. The blood had settled into the lower regions of her body due to the pull of gravity. A purple discoloration was noticeable on the lower sides of her arms, hands, and neck—all of which were bruised from blood vessels filling with red blood cells and coagulating inside her veins, skin, and muscle. There was no pulse. Her skin was cool to the touch. Her pupils were of differing sizes. The position of the body had been compromised. Because of Brandon's actions, there was the possibility of cross-transfer of prints, fibers, and hairs. Natalie placed the body back where they'd found it originally—or as close to that position as she could recall. Daisy had been dead for several hours now.

Her heart began to pound with an explosive mixture of adrenaline and fear. She tamped down her anxiety and had a flash-memory of the boy in the woods. *The stick. The dead rdccoon.* A sour taste filled her mouth. A snowy dullness crept over her.

Natalie shook it off. She had to stay focused. For a few miserable seconds, she couldn't pry her eyes away from the refrigerator magnets that had slid off the stainless-steel door and landed in a darkening pool of blood. SpongeBob, Lisa Simpson, Wonder Woman.

Focus.

Thirty-six-year-old Daisy Forester Buckner was a petite redhead, five foot four, maybe a hundred pounds soaking wet. She looked like a Barbie doll come to life, with her perfect teeth and hair. Her gemlike eyes drew you in. Her sleek red hair was cut short, and she wore very little makeup. It was common knowledge around town that Daisy had been having trouble getting pregnant. Finally, she'd managed a small triumph. Now she and the baby were dead.

Natalie had known Daisy Forester all her life. They'd grown up on the same street together. BFF's Daisy and Grace were the same age and had always been close. Now they were teachers at the same school, but when they were younger, they'd wanted to be Olympic gold medalists, swimmers as famous as Janet Evans. They were self-proclaimed water nymphs. For Natalie, who was eight years younger than Willow and six years younger than Grace, it felt like having two extra moms. Cool moms. And Daisy was a bonus mom. The three older girls had spoiled her silly. They'd piled on the love. They'd doled out Skittles and Reese's Pieces and brushed her hair and dazzled her with tall tales about witches and princesses trapped in towers, but as the years passed, they had gradually slipped into adulthood without her.

Natalie doubted the killer was still on the premises, but you never knew, and besides she had to follow procedure—first, secure and isolate the crime scene. "Brandon, wait here. I have to secure the area. Don't touch anything."

She unbuttoned her jacket, unfastened the safety strap of her shoulder holster, and lightly rested her fingers on the butt of her gun. Her clothes were clammy and damp. Natalie had a talent for shooting. On the practice range, she actually liked the smell of gunpowder and the "surprise" sound of shots ringing out. But she'd never had to fire her weapon in the field. *When to use your weapon, that's the big question,* her father used to say. Because the answer was vital to the soul of all law enforcement personnel. It was the final solution, and only after every other option had been exhausted. Despite all her years of training, Natalie had no idea when that line would be crossed.

Now she searched the second story. Three bedrooms, two bathrooms. The second floor was clear. She went downstairs and swept through the dining room, the half bath, the living room and den. The basement was empty. There appeared to be no secondary crime scene, no blood or disarray found anywhere but inside the kitchen, the primary scene. This wasn't a botched robbery, she decided, since all the things a thief might've taken were still there—computers, mobile devices, audio system, cash, jewelry, a thirty-year-old bottle of scotch.

The only disturbance was a cluttered desk in the living room. Daisy kept a fairly neat household, but it looked as if someone had rummaged through the desk recently. Drawers were open. Desktop items were askew. Messy paperwork—mostly test papers and student essays—littered the surface, with a few pieces coming to rest on the seat of the chair. Natalie tucked this observation away for later rumination and headed back into the kitchen.

The sliding glass doors overlooked the backyard. They weren't locked. She stepped out onto the cedar deck, letting in the chilly night air along with a curl of moonlight. There was Brandon's new top-of-the-line barbecue grill. She took out her iPhone, activated the flashlight, and illuminated the expansive backyard with its old-fashioned gazebo and flower beds bordering the perimeter. A tall cedar fence separated the three-acre property from the Buckners' nearest neighbors. The backyard was great for summer barbecues, recessed about thirty yards from the road and surrounded by dense woods. Very isolated.

Back inside the kitchen, Natalie fastened the safety strap of her holster and looked around for Brandon. She found him in the living room, rummaging through his wife's desk. "What are you doing?"

"Son of a bitch." He held up a piece of paper. "Riley Skinner. He's in Daisy's class. The stupid prick was flunking out of school, and she was trying to help him. Daisy thinks she can *reason* with these animals. . . ."

"Whoa, back up. You aren't making any sense," Natalie told him. There was only one Riley Skinner in town—a sixteen-year-old troublemaker, well known to the police, whose father was an ex-felon.

"See this F?" he said, pointing at the test paper. "See Riley's name on top? Daisy jumped through hoops getting him to retake the midterms last February, but he didn't care. He never showed up. You know Daisy, right? She only tries harder to help these drug-addled bastards . . . Jesus." His voice broke with raw despair. "Riley threatened her a few weeks ago. . . ."

"He threatened her? What happened?"

"He's flunking out of school, and he blamed her for the whole fiasco." His eyes blazed. "I know where to find him, Natalie. We could pick him up right now. He's either at Haymarket Field or Munson's Lane, one of those two places . . ."

"Slow down." She struggled to understand. "I'll call Dispatch and tell them to put out a BOLO for Riley's vehicle, okay? In the meantime, you're in no condition to do anything . . ."

"I'm telling you, this asshole threatened Daisy's life. *He did this to her.*"

"We don't know anything yet."

He nodded numbly. "Fuck that." He scooped up a set of keys from Daisy's desk and bolted out the door.

"Brandon, wait!" She chased after him, but by the time she got to Daisy's minivan, he'd locked himself in. She pounded on the driver's side window. "You're drunk!" she shouted. "You're in no condition to drive. Get out of the vehicle, now!"

He hit the gas and sped off in a cloud of dust, leaving a nasty patch of rubber on the road.

5

Natalie felt an avian fluttering in her heart as she got in her car and fastened her seat belt. She tore out of the driveway and headed south—Brandon had mentioned either Munson's Lane or Haymarket Field, two popular hangouts for troubled teenagers. She dug her shield out of the glove box, clipped it to a chain, and slung it around her neck. During a high-speed chase, you didn't want to be mistaken for a criminal by the state highway patrol.

With trembling hands, she called Luke. "Daisy Buckner's dead," she told him. "Possible homicide. We found her lying in a pool of blood on the kitchen floor. Front and back doors were unlocked. No secondary scene. No defensive wounds."

"Daisy?" Luke exclaimed. "Jesus, is Brandon okay?"

"He took off before I could stop him. He thinks Riley Skinner might've had something to do with it, because he's been threatening Daisy at school. Brandon mentioned Haymarket Field and Munson's Lane . . . I'm heading for Munson's Lane now."

"Okay. Meet you there in ten minutes." Luke hung up.

Sweat beaded on Natalie's neck as she took a left onto Daniel Boone

Lane, a lonely stretch of hills that eventually connected to Route 151, a busy thoroughfare. Winding around the lake, she ribboned past roadside diners and motels selling on-demand porn. Every time the road turned sharply, her discount tires hugged the asphalt. Soon the establishments gave way to the woods. On either side of the road, gray trunks tapered into swirling darkness. Deep in the underbrush, Natalie caught sight of a pair of animal eyes that didn't blink.

Now Dispatch radioed through the stuttering static. "There's been an altercation on Granite Falls Road behind the old Shell station."

She scooped up the mike. "Who called it in?"

"Unknown female. Looks like Detective Buckner and the suspect took off on foot into Haymarket Field . . ."

"Okay. I'm on my way." Natalie hit the brakes, made a U-turn, and headed west. She grabbed the portable beacon, slapped it on the hood, and switched on the siren. The police occasionally patrolled the vacant field behind the old Shell station, on the prowl for drug deals.

Natalie phoned Luke again. "A witness just spotted Brandon and Riley Skinner in Haymarket Field."

"Okay, I'll meet you there," Luke said and hung up.

Natalie approached the next intersection going eighty and blasted her horn as she charged through the red light, siren blaring. Her face felt stunned, frozen. Her nerve endings hummed. It was easy to understand why cops overreacted. The adrenaline rush was a huge factor. It could seriously mess with your head. There was an unshakeable sense of disconnect, like a trolley uncoupled from its driver.

Joey had warned her about moments like this, when the pressure mounted and the obstacles popped up and the seconds flew past, and it was totally up to you not to make any strategic errors. *We're only human, remember that. Do your best. Breathe deep and slow. Remain calm and steady, even though it seems like you should be speeding up.* Whether it was hiking up Dix Mountain, learning to shoot a bow and arrow, or standing up for what she believed in, her father had taught her how to maintain a cool head.

Natalie slowed down at the next intersection and took a right onto a gravel road that dead-ended into Haymarket Field, an overgrown stretch of scrub and rubble where early settlers had built their log cabins. Now it was a playground for derelicts getting high in the crumbling foundation of the old Shell station and passing out in the weeds.

The vacant field was partially fenced off, and beyond the chicken-wire fence were the ever-present woods. Soon Natalie was rolling over dirt and coming to a bumpy stop at the edge of the field, where half a dozen cars were parked crookedly in the weeds.

She burst out of the car like a trapped animal and spotted Daisy's green minivan parked in a ditch not far from Riley Skinner's 1967 renovated candy-apple red Camaro, Trash Talk and Drake stickers plastered over the back bumper.

"Brandon?" she shouted, announcing her arrival. She could hear a commotion in the distance. Something was going down about thirty yards ahead, but she couldn't see anything, due to the ground fog and heavy overcast.

Behind her, tires crunched over gravel and she turned just as Luke pulled up in his midnight-blue Ford Ranger, which was outfitted with the latest equipment—police radio, video surveillance system, portable data terminal mounted on a swing arm. He got out and moved swiftly toward her. "What's up, Natalie?"

"They're in the field. Dead ahead." She pointed in the direction of the commotion, which had stopped.

"I'll go behind the fence in case he runs," Luke said, taking off in a westerly direction, while Natalie headed straight into the field.

She pounded over the uneven terrain, each consecutive footstep sending another shock wave up her spine. The ragweed-strangled site was a strip mall waiting to happen. The chicken-wire fence was plastered with real-estate signage. As she left the streetlights behind, the night came alive with deceptive shadows. A few kids were shouting and running toward her. Scattering. Not a good sign.

She could feel her heartbeat parking itself at the base of her throat as she spotted a lone figure standing in the fiddlehead ferns about ten yards ahead.

"Brandon?" she said. "What's going on?"

Detective Buckner loomed over a prone body, his fists clenched. His chin thrust out. Natalie tried rearranging her thoughts in order, but it was like corralling kittens. She narrowed the gap between them, ferns sloshing against her calves. "Brandon?"

He turned with a puzzled look. "I swear to God I didn't touch him."

"What happened?"

"He just collapsed."

She approached with caution. Riley Skinner was lying on his back. He was twitching spasmodically, hands pawing at the air, and she realized he was having a seizure. "Does he have epilepsy? Is there a medical bracelet?"

Brandon knelt down and checked the boy's wrists for a medical bracelet. "No, nothing."

"When did he collapse?"

"Just a few minutes ago."

"Did you call 911?"

He nodded. "They're on their way."

She knelt down beside them and could feel the boy's pulse stuttering in the veins of his neck. There wasn't much you could do for a seizure besides comfort measures, until the ambulance arrived—remove the eyeglasses, loosen the collar, check the airway. "Help me roll him onto his side," she said. "It'll help with the breathing. We have to keep his head elevated."

Brandon helped her roll Riley over, then he cradled the boy's head in his hands.

"Was there an altercation? Any shots fired? Is he injured?"

"No," Brandon said, breathing hard.

"What happened?" she asked.

"He and some friends were smoking weed," he explained. "Riley dropped the joint and fled, so I gave chase, and when I caught up with him, he resisted arrest."

"Resisted? Did you grab him? Tackle him?"

"No, nothing like that. He was spouting gibberish, throwing punches."

"He punched you?" she asked.

"Nothing landed. I didn't lay a hand on him, Natalie."

"Did you fire your weapon at any point? A warning shot?"

"Hell, no," Brandon said angrily. "Quit asking me that."

Luke approached them, his face tense and expressionless. "What's going on?"

"He was smoking marijuana, Lieutenant," Brandon explained again in a shaky voice. "He fled the scene. I gave pursuit and told him to surrender, and that's when he collapsed on the ground."

Luke turned to Natalie and asked, "You got this?"

"Yeah. Got it." She took over for Brandon, cradling the boy's head in her lap and checking for a pulse. Riley's eyes were rolled toward the back of his head and his torso was jerking every couple of seconds. She checked her watch, timing the length of the seizures, knowing that the paramedics would find it helpful.

"Brandon, step over here," Luke commanded. "Come stand next to me."

Brandon did as he was told. "I wanna talk to my union rep," he muttered.

"Duly noted."

Just then, an ambulance came wailing up the dirt road toward the abandoned Shell station, clouds of dust puffing up as it braked. Two paramedics hopped out and fetched their equipment. Soon, they were rolling a gurney across the field through the tangled weeds.

"How's he doing, Natalie?" Luke asked.

"The seizures are winding down." She performed a quick inspection of the boy's scalp, searching for any signs of blunt trauma. She checked his arms and hands for defensive wounds, lacerations, or abrasions, but she couldn't find any. They were going to have to corroborate Brandon's story, since he was drunk and off-duty tonight, distraught about the death of his wife. He shouldn't have been out here arresting anyone. The media would be all over the story if the police weren't careful. Accusations of excessive use of force were a nightmare scenario for the department.

All she could find preliminarily was a single bruise on Riley's right cheek that could've happened during the fall. Perhaps the teenager had epilepsy or some other medical condition.

All of a sudden, the boy became unresponsive. "Riley?" She checked his eyes and took his pulse again.

"What's happening?" Brandon asked nervously.

Suddenly, Riley's muscles clenched, and he became rigid as a board. Next came a series of grotesque jerking movements—arms flailing, face twitching.

"He's having another seizure," Natalie said, holding his head in her lap until the paramedics arrived. She smoothed the hair off his brow, and Riley regained a moment of clarity and gave her such a fiercely hateful look, it chilled her to the bone.

The boy in the woods. The raccoon. The stick.

She pushed the bad memories aside and finally the paramedics took over.

6

By two o'clock in the morning, the crime scene was secured and Daisy's body had been transported to the morgue. Two teams were working simultaneously—one in Haymarket Field; the other at the Buckner residence. Detective August "Augie" Vickers, a hardworking but unimaginative grinder, was in charge of Haymarket Field. Since Natalie had caught the case, she was the detective-in-charge of Daisy's homicide, and the stakes couldn't be higher.

Not that she hadn't seen plenty of dead bodies before. As a patrol officer, she'd caught her fair share of suicides, car accidents, assaults, rapes, and carjackings. She'd made hundreds of arrests and filled out plenty of run sheets, but she'd never led a murder investigation beyond a couple of suspicious drug-related deaths. As the newbie and the only female in the unit, she didn't have the luxury of fucking up.

Luke was supervising both sites. He'd been traveling back and forth between them for hours now, issuing orders and getting updates. "Stay focused," he'd advised her earlier that evening. "A little adrenaline is good. Stage fright keeps your performance sharp." The adrenaline was still coursing through her veins, making her temples pulse and heightening her senses.

There were other voices inside the house. Detectives Lenny Labruzzo and Mike Anderson were methodically working their way through the first floor—photographing, fingerprinting, bagging and tagging. The BLPD couldn't afford a CSI unit, so the detectives had to process the scenes themselves.

Natalie went into the kitchen and hit a wall of decomposition—the putrid smell of decaying flesh you never got used to. The chalk outline on the floor looked cartoonish, not dignified. The puddle of blood had coagulated into a jellied pool, and Natalie felt a rush of outrage for her old friend. No one deserved this.

Lenny had been over every surface of the kitchen already, looking for latents, visibles, smears, and plastics. The primary scene was dusted in red, white, and black fingerprint powder—everything but the stove dials. Natalie stood in front of the Bosch gas-range stove and studied the burners. Daisy had been in the middle of cooking dinner when she was attacked—there was a tepid pot of noodles on the back burner and chopped vegetables on a cutting board. But someone had turned the burners off before Natalie and Brandon entered the scene. The question was—who? Daisy or her attacker?

"Lenny?" she called out. "When you're done in there, I need you to process these stove control knobs for me."

"I already dusted the kitchen," came his bone-tired response.

"Yeah, but we forgot about the stove dials."

Detective Labruzzo came shuffling into the kitchen. He had a receding hairline and a pruney face, and he often transported his stuff around in a rolling briefcase that looked silly but saved him a lot of back pain. "How the hell did we miss that?" He scowled, opening up his fingerprint kit.

Sometimes you missed an important clue the first time around, but Natalie couldn't help feeling a child's disappointment. It had taken her longer than most of her friends to learn things—reading a primer, tying her shoes, riding a bike—but once she learned, she excelled. She hoped this case wouldn't present too steep a learning curve, because she needed to be on top of it—right now.

The cast-iron skillet on the floor had been bagged and tagged, since chain of custody was vitally important. The skillet contained a greasy residue, and its contents—a messy pile of cooked, ground beef—was cool to the touch, with orange evidence placards placed around it. The saucepan of water and tortellini noodles sat on a back burner. There was an empty tortellini box on the granite countertop next to a water-stained recipe card for Ground Beef and Tortellini Casserole, a wedge of parmesan cheese wrapped in cellophane, and two cans of tomato sauce. On the cutting board were diced carrots, a sliced red onion, and a three-inch vegetable knife with a rosewood handle.

The slotted wooden cutlery block next to the microwave held an assortment of chef's knives by Victorinox. A set of eleven. Natalie counted ten rosewood handles inside the wooden block, plus one empty slot, which matched the vegetable knife on the cutting board—meaning that all the Victorinox chef's knives were accounted for.

Natalie reviewed her mental checklist, ticking off the boxes. They'd cordoned off the scene and notified the medical examiner. They'd taken hundreds of photographs while combing through the house, looking for blood, hair, and fiber evidence. They'd scoured the yard and driveway, searching for footprints and tire impressions—although tonight's rain was making that difficult. They'd recovered DNA samples from the body and sent them to the state lab for testing. They'd emptied the wastebaskets in search of discarded wads of chewing gum, rumpled cigarette packs, or other telltale evidence. They'd swabbed the telephone mouthpieces for saliva—both landline and cellular. The errant soda can—Coke—had been bagged for testing. They'd documented the angle and degree of coagulation of all bloodstains, including the arcing spatter-pattern on the refrigerator door, the recessed-panel kitchen cabinets and glass-tiled backsplash. The medical examiner had signed the death certificate. The official cause of death was blunt-force trauma.

Five hours ago, Natalie had instructed half a dozen patrol officers to canvass the neighborhood, checking door-to-door for any suspicious sightings in the vicinity. Nothing had come of it yet. Too many working professionals with zero kids in this upscale neighborhood. Around midnight, she sent the officers home, but they would be back tomorrow, bright and early, to resume their canvassing duties.

Due to the direction of the blood spatter, Natalie surmised that Daisy had been standing in front of the refrigerator, reaching for a can of Coke, when she was attacked. As soon as her back was turned, the killer must've picked up the skillet and swung it at her head, using one crushing blow to annihilate her. A single injury to the right side of the skull—which meant the perpetrator was right-handed.

First order of business: Was Riley Skinner right-handed?

Second: Could it be someone other than Riley? Were they already on the wrong path due to Brandon's high emotions?

Third: Did the killer prefer Coke over any other beverage in the fridge?

Fourth: Was the Coke meant for Daisy instead?

Natalie knew the answer to this last question. Daisy was strictly a diet soda girl—diet ginger ale, diet Fanta, Diet Coke—never Diet Pepsi, though. She preferred Coke over Pepsi and watched her figure like a hawk. But a pregnancy could alter a woman's cravings. Daisy's drinking and eating habits may have changed without Natalie ever knowing about it. After all, Daisy was Grace's best friend, not Natalie's. And although Daisy had been wonderful to Natalie when she was little, the two of them rarely got together socially anymore. When they did bump into each other at a party or on those rare occasions when she accepted Brandon's dinner invitations, they had a casual but polite relationship, always encouraging each other but never treading on each other's lives. It was as if their once-close bond had been stretched into obliviousness. In truth, Natalie was closer to Brandon than to Daisy, who'd become more of a warm acquaintance.

She stepped around the minefield of evidence placards on the floor, opened the refrigerator, and examined its contents—a gallon of low-fat milk, an unopened six-pack of Rolling Rock, various bottled waters, and a generous assortment of canned sodas—Coke, Seven-Up, Canada Dry Diet

Ginger Ale, Dr Pepper, Pepsi, Fanta, Diet Coke. There were several packages of deli cold cuts and gourmet cheeses, a carton of eggs, and a stick of butter—nothing unusual there. Half a dozen chicken breasts marinating in a glass dish. A bag of carrots and a head of broccoli in the vegetable drawer. Designer stoneware dishes in the cupboards. Oreos and Doritos. Organic soups and protein bars. Wheat Thins and graham crackers.

Natalie walked over to the breakfast table and studied the crime-scene photos spread across the polished oak surface. Along with hundreds of digital pics, Lenny had taken dozens of tamper-proof Polaroids as well. She scrutinized Daisy's debilitating injury—the single blow to the head, an ugly gash located approximately two inches behind her right ear. The curved surface of the wound was an exact match for the curved edge of the cast-iron skillet.

The eight-inch, medium-size skillet—weighing about five pounds with a sturdy handle and a hole for hanging—was part of a three-piece set. The two other skillets—one large and one small—were suspended from a hanging pot rack in the coffered ceiling. A couple hours ago, Lenny had preliminarily ID'd the medium-size skillet as the murder weapon after spraying it with luminol and finding traces of human blood. There weren't any prints on the handle, though—not even Daisy's—which indicated the killer must've wiped the skillet clean. That was smart.

Natalie straightened up too quickly, then took a balancing breath. When sketching out a scenario, you had to be careful not to leap to conclusions and stick to the facts. Like her father used to say, *You can't choreograph reality.* But Natalie felt she had enough facts within her grasp to paint a scenario of the murder as it might've unfolded.

Starting with the assumption that Riley Skinner was the killer . . . okay, something was wrong with that picture. First of all, most teenage boys weren't known for their maturity or patience. If Riley was upset enough to kill Daisy, then she would've been alert enough to run out the unlocked back door or grab a knife to defend herself with. She would've seen his aggression coming. At the very least, there would've been a struggle, resulting in defensive wounds on her body. But no. There was nothing—just the single lethal blow.

Another question. Why would Daisy offer Riley a Coke in the first place if he'd been threatening her life? Why would she even let him into her house? This had all the markings of a crime of passion—nothing premeditated about it. Most crimes of passion were committed during the heat of an argument. If Daisy and Riley had been arguing, then why would she turn her back on him and offer him a soda?

Okay. Back up a little.

A more likely scenario was that Daisy knew her attacker and felt comfortable enough to invite this person into her house. The two of them had been talking in the kitchen, when Daisy—not at all concerned for her safety—had offered her guest a soda. The killer said yes. Once Daisy's back was turned, the killer grabbed the skillet off the stove and struck the disabling blow, rendering her dead. Clobbering shot. End-of-life blow. Daisy collapsed instantly, blood dripping from her skull, while the soda can went flying out of her hand and across the floor. The skillet was dropped. Perhaps the dish towel on the floor was used to wipe away the prints.

A single blow. Crime of passion. Pent-up fury.

Alternatively, the killer could've been a stranger, unknown to Daisy. After all, both doors were unlocked. But if someone managed to sneak inside while Daisy was cooking in the kitchen, wouldn't she have heard them coming? You grew alert to any stray sounds in the house when you were alone. Natalie knew this from personal experience.

She tested out her hypothesis—the hinges on the front door squeaked, the floorboards in the front hallway creaked, the sliding glass door in the kitchen wouldn't open without a sucking sound. The first floor was open concept, which meant that Daisy had a good line of sight into the living room. She would've had plenty of time to react, either by fighting or running. But Daisy had invited the killer in. She'd offered this person a Coke.

Luke came into the kitchen just then, breaking Natalie's concentration. He had a concerned look in his eyes. "How're you holding up?"

"Fine," she lied, catching a glimpse of her reflection in the kitchen window. Her mahogany-colored hair was frazzled and her pale blue eyes were rimmed red with fatigue. Natalie, the baby of the family, took after her blue-eyed Sicilian dad, whereas Grace had inherited their mother's Nordic genes. "How's Brandon holding up?" she asked.

"Grieving," Luke said softly. "Sedated. He's with his family."

"There'll be an internal investigation?"

"Has to be. His blood alcohol content was elevated. His actions tonight could've contributed to Riley's seizures, we don't know yet. We can't rule it out."

She nodded. Riley's family was within their rights to issue a complaint against Detective Buckner, whether there was evidence of assault or not. He was off-duty and driving under the influence. They could also add other charges—no arrest warrant, threatening conduct, abusing a suspect's civil rights. Brandon might be in serious trouble, and unless the evidence was on his side, they wouldn't be able to protect him. He'd sealed his own fate.

"How's Riley Skinner doing?" she asked.

"His brain began to swell in the ambulance, and he lapsed into a coma. He's listed in critical but stable condition. It's possible he could have brain damage, they won't know until he regains consciousness."

"God." Natalie frowned. "That's bad news."

"The worst."

"Was there a history of seizures?"

"No. The doctors think it could be drug related. They've ordered an extensive tox screen, along with an MRI and other neurological tests. In the meantime, the hospital won't release Riley's outfit without a warrant. Augie was able to send me some pictures, though." He took out his phone and swiped through the images. "Possible blood on the hoodie," he said, pointing at the screen. "Just a couple of drops on the sleeve. See there? Could be cross-contamination from Daisy's body."

Natalie squinted. "Or else blood from the seizures."

Luke nodded. "We found contraband at the scene, which we're processing for prints and saliva. A witness came forward, and we're using his statement to get a warrant for Riley's outfit. If the blood drops on the hoodie are a match for Daisy's blood type, I'll instruct Augie to file affidavits for a blanket search warrant for Riley's vehicle and the Skinners' residence. In the meantime, Brandon's lawyered up. Not an unwise move, given the circumstances."

Natalie drew a hand across her damp forehead and said, "I checked Riley for defensive wounds or other signs of assault. The only concern was a small bruise on his cheek, which could've happened during the seizures."

"Dr. Swinton came to a similar conclusion. No evidence of assault, just a lot of bruising from the resuscitation efforts in the ambulance. Hopefully, we'll find out what caused the seizures soon. But there's no excusing Brandon's behavior tonight. He acted impulsively. He's been trained like the rest of us to set aside his emotions during the heat of the moment. Daisy's death, no matter how tragic, doesn't excuse the fact that he drove drunk and chased down some punk-ass kid in a park. We'll have to let the investigation take its course. Meanwhile, Brandon's father has hired Frank Moorecraft and Associates, one of the top law firms in Syracuse. I'm guessing he's bracing for things to get ugly."

"Do you think it'll get ugly?" Natalie asked, the thought twinging through her.

"Who knows. Dominic Skinner isn't the easiest person to reason with." Luke checked his watch. "Two thirty. What's the latest, Natalie? What else you got for me?"

"I found something on Daisy's laptop."

"Show me."

She led the way into the living room, where she took a seat behind the designer desk in the corner, its glass surface littered with fingerprint powder. The scattered paperwork had been bagged and taken away for processing. Moonlight spilled in through a nearby window—the clouds had blown away, and you could see bright constellations in the sky. Daisy's mouse pad was illustrated with a basket of kittens. Her laptop was open.

"She kept track of her daily schedule in a folder labeled 'School Notes'—mostly tracking her class syllabus, school activities, faculty meetings, stuff like that. But there's also a running commentary on events, like a daily progress report." She double-clicked on the icon, and up popped twelve Word docs, one for every month of the year. "So I opened the April file and scrolled across . . . see here? Under 'last date modified,' the time is two fifty-eight this afternoon."

"So she was home at two fifty-eight?" Luke repeated with interest. "Alive at two fifty-eight?"

Natalie nodded. "School lets out at two thirty. It's about a fifteen-minute drive."

"So we can place her inside the house as early as two forty-five P.M.?"

"Teacher's hours. Now check this out." Natalie opened the "March" document and scrolled through Daisy's notes. "About four weeks ago, Riley Skinner was issued a warning. He was already flunking two other classes, but after receiving a warning from Daisy, things seemed to escalate. Three and a half weeks ago, he verbally threatened her. 'You're gonna be sorry.' 'I know where you live.' Stuff like that. She had a meeting with the principal about it the following week."

Luke stroked the nape of his neck. "I want copies of everything."

"I've sent the attachments and print screens to my phone, and as soon as I've downloaded everything, I'll forward them to you. Now check this out." Natalie opened Daisy's tabbed email account. "She was answering emails between three oh-five and three seventeen P.M. I've skimmed through them, and there's nothing pertinent so far. No signs of distress or reaching out for help, nothing unusual. She didn't come across as overly concerned. So I checked out her phone logs. Brandon texted her a couple of times this afternoon, and she texted back. Again, nothing out of the ordinary. According to Brandon, she wasn't expecting him home until eight o'clock. But then, there's no more activity after three seventeen. No texting, no phone calls, no emails."

Luke nodded. "Maybe that's when the killer arrived."

"Or else she went into the kitchen and started cooking. Something else," she said. "I checked out her online search history. She was looking up baby stuff online. Car seats, strollers, baby announcements. But also . . . get this. Advice on broken relationships."

"Yeah?"

"So I went to her Amazon account, and look here . . . she purchased two Kindle ebooks. *The Breakup Bible* and *Getting Past Your Breakup*."

"That's odd." Luke scratched the back of his neck.

"Right? Brandon confessed on the ride over that he and Daisy were having marital problems, but this looks as if she wanted to end the relationship, not fix it."

Luke arched his eyebrows. "Marital problems? Seriously?"

"I know. It surprised the hell out of me, too. Long story short, he didn't sound all that thrilled with their sex life . . . he indicated they'd been having sexual problems."

"Maybe their marriage was rocky as hell? Maybe he's been lying about it?"

"The point is . . . even if she was thinking about getting a divorce, wouldn't you buy this type of book *after* a breakup? Not before. They're written for the post-breakup period—how to mend a broken heart. How to move forward."

Luke drew back. "So what do you make of it?"

"I honestly don't know. Maybe a student needed advice in that department?"

He rubbed his chin. "When Audrey and I were trying to get pregnant, the sex became pretty routine. If Daisy and Brandon were on a sex schedule while she was ovulating, that could explain the big turnoff. Being compelled to have sex during a fertility window can take all the fun out of it."

"Yeah, but . . . mission accomplished," Natalie argued. "Daisy's three months pregnant. No more fertility window or sex schedule. And yet Brandon implied they were having difficulties now." She realized how coldly professional that sounded. They were talking about people they knew and cared about with such clinical detachment, it saddened her. "Anyway, I'll keep poking around in her social media accounts, see if anything pops up."

"Not tonight, Natalie." Luke checked his watch. "We're done here."

She leaned back. "I couldn't sleep if you paid me."

He shook his head and said, "The forty-eight-hours thing is a myth. Eventually the clock runs out. You gotta sleep."

She rubbed her tired eyes. "If I go home now, I'll only start thinking about how fucking awful and heartbreaking this is."

"It's not like I'll be able to sleep, either," he admitted. His hair was slightly wavy and amber-colored, like his father's, but he had his mother's intense eyes. They were crystal blue and thick lashed, and his mouth turned down on one side whenever he grew pensive, like he was now. "But you go home. You take a shower. You snack on something. Then you lie down and close your eyes. You try not to run the investigation over and over in your head. You let your body relax. Then you come back tomorrow morning and start all over again."

She frowned. "I almost forgot." She took out her phone and swiped through the images. "Today at the cemetery, I found something rather disturbing. I took pictures before the rain washed it away."

He studied the screen, all his worries congregating into a bunched square of real estate between his eyebrows. "Teresa McCarthy's headstone?"

"You can barely decipher the handwriting, but whoever did this is clearly fucked up."

He rubbed his chin. "I've seen something like this before."

"Really?"

Luke nodded solemnly. "Do you remember the seventeen-year-old who got raped in Haymarket Field two years ago?"

"Hannah something," Natalie responded. "Her ex-boyfriend's doing time."

"Right. While we were investigating, we did a grid search of the area and came across some similar-looking graffiti written on one of the old stones in the foundation of the Shell station."

"How similar?"

"Just like that," he said emphatically. "And the weird thing was, that corner of the foundation was the exact location where Minnie Walker was last seen alive."

"Minnie Walker? One of the Missing Nine?"

He nodded thoughtfully.

Prickles crept across Natalie's scalp. Minnie Walker was a thirty-eight-year-old alcoholic, last seen four years ago giving a blow job to an unknown male, possibly identified as a long-haul trucker, in the foundation of the old Shell station at Haymarket Field. Minnie was one of the nine cold-case files sitting on Natalie's desk back at the office. One of her back-burner cases. Minnie had an anemic face and veiny eyes that mistrusted everyone. She was a paradox—a beggar with expensive shoes and Ray-Bans. She begged on the street corners every day. She was hostile to the working women who refused to give her any more of their hard-earned cash. She lied and said she had children to support. She had no children. She disappeared one autumn afternoon when the fog pooled in the valley and the lake rose ten feet from the weekend rains.

"But you said this happened two years ago," Natalie told him, "whereas Minnie disappeared *four* years ago. And there's nothing in her case file about this type of graffiti . . . investigators went over the scene of her disappearance with a fine-tooth comb, interviewing dozens of witnesses . . . nothing ever came of it. Dead ends all the way."

"That's because it's not in Minnie's file," he told her. "The graffiti showed up two years later. Written in chalk. Just like that. Practically illegible, but some of the obscenities were crystal clear. Just like that."

"Did you take pictures?"

"Yeah, they're in Hannah Daugherty's file."

"Great. Let's go." She stood up and grabbed her jacket.

"Whoa. Not tonight."

"Why not?"

"It could be packed with meaning, or it could be nothing. A prank."

"But it's worth investigating, either way."

"I agree." He handed Natalie her phone back. "But Daisy's case takes priority. The cold cases can wait. I'm not telling you to stop or even slow down on the Missing Nine. This is a significant lead, Natalie. We'll follow up, for sure, but it's a matter of priorities. Simple, really."

"Simple for you, maybe."

Silence surrounded them. She realized Luke had sent the guys home already. They were alone in the house, where Daisy's ghost drifted, lost and confused, all her hopes and dreams having been crushed in an instant. Natalie felt an unpleasant throbbing in her chest, an upside-down ache.

"Good job today, Natalie."

She studied his sincere, etched face. "Don't you think it's strange? Daisy's homicide took place on Willow's deathiversary—same day, twenty years later."

"Our brains operate that way," Luke said. "We see patterns and try to fit all the pieces together. Random facts. Coincidences. Unrelated incidents. Which is why we have to go where the evidence leads us."

So much history had passed between them. He'd witnessed her first bike ride. He was there when she'd switched from cartoons to MTV, from dolls to makeup. He'd seen her laugh and cry and throw up and do cartwheels.

She sighed and said, "Remember the first time we met?"

"Met?" He grinned crookedly and said, "You mean, the day I crawled through the fence in your backyard and introduced myself, and you threw a rock at my head?"

"A pebble."

"You were—what? Five? Six?"

She laughed. "A little brat."

"Willow came over and said, 'Welcome to Hell.' I thought that was cool."

Luke had moved into a run-down ranch house with his hippie mom. He was an only child with no father, and he came over to play with Natalie and her sisters in their big backyard, climbing trees, instigating snowball fights, building leaf forts. He had spiky hair and super-calm eyes, a steadying way about him. He used to call Natalie "pipsqueak" because of their age difference—eight years.

It had taken thin-skinned Luke a long time to fully mature. At some point, Joey noticed the scrawny, fatherless boy hanging around the neighborhood and took him under his wing. Joey taught him how to fight, how to build a six-pack, how to spot a bully and lay him out. In a funny way, Joey finally found his son, and Luke found his missing dad.

Years later, Luke went away to college and got married. It was a rebound relationship. He admitted this to Natalie during one of the department Christmas parties. His smarty-pants, Ph.D. girlfriend of two years had just broken up with him, and he'd never felt so bitter about anything in his life. But then, along came Audrey Peeley, so petite and flirtatious she made him feel manly. She'd seduced him. She came on strong. She was sensual in the beginning, before the baby. But then, after the physical attraction faded away, he realized they didn't have much in common, except for their daughter.

Luke got a divorce, joined the United States Army, did a couple of tours of the Middle East, and came home prison hard. Soon he'd joined the ranks of the Burning Lake PD, where he eventually became lieutenant detective of the fucking unit. Nobody messed with him now. At six foot one, Lieutenant Pittman had zero timidity.

Except around Natalie, when it came to their shared history. When they were kids, they used to sit in the hot summer sun or on a snow-dusted porch, and he would confess his deepest fears and biggest dreams to her—how badly he'd been bullied at school, how he was going to avenge himself someday, how deeply humiliating his family's poverty was for him, to have a single mom and no dad, what an indelible scar that had left on his heart. He'd confided all his deepest secrets, never once suspecting that she'd grow up to become a rookie detective under his wing.

"Let's pick this up in the morning," he said, heading for the door. "Don't forget to lock up."

7

Back home, Natalie's sister had left several distraught messages on her answering machine. Earlier that evening, Natalie had delivered the bad news to Grace and promised to call her back, but in all the chaos, she'd forgotten to check in on her again.

Now Natalie turned on the house lights, dropped her bag on the living-room sofa, dug out her phone, and dialed Grace's number. "Hey, it's me," she said. "I just got home. Did I wake you?"

"No. Can't sleep," Grace said hoarsely.

"How are you feeling?"

"Jesus, it hurts . . . she was my best friend in the world. I'm still in shock. I can't stop shaking."

"How's Ellie?" Natalie asked.

"Hysterical earlier, until I gave her one of my Valiums. I don't know what I'm supposed to do now."

"Just take care of yourselves, okay?"

There was a pause. "It said on the news that Riley Skinner's a suspect . . . and I know Daisy was having problems with him."

"Listen," Natalie said, taking a deep breath, "what can you tell me about it?"

"He was flunking her sociology class, but what could she do? Her hands were tied. All he had to do was write a few essays, but he never completed the assignments. She was under an enormous amount of pressure from the administration to hold him back a grade, otherwise it could've effected JFK's overall performance," Grace explained. "You can't have too many students flunking the statewide tests, or else it'll reduce the funding levels. Nobody wants to hold back a student, least of all Daisy. She took it as a personal challenge. And for these kids, it's humiliating. Most of the holdbacks never get over it."

"Did you witness any altercations between them?"

"No, but he called her a cunt once. Daisy told me about it afterwards."

"A cunt?" Natalie said, alarmed. "When was this?"

"Three or four weeks ago."

"What were the circumstances? Did he use any other abusive language? Did he threaten to hurt her physically?"

"All I know is, they were alone after school one day, and he was upset about his situation, and in typical Daisy fashion, she tried coming up with a last-ditch effort to save him. He reacted by blaming her instead. He said some pretty nasty things, but then he apologized—profusely, she said. He was ashamed of himself for lashing out like that. After all, she was the only adult in his life who seemed to care. She didn't report him, not officially. She's very forgiving that way."

"But she talked to the principal about it, correct?"

"She told me she withheld the worst of it, though. Because that would've been the end of it. Ironic, isn't it? She protected Riley from himself."

"What kind of last-ditch effort?" Natalie asked.

"Gee, I don't know. She was running out of options. She'd already given him plenty of opportunities to retake the tests, but he never followed through."

Natalie frowned. "Why not?"

"I don't know. Probably wishful thinking. Some of these kids imagine they're destined for greatness—you know, they're going to be famous rock stars or rich athletes or whatever. Their heads are full of garbage. Grades aren't important until the threat of being held back looms on the horizon. But Daisy wasn't afraid of unruly boys. She used to tell me, no matter how rotten some of these kids are, they're still kids." She paused. "Oh God. Do you think he killed her, Natalie?"

"We don't know anything for sure yet. The investigation's ongoing."

Grace took a steadying breath. "It's so fucking unfair. Daisy and I were best friends for as long as I can remember. We got our teacher's certifications at the same time. We used to finish each other's thoughts. . . ."

Natalie paused to let her have a moment. She checked her watch. Half past three in the morning. "Listen, I'll be dropping by the school tomorrow. Can I get a statement from you then?"

"A statement?"

"We'll be interviewing everyone who knew Daisy—students, faculty, staff. We're looking for any information that might be pertinent to the case."

"Oh. Yeah, of course. You sound tired, Natalie."

"There's nothing more we can do right now. Get some sleep, okay?"

"You, too, sweetie."

"G'night, Grace."

"Night." She hung up.

Natalie went upstairs, where she peeled out of her clothes, put on the extra-large BLPD T-shirt she used as a nightgown, and collapsed on top of her bed, too exhausted to turn back the covers. *Never take it home with you,* Joey used to say. *Some of these cases will haunt you if you let them. Fucking ghosts.*

Her nerves were frayed beyond belief. Tonight, she would have to keep a distance between herself and reality if she hoped to get any sleep at all. When you dealt with mangled bodies at the scene of an accident, grisly suicides or domestics where the woman's jaw was broken or the child's eye socket was fractured—the best way to cope was to pretend it never happened. Face it in the morning.

She sighed and closed her eyes, on the verge of floating away.

The boy in the woods. The raccoon. The stick.

She opened her eyes and lay there, struggling with the old horrors.

A long time ago, when Natalie was nine years old, a teenage boy attacked her in the woods. She'd managed to escape, but not before catching sight of the telltale birthmark on his left arm—at the crux of the elbow, on the fleshy inner part of the arm where the skin was most tender and vulnerable. A striking purple birthmark the size of a quarter. It looked like a startled butterfly. She knew that didn't make any sense, but it was the best way to describe it—a startled butterfly, freaking out in midflight, flapping its wings and shaking its antennae. As if a Disney cartoon and a Rorschach blot had a baby. Natalie managed to escape that day, but they never found the boy who attacked her, despite months of searching, and this traumatic incident had left an enduring scar on her psyche.

The dead raccoon, swollen with rot. The strange boy poking it with a stick.

Now she tossed and turned, growing alternately feverish and freezing cold.

It was early autumn, and nine-year-old Natalie had taken a shortcut through the woods. The hawks were circling overhead, trying to flush the field mice out into the open. She got lost on the crisscrossing deer paths. The giant oaks were like haunted house trees, their crooked branches pawing at the sky. The wind made the slowly turning leaves flutter. It sounded like rain.

Eventually, she came to a clearing, where she spotted a boy about Willow's age kneeling on the muddy bank of a stream. He wore jeans and no shoes. He'd taken off his T-shirt and wrapped it around his head like a voodoo mask, with a slit for the eyes, two glints inside a smeary darkness. His naked torso was painted with mud. He held a stick in his hand—a sturdy branch with a pointed tip—and he kept poking the dead raccoon with it, lancing its bloated belly and stabbing deeper and deeper until the intestines gushed out.

"Fuck," he muttered to himself. "Fuck."

Natalie trembled with terror on the edge of the clearing, while the bogeyman stabbed and stabbed. She couldn't rip her eyes away. Couldn't escape her growing nausea. All of a sudden, she screamed.

He turned and spotted her, then slowly stood up. His eyes seemed to smile behind the mask. Natalie froze, trying to make herself invisible, but the bogeyman came charging after her. He chased her through the woods—silently, never calling for her to stop, never speaking. They zigzagged through the trees, and whenever she stumbled he gained speed. She took one path after another, until she no longer recognized where she was.

Finally he caught up with her and threw her down on the ground. She couldn't breathe. He tightened his grip, and the pain was astonishing. He sat on top of her. He was going to kill her. He would rip her apart like a coyote. He would split her open like a piñata and spew her guts all over the place like stale candy.

Natalie kicked and clawed at the air, trying to scratch his face, but the boy was too strong. In thrashing glimpses, she saw pieces of him—his sweaty bare chest, the strained tendons in his neck, the butterfly birthmark on the inner part of his elbow. Like a startled butterfly, it trembled all over, trying to escape, just like Natalie.

She swung her fists wildly, fending him off every step of the way. When he swiped at her again, she caught his arm between her teeth and bit down hard enough to draw blood, a warm liquid pooling inside her mouth.

He cried out in pain and released her.

Natalie leapt to her feet, then looked around for something to defend herself with. She picked up a rock and flung it at his head, and he dropped like a sack.

Natalie ran for her life, tripping and stumbling through the woods, a crazy pattern to her breathing. She veered off the trail and crawled through the underbrush, scratching her arms and face on the thorny bushes. Ten minutes later, she pitched herself out of the woods and crossed a field full of bluebells, finally recognizing where she was—behind Luke's house. She entered the Pittmans' backyard, where Luke's mom allowed the grass to grow wild and the sagging bamboo chairs looked like a herd of cows. Natalie hammered on the back door, calling for help. Mrs. Pittman was at work, but Luke was home, and he took her inside and comforted her, then drove her to the police station, where her father asked her what exactly had happened in those woods?

The dead raccoon. The slit for his eyes.

The police never found the boy with the stick. It was as if she'd made it all up. There was no dead raccoon, no bogeyman, no evidence of rape or sexual assault; just scrapes and scratches from where she'd clawed her way through the brambles.

She never saw the bogeyman again, even though he haunted her dreams and poked holes in her memories. It made her furious to have him lodged inside her head like a land mine, ready to explode. Like a cold spot on her brain.

A wise man once said, when you close your eyes, you die for just a bit. For a split second, you cross a barrier, and there it is, in the viscous membrane between waking and dreaming—your true self.

8

Seconds later it seemed, the alarm clock was blaring in Natalie's ears—that cheap, tinny, big-box-store blare. She rolled over and smacked it off. Her eyes felt glued shut. Her head was throbbing. Her father had a name for this—a crime-scene hangover. Joey would've been proud.

She crawled out of bed and staggered into the bathroom, where she swallowed two Aleves with a glass of tap water and took the hottest shower in the world. She tried to squeeze all the grief and confusion out of her heart. She scrubbed herself vigorously with a soapy washcloth, rubbing out the stench of death until her skin was velvety pink.

She left the bathroom ventilation fan running and opened a window. The lacy trees were budding out. A gorgeous perfume filled the air. Her stomach clenched. Fresh from her shower, Natalie grew clammy all over. This was no ordinary day. Something ugly had happened last night. Daisy had lost her life—Grace's best friend, Brandon's pregnant wife, the students' beloved Ms. Buckner. Something inside Natalie stirred—a fresh awareness that the world wasn't as safe as it seemed. Forces greater than yourself could carry you into a realm where all color was sucked out of the landscape—a realm where butterflies became symbols of evil. How could that be?

Natalie skipped her morning run and went downstairs to start the coffeemaker, grab a Pop-Tart for breakfast, and load the dishwasher. She'd inherited this sunny, drafty hundred-year-old house from her parents. She let the sadness wash over her as she glanced around the old-fashioned living room. She'd taken a stab at renovating last year, sanding and repainting the walls, but the end result was a mixed bag of awful. She'd donated some of the ugly-ass furniture to the Goodwill and had moved the rest of her parents' belongings up into the attic, big orchestrated piles of boxes and scarred sticks of furniture she couldn't bear to part with. Now she could feel her mother's resentment boring into her—*That's a perfectly good chair, why aren't you using my hutch?*

Deborah Lockhart had been a smart, well-educated woman stuck in a domestic role she both relished and resented. Raising three girls had been fun for a while—until it wasn't. According to Deborah, she'd fallen in love with Joey at a friend's graduation party. Joey had a cleft in his chin she was tempted to push the tip of her finger into. He wore a look of intense introspection, and his piercing blue eyes, elegant face, and wolfish ears made her heart skip a beat. She had a fleeting desire to lose herself in him, or at least to misplace herself for a little while.

"A little while" turned into a lifetime of housekeeping and motherhood. On her deathbed, Deborah told Natalie, "When you girls were growing up, the days just flew by. I was always doing laundry or shopping or housework, and three times a day, seven days a week, I had to figure out what to feed the hungry people who showed up at my door. You girls and your father. Four hungry mouths." To make life simpler, Deborah had assigned each girl a color: Willow was pink, Grace was purple, and Natalie was as blue as her father's uniform. They all had plastic dishware in their own color, socks and pajamas in their color, headbands and sweaters in their color. Even the walls of their bedrooms were painted pink, purple, and blue. Deborah encouraged her daughters to pursue a career in the fine arts, since her dream had been to become a dancer. Therefore, it was decided early on that Willow would be a ballerina, Grace a writer, and Natalie an artist (since she'd shown talent for it early on). Deborah believed all her girls were gifted, and it upset her deeply when Natalie chose Joey's dangerous profession over her own preference.

Now Natalie chewed on her Pop-Tart and noticed the cardboard box in a corner of the living room, gathering dust. It was full of Zack's stuff. She kept finding little things he'd left behind and tossing them in there—cutesy trinkets, an old sweatshirt that smelled just like him, a coffee mug that said SH*T HAPPENS, a disposable razor, stray socks. Eight months' worth of crap.

Put a fork in us, we're done.

Okay. She put down her Pop-Tart and carried the box outside, where she upended it into the trash. Her relationship with Zack Stadler hadn't just happened—he'd hunted her down, if hipsters could hunt. More accurately, Natalie had let herself be captured. Big mistake. She was drawn to him initially because of his bookish levelheadedness. She thought it was cute how studious and argumentative he was. They met at a juice bar, and it was love at first sight. Zack was teaching art history at the local community college, and he used a lot of big words and was truly impressed by her gun. He detested her world, and yet he couldn't stop asking her about it. Of course they argued. There were tears. Every couple had their meltdowns. But it was his tendency to behave like a petulant child instead of an adult that finally got to her, as if he'd been pushed halfway out of the nest by his parents but somehow managed to cling to the sides and never let go. She grew sick of his self-absorbed tirades over the years.

What was worse, Zack hated Burning Lake. He called it a "bucolic fucklet," but Natalie loved this town, warts and all. Neither one of them was strong enough to endure the final stages of their relationship, and so it had collapsed like a poorly constructed building. All that was left was a smoking cloud of dry rot and regrets.

She remembered the day it was over—her birthday last year. The memory of her ex-boyfriend's aloofness hit her with a soft impact—Zack in his Clark Kentish glasses, dressed in flannel like a throwback to the golden age of Seattle grunge. They celebrated her birthday in a restaurant that had the best shrimp pad thai in town. He leaned in for a kiss, and their lips bumped together. There was a stiff formality about the way he moved that disturbed her and put her on edge.

"Natalie?" He sat down opposite her in the booth, and she noticed his heavily lined forehead—evidence of sleepless nights. "Don't say anything for a second. Let me talk. I've been thinking about us lately. . . ."

As he spoke, he kept glancing beyond her into the depths of the bar. He told her things that she'd been thinking about herself but had never said aloud. Basically, what it came down to was that Zack wanted to run away, from this place, from her, from the things he no longer felt—that initial excitement, that spark, that sizzle, the tingle that had once driven them both physically crazy. Lust. Desire. It'd gradually evaporated until all that was left was a bunch of excuses. I'm busy, I'm exhausted, it's my job, I'm sorry. Plenty of *sorries*.

It all boiled down to the fact that they'd fallen out of love. That each of their habits had become so annoyingly familiar, there was nothing left to explore. "You could've been anything you wanted to be," Zack told her one night. "You're an exceptionally talented woman—those drawings you showed me from your childhood. You were so gifted. Why did you throw it all away?"

If you wanted to get psychological about it, Zack was too much like Natalie's mother. Deborah was a snob, an elitist, who wanted the girls to follow a certain narrow path in life. An artist—that's what Natalie's mother wanted her to be, not the choice she'd ultimately made. But Natalie's early passion for painting had been smothered by the actual study of art. So boring—color charts, perspective, acrylics, stretching your own canvases. She used to look at her drawings and wonder what on earth she would do with an art degree? Teach? Ugh. Please.

Joey used to leave Natalie little made-up mysteries to solve—notes at the breakfast table; a message on the answering machine at home. She loved solving puzzles. She could see patterns everywhere—patterns of behavior, patterns of ritual and habit. Soon she began to observe people on her own. She caught Grace hiding condoms in her backpack. She found out Deborah had wanted only one child, not three—and that Grace and Natalie were accidents. She found out about Willow's relationship with Justin Fowler before anybody else. The art—sure, Natalie was good at it, but her passion lay elsewhere. Besides, her artwork sort of embarrassed her, it was so nakedly revealing of her innermost secrets. What good was that? Natalie had felt forced and pressured into taking art classes by her mother, and so naturally, as a wildly independent teenager, she'd rebelled against this manufactured "destiny" and decided to follow in her dad's footsteps instead. Despite Deborah's heavy-handed pushback.

Natalie's relationship with Zack seemed to reflect a similar tension—whether to become a cop or an artist, two radically different things. Zack represented her mother—refined, intellectual, judgmental. But Natalie sided with her father—down-to-earth, loyal, funny, ironic, always wanting to help out. Not that she didn't appreciate art, music, books, culture. She adored the Whitney Museum and the Metropolitan, and she'd inherited Joey's love of music—jazz and classical, Motown and Mozart, Frank Sinatra and Chet Baker, 1970s punk and 1990s grunge. She still sketched sometimes—absently, while thinking about a case. But she hadn't chosen art as her profession, and Deborah and Zack would never forgive her for it.

Now Natalie felt a strong sense of closure and relief as she clamped the garbage lid shut. Good riddance. She rubbed the morning chill off her arms and looked around the property. This modest plot of land was isolated, bordered on three sides by thick woods. Some mornings, a doe and her fawn would step out of the shadows to nibble at the crab apples on the edge of the lawn. The fruit fell off and rotted on the ground, attracting honeybees in the summer. The forsythia bushes were in desperate need of pruning. The Creeping Jenny had spread into her mother's old garden. A plastic watering can hung upside-down on a branch Deborah had pushed into the lawn thirty years ago. Her mother's old gardening gloves were around here someplace, buried under countless fallen leaves.

Natalie's parents had had an old-fashioned, blond-wood relationship with clearly defined boundaries and a cemented sense of duty. Just like the furniture that wasn't pretty but lasted forever. Her mother had names for all the houseplants, which infuriated Grace, because Grace thought Deborah should love her children a thousand times more than she loved her stupid plants. And Deborah couldn't seem to get rid of the girls fast enough, always kicking them out of the house to go play so that she could have a little peace-and-quiet time—nothing wrong with that—listening to her favorite Broadway musical soundtracks and eating vanilla yogurt mixed with fresh blueberries. "As if us kids were a burden, and not a privilege," Grace said petulantly at their mother's funeral. "Willow was her angel, and since God lets children die, then the two of us weren't worth the trouble of loving and possibly losing."

Natalie's parents weren't exactly what you'd call happy, but they were settled and comfortable. They nested together. Happiness was for other, more frivolous people.

Now her phone buzzed. It was Luke.

"Hey," he said, "I'm heading over to the high school now."

"Okay."

"Meet me in front of the bulletin board." He hung up.

She went back inside and turned on the dishwasher.

9

John F. Kennedy High School consisted of three large buildings—a field house gymnasium, a science center, and an imposing three-story main building constructed in 1972. Natalie parked her car in the school lot and retrieved her notebook and pen from the glove compartment. Today they were tasked with gathering as much information as they could, while people's memories were still fresh.

She got out and crossed the courtyard, where discarded wads of chewing gum filled the cracks between the stones. The flag was at half-mast. She entered the 300,000-square-foot main building and found herself gazing into a hundred pairs of distracted eyes as she walked through those all-too-familiar doors. She'd arrived between classes, and the corridors were clogged with kids. Roughly 1,500 students went to school here, and nothing had changed since Natalie was a freshman.

Today, the entire student body appeared to be in shock. The atmosphere was subdued. The PA system issued a bunch of fuzzy announcements—grief counselors were available, a school assembly was planned for later that afternoon, memoriam speeches for Ms. Buckner were being prepared, and volunteers were welcome.

Natalie's phone buzzed in her pocket. It was Ellie, texting her.

Mom stayed home sick today. Where are you?

At JFK. Interviewing witnesses, Natalie texted back. *Can I give you a lift after school?*

Okay. We'll talk then. Sad emoticon.

Natalie put away her phone and found Luke waiting for her in front of the bulletin board, and when he turned to look at her, she felt that zing again. In unguarded moments, Luke's eyes cupped her like a fresh peach.

"How'd you sleep?" he asked.

"Not great. But I'm upright, aren't I?"

"Hmm. Hard to tell. I'm still half asleep myself. Coffee?"

"Miracle worker."

He handed her one. "It ain't my first rodeo."

She took a sip. "Any news about Riley?"

"No change in status."

"Shit."

"Word of the day. Shit," Luke said. "Let's go."

They walked past rows of banged-up metal lockers that seemed so small to her now. Natalie used to grapple every day with her unyielding, clanking locker with its finicky combination lock. She listened to the familiar slap of feet against the linoleum floor. Every turn down another hallway brought back more memories—art class, chorus, gym, lunch, study hall. Her high school self dogged her like a shy shadow.

On the first floor were the administrative offices, the cafeteria, and the auditorium. On the upper two levels were the classrooms. Natalie could feel the old humiliations throbbing from the cement-block walls. She never used to care what she looked like until she'd entered high school, when the popular girls started snickering about her hand-me-downs. Back then, Natalie radiated a kind of self-possession that garnered instant suspicion. She bought a pair of cheap sunglasses and grew her hair so long, it fell like a plank down her back. She hid behind her shades and long dark hair and ill-fitting clothes until eventually she found her own tribe—a small group of "gifted" misfits who excelled academically and rebelled against their parents' hopes and dreams by listening to Nine Inch Nails and dying their hair funny colors. She became so enmeshed in this tight-knit clan that it felt like an explosion when Bella ran away, and nothing was ever the same for them again.

Some of the students were watching the two detectives with guarded eyes, their youthful faces registering adult skepticism. "God, it's like a John Hughes movie in here," Natalie said in a subdued voice. "You've got your jocks, your class clowns, your druggies, your Goths . . ."

Luke glanced at the impressionable faces swimming all around them and said, "High school felt like it would last forever. Thank God it didn't." It was funny, he pretty much had the world by the balls. He was handsome, charming, successful, a decorated detective, and yet he constantly saw himself as the ninth-grade loner he used to be, a moody fatherless boy who seemed destined to crash and burn in the real world. Well, news flash, Natalie thought—just the opposite.

They walked past a mural of the Founding Fathers and stopped in front of the principal's office. Luke knocked on the etched-glass door and Gilda, the administrative secretary, waved them inside, waddles of fat jiggling under her arms.

"Go right in, he's expecting you," she said as she beamed at them.

Principal Seth Truitt had deep-set eyes, manicured gray hair, and the sour disposition of a man who'd spent too much time hunched over his keyboard, dealing with the banality of bureaucracy. "Good morning, Lieutenant. Good morning, Detective." He stood up and shook their hands.

"We appreciate your cooperation," Luke said.

"Of course. Whatever you folks need. Please. Have a seat."

They sat in a pair of matching vinyl chairs angled in front of Seth's broad, mahogany desk. The office was drafty and sunny, full of period trim and knotty pine built-ins, decorated with somber portraits of past administrators.

"We're in shock, the whole school," the fiftysomething principal said. "Daisy was extremely popular with the students. It's such a tragedy." He shook his head. "So. How can I help? What can I do for you, Lieutenant?"

"Whatever you can tell us about Riley Skinner would be great," Luke said.

"Of course." He opened a dog-eared file on his desk. "Troubled kid, into drugs, on the fast track to nowhere." He sighed. "Riley was brought up in a dangerous household, where the potential for violence is always a risk. Ms. Buckner . . . Daisy was trying to help him overcome these obstacles. I'm not sure if you know this, but she'd helped other troubled students before, and this time was no different."

"Did he ever threaten her physically?" Luke asked.

Seth shook his head. "No. But he became verbally abusive about a month ago, and I take any threats to my teachers very seriously. She was upset by the incident, but Riley apologized, and she figured it was just teenage bravado. Daisy was determined to help him pass her class. The boy's no dummy. He just has issues, that's all." Seth leaned forward. "Confidentially, a lot of my teachers are good at crowd control. They're good at lecturing and hectoring . . . what I call lifers. They're in it for the pensions and the summer vacations. But Daisy actually enjoyed teaching, which is why she got some of the highest scores on our student review site at the end of the year."

Natalie nodded. "Why was Riley flunking out of her class?"

"He was failing several classes, actually. Let's see." Seth thumbed through the file. "Misbehavior, lack of impulse control, absenteeism, failing grades. He was a dropout waiting to happen. His grades were terrible this year. But the deciding factor was Daisy's class. He was about to flunk out of her humanities course, which is a relatively gut-level course, and if that happened, then we were under tremendous pressure to hold him back a grade. It would've been humiliating for Riley, though."

"Humiliating enough to push him over the edge?" Natalie asked.

"Anything's possible," Seth acknowledged. "All of his friends were moving on. When a student gets stigmatized like that, it's easier to drop out of school. That was Riley's future."

"He couldn't recoup?" she asked. "It's only April. Wasn't there enough time to turn things around?"

Seth folded his hands on the desk. "We typically respond to an academic crisis with increased parent-teacher communication. Daisy reached out to Riley's father, and we were hoping Dominic would get more involved, but he never responded to our phone calls or emails. So I offered her my recommendation."

"Which was?"

"You don't pass an underachiever and hope for the best. It's not good for the school, and it certainly isn't good for the student."

"So you recommended he repeat a grade," Natalie said. "How did Daisy respond?"

"Some of these teachers don't care enough to think it through. They'd rather take the easy way out. But Daisy wanted to do what was best for Riley. So she offered him several solutions. She handed the boy a lifeline, but he didn't take it."

"What sort of lifeline?"

"Oh my gosh, she went above and beyond the call of duty. She asked him to write a paper that could've pushed his grade up to a C, if he'd bothered to hand it in. She gave him every opportunity to redeem himself, but he was full of excuses. She was more than fair."

"In your opinion," Luke said, "was Riley a danger to himself and others?"

"Oh, he was trouble," Seth admitted. "There were fistfights."

"Is he capable of murder, in your opinion?"

Seth closed the manila folder. "Honestly? I can't imagine it. But if you think about it—raging hormones, academic pressures, neglect at home. It's all there."

Natalie nodded. "We'll need the names of the kids he hangs out with."

"Sure," Seth told them. "It's not a very long list."

10

They split the list. Three names each.

Down at the eastern end of the building, Natalie passed a group of rowdy boys who acted as if they owned the place, high-fiving and making a lot of noise as they stormed the corridors. Some of the shyer ones stuck to the shadows, ignored or barely acknowledged, the ache of alienation plastered all over their young faces.

Natalie found two of Riley's friends hanging out in the quad between periods, a rectangle of lawn surrounded by weathered picnic tables. She recognized sixteen-year-old Kermit Hughes, a pasty-faced Goth who couldn't stop touching his pimples. His father worked at a gas station and his mother was a housewife who sold Mary Kay makeup.

Fifteen-year-old Owen Kottler was a wide-eyed boy with scruffy brown hair and a skinny frame. His father was on disability, and his mom was a waitress. As a rookie cop, Natalie had gotten to know many of the residents of the west side. She loved these people. She'd earned their trust. She knew their families and the troubles that plagued them. Like so many west side teens, these boys wore army-navy surplus, drove around in their father's battered pickup trucks, and dreamed big when they weren't feeling small.

Now she showed them her badge. "Detective Lockhart. Remember me? Mind if I ask you boys a few questions?"

"Guess so, yeah," they muttered, averting their eyes.

"I hear Riley Skinner threatened Ms. Buckner about a month ago. Do you know anything about that?"

Kermit balled up his fists and said, "Riley never threatened anyone."

"Are you sure?" She looked over at Owen. "Maybe he was upset because he was flunking out of school? Did he ever talk to you about that?"

"He called her a ho once," Owen blurted, to the dismay of his friend.

"Shut up," Kermit muttered, shoving Owen off balance.

Natalie took out her notepad and pen. "Riley called Ms. Buckner a whore? When was this?"

"It never happened," Kermit insisted, glaring at his friend.

Owen clammed up.

Natalie had learned over time that if you approached a witness with an obvious agenda, they'd be more likely to lie to you. So she put her notebook away and said, "Kermit, how's your mom?"

"Okay, I guess," he said with a shrug.

"Is she still selling Mary Kay?"

"Yeah." He smiled.

"I need a new lipstick," Natalie said. "Tell her I'll swing by sometime."

"Okay," he said.

"Now, in the meantime, I'm trying to figure out what happened yesterday, that's all. When was the last time you saw Riley?"

"After school," Kermit said. "He gave me a lift home."

She got out her notebook and pen and jotted it down. "When was this?"

"Quarter to three."

"Did he say where he was going after that?"

"No."

"Were you at Haymarket Field last night?"

The boys glanced at each other and shook their heads. She felt sorry for them. Their parents struggled to make ends meet. They clipped coupons and went without. They shopped at the 99-cent store and attended church on Sundays, dropping their hard-earned cash into the collection plate. Their older brothers and sisters were into drugs. Kermit's cousin had been caught shoplifting. Owen's uncle was in jail for petty theft. Life hadn't exactly treated them fairly.

"No?" Natalie said. "Because I can check it out. Hold on." She got out her phone and did a search of Owen Kottler's social media, found his Instagram page, and scrolled through the postings. "Well, look here, Owen. What about this?" She showed him a screenshot of himself, Kermit, and Riley, down by the old Shell station. "You posted this at seven thirty last night."

Owen's eyes widened. "Well, um . . ."

"It's okay. You can still change your statement," she told him gently. "It's not too late. I'm looking for any information that might be helpful to the investigation."

"We rode our bikes over there around seven," Owen confessed.

She glanced at Kermit. "You were there at seven o'clock? Riley, too?"

The school bell rang, and both boys grew tense.

"I can't be late for class," Owen pleaded, wiping his sweaty forehead.

"Don't worry, I'll talk to your teachers," she reassured them. "You won't get into trouble, okay? When did Riley arrive at Haymarket Field exactly? Do you remember?"

Kermit shrugged. "We got there around seven. Riley came a little later."

"How much later?"

"Seven fifteen. Seven twenty."

Natalie jotted it down. "I see from your Instagram page, Owen, that Riley wore a gray hoodie and a green flannel shirt over a pair of jeans. Is that the same outfit he wore to school?"

"I don't remember," Owen said.

"Kermit? Did he wear this outfit when he dropped you off yesterday?"

"No. He had on a T-shirt that said 'Dumbnation.'"

"'Dumb Nation'? What color?"

"One word. 'Dumbnation.' Black with yellow lettering."

"What else? Jeans or chinos? Sneakers? What?"

"Cargo pants," Kermit said.

"Right," Natalie said. "Lot of pockets. What color were the cargoes?"

"Black."

"Black again. Anything else? Type of footwear?"

"Vans slip-on checkerboards," Kermit said. "Like mine." He showed her.

"Nice. And while the three of you were at Haymarket Field last night, did you see Detective Buckner arrive at any point?"

"Yeah," Kermit said.

"When was this?"

"Eight thirty, I think."

"And then what happened?"

"We heard tires squealing, and a car came swerving into the field. Detective Buckner got out, and he was shouting at us. He said we were holding, but there's no way he could've known what we were up to from that far away. Then he got in Riley's face and started yelling something about Ms. Buckner . . . we were all freaking out."

"What did Detective Buckner say about Ms. Buckner?" Natalie asked.

"Crazy stuff."

"Do you remember specifically?"

Kermit shrugged. "Something about . . . did you kill her? And we said, 'Kill who?' It made zero sense, because like . . . who would kill Ms. Buckner?"

Natalie nodded. "Then what happened?"

"Riley took off running. So Detective Buckner tore after him."

"I have to go now," Owen said urgently. "I've got a test."

"Don't worry, Owen, I'll talk to your teacher. Just a few more questions." She took a breath. "Backing up, Kermit, after Riley dropped you off at your place around quarter to three yesterday, did he say where he was going?"

"Just that he was gonna see India later," Kermit said.

Natalie masked her confusion. "India Cochran?"

"Yeah. He said he was going over to her place."

Natalie had known sixteen-year-old India ever since she and Ellie attended daycare together. India was just like Ellie, top of her class. College-bound. What was she doing with a troubled kid like Riley Skinner?

"Riley didn't kill anyone," Kermit insisted. "I mean, yeah, he likes to talk trash, and he's messed up, but he'd never hurt Ms. Buckner. He was trying to make a name for himself, and Ms. Buckner was helping him. Why would he kill her?"

"How was she helping him?" Natalie asked.

"With his music. He's a rapper. It's totally lit." Kermit unzipped his backpack, took out his phone, and showed her an amateurishly produced video. The track had a good beat.

I look into your eyes and see lotta regrets,
Not your typical bullshit teacher ignorance,
No more Dumbledores or Dead Poets Society.
You tryna be good, but I wanna be free.
Flunk or pass? I don't know. Too many questions to ask,
Too many tests to take, too many pointless essays to hack.
Do my grades tell you who I am?
Do they make me a better man?
Can you see into my soul, Mrs. B.?
Do you know who I am from my Fs and my Ds?
What the hell? How'd I get myself into this jam?
It's a mess. So much stress. I don't know who I am.
What makes you so confident? So positive? So damn sure?
Where'd you get that big bleeding heart of yours?
Do you shop in the mall for your Jane Goodall tees?
Where'd you get those eyes that into-the-future sees?
How do you know so much, Mrs. B? Tell me.
Is this real? What if I can't live up to your ideal?
Maybe I'll piss you off? Eventually pull a Mom, hit a vein . . .
We're talking seppuku, or a run-of-the-mill hang.
Here's lookin at you, kid. I'll commit hari-kari.
You do you, I'll do me—only you will be sorry.
Whaddya think of that, Mrs. B? How's your plan sounding now?
I'm lost in a forest of tears and phonies, I wanna bow out.
Are you gonna let me go? Or are you gonna hold on?
How will you live with yourself once I am gone?
You'll be what—sad? Glad? Relieved?

No more flunkies to worry about. No more deaf ears and pleas.

I can't picture that. Who's your next loser gonna be?

Not me. I'll be floatin up there, in the air, where I'm free.

Kermit turned off the video and crossed his arms.

Natalie felt the surprise in her solar plexus—Riley had given a confident performance. Here was an angry young man, writing about suicide and self-harm with more insight than she'd expected. It revealed feelings of failure and acquiescence, perhaps even grudging gratitude for Daisy's concern.

She couldn't square it in her mind with the theory that she and Luke had been floating about a sociopathic student who'd brutally murdered his teacher. Although you never knew. Reality didn't have to make sense.

"Kermit," she said, "I'd like a copy of the video."

"Where should I send it?"

She gave him her department email address, then said, "Okay, guys. Let's go. I'll explain your absence to your teachers."

11

Upstairs on the third floor, Natalie found Daisy's old classroom, where twenty-five bored-looking students sat fidgeting in their seats, jiggling their feet, and tapping their pens. The substitute teacher wrote instructions on the whiteboard, her silver-rinsed hair cropped short and layered like rose petals.

Outside the door, a makeshift memorial covered a small area of space on the floor—an overflowing pile of flowers, stuffed animals, unlit candles, and thoughtful handwritten notes. Natalie picked one up at random. "I will miss your beautiful smile and your encouraging words." Nearby were five items carefully arranged in a circle—a bird feather, a stone, a votive candle, a Dixie cup full of water, and a picture of Ms. Buckner cut out of last year's yearbook.

Natalie recognized the Wiccan ritual honoring the dead. The four items surrounding Daisy's picture represented air, earth, fire, and water. Natalie and her friends used to perform a similar ritual on occasion. You sat in a circle, holding hands and chanting, "I call upon the elements, and invite the powers of the four directions to watch over Ms. Buckner's soul. By air and earth and fire and rain, we will remember you."

There weren't that many actual witches in Burning Lake, although Wicca was a legitimate religion now. It had been legal to practice since 1986 due to a landmark court decision, but the local Wiccans made sure everyone understood they only did white magic, and that they had nothing to do with Satanism, which was another breed altogether. There were two official adult covens listed in the phone book, with about eighty members each, but there were many more unofficial covens hidden from public view. On the surface, it would appear that Burning Lake had a sparse Wiccan population, but that was due to the fact that many of them were still in the broom closet.

Conversely, no one knew exactly how many practicing Satanists there were in Burning Lake, except for the small group of about two dozen adherents who'd planted their church here. Rumors of animal sacrifices and devil worship had floated around for years, but the police investigations into, say, last year's spate of missing pets, had subsequently exonerated the church members, who seemed for the most part to be nice people.

During her sophomore year in high school, Natalie had formed her own coven with her best friends Bobby, Adam, Max, and Bella. The love, the bond between these five friends, had once been so solid, so unbreakable— *never* would they not be linked somehow, they swore, across time and space, regardless of where life hurled them. They would be like quantum particles, always feeling what the others felt, even if they were thousands of miles apart. This just had to be true. Sixteen-year-old Natalie couldn't imagine it otherwise.

For Natalie, high school had been a living, breathing nightmare. Rumors spread like wildfire. Nobody trusted anybody else. Natalie and her artsy friends knew that they sucked—but at least they sucked with integrity. They prided themselves on standing up for the underdog. Their defensive weapons of choice were snark and derision. They called themselves "brilliant misfits"—in private, where there was no need for modesty. They amused themselves by boasting about how talented they were, since it boosted their morale. On the outside, they were losers. On the inside, they outshone the entire school.

During Natalie's witchy phase, she and her friends would stay out long after sunset, watching dusk dissolve into twilight, and twilight disappear into a velvety blackness, where the stars blinked on one by one, and they worked their magic—hexing other kids who picked on them, wishing luck to those in need, relishing their newfound sense of empowerment. But the deeper she and her friends got into the concept of evil, the more her thoughts touched on the wet, squishy sound of a stick stabbing into the bloated guts of a dead raccoon . . . the one thing she wished to erase from her mind.

Of course, reality was vastly different from adolescent hopes and dreams, and Natalie hadn't heard from any of her old pals in quite some time. After Bella ran away, they all took off for college, scattering across the country. Occasionally, she'd bump into Bobby Deckhart, who was working as an accountant now, or Max Callahan, who was developing some sort of music app. But Bella was gone. Drugs took Adam.

Now she continued down the hallway, looking for room 312. She paused in front of Ethan Hathaway's English lit class at the end of the corridor. The room was filled to capacity. The students were mostly silent. Not a lot of foot-jiggling. All eyes were on Mr. Hathaway, a tall handsome man who leaned against the lectern and read aloud from a book of poetry.

Natalie didn't know much about Hathaway, only what Grace had told her. He was fortysomething and unhitched—a prize catch in this town. Except that, according to Grace, he'd gotten mixed reviews from some of the ladies he'd dated. They called him antisocial, standoffish, bookish, too serious.

Now she observed the sophomore class through the glass panel. Most of the girls were paying rapt attention, but not everyone was impressed. The boys in back looked bored, propping their chins in their hands and slouching over their desks, idly tracing flaws in the varnished wood.

The English teacher was a good-looking man. Tall, bespectacled, and square-jawed, with toned, sinewy limbs. He spoke calmly, with conviction, and possessed the kind of dignified sincerity that wasn't easy to fake. No wonder some of his students had crushes on him. He paused for dramatic effect before turning the page and continuing in a stage whisper, "'O, that you were yourself! But, love, you are . . .'"

Some of the girls practically swooned.

Ellie was seated up front between her two best friends, India Cochran and Berkley Auberdine. Another close friend, Sadie Myers, sat next to Berkley. India's black skirt was inappropriately short, and she swung her long leg with seductive synchronicity, while nodding to the sound of Hathaway's voice. Ellie, Berkley, and Sadie were doing variations of the same theme. Four hypnotized seductresses. And yet, despite the Goth attire, Natalie was struck by Ellie's clean-scrubbed earnestness.

She'd known these girls since they were fat little babies. She'd been to all of Ellie's birthday parties and had witnessed many dramas. She recalled sitting in the kitchen with Grace and overhearing little blooms of laughter followed by little outbursts of disagreement. During the sugar highs, Ellie and her friends would run around the yard, twirling their colorful skirts like flowers that had grown legs.

Today, they were dressed head-to-toe in witchy black—okay, so this was the coven. Ellie, India, Berkley, and Sadie. Four fast friends. Hanging out in New Age bookstores and metaphysical shops after school, just like Natalie and her friends had done.

Funny—her niece had never mentioned Riley before, and Grace monitored Ellie's friendships closely. If Riley knew India well enough to drop by her house after school, then Ellie would certainly know about it.

Natalie checked her watch. Fifteen minutes to kill before next period. She logged on to Instagram and perused India's social media pages. It felt wrong to be spying on them, like a transgression. They still called her Aunt Natalie. Once upon a time it was Auntie N. She knew their lovely mothers. It troubled Natalie deeply, but she knew she would have to reconcile her dual roles in their lives going forward.

There was nothing posted on India's Instagram or Facebook pages yesterday, which was odd, because she posted something almost every day—plates of food, shoes in her closet, selfies. Next Natalie scrolled through Ellie's social media pages, feeling rather sick about it. How many times had she advised her niece to use caution? Twitter, Instagram, Snapchat, Facebook. The internet was forever.

Natalie didn't find anything of significance on any of the girls' accounts and put away her phone. Hathaway's class was winding down. The girls in the front row were still mesmerized—India with her jet-black hair and strangely adult gaze, more mature than the others; Sadie with her pixie lisp and multiply pierced ears; lithe, aristocratic Berkley, whose single flaw was her slightly droopy eyelids behind designer glasses. These weren't the school misfits or cast-offs, nerdy losers or artsy types. They were the brightest, smartest, and cleverest of the bunch. Churchgoers and members of the Honor Society. Straight-A students. Natalie had always been amazed by them. She adored them—although some of their personality traits could use a little improvement. For instance, India could be manipulative; Berkley could be surprisingly cold; Sadie wasn't as intellectually curious as she needed to be; and Ellie could be honest to the point of rudeness, like her father, Burke.

Natalie had a flash of Ellie as a toddler in the wintertime, walking stiffly in her quilted jumpsuit, like an astronaut taking her first steps on Mars. God, they grew up fast.

The bell rang.

The students grabbed their backpacks and shot up from their seats.

"Just remember," Hathaway said above the ruckus, "switch off your phones and open your minds. I want summaries of chapters nine and ten on my desk by noon tomorrow." He closed the book of poetry and smiled at the stream of students flowing out the door, and Natalie had to step back to avoid getting bowled over.

A handful of girls lingered after class, including Ellie and her friends. Natalie listened in on the conversation. They were devastated by Ms. Buckner's death, grief-stricken and seeking comfort. Lots of flushed faces and choked voices. At one point, they all spoke at once, then laughed awkwardly and tried again.

Hathaway responded warmly and earnestly, like a favorite uncle. He was good at this. He quoted Edna St. Vincent Millay and Toni Morrison. They ended in a group hug—with one another, not with Mr. Hathaway. He was careful not to touch them.

Finally, the girls filed out the door.

Natalie tapped India on the arm. "Can I speak with you a second?"

The sixteen-year-old seemed startled. "Aunt Natalie? What's wrong?"

"Let's go back into the classroom, I'm sure Mr. Hathaway won't mind."

"Um . . . okay."

"Go on, I'll be right in," Natalie told her.

Puzzled, India said good-bye to her friends while Natalie turned to Ellie and asked, "How are you feeling?"

"Not great," her niece confessed with taut jaw muscles. "Mom's an emotional wreck, and I just lost my bracelet." She showed Natalie her pale wrist. "The one you gave me last year. It's my favorite."

"I'm so sorry, Ellie," Natalie said with disappointment. The scarab-link bracelet was a museum reproduction made of turquoise, pewter, and brass. Ellie had always been fascinated by mummies and archeology, and she'd read that scarabs were an ancient Egyptian symbol for immortality. When Natalie saw the bracelet, she just knew Ellie would love it. "Did you retrace your steps?"

"Yeah, I've looked everywhere." Ellie rubbed her wrist. "I *love* that bracelet."

"What about the lost-and-found box?"

Her eyes lit up. "I'll go check it out. Thanks, Aunt Natalie. See you after school."

"Two thirty."

"Bye." Ellie took off after her friends.

Natalie joined India inside the vacant classroom. "Sorry to barge in on you like this," she told Hathaway. "I'm Detective Lockhart. I don't believe we've met. I need to borrow your classroom for a few minutes. Is that okay?"

He glanced at his watch. "Sure. My next class starts in fifteen minutes, though."

"Just enough time."

Hathaway at a distance was easy on the eyes. But upon closer inspection, he seemed worn-out this morning—gaunt cheeks, a pallid complexion, a few missed spots shaving. "You're Grace's sister, right?" he said.

"Natalie." They shook hands.

"I've heard a lot about you."

"All good, I hope." She smiled.

"Are you kidding me? Grace won't stop bragging about you in the faculty lounge. Anyway, I'll go fetch a cup of coffee," he told them, and left the room.

India touched her damp forehead. "I really can't be late for class."

"That's okay, I'll make it quick," Natalie said, closing the door. "Have a seat."

Despite the fact that Natalie had known India forever, she didn't really *know* her. Sixteen-year-old India Cochran was a bit of a mystery. She looked like a model for *Teen Vogue* in her fitted black skirt with the metal zippers down both sides, her retro boots, her slim black T-shirt, and tailored velvet jacket. India's face was narrow and catlike, with sly, curious eyes. Whereas Ellie wore her heart on her sleeve and gave you her opinion on everything from world peace to ketchup, India was more circumspect, as if she were afraid to reveal her true self. Natalie had observed the four of them for years, and she occasionally caught India bossing the other girls around when she thought nobody was looking.

Now India tugged on her skirt and swung her leg with barely veiled impatience.

"Did you see Riley Skinner after school yesterday?" Natalie asked.

"Riley? No. I was over at Berkley's house," she said, blinking a little. "Why?"

"Just you and Berkley?"

"No, we were all there. Me, Sadie, Ellie, and Berk."

Natalie grew vaguely troubled. She recalled Grace saying yesterday that Ellie had "a thing" after school, and realized this was what she meant.

"And you're sure you didn't see Riley after school?" Natalie pressed.

"No, Aunt Natalie."

"I'm speaking to you as a police detective now. You don't have to answer my questions, India, but I'm trying to find out what happened to Ms. Buckner. Does Riley drop by your house often?"

"God, no. He doesn't drop by. He's, like, my stalker," India explained.

"Your stalker?"

She nodded. "Yeah. He'll drive past my house a dozen times a day. Or else he'll hang around the hallways after class . . . waiting to catch a glimpse of me, I guess."

"Okay. Well, someone told me Riley was planning on visiting you after school yesterday," Natalie said. "Was that misinformation?"

India twisted her long black ponytail around her slender fingers and smoothed a few wisps of hair off her damp neck. "Who told you that?"

"I can't reveal the information, sorry."

"Because it's not true. No way. I mean, maybe he drove past my house, but I wasn't there," she said with a shrug. "I was at Berkley's, like I said."

"You said he's your stalker? Have you contacted the police?"

"No." She shifted uneasily.

"Why not, India? Does your mother know Riley's stalking you?"

"It's not like that, Aunt Natalie. It's . . . complicated."

"Complicated how?"

"We used to be friends," she admitted, glancing at her nails. "But he wanted to take it to the next level, and I didn't."

"Oh. So when you say 'friends,' how close were you?" Natalie asked.

"Just friends." There was a sheen of sweat on India's face.

"Maybe he drove over to Berkley's house then?"

"He didn't even know I was there," India said, visibly upset. "Unless someone told him. In which case, I suppose he could've driven past Berk's house, but he didn't stop by to say hello or anything."

"Then it's possible Riley may have driven past Berkley's house, stalking you, as you say . . . but you never actually saw him or spoke to him?"

"That's right." She adjusted the black leather bracelet around her wrist, sliding it down, and Natalie noticed a small tattoo on the inner part of her wrist. A small red rose surrounded by twisted barbed wire.

India quickly tucked the leather bracelet back in place and heaved a sigh.

Natalie leaned forward. "India, has Riley ever threatened you?"

"No. That's stupid. Was it Kermit who said that?" She tipped her head furiously. "Did he tell you Riley was coming to see me? Because, seriously . . . that guy is such a loser."

"You said Riley was stalking you . . . do you ever feel unsafe?"

"Well, yeah. I mean, he'd rap about us sometimes."

"Rap about you?"

"In his songs." Her eyes glazed over. "He made it sound like I'd betrayed him, but that's the furthest thing from the truth. We were never a 'thing,' except in his head."

"Did you ever feel threatened by the lyrics in his songs?"

She shrugged it off. "Just because he raps about us doesn't make it true."

"Do you think Riley was stalking Ms. Buckner, too?"

She crossed her arms tightly. "Why would he?"

"I don't know."

"Well, I mean . . . maybe. Riley is totally self-sabotaging." Tears sprang to her eyes. "I'm sorry, Aunt Natalie, but I'm under extreme stress right now. I don't exactly feel safe."

"Why not?"

She tapped her foot nervously. "Because you keep asking me all these questions, and I don't know what you're getting at."

"Oh." Natalie drew back. "Sorry. I didn't mean to confuse you. I've been asking people questions all morning. You're just one of those people."

India sighed hard. "Well, look, we all loved Ms. Buckner, are you kidding me? She was totally cool. If you ever needed extra credit or wanted to throw a bake sale or something, she'd be there for you. She was helping us raise money for the girls' athletic scholarship, and she hosted the prom committee at her house, where she served us tea and cookies. It was really nice."

The bell rang.

India sat forward, palms open. "I can't be late for class, Auntie N."

It was the first time India had called her that in many moons, and it tugged at Natalie's heartstrings, but at the same time, it felt slightly manipulative.

Natalie handed the girl her business card. "Tell your teacher I detained you, okay? If she needs anything else, have her call me."

"Okay, I will. Thanks. Bye." India scooped up her book bag and hurried away.

Natalie's phone buzzed, and she checked the number. It was Luke.

"Any luck?" he asked.

"Owen Kottler forgot to delete his Instagram posts showing that he and Kermit Hughes were with Riley last night at Haymarket Field."

"Good. Let's see if we can get the boys' parents to bring them in for a formal interview. In the meantime, the autopsy's in fifteen minutes."

"Meet you at the morgue," she said and hung up.

12

The autopsy took place in the county health building, a few blocks east of the police station. The morgue was dank and chilly, full of dripping pipes and mechanical sounds. Coroner Barry Fishbeck was a fellow of the American Academy of Forensic Sciences, a man possessed of country humor and shrewdness. In his midsixties, he was stooped and dignified-looking with a silver goatee and a bulbous nose.

Daisy's clothes had been bagged and sent to the state lab for testing. Her body lay on a chrome table in the autopsy suite, and it shocked Natalie all over again to see her lying there dead. Daisy was slender and pale, with a dusting of freckles over her elfin nose, and she looked younger than her thirty-six years. There was a slight baby bump above her pubic bone, as well as evidence of meticulous grooming—manicure, pedicure, leg wax, bikini wax. Natalie recognized the faded, red and black starfish tattoo above her left breast—Grace had an identical tattoo. They'd gotten them when they were seventeen and stupid, and showed Natalie the results, giggling and drunkenly insisting, "Don't tell Deborah! Don't tell the Momster!" Natalie never did.

She'd learned to suppress her emotions during an autopsy, but this one was tough. Daisy Forester used to live down the street from them—a galloping girl with curly red hair and Kewpie doll eyes who liked to sing "Baby, I Love Your Way" on karaoke nights. Grace and Daisy were best friends forever. In the eighth grade, they'd worn identical overalls and black pullover sweaters. In the ninth grade, they joined the girls' swim team and developed deep tans, strong arm muscles, and cheerleader smiles. In the tenth grade, they dabbled in the occult—looking for their future husbands in a crystal ball and casting spiteful curses on their frenemies. In the eleventh grade, they got identical tattoos—the brittle star had a talent for regrowing its limbs. It was a powerful symbol of hope. It meant that happiness could regenerate over time. In the twelfth grade, they went a little wild, smoking pot and sleeping with boys. They were so close at times, some of the girls at school called them conjoined twins.

Barry Fishbeck made a show of removing his jacket and putting on his white coroner's coat, his surgical mask, and latex gloves, like an athlete preparing for the big game. Natalie could barely breathe. She hated the autopsy room's foul chemical smells. Here the cadavers were studied, X-rayed, and cut open, before being stacked in a forty-degree cold room, where you could see their waxy feet through the clear plastic body bags.

Daisy's head was turned sideways, and part of her scalp had been shaved so that the wound behind her right ear was exposed. Natalie couldn't stop staring at it. It held a peculiar fascination. The geography of the human body never ceased to amaze her. The cast-iron skillet had impacted the right parietal bone, approximately five inches from the top of the skull, resulting in a deep laceration with ragged, swollen edges. Were it not for this grotesque head wound, Daisy would be teaching her fourth-period humanities class right about now. Natalie struggled to comprehend how she could be walking around in her own skin, while this person she'd known her entire life was gone.

Now Barry clipped a digital recorder to his belt, slipped on his headset, and chose from an assortment of tools. "Victim's name is Daisy Forester Buckner," he began, while Luke took out a roll of Peppermint LifeSavers, popped one in his mouth, and offered one to Natalie.

"Thanks." Only human blood had that sharp, coppery odor that invaded your psyche and lingered for days. Everything Natalie had touched last night—body fluids, blood spatter, unknown substances—all those scent molecules had clung to her skin and clothes. Despite this morning's shower, despite the extra laundry detergent she'd poured into the washer, the smell of last night's crime scene would die a slow, hesitant death. As a homicide detective, you risked carrying a whiff of decay around with you wherever you went. To counter this effect, the guys in the unit wore cologne, and sometimes the office smelled like an air-freshened graveyard.

"Okay, now for the coronal mastoid incision." Barry picked up a scalpel and made an incision across the top of the head. He peeled back the scalp and exposed the cranium, which was fractured like an egg.

Natalie's stomach seized, and her nostrils flared with revulsion at the raw smells. Human beings weren't meant to be cut open and exposed for all the world to see. The dead were supposed to be honored, laid out in their absolute finest, and mourned by candlelight. The Victorians had it right.

A memory pulsed before her. Natalie and her friends used to hold their breath whenever the school bus drove past the graveyard. You had to hold your breath until there were no more headstones left to see, and when Natalie couldn't hold her breath any longer, she would pretend. She was pretending now.

She reached for the roll of LifeSavers on the counter, popped another mint in her mouth, and crunched down hard. Daisy's skin was flawless, except for the starfish tattoo above her left breast and . . . wait. What were those marks on her wrist?

Natalie carefully lifted Daisy's left arm and examined the faded old scars on her inner wrist—three small irregular scars, each about an inch in length, parallel and close together. They looked like three baby earthworms.

"Hesitation marks from a failed suicide attempt," Barry explained. "Although there's no mention of it in the medical records."

"Really? Her family doctor kept it a secret?" Natalie said, surprised.

"Or else Daisy kept it secret. Those wounds are superficial. They could've healed on their own. This wasn't a serious attempt, but it was enough to leave scars."

"I never noticed before," she admitted, gently placing Daisy's arm back on the chrome table. It explained some of Daisy's fashion choices. She favored wrist cuffs—lace, wrap, leather—or long sleeves year-round. "How long ago did this happen?"

"Well, from the looks of it . . . raised and faded keloidal scarring means the scar tissue continued to grow larger over time, until the overgrowth eventually became larger than the original wound. Probably late teens, early twenties, but I'm guessing."

Natalie vaguely recalled some drama when Daisy was eighteen—there were rumors about a bad breakup, something to do with a boy, but she couldn't remember the details. Brandon had come into the picture around the same time. It was sort of an abrupt transition from Grace to Brandon, as if they'd handed Daisy off like a baton.

Now the harsh overhead lights exposed the radial cracks in Daisy's cranium. The fractures reminded Natalie of a hawk's talons, gripping the glistening white skull, with dark blood folded into the most severe cracks. On the counter, a few feet away from the chrome table, was the murder weapon—the medium-size cast-iron skillet, bagged and tagged, lying on a fresh clean towel. Preliminary results were in. The skillet contained traces of type A-positive blood. Daisy's blood was A-positive. Further DNA testing was being done at the state lab, but it would take a couple of weeks to get the results back. Still, the preliminary findings were significant. Even though type A-positive was fairly common, it was clear to everyone in the room that the skillet was the murder weapon.

Now Barry removed the calvarium and the brain, then stripped the dura away from the cranial cavity and examined the interior of the skull, tracking the weapon's trajectory. "See here . . . where the bones are shattered in a curved pattern?" He pointed at the site of impact with his scalpel. "This pattern has the same characteristics as the edge of the skillet." He picked up the skillet and did a side-by-side comparison. "They match almost exactly."

Luke leaned forward and studied the exposed skull as if it were a piece of sculpture, while Natalie shuddered, no weight in her stomach.

"Method of death?" Luke asked the coroner.

"MOD would be impact with a heavy object," Barry said, "resulting in the underlying dislocation of the skull. Projectiles of bone fragments penetrated into the brain, causing massive damage. Proximate cause of death is acute blunt-force trauma, resulting in complete and instantaneous disability and death."

At least it was quick and painless. Small comfort.

Luke crossed his arms. "So a single blow to the skull with a medium-size skillet killed her? How much strength would that require?"

"Upper body strength? Not a lot," Barry said. "An injury to the back of the skull is statistically more lethal than a blow to the front of the head. Which means, if the skillet was swung with great speed, then speed beats size. Not a lot of strength would've been required. I've seen this type of injury before in crimes of passion. All it takes is one blow."

"What's your TOD?" Natalie asked.

Barry picked up the chart and flipped through the fluid-stained pages. "By the time I arrived at the scene last night, around nine o'clock . . . the skin was waxy and translucent. Purple striations over the lower extremities. Eyes not yet milky—that usually occurs eight to ten hours after death. Body temperature was incrementally lower. Rigor mortis was just beginning. Limbs were flaccid. Stiffness of the jaw. Clear signs of postmortem lividity throughout the body. I'd say . . . three to five hours before my arrival."

"So then . . . between four and six o'clock?" she clarified.

"I can't pin it down precisely—nobody can—but that's my best estimate." Next he performed the Y-incision and removed and weighed each organ, dissecting the stomach contents and recording his findings. "A few partially digested pecans . . . the remnants of a peanut-butter-and-jelly sandwich . . ." He paused with his instruments hovering over the victim's pelvic cavity. "Okay," he said softly. "Now for the fetus."

The room grew still.

Daisy's face was disturbingly peaceful.

Forgive us our sins.

The sorrow was stuck in Natalie's throat like a handful of sand. When they were young, Daisy's favorite CD was *The Monkees Greatest Hits*. She was a no-BS kind of girl. She used to give Natalie beauty makeovers. "Hey-ho, future movie star. Get ready for your close-up!" She'd curl Natalie's long hair with a flat iron and let the little rug rat ask her a ton of pesky questions. But shortly after Daisy and Grace formed a coven with Lindsey Wozniak and Bunny Jackson, they no longer wanted the nine-year-old tagging along. They became supersecretive. Grace even put up a sign on her door that read "Gnats (that means *you* Natalie) Not Allowed."

But none of that mattered anymore. Death was final.

The coroner made his first incision into the abdomen.

All of a sudden, for Natalie, it made perfect, haunting sense. One blow. Impulsive. Disorganized. A crime of passion. Sexual problems between Brandon and Daisy. *The Breakup Bible.* Manicure. Pedicure. A bikini wax.

"We need to confirm who the father is," she said.

Barry looked up. "Why? Do you think she was having an affair?"

"I'm beginning to suspect it." She couldn't help feeling, deep in her gut, that Brandon wasn't the father. She told Barry, "You'll be running a DNA test on the fetus?"

Luke nodded. "Good point."

"It'll take a few weeks to get the results back from the lab," Barry said.

For the second time that day, she felt as if she'd betrayed someone close to her. What did the dead think of us? What if they haunted the living out of spite?

13

Thirty minutes later, Natalie pushed through the heavy double doors and entered the bustling intensive care unit at Langston Memorial Hospital. The ICU was one big room where the patients' beds were separated by royal blue curtains. You could hear the blipping and buzzing equipment, the ventilators whooshing up and down.

She spotted Dr. Russ Swinton over by the nurses' station. He was a no-nonsense professional in his midfifties, saddlebag-tough and emotionless, which made him exactly the kind of person you wanted during an emergency. His dark bushy eyebrows gave him a perpetually glum look. Twenty-one years ago, Russ had examined Natalie after she'd been attacked in the woods. He was younger back then, with a kinder demeanor, but time and experience had taken away his warmth.

"Natalie," he said crisply. "How can I help you?"

"I came to see how Riley Skinner's doing."

"No change in status," he said with a regretful shake of his head. "We've got him on steroids to help with the swelling. No history of epilepsy or any other neurological disorders. He came to us dehydrated, with an elevated temperature and heart rate. He had a small contusion on his right cheek, but no other signs of injury. No body blows or head wounds. No evidence of a physical altercation of any kind."

"What happened? Why did he start seizing?"

Russ frowned. "We don't know yet. So far he's tested negative for epilepsy, meningitis, encephalitis, parasites, brain abscesses, and various other diseases. We've also screened for heroin, cocaine, MDMA, amphetamines, antidepressants, convulsants, and psilocybin. He did test positive for alcohol, and now we're screening for synthetic drugs, which are much more difficult to detect—"

"Synthetic?"

"It's a possibility. We've seen a number of similar cases in the ER this year."

Synthetic drugs were unregulated, and the ingredients were unknown. Synthetic marijuana, for instance, had very little in common with organic marijuana. Cheap and easy to obtain, these drugs didn't show up in the most common drug tests and often contained powerful stimulants—it would be like snorting high-grade cocaine times ten.

"Until we can pin it down, we'll be treating him with antianxiety medication to slow his heart rate and lower his blood pressure, reduce the frantic activity in his brain. There's something else you should know," Russ said. "Riley had about three hundred dollars in his pockets, mostly tens and twenties."

Which implied he was dealing, she thought. "What's his prognosis?"

"That all depends." Russ scratched his neck with his finger. "One of my patients was in a coma for six months before waking up with no deleterious effects whatsoever. Others haven't been so lucky. We'll have to wait and see. Every case is different."

Natalie tucked a strand of hair behind her ear. "Any good news?"

Russ picked up a chart. "The CT scan shows no structural abnormalities, such as a stroke or a tumor. His blood pressure is normal, his vitals are stable. So far, we've prevented his organs from shutting down. That's what I'd call good news. We'll know more once the swelling recedes. We're dealing with a dire situation, but we're monitoring it closely."

"Thanks, Russ. I'm here to pick up the medical records." She handed him the subpoena. "And collect the outfit he was wearing last night."

The doctor skimmed through the paperwork—he knew how thorough the BLPD was. "Looks in order. I'll have Sofia forward you the patient's medical records. And Monica will fetch Riley's clothing."

"Thanks. When will you get the results on the latest tox screen?"

"Hopefully in a few days. I'll keep you posted." He pivoted on his heel and was gone.

Five minutes later, one of the nurses came over with a sealed plastic bag full of Riley's clothes—Levi's, a pair of scuffed Doc Martens, a plaid flannel shirt, and a gray hoodie with pinprick drops of something dark on the right sleeve, along with Riley's wallet and keys. Natalie signed the chain of custody form and accepted the bundle. She checked the bag for a cell phone, but there wasn't any. "Did he have a phone on him when he was admitted?" she asked.

"No, Detective. Just what's in the bag." The nurse pointed toward the rear of the ICU. "He's back there. The last bed at the end."

Natalie thanked her and headed over. She parted the privacy curtain and stood at the foot of the hospital bed with the heavy bundle in her arms.

Riley's eyes were closed. There was an endotracheal tube taped to his mouth and an intravenous needle stuck in his arm. His scalp was shaved, and over a dozen electrodes on his head were wired to the EEG machine. A monitor displayed his brainwaves—rolling like ocean waves. Maybe that was what being in a coma felt like, she thought—floating in the middle of the ocean with no land in sight. His ventilator made a rhythmic sucking sound, while the IV bag dripped stabilizing drugs into his system.

In a perverse way, Riley was royalty. Riley's father had once been a formidable force in this town, a drug kingpin on the west side, trafficking in meth and enjoying the sense of power he got from intimidating others. Then Dominic got busted for drug trafficking and was sent to prison for seven years, and now, as a parolee, he was forbidden to own a weapon, fraternize with other ex-felons, or leave the area. But you never knew when Dominic might try to circumvent the restrictions. On the surface, at least, he'd given up a life of crime for the rustic rewards of farming, just like his father and grandfather before him. But Brandon was convinced it was all an act, and they just hadn't caught him yet. Now Dominic would be coming after Brandon, despite whatever might've caused Riley's seizures. West side justice was nothing to mess with.

Natalie watched the suction ventilator moving up and down as it kept the boy's heart alive, while his body remained unresponsive. There was a point at which you sensed the personality, the soul, or whatever you chose to call it, had left the building. All that remained was a beautiful corpse hooked up to a machine. She fervently hoped that he would step back from the abyss.

One of the nurses interrupted, murmuring "sorry," and made a few adjustments, fluffing the pillows, checking the stats, jotting a few notes on a medical chart. Natalie stepped aside and let her perform her duties.

As the nurse shifted the patient's johnny off his shoulder, Natalie caught sight of a tattoo—a small red rose surrounded by twisted barbed wire. Identical to the one on India's wrist.

14

Natalie pulled into the high school parking lot and cut the engine. The main building was composed of once-fashionable yellow brick with granite columns and archways. JFK had an excellent reputation. Their SAT average was outstanding, according to Grace, and their ACT average was one of the highest in the state. Sixty-five percent of the graduates went on to college, and every year more than a dozen seniors got into Harvard, Princeton, and Yale. In that sort of competitive climate, the Rileys of this world simply couldn't cut it.

She checked the time: 2:30 P.M. The final bell rang, the doors shot open, and the yellow brick building burped out an endless parade of students wearing the same elated look. Natalie spotted Ellie and waved.

Ellie said good-bye to her friends and came right over. "Hey, Aunt Natalie," she said, getting in and slamming the door, depositing her book bag on the floor and buckling her seat belt. "Thanks for the lift."

"No problem. How'd it go today?"

Ellie's shoulders slumped. The only touch of color in her all-black outfit were two pink barrettes taming her wild black hair. "We had the remembrance ceremony. Everyone was crying. It was really sad. They told us there was a grief counselor available, but I didn't feel like talking to a stranger about it." Ellie chewed on her thumbnail and glanced over at Natalie. "Do they know what happened yet?"

She shook her head. "We're still piecing it together."

"But you're going to find out who did this to her, right?"

"Absolutely," she reassured her.

Ellie rubbed her wrist and stared transfixed out the window. "I couldn't find my bracelet. I looked everywhere for it. Chemistry, gym class, homeroom. The lost-and-found box was full of these disgusting sweaters and scarves from last winter."

"Maybe you left it at home?" Natalie suggested.

She shook her head. "I wore it to school this morning."

"And you don't remember losing it?"

"Well, I had gym for second period. When I looked in my locker, it was gone."

"I'm sorry, Ellie." Natalie had already decided that she would surprise her niece with another scarab bracelet for her sweet sixteen. She took a deep breath, reluctant to use this ride home as an opportunity for another interview, but she had no choice. "I heard you were at Berkley's house yesterday afternoon. Did Riley Skinner show up there?"

"No." Ellie said, wrinkling her nose. "Why?"

"What can you tell me about him?"

"Riley?" The girl powered down her window and let her hair blow loosely around her shoulders. "Riley does whatever he wants. He doesn't live by the same rules as the rest of us. He's got this . . ."

"What?"

Ellie stared blankly at the passing scenery. They were driving past the lake, visible through the thinning trees, where road signs warned about the dangers of cliff diving on Devil's Point. To the north of the cliffs were miles of thick, desolate woods, part of the vast state forest.

"What is it, Ellie?"

The girl shifted uncomfortably, tugging on her seat belt. "When I first met him, he sort of scared me. He was reading this book called *American Psycho*, mostly to intimidate people, I think. He's from the wrong side of the tracks, and his father went to prison, so I tried to avoid him. But he and India were friends, so I couldn't ignore him every single time. And after I got to know him, I realized he wasn't as crazy or weird as most people thought. It made me realize how much we judge others by their appearances and . . . I don't know." She shrugged. "We're all so locked into our own tribes. Jocks, geeks, witches, stoners, nerds . . . it's depressing, when you think about it."

Natalie nodded empathetically. "So Riley and India are friends?"

"They used to be pretty close last year," Ellie said. "But India didn't want to hang out with him anymore, so she told him to give her some space, and now she treats him like he's her stalker. No means no, right? But I can sort of understand his confusion."

"You sympathize with him?"

"A little. She led him on for a long time, then just dumped him."

"How close were they before? Boyfriend and girlfriend close?"

Ellie gazed out the window while the wind blew her hair around, and Natalie could see the tips of her ears burning. "You know what I hate, Aunt Natalie? I hate how judgmental people can be. Too many kids at school size you up by how much money your parents have. Do you wear the right clothes? Listen to the right music? Think the right thoughts? Are you worthy of their company? There's this girl in my history class who gets picked on all the time for wearing knitted-by-mom sweaters. But I mean, her mother did it out of love."

"Some things never change," Natalie said softly.

Ellie's hair caught the sunlight. "Was it like that when you were growing up?"

Natalie nodded. "Human nature can be very predictable."

"It sucks."

"Big-time."

Ellie's phone buzzed, and she checked her messages. "It's Mom." Her fingers danced over the buttons. After a quick exchange, she put her phone away.

Natalie glanced expectantly at her niece. "So Riley isn't part of India's tribe?"

"She used to *really* like him. But not anymore."

"Is that why they have the same tattoo?"

The girl's eyes widened with alarm. "How do you know about that?"

"I saw it on her wrist—a rose surrounded by barbed wire. I saw Riley's, too."

Instead of answering the question, Ellie asked, "How is he?"

"Stable but critical condition."

"What does that mean? Is he going to be okay?"

"Dr. Swinton doesn't know yet. But Riley's getting the best medical care possible." She glanced at her niece with deep concern. "Ellie, is it possible Riley could've hurt someone? Out of a sense of rejection?"

"No," she said, hugging her slender arms. "I don't get it, how people can say he killed Ms. Buckner, because she cared about him and was trying to help him."

Natalie nodded. "Is there anybody else at school Daisy was having problems with? Any other students or teachers? I'm just wondering if—"

"We had a debate in Ms. Buckner's class last week about the executions."

"Executions?"

"Those three witches weren't burned at the stake," Ellie said a little feverishly, brushing the hair off her forehead. "It was illegal to burn people at the stake . . . in England and all the colonies, including America. Which is why at the Salem witch trials they hanged the accused, or else they pressed them to death with huge stones. I mean, they burned witches in other parts of Europe, but not here in Burning Lake. Those three women were hung to death, and then afterwards their bodies were burned on the pyre."

"Right. That's true. But what does this have to do with Daisy?"

"We had a big argument about it in class, and people took sides, getting really emotional and almost yelling. It was so stupid. Half the class believes they were burned at the stake, despite all the evidence to the contrary."

"It's one of the most hotly debated topics in town—"

"There's nothing to debate," Ellie interrupted, rolling her eyes.

"History is loaded with myths," Natalie told her gently.

"Loaded with BS, you mean."

"Myths can be stronger than facts."

"Well, I guess it's trendy to burn witches nowadays. I mean, where the hell would we be if we couldn't burn witches in effigy every Halloween? How would the town survive? Who'd come to see them hang a bunch of mannequins?"

"Good point." Natalie tried to think of something wise and comforting to say, but she was worried for Ellie—where was all this deflection coming from? "Are you saying that one of the students got angry at Daisy during this debate? Did one of the students act out inappropriately?"

"No," she said, her face flushing. "Half the class was pissed off at the other half. Ms. Buckner tried to remind us that not every disagreement has a resolution. It's just that . . . I think we should honor the dead by telling the truth about how they died, rather than capitalizing on their pain." Ellie looked sorrowfully at Natalie. Tears in her eyes.

"What's wrong, sweetie? Why are you so upset?"

"I've been having awful dreams lately, where I'm tied to the stake like a witch, and I'm standing on a pyre of wood, and there's no escape. People are laughing at me. They're holding torches, and they want me dead."

Natalie nodded, concerned for her.

"Then one of them lights the fire, and flames shoot up all around me, and I can hear my flesh sizzling . . . and I wake up screaming."

"It's just a nightmare," Natalie said, not wanting her niece to hurt like this but wondering what was behind it.

"The worst part is—" She shook it off. "Never mind."

"What, Ellie? Tell me."

She turned away and said, "We're here."

Natalie pulled into Grace's driveway and parked behind the Mini Cooper. "Ellie, why did you bring this up? What are you trying to say?"

"It doesn't matter." Ellie unbuckled her seat belt and got out.

Too much too soon, Natalie realized. She had crowded her niece. Ellie needed time to process her emotions, and yet Natalie couldn't stop hammering her with questions.

Out here on Crenshaw Road, the woods nibbled at the edges of the green suburbs. Grace's handsome post-and-beam-style home had three bedrooms, two and a half bathrooms, and a heated garage. Open-concept living/dining/kitchen. A beautiful marble en suite on the upper level. Vaulted ceilings and natural woodwork. The house was ten years old. The fluffy clouds had blown away, and the air was crystal clear.

Grace greeted them at the door, but Ellie brushed right past her mother and disappeared into the house. "How was school?" Grace called after her.

"Lousy," Ellie said before hurrying up the stairs.

"How was the remembrance ceremony?" Grace asked.

"Terrible, Mom. Everyone was sobbing. I could hardly breathe. Thanks for the ride, Aunt Natalie," she said from the top of the stairs. Moments later, her bedroom door thumped shut.

"Sorry I missed it," Grace said softly. "Come on in, Natalie."

"Thanks." Natalie wiped her shoes on the welcome mat.

Grace led the way inside, saying, "Sorry, but I'm an emotional wreck today. I can't seem to focus on anything. Want some coffee?"

"Love a cup."

"Follow me."

They went into the kitchen. Top-of-the-line stainless-steel appliances. Italian marble backsplash. Teak-and-leather bar stools hugging the kitchen island. Grace lived in one of the wealthier neighborhoods, along with people who yielded considerable influence in this town—doctors, bankers, lawyers, managers, consultants. Burke's alimony and child support payments provided Grace and Ellie with an effort-free lifestyle, but it didn't guarantee happiness. Grace was comfortable and her future was secure, but she wasn't exactly Ms. Happy. Sometimes Natalie detected an aura of melancholy tremoring around Grace's edges.

"Is now a good time to talk?" Natalie asked, hoping her sister wouldn't say no. Grace was the only person besides Brandon who knew almost everything there was to know about Daisy.

"Yeah, sure." Grace didn't look well—disheveled hair pulled into a sloppy ponytail, nails bitten to the quick, eyes swollen from crying.

Natalie took out her notebook and pen, and Grace handed her a steaming mug of coffee.

"Let's go into the living room."

She followed her sister into the living room, juggling everything in her hands—coffee, napkin, spoon, pen, notebook.

"I really wanted to be there for my students today, but I didn't want to melt down in front of them," Grace explained, curling up on the sofa. "Ellie's handling it pretty well, but I didn't sleep a wink."

Natalie took a sip of her French roast and put everything down on the glass-topped coffee table. "Walk me through Daisy's schedule. Tell me about her typical day. What happens?"

"Oh God." Grace folded her slender legs underneath her. "What happens? Let's see. Daisy and I are usually the first to arrive. We're the early birds, I guess. We get to school around six fifteen, make a pot of coffee, and vent in the faculty lounge. That's our together time. We trade war stories and laugh a lot. Sometimes we get frustrated at the administration, because they keep changing the rules on us. So many forms to fill out. So much paperwork. We gripe and kvetch. Then we wish each other luck and go our separate ways."

"And then what?"

"I head upstairs to my classroom and run around like a crazy person, trying to get things organized before the kids show up. Plug in my laptop, check my emails, stack the class assignments, write the highlights on the board."

"What did you and Daisy talk about yesterday morning?"

Grace shrugged. "Nothing special."

"She didn't mention her problems with Riley?"

"No." She shook her head. "We talked about things that would've been boring to anyone but us. Class size, student-teacher ratios. She mentioned her new barbecue. The baby, of course. By the way, she swore me to secrecy, Natalie, otherwise I would've told you right away. But anyway, the subject of Riley never came up."

"Why not?"

"Well, the outburst happened a few weeks ago, and things had quieted down since then. I figured everything was chill. Guess I was wrong."

Natalie nodded. "So what happens on a typical Wednesday?"

"The buses pull up, the kids come pouring out, and it's chaos from that point on." Grace smiled sadly. "My first class is at seven thirty. They last about fifty minutes. There are four periods before lunch, which is at eleven thirty. After lunch, there's a planning period for teachers and a study hall for the students. I usually grade papers during that time."

"When did Daisy leave school yesterday?"

"Gee, I don't know." She frowned. "I think she left around the same time I did."

"When was that?"

"Two thirty on Mondays, Wednesdays, and Fridays. But on Tuesdays and Thursdays, we'll stay until three thirty to help those kids who are struggling with the material. At the end of those extra-long days, Daisy and I will meet up again to chat. But yesterday was Wednesday, so we didn't stay late."

"And you didn't see her leave the building?" Natalie asked.

"No."

"Was her car in the lot?"

"I didn't see it there."

"So she may have left before you?" Natalie asked.

"It looks like it."

"And you didn't contact her afterwards? No phone calls or text messages?"

"No. I had a lot of errands to run. I was preoccupied with the deathiversary."

Natalie nodded. "Right."

Grace plucked a tissue out of the box on the coffee table and said, "Can we get this over with? Do you mind, Natalie? Is that selfish of me?"

"No, I'll try to keep it brief," Natalie promised. "Did Daisy ever fear for her safety around Riley or any other students?"

"Fear? No."

"She wasn't afraid to be alone with Riley, for instance, after class?"

Grace reached for her big leather bag on the floor, then plopped it on the sofa next to her, and rummaged around for her cigarettes. She held the pack in her hand. "Maybe. I don't know. I mean, Daisy wasn't naïve, but she believed in second chances. She trusted in her ability to reach even the most troubled kids. Remember Jenny Barber and Dunham O'Brien? Everybody had written them off for good, but Daisy got them into college. She was such an empathetic person. She hated giving up on anyone. So if Riley wanted to talk to her after class, despite the issues between them, then yes . . . I can picture her feeling okay with that."

"Even after he called her a cunt?"

"No, I think after that incident, she became a little wary of him. But that didn't stop her from trying to help him. Daisy was pretty fearless. I'm not saying she'd embrace him or anything like that, but . . ." Her voice trailed off.

Natalie jotted it down. "Are the Buckners in the habit of keeping their doors unlocked?"

Grace leaned back. "You remember the Foresters, right? They hardly ever locked their doors. It wasn't so unusual back in the nineties. Daisy's mom loved having people over, and a bunch of us kids used to traipse through the house without knocking. They'd only lock their doors at night, or if they went on vacation. Daisy's the same way."

"No other difficult students? No other problems or concerns?"

"Well, there are always problems and concerns. There are always difficult students. But nothing that comes to mind." Grace put down the pack of cigarettes, reached for her coffee, and took a small sip. "I heard Riley was in a coma. Is he going to make it?"

"It could go either way."

"Really?"

"Dr. Swinton says he doesn't know."

"Maybe it's karma?" Grace put down her coffee and wrung her hands. "Oh God, I don't want to be *that person* . . . it's not like I want him to die or anything."

"We're all that person sometimes," Natalie said sympathetically.

"I mean, *if* he killed her . . ." Her eyes teared up. She plucked a tissue from the box and pressed it to her runny nose. "But who else could've done it?"

Which led Natalie to her next question. "Was Daisy happy in her marriage?"

"Happy? Yeah, of course. Why?" she asked apprehensively.

"No complaints? Just covering all the bases."

"As far as I know, she was thrilled to be pregnant. It was a significant milestone for her, given her history. It was a blessing."

"No marriage is perfect," Natalie countered. "She must've complained a little . . ."

"She hardly ever complained about Brandon. She loved him, Natalie. He's a good provider, very loyal. Sure, he has his faults, but he made her laugh. It's so fucking tragic. She would've made a great mom."

Natalie's phone buzzed. It was Luke. "Sorry, I have to take this."

"Sure." Grace daubed at her eyes.

"We've identified the blood on Riley's hoodie as A-positive, same blood type as Daisy's," Luke said. "Riley is AB-positive, and Brandon is O-negative—so we can rule them both out as the source. We also found blister packets at Haymarket Field with Riley's prints on them. And a witness came forward identifying a vehicle speeding away from the Buckner residence last night that matches Riley's Camaro. It's enough to get a warrant. We're about to serve papers on the Skinner residence, and I need you to be there. Meet me two blocks west of the property on O'Dell Road."

"Okay, on my way." She hung up. "Sorry, Grace. I have to go."

Her sister walked her to the door. They paused on the threshold, and Grace gave her a heartfelt hug. "I worry about you, kid."

Natalie smiled. Grace hadn't called her "kid" in years. "You, too, Grace."

"Be careful out there."

Grace was the person who taught Natalie how to insert a tampon, how to get past Deborah's rules. Grace showed her how to tie her hair in a French knot and buy the most ironic T-shirts at Walmart. When Natalie was twelve, before Grace went off to college, they'd sit by the open window, blowing the cigarette smoke outside and waving their hands so their mother couldn't smell it. Grace and Deborah didn't get along. Grace felt unloved, but Natalie loved her sister with all her heart and soul.

Now Natalie wiped the sweat off her brow and said, "Get some rest, sweetie."

15

The Skinners lived a mile and a half past the old railroad depot on the west side of town, where the burdock and pigweed grew mangled and thick. Natalie knew every junker, every ailing family farm, every halfway house, every abandoned shed where drugs were sold, every trailer up on cement blocks. There were violent crimes she still couldn't talk about without her voice cracking—the abduction of a young girl by an animal she'd helped put away; a baby so thin from parental neglect they all worried he might not survive (but he had); a seventy-year-old woman who'd been robbed and beaten by a thug with an angel's face. But she'd also witnessed countless acts of kindness here. The west side was both a sick and a hopeful place. Beauty and ugliness cohabited side by side. *A paradox*, Joey used to say. All sorts of nefarious dealings took place in this neck of the woods, and if they were going to serve a warrant today, then it would have to be handled delicately.

Luke was waiting for her on O'Dell Road, along with a couple of patrol officers. She got out and greeted them, and the four of them stood strategizing by the side of the road.

"I have no idea how Dominic's going to handle this," Luke explained, "so I'd like you to serve papers, Natalie. We all know this guy and his temper. But whenever there's a woman present, he mellows out."

It was common knowledge that Dominic's grandmother used to administer regular ass-whoopings, and if there was one thing the cagey ex-con feared to this day, it was a lady with a stick. He became polite and close-lipped whenever it came to the "fairer sex," and so, having Natalie serve the warrant would give them a distinct advantage.

"No problem," she told Luke. "I've dealt with Dominic before."

"We'll hang back but stay within range." Luke gave her the paperwork. "Okay, let's roll."

They got back in their vehicles and drove past struggling farms and pastures full of dairy cows. The Skinner family had deep roots here. Its branches sagged with bushels of motherfuckers. Dominic didn't just have a chip on his shoulder, he had a whole freaking iceberg. The kids in this neighborhood felt stuck in a nowhere town. They didn't want to become farmers or tour guides like their parents, they wanted to have their own YouTube channels. Out here, you could sense the hopelessness of the disadvantaged youth and their desperate search for meaning. There were good people fighting off the darkness—ministers, teachers, cops, priests, social workers. They stood up to drugs, thievery, debauchery, and "darker things" like cults and prostitution. But it was an ongoing struggle.

Now Natalie pulled into the Skinners' driveway, flanked by Luke and the cruisers, and got out of her vehicle. As she approached the house, Luke and the officers hung back. The Skinners lived in a crumbling wedding cake of a home, a sad-looking Gothic laced with rotting gingerbread trim and a sagging front porch. She rang the doorbell, and after a moment Riley's younger brother, Peter, answered.

"Hi, I'm Detective Lockhart," she said. "Is your dad home?"

"He's asleep," the recalcitrant ten-year-old said.

"I'm here on official business. Can I come in?"

The boy stepped aside.

The living room was stuffy. The shades and curtains were drawn. The house was decorated with blocky bargain furniture. There were dirty glasses and cereal bowls everywhere you looked. The flat-screen TV dominated the living room, and a stale pizza box yawned open on the crumb-strewn coffee table.

"Go wake your dad," she said, and the boy disappeared down the hallway.

Luke and the officers stepped inside, but stayed close to the entrance.

A few minutes later, Dominic Skinner stumbled out into the living room, barefoot and wearing a faded gray robe. One of his eyes was swollen shut. He had a meth-ravaged face, a gaunt body, and a tangle of greasy blond hair. Years of addiction made him look decades older than his early forties. It was hard to believe he used to be one of the cool guys back in high school. Now he was a hard-core ex-felon with bad knees and bad breath.

"What d'you want?" He scowled.

Natalie handed him the paperwork. "We have a warrant to search the premises."

Dominic took it and said nothing. His face was mottled with grief. Beneath the open robe he wore a pair of blue cotton boxers and a T-shirt that read I LUV NEW YORK. His arms were covered with prison tats, mostly skulls, daggers, and serpents. Years ago, when she'd first entered the force, Natalie had privately—after hours—combed through Dominic's arrest records in search of any incriminating birthmarks that might've ID'd him as the bogeyman, but there were no startled butterflies to be found on his drug-ravaged body.

"We'd like to start with Riley's room," she said. "These two officers will search the front and back yards, while the lieutenant and I go through the rest of the house. We appreciate your cooperation. We're very sorry about your son. We're here to gather evidence, that's all."

Dominic dropped the warrant on the floor. "Evidence of what?"

"Riley's potential involvement in the murder of Daisy Buckner."

His shoulders sagged as if the world had just crushed him flat.

"Are you carrying?" she asked.

"No, ma'am. You won't find any firearms in my home," he said, taking his hands out of his pockets and showing her his palms. His bathrobe pockets contained no suspicious bulges. His feet were bare. There was nowhere else to hide a gun on his person. "I went through a court-mandated drug program," Dominic said. "I'm off opioids for good. I don't use anymore. That's all in the past."

"I'm glad to hear it," she said truthfully.

"I'm back to farming, like my dad and granddad. I'm an ex-con and an ex-user who's cleaned up his act."

"What about Riley?" Natalie asked.

"Absolutely not." He glared at her. "Don't you think I would've noticed?"

"Maybe he's not using. Maybe he's dealing?"

"Hell, no." He shook his head with furious eyes.

"Are you sure? Did you know he was flunking out of school?"

"I knew he was in trouble, but Riley didn't want his old man getting involved. I was a major fuckup when he was a little kid, and I think he's ashamed of me now." He rubbed his swollen-shut eye vigorously. "You wanna know how I got into drugs in the first place, Detective? I needed a new combine-harvester. Couldn't afford one, and the banks wouldn't approve my loan applications, so I started to deal part-time. I told myself I'd stop once I'd raised enough for the combine, but then the money was too damn good."

"Riley may not have wanted your help, but he needed it," she said. "Didn't you get the school notices asking you to contact the administration?"

"I did. But like I said . . . he didn't want me involved. He told me not to worry about it. He respected Ms. Buckner. There's no way he would've killed her." Dominic glared at her for a long, miserable moment. "They tell me he's in a deep coma."

"Rest assured," she told him gently, "the doctors are doing everything in their power to pull him through."

His pale gray eyes were embedded in a rich web of wrinkles, and his mouth was curled into a cantankerous scowl. "Peter, come here," he said, taking a seat on the sofa and folding the boy into his arms. He nodded down the hallway. "Make it quick."

There was a large red STOP sign on Riley's bedroom door. Luke did the honors, cracking it open. First, the reek hit her—locker-room stink. It was dark in here. The miniblinds and burlap curtains were closed. Natalie crossed the cluttered floor and snapped them open, and a strong, cleansing sunlight poured into the room.

A sloppy mess greeted her eyes—soiled laundry on the floor, abandoned schoolbooks, legal-size pads full of scribbled rap lyrics, crumpled food wrappers, dirty towels.

They tossed the room for contraband, searching for any evidence of drug-dealing or possession—pills, powder residue, cannabis, cash, works, a scale, a pager. Most high school dealers lived with high levels of stress and had more than the police to worry about. Other kids at school could rat them out or steal their drugs. Riley would've had different hiding places, both at school and at home, to stash his supply and keep it safe. Natalie and Luke got to work, rummaging through everything, but came up empty-handed.

Next, they sprayed the surfaces with luminol, searching for blood evidence, and came up positive for the doorknob and the light switch. Natalie also found a loose bundle of clothing shoved into the far corner of Riley's closet. She held up a pair of black cargo pants, the Dumbnation T-shirt, and Vans slip-ons—the outfit he'd worn to school yesterday, according to Kermit. She didn't detect any visible bloodstains, but Lenny would test it for blood and fibers back at the station.

They confiscated all of Riley's devices—laptop, tablets—but couldn't find his cell phone. They emptied the trash receptacles and sorted through the garbage. They vacuumed for any possible cross-transfer of hairs and fibers.

"Excuse me, Lieutenant?" Officer Bill Keegan, an intimidating presence, came into the room and showed them an evidence bag holding four quarter bags of marijuana and more than a dozen marijuana joints. "We found these hidden in one of the old shacks out back." He held up a second evidence bag. "And we found this in another shack."

Natalie peered at the dead bird—a skeletonized crow with iridescent black feathers covering its leathery, desiccated flesh. There was a thick piece of butcher's twine knotted around its neck and a number-two pencil driven through its mouth and penetrating its anus. Animal mutilations were a bad sign. It was symptomatic of a deep mental disturbance.

"Where did you find the dead bird, Bill?" Luke asked Officer Keegan.

"Out back in an old toolshed, hidden behind some crates. The drugs were in the equipment shed, tucked under a loose floorboard."

"Did you document everything?"

"By the book."

Due to staff constraints, all the uniformed officers in the department had been cross-trained to handle certain preliminary aspects of a criminal investigation—they could run a grid search, secure evidence, document the scene, and testify in court as well as their hardworking counterparts in the Criminal Investigations Unit.

"It's time to talk to Dominic," Luke told Natalie.

Five minutes later, she was seated in the living room with Dominic and his son. Peter had the roundest face she'd ever seen, like a tambourine with blinking brown eyes.

"Did you see Riley after school yesterday?" she asked Dominic.

"No," he said. "One of my heifers was giving birth."

"What about you?" she asked Peter. "Did you see Riley after school?"

The boy nodded shyly.

"What time did he get home?"

"Around three, I guess."

She jotted it down. "When did he leave the house again?"

"Ten minutes later," Peter answered.

"Did he say where he was going?"

"Nope."

"Did he take anything with him?" Natalie asked.

"Just his phone."

"What kind of phone?"

"His Samsung."

"And he drove off in his Camaro?"

"Yes," the boy answered.

"And he didn't tell you where he was going? Did he mention India Cochran?"

"No."

"Did he mention his teacher, Ms. Buckner?"

"Nope."

"Did he change his clothes after school?"

Peter shrugged. "I dunno."

"What was he wearing when he left the house?"

"He says he doesn't remember," Dominic said protectively.

"Riley was in trouble," Natalie explained. "He was flunking out of school. That must've been humiliating for him, having to repeat a grade when all his friends were moving on. He was under a tremendous amount of stress. I'm trying to piece together his actions yesterday, where he went and who he talked to . . ."

Dominic smoothed his hand across his thinning hair and said, "All I know is my son had his whole life ahead of him, and now he's lying in a coma, and he can't talk to me or even open his eyes." His voice cracked.

She didn't know what to say. The news was grim, either way—whether Riley came out of the coma or not. She glanced out a nearby window. Luke and the officers were loading evidence boxes into the back of a cruiser. "We found marijuana hidden in one of the sheds out back," she said.

"Yeah?"

"You don't sound concerned."

"Oh, come on. What teenager doesn't smoke a doobie now and again?" he argued. "Weed should be legalized. Everybody knows that. There's a big difference between possession of a controlled substance and possession with intent to supply, and my boy isn't dumb. I'm telling you, there's no way he's dealing. He's seen me at my worst. Crazy wasted, pissing at the moon. I warned him . . . don't you take the wrong road, like I did. He witnessed my transformation. Hell . . . I gave up drugs for life. I saw the light in prison. That's why I joined Narcotics Anonymous. It's helping me with my issues. I took up farming, and I've revived the family farm, and now I'm raising a herd of cattle, and my boy . . . my Riley . . . just because he's doing poorly at school, why would you assume he must be dealing?"

"We found quarter bags and a dozen or so joints," she told him.

"Fuck that." He cinched his robe tighter and folded his hands together in his lap. "Back when I was dealing, you know who my best customers were? Nice, well-dressed middle-class folks. I guess their lives must be pretty boring, huh? They flagrantly break the law. North side, south side, east side—you're okay, buddy. To the contrary, everything on the west side's a crime." He shook his head. "Maybe it's time to call my lawyer. My son isn't here to defend himself."

"We also found a dead bird," she interjected, "a crow with twine knotted around its neck and a pencil driven through its innards. Do you know anything about that?"

"That's mine," Peter blurted.

Dominic touched the boy's arm. "Hush up."

"But I found it!" Peter protested loudly. "It's mine!"

"Where'd you find it?" Natalie asked him.

"Over by the gravel pits, behind Big Rock."

She knew what he meant—an ancient boulder on the dirt road leading into the abandoned gravel pits, located about a mile and a half north of the lake. Locals referred to the huge boulder as Big Rock.

"Did you put the pencil through it?" Natalie asked Peter, who shook his head.

"I found it like that."

"Peter, that's enough," Dominic said. "You don't have to say anything."

Natalie asked Dominic, "One more thing? I need to know more about Riley's relationship with India Cochran."

"Relationship?" Dominic scowled. "He's known her since middle school. Why? What's that got to do with anything?"

The front door creaked open, and Natalie's stomach clenched. Officer Troy Goodson stepped inside. A big guy, tall and broad-shouldered, with cautious eyes. "We're all set, Detective."

"Thank you," Natalie said. "I'll be out in a minute."

"S'okay, I'll wait." Troy adjusted his duty belt and hooked his thumbs into his waistband, looking like he wanted to kick the crap out of Dominic. An old grudge perhaps. There were plenty of unresolved grudges in this town.

"Okay, we're all done here, Detective," Dominic told Natalie, and she could feel the tension in her facial muscles as she tried to maintain her composure. "You can contact my lawyer, Vinnie Patalino, for anything else you need."

She closed her notebook and stood up. "Thanks for your cooperation."

He gazed at her pleadingly. "Riley's fighting for his life. He needs your prayers."

She nodded stiffly. Someday, she would keep her promises to the victims' families. She used to pray all the time, but she hadn't forgiven God yet for taking Willow away so young.

16

The police station was located in a three-story granite building at the heart of downtown, nestled between an Olive Garden and the town hall. Due to its proximity to the restaurant, the station sometimes smelled of garlic and tomato sauce. Natalie pulled into the parking lot around back and sat for a moment, her head throbbing as if a thousand pneumatic drills were boring into her skull. She hadn't had her third cup of coffee yet and was struggling with caffeine withdrawal. She gathered her energy, got out of her vehicle, and headed for the back entrance.

Seventy-five sworn law officers made up the rank and file of the Burning Lake Police Department. There were twenty support staff, and whenever things got a little heated around here, like they were now, everybody chipped in by taking a heavier caseload and volunteering for overtime if necessary.

Natalie stopped by the kitchen for a cup of coffee before grabbing her mail and heading for the elevators. She took a steel car up to the third-floor detective's unit, where her desk was situated across the aisle from Detective Buckner's. Brandon was on unpaid leave pending the internal investigation. He was staying with his father across town and hadn't returned any of her messages yet. She sat down at her desk and answered a few emails. Her mouse pad said PROPERTY OF BLPD. Her ivy plant had died a few days ago because she kept forgetting to water it, and now the leaves were brown and curled. The only other personal touches on her desk were two crayon drawings by five-year-old Ellie and a framed picture of ten-year-old Natalie and her sisters dressed as witches one long-ago Halloween.

"Hey, Natalie." Detective Augie Vickers, a bland-looking man in his late forties, came over and stood so close to her desk, she could smell the liverwurst on his breath. His exhaustive reports were no fun to read. You got lost in a sea of details. "We didn't get the tox results back from the hospital yet, but my contact at the state lab says some of the contraband we found at Haymarket Field was Kush, not marijuana."

K2 was a synthetic cannabis that went by a hundred other names— spice, black mamba, fake marijuana, blaze. Synthetic cannabis was created in homegrown labs, combining noncannabis herbs with chemical compounds that could be highly toxic. It was easy to overdose on K2, because it wasn't anything like marijuana, more like amphetamines, and could lead to hallucinations, seizures, convulsions, tachycardia, stroke, acute psychosis, brain damage, and even death.

"Confirmed Kush? That might explain Riley's seizures," Natalie said.

"Exactly. I'll head over to the hospital after the team meeting and find out if the tox results are back, but I'd bet my left nut that's what caused them. We found two other witnesses who attested to the fact that Brandon didn't touch Riley, was in fact nowhere near him when he collapsed. So I think we can rule out the use of force. Fuck it, Natalie. How do you spell *relief?*"

"Let's hope so," she said, her desk wobbling just a little.

"Oops. Gotta fix that," Augie joked and walked away.

"Hey, thanks," she said cynically. Her first day on the job—as was the custom for all rookies—the guys had given Natalie the worst desk in the unit, the one with the wobbly legs. She kept a matchbook tucked under the shortest leg to keep it from driving her insane, but once in a while it slipped out of place.

The afternoon sun glared through the office's wide, old-fashioned windows. She got up and closed the nearest set of blinds. The air vent above her desk cooked her head in the wintertime and froze her scalp in the summer. Today she had a pounding headache, and the drone of background noise drilled into her skull.

On the far wall, next to an old-fashioned clock, was a large-print calendar, big enough to read from across the room. All the significant information was posted there—team meetings, interviews, appointments, court appearances. The Criminal Investigations Unit consisted of seven detectives and a supervising lieutenant detective. The unit handled homicides, suicides, non-traffic-related accidental deaths, in-custody deaths, and any other suspicious incidents resulting in life-threatening injuries. Traffic accidents, however, were handled by a small team of qualified officers.

A row of heavy-duty binders lined the shelves to Natalie's right, and her active investigative files were spread across her work table. A case was declared "cold" when the detective-in-charge had reached a dead end and her more current cases were piling up. It was a matter of priorities.

The Missing Nine were different, however. Special. They'd been passed from detective to detective inside the unit for years in order to get new eyeballs scouring through the voluminous information. Why had they failed so far? Conflicting stories, few verifiable facts. The homeless population was afraid to talk to the police, whether their apprehension was justified or not. Details were scarce. Witnesses scattered. Leads dried up. Transients were almost impossible to track.

Natalie had been studying the nine case files for months now, searching for any new links or leads. A few weeks ago, she'd found something that appeared to connect at least *two* of the cases together—but hadn't informed Luke about it yet, preferring to dig up more evidence to support her theory first. And today, she'd gotten an intriguing third connection.

It all began with Dustin Macgowan, a transient so covered in dirt he looked like a paperdoll-cutout come to life, limbs and clothes covered in earth, two radiant eyes lined with cracked mud. He disappeared nine years ago, simply vanished from an alleyway that smelled of urine and garbage. All that was left of Dustin was a paper bag in the shape of his hand wrapped tightly around the neck of a pint of whiskey and a bloodstain pattern on the brick wall.

Natalie had recently discovered an overlooked clue in Dustin's file, however—something that wasn't mentioned in any of the police reports. A dead crow was visible in one of the police photos of the cluttered alleyway Dustin once called home.

Now she opened the binder and leafed through its careworn pages. There. She used a sticky note to mark the spot, then pulled down a second binder. Like Joey used to say: *Reduce it down to the basics—beginning, middle, end.* Natalie carried both binders with her down the hallway and knocked on Luke's door.

"Come in," he said, hanging up the phone.

"Got a minute?"

"Sure, Natalie. What's up?"

She closed the door behind her and took a seat. "King Edward," she said, handing him one of the binders and opening it to a specific page.

Luke's office chair squealed as it rolled over the antistatic floor mat. "Edward O. King," he repeated, looking down at several color photographs in their transparent sleeves. "Yeah, I remember this guy. One of our Missing Nine. Used to wear a fright wig, mumbling to himself and scaring the tourists. Disappeared five years ago. What am I looking at? Pictures of his shopping cart?"

"He vanished without a trace and left the cart behind. These pictures were taken about a week later, after his social worker reported him missing. See here?" She pointed at one of the photographs. "There's a dead crow in the cart, underneath all that junk. You can only see its wings in this picture, so we don't know if it was mutilated or not. It could be roadkill."

Luke nodded. "King Edward was certainly a hoarder."

"Now check this out." She handed him the other binder and opened it to a bookmarked page. "Here's a photograph of the alleyway where Dustin Macgowan used to sleep before he disappeared nine years ago. See the dead crow next to the dumpster? It wasn't mentioned in any of the police reports, because it was just a dead crow on the ground, but cumulatively, if you look at these two cases, plus today's find—"

Revelation bloomed in Luke's eyes. "Peter Skinner found the mutilated crow at Big Rock, which was the last place Juan Navarro was seen alive, sitting on top of Big Rock, before he disappeared fifteen years ago."

"That's *three* of our Missing Nine," she said.

"Are you suggesting it's a calling card?"

"Could be." Juan Navarro had probably three whole teeth in his head. He used to hang out at the shelter on Palmer Avenue, drumming his fingers on the tables and listening in on other people's conversations. An anorexic guy with greasy hair down to his waist, he'd turn up his nose at the hot meals, because he just wanted to be around other folks. He'd warm his hands on their company, like a wood-burning fireplace. "In the meantime," Natalie said, "I'll keep looking through the archives for any other photographs or mentions of dead birds, but as of now . . . we have three dead crows associated with three disappearances. Add to that the handwriting on Teresa's grave," she continued, "which you said was similar to the graffiti you and Mike found on the spot where Minnie Walker disappeared . . ."

Luke nodded. "I've asked Mike to dig Hannah Daughtery's file out of archives."

"Thanks."

"But don't get your hopes up. The timing of the Juan Navarro case is off. I doubt that a mutilated crow has been out there behind Big Rock for fifteen years. Which means that somebody put it there more recently. Maybe some sicko who's obsessed with the disappearances, or who's into witchcraft—not necessarily the perpetrator of the abductions. Same with the handwriting. This could all add up to nothing. At any rate, it's definitely worth investigating. See where it takes you, and keep me apprised. At some point, I may want to get involved."

"Great," she said.

"Good job, Natalie. But remember your priorities." He checked his watch. "Ready for the team meeting?"

Natalie nodded. "Be right there."

17

Natalie went back to her office, where she gathered up her notes and bit her cheek out of nervousness, a salty warmth surging into her mouth. She noticed that her ID badge had a spot of something on it. She wiped off the spot with shaky fingers, then straightened her clothes. *You can do this.*

Conference room A was reserved for monthly staff meetings and department trainings. Conference room B was reserved for team meetings and strategy reviews. She walked into a room full of grim faces, subdued voices, and notebooks full of details. All the guys sat around the polished laminate table, watching her expectantly. The fluorescent lights weren't flattering to anyone. Foam coffee cups were strewn about, along with pens and extra pads of paper.

Natalie took a seat and spread out her case file before her. *Daisy Forester Buckner: Homicide.*

Luke took a seat at the head of the table. "Good afternoon, everyone."

"Afternoon, Lieutenant," came the muffled response.

"I'm going to be asking a lot from you in the coming weeks. The department is stretched thin, which means we're going to have a lot of overlap.

There'll be plenty of overtime available. It can't be helped. The chief has authorized it. Budget's tight, but he's made it a priority. So let's all pitch in. Natalie? Why don't you begin."

Chairs inched forward as the men reached for their notebooks and coffees.

"Here's what we know so far," she said. "At nine o'clock last night, the coroner made his TOD determination, which the autopsy confirmed. The victim died of blunt-force trauma to the head, between four and six P.M. on Wednesday evening. The homicide appears to have been unplanned and spontaneous. No sign of premeditation. Daisy was reaching into the refrigerator for a can of Coke when she received a blow to the right side of her skull with the medium-size skillet. No defensive wounds. No sign of a struggle. She wasn't expecting the attack.

"Other than the bloodstains inside the kitchen, luminol showed no other hits, with one exception—a minute amount of blood was found on the front doorknob, both inside and outside. Type A blood, which matches Daisy's. It looks as if the front doorknob was wiped clean of prints—so it's a mystery as to how the blood trace got there. No other latents were found at the primary scene that didn't match Daisy's or Brandon's—but we're still processing the voluminous trace. No prints were found on the handle of the skillet—we can deduce it was wiped clean. No prints on the stove dials . . . also wiped clean. Back doorknob, no viable prints were captured except for Daisy's and Brandon's. We can assume the killer didn't walk into the house wearing latex gloves, so the prints must've been eliminated after the fact— or else Daisy let the killer in. There was a rumpled dish towel on the floor next to the skillet—we found traces of blood on the towel, so it was most likely used to wipe off the prints. Considering this wasn't a preplanned attack, the killer kept a very level head.

"We canvassed the neighborhood. Nobody saw or heard anything unusual during the time frame, although most of the neighbors weren't home between four and six o'clock. A lot of working professionals with no kids. Those who were home during the time frame didn't report anything unusual, with three exceptions—" She paused to flip through the pages. "A resident two streets over reported seeing a UPS truck dropping off packages in the neighborhood, while another resident ten blocks south of the Buckner house said she noticed a white GMC van in the area that afternoon, parked by the side of the road for a few minutes. Another witness several streets over claimed she saw a red Camaro speeding past her home at around six thirty P.M., which is outside the TOD estimate. We've impounded Riley's vehicle for further testing, but haven't found any trace linking him to the scene so far. We'll follow up on those vehicles, and also look into surveillance footage, which I'll touch upon in a minute.

"The Buckner residence is recessed from the road, and there are plenty of trees in the fenced-in yard, with thick woods all around. The properties in this area consist of one- to three-acre lots. The Buckners' closest neighbor is two hundred feet away. Nobody lives across the street from them— just an overgrown field and woods. The state park abuts the property, and there are thickly wooded conservancy lands back there for at least a mile or so. The perp could've come and gone without notice. Due to yesterday's rain, we didn't find any footprints or tire tracks on the property.

"Which brings us to surveillance cameras," Natalie said, turning the page. "Bear in mind, despite the rural surroundings, Wolf Pass is one of our busier roads, since it's the quickest route from Elizabeth Falls to Burning Lake. They get a fairly steady rate of traffic. It will take a while to collect all the pertinent traffic tapes, and we'll need volunteers to search through the material. This will be time-consuming. Most of the cameras monitoring traffic are located in the downtown area, which doesn't help much, but it's a start. I've assigned Officer Troy Goodson to retrieve all available video footage from the intersections and businesses closest to the residence, for expediency's sake. The time frame will fall between three and seven P.M., just to be thorough. We'll be looking for Riley's vehicle on the surveillance tapes, along with any other unusual vehicle sightings, plus the two others on our witness list.

"Small traces of blood were found on the hoodie Riley was wearing last night when he was transported to the hospital. The blood type matches Daisy's, not his or Brandon's, and the state lab is performing a DNA test to see if it's a match for Daisy Buckner. No other blood type was found on the clothing. Daisy's is type A-positive blood, which is shared by about thirty-four percent of the population. We've sent the rest of Riley's clothes—both outfits he wore that day—to the state lab for further testing, along with the evidence we gathered from the Skinner household. It'll be processed in the coming days."

Natalie took a pause, while the men shifted in their seats and sipped their coffees.

"As far as we can piece together," she went on, "the victim got home from her job around two forty-five, changed out of her work clothes, took a shower, answered emails until three oh-eight P.M., and perused the internet until three seventeen P.M. She was looking at baby things on her computer, but she also purchased two ebooks, *The Breakup Bible* and *Getting Past Your Breakup*. We believe Brandon might be able to shed some light on these purchases, and we're negotiating with his attorney to set up a formal interview. All activity stops around three seventeen and, at some point, Daisy went into the kitchen to cook a casserole. That was her last known activity." Natalie turned the page. "We did a grid search of the property and found a few items in the backyard which may or may not be pertinent. A gardening glove, a trowel, and over a dozen wooden stakes tied with rags, all of which appear to be related to a landscaping project. We're reviewing all of this trace." She sat back. "Any questions?"

Detective Lenny Labruzzo spoke up first. "This is where Brandon's cooperation would be enormously helpful. So why'd he lawyer up? What's he afraid of?"

"It's a precautionary measure in response to his suspension," Natalie said. "He was over the alcohol limit and he shouldn't have been driving. We all know this."

"Brandon's actions are totally relatable," Mike Anderson said. "His wife had just been murdered." Squat as a bulldog, the thirtysomething detective had a disgruntled disposition and sad-sack eyes as gray as the residue at the bottom of a shot glass.

"Rather than jump to any conclusions, let's wait until Brandon comes in for an interview," Natalie suggested.

"When will that be?" Lenny asked.

"We're working on it," Luke told them. "Moving on."

"So we're homing in on Riley Skinner as our primary suspect?" Augie asked.

"Yes," Natalie said. "But we want to dot all our i's and cross all our t's so we can't be accused of not being a hundred percent thorough. If Riley is guilty, then we need to present a solid case to the DA for successful prosecution. Which is why we're in the process of interviewing all of Daisy's friends, associates, colleagues, and employers, as well as any electricians, plumbers, or delivery men who might've been to the house recently . . . plus any and all registered sexual offenders in the neighborhood."

"What happened to Riley's phone?" Mike asked.

"We haven't located the Samsung yet," Natalie told him, "but Augie's working on a court order for the service provider."

"The sooner the better," Luke told Augie, who jotted it down in his dog-eared notepad. "What about the hotline?"

Natalie nodded at Detective Anderson. "Mike's in charge of the hotline."

"It's been ringing day and night," Mike told the team. "We've been deluged with information, mostly speculation. A lot of sludge slows down the entire investigation, in my estimation. All that manpower on the phone lines could be put to better use."

"So nothing to report?" Luke asked.

"Nothing so far, Lieutenant."

"I have a question." Detective Jacob Smith was the kind of guy who'd peaked in high school and was paunching out, but he viewed himself as a cool dude. He had a reputation for executing an impressive number of drug busts and recruiting informants. "Why was Daisy Buckner buying books about a breakup when she's married and three months' pregnant?"

"We're still trying to determine that," Natalie answered.

"Exactly," Lenny said with exasperation. "Brandon could really clear things up right about now. When exactly is he coming in for an interview?"

"Unknown at this time," she said.

"He's doing what any of us would've done," Augie said, coming to Brandon's defense. "He's lawyering up. What the hell would you do in that position, Lenny?"

"Okay, since you asked, the way Brandon went gunning for that kid is highly suspicious to me," Lenny said. "Right away, he blames the punk."

"What are you implying?" Augie said heatedly. "People do stupid things when they're in shock."

"We never found any of Riley's prints inside the house. Not even a partial," Lenny went on. "Whoever did this wiped the skillet clean, the stove dials, the doorknobs, all points of entry. Would a teenage boy who'd just killed his teacher in a frenzy clean up after himself? He'd have to be extremely calm and levelheaded. Is Riley Skinner levelheaded? I don't think so. Impulsive, reckless, disorganized."

Augie shrugged. "They pick up a lot from *Criminal Minds* nowadays."

"No prints," Lenny went on. "Which means he's either extremely self-aware, or else he brought latex gloves to the scene—which implies premeditation, which this was clearly *not*. Unless it was staged to look that way."

"You think it was staged?" Augie asked.

Lenny shrugged. "There's elements to the crime scene only a cop, or somebody like that, would have knowledge of."

"I've been wondering the same thing myself," Natalie admitted, and the room fell completely still. All eyes were on her. "It doesn't add up. Daisy was in the middle of cooking dinner. Why would she turn off the stove burners? And if she didn't turn them off, why would the killer do it? Wouldn't the perpetrator be more focused on covering his tracks and fleeing the scene? A teenager, especially."

"What else you got?" Augie said. "Because stove burners isn't enough. You're forgetting all the evidence we have against Riley Skinner—blood on the hoodie, the sighting of his Camaro in the vicinity, the altercation with the victim, drugs. Solid stuff."

"Right, but type A-positive blood is one of the most common," Natalie countered. "We don't have a DNA match yet. The neighbor saw a car fitting the description of Riley's Camaro around six thirty P.M. That's outside the time of death estimate. I know it's a long shot, but what if he dropped by to talk to Daisy about his problem *after* she was dead? The front door was unlocked. What if he touched the body, just like Brandon did, and got blood on the sleeve of his hoodie? After all, she was the most sympathetic adult in his life. The only one who truly believed in his potential. I listened to his rap song, and the lyrics about Daisy sounded more sorrowful than angry. As if he blamed himself for his failings, not her. And we still don't know yet if Daisy was having an affair."

Luke nodded. "These are great points, but maybe she was having an affair with Riley. Has anybody thought of that? What if we're underestimating the intelligence of this kid? Maybe he did have a level enough head to wipe off his fingerprints. After all, teenagers can be quite sophisticated nowadays."

"Okay, but he wasn't in love with Daisy," Natalie argued. "All signs point to him being in love with India Cochran to the point of stalking her."

"So you're suggesting he went over to Daisy's house to talk to her around six thirty," Luke said, "and found her dead? Then touched the body, and fled the scene?"

"Her front door was unlocked. He went inside. Found the body in the kitchen. Discovered she was dead. Fled the scene, stopping long enough to wipe his prints off the doorknob with his hoodie sleeve, and therefore cross-transferring traces of blood onto the doorknob, but no prints. He didn't report the crime, because he thought the police would suspect him."

"We do suspect him," Augie admitted.

"Okay, what if Daisy was having an affair—not with Riley, that's far-fetched, but with another adult," Lenny said, picking up the thread. "Taking things a bit further, what if Brandon *knew* that his wife was having an affair? We're talking about a crime of passion, right? Maybe Brandon found out about the affair and killed her, and then he tried to pin it on Riley? Maybe that's why he went gunning for the kid. To divert attention away from himself. Law enforcement teaches us we don't really know anyone. Are we all convinced that Brandon didn't pop that kid at least once? Riley's in a coma. Who would benefit from that? I'm not saying I believe it or think it's true. But we need to broaden our search to include the victim's spouse and potential lover. I don't want to believe it—no way—but I can't help it. The idea is stuck in my head like fruitcake. Tastes horrible, but I can't stop picking at it."

Once again Augie leapt to Brandon's defense. "You know, I've been sitting here this whole time listening to your crap . . . why *wouldn't* Brandon go gunning for the kid who called his wife a cunt? That'd be reason enough for me. Also, we have two eyewitnesses who say Brandon didn't lay a hand on the kid."

"I'm just saying—"

"Fuck you and your fruitcake," Augie said. "Go fling your poo elsewhere."

"I'm speculating, like any *responsible* detective would," Lenny argued.

"Are you calling me irresponsible?"

Others leapt to Brandon's defense. The argument escalated—overheated faces, overlapping conversations. Tension crackled off the walls.

"Okay, gentlemen. Settle down. That's enough," Luke commanded, and the room fell silent. The detectives shifted in their seats, their anger slowly dissipating. Luke glanced at Natalie. "Why don't you conclude the meeting for us."

She smiled at him and, tucking a lock of hair behind her ear, said, "We've just started our investigation. However, the blood type evidence points to one suspect at this time. Until we hear from the lab regarding the DNA results, Riley Skinner's our primary suspect—for the time being. In the meantime, we'll be following all other leads."

"Thank you, Natalie." Luke looked around the table. "Any other questions?"

Cups were drained. Notebooks were put away.

"Good. Here are your assignments." He passed around the assignment sheets. "There'll be plenty of time to speculate about the bigger picture. Just remember, we have our work cut out for us in the coming weeks and months. It's time to focus on the minutiae—eyewitness reports, suspect interviews, hotline tips, trace evidence. Leave no stone unturned. I want facts, people. Give me facts that I can hold in my hand."

18

Natalie gathered up her paperwork while the rest of the guys headed back to their cubicles and Luke remained seated at the conference table. He was on the phone. He prevented her from leaving, motioning for her to sit back down. She figured he wanted to discuss a few more details of the case with her, so she took a seat and waited.

Soon her phone buzzed—it was Brandon. All she could hear was his cotton-mouthed breathing. "Brandon? Is that you?"

He hung up.

Natalie phoned him back, but the call went straight to voice mail. She left a message. "If you want to talk, Brandon, seriously . . . I'm here for you." She hung up.

Luke was gesturing for her notebook and pen. She handed them over, and after a few moments of scribbling, he hung up. "That was Benjamin Lowell, one of Riley's buddies I talked to this morning. Seems Riley was planning to meet up with some friends at the Mummy's Cabin on Wednesday afternoon. To sell drugs."

"Great." Natalie stood up. "Let's go."

The Mummy's Cabin was named after Frederick Moth, a mentally imbalanced drifter, who'd holed up inside the remote cabin in the woods one long-ago winter and killed himself the following spring. It was a gruesome suicide—he'd wrapped his entire head in duct tape, like a mummy, and consequently choked on his own vomit. The police found bottles of Carlo Rossi lying around. The sensationalized newspaper headlines at the time declared, DERELICT MUMMIFIED IN CABIN. The name stuck.

Now Natalie followed Luke's Ranger northwest of town through a complex topography of cliffs, valleys, ponds, and forest-covered hills. Fifteen minutes later, they parked by the side of a fire road and stepped into the breezy April late-afternoon.

They took a serpentine footpath into the forest, where the trees creaked and rubbed in the wind. White spruce, red pine, bear oak, American beech, and balsam firs all thrived in the conservancy lands and protected woods. The sugar maples grew to seventy feet tall and lived for three hundred years. Burning Lake could feel as quiet and remote as the Canadian outback, with its sun-drenched meadows, panoramic vistas, and miles of hiking trails. In the spring, the forest bloomed with frothy myrtle and patches of sea lavender nestled along the creek beds. By the fall, everything turned as golden and fragrant as honey.

After a strenuous ten-minute hike, they came to a small clearing where a bevy of wild roses and sweetbrier grew. The Mummy's Cabin was nestled on the edge of the woods, looking blown-out and desolate, overrun with weeds and caught in a net of climbing hydrangea. The windows were broken. The splintery door stood open. Natalie could hear voices coming from inside. Chants. A soft, eerie sound.

She unfastened the safety on her gun—just a precaution. Scattered throughout these hollows were dozens of abandoned cabins where drug deals were known to take place, and violence could erupt at any second. Still, she kept her arms down by her sides and didn't draw her weapon. Luke kept his weapon holstered but unfastened.

"Police," the lieutenant called out. "Come out with your hands up."

The chanting stopped. The voices fell silent.

"Step out of the cabin with your hands over your heads," Luke demanded, the strain showing in the tendons of his neck.

Shadows stirred inside the cabin. Moments later, six teenagers filed out with their arms in the air—Kermit Hughes, Owen Kottler, India Cochran, Berkley Auberdine, Sadie Myers, and Angela Sandhill. Angela was one of Ellie's second-tier friends who got invited to all the sleepovers and parties, but who wasn't part of her inner circle. The six of them were dressed in black, like a flock of ravens.

"Keep your hands out of your pockets where I can see them," Luke cautioned. "Do you have any drugs in your possession? Any weapons?"

"No," the raven-haired India responded, speaking for the entire group.

"What are you doing up here?" Luke asked.

"Holding a séance."

Natalie fastened the safety on her gun and glanced at the open door of the cabin. "Is that all of you?"

"Yes," India told her stiffly.

She was relieved Ellie wasn't among them, but couldn't help wondering where her niece was, since Ellie and India did everything together.

Luke walked over to the cabin door and peeked inside. "You lit candles," he said. "That's against park regulations. And I see a couple of liquor bottles in there."

"Sorry about the candles," India said. "Those liquor bottles aren't ours."

"A lit candle started a forest fire in Elizabeth Falls seven years ago," Luke reminded them. "Empty your pockets, please."

"What for?" India asked, blinking innocently.

"Just a precaution," he said, but when that didn't seem to convince them, he added, "Drug possession and underage drinking are still illegal, as far as I know."

"We weren't drinking or taking drugs, Lieutenant Pittman, I swear. We were holding a séance, that's all."

"Empty your pockets, please," he repeated—leaving little room for argument.

The teenagers emptied their pockets and put everything on the ground.

Spare change, smartphones, keys, wallets. Sadie Myers placed two phones on the ground—her iPhone and a Samsung—and Natalie grew immediately suspicious.

"Why do you have two phones, Sadie?" she asked.

"I . . . um . . ." Sadie's eyes welled with tears. Freckled and elfin, she had enough facial piercings to set off a metal detector—earrings, nose rings, a tongue stud that exaggerated her natural lisp. "I don't know."

The teenagers grew visibly nervous as Natalie picked up the Samsung. The battery was low. She scrolled through the call logs, then opened up the contact list. She tapped on India's name and held the phone to her ear.

India jumped when her ringtone burst to life—Selena Gomez's "Wolves."

"Who does this phone belong to?" Natalie asked, already knowing the answer.

"It's Riley's," Sadie quickly confessed, blushing crimson.

"Why do you have Riley's phone, Sadie?" Natalie asked her, hanging up.

"Kermit wanted me to hold it for him. He was afraid he'd get caught with it."

They all nodded their heads. Kermit shuffled his feet. India averted her eyes.

"How did you get Riley's phone, Kermit?" Natalie asked him.

"He told me to hold it for him, right after Officer Buckner showed up at Haymarket Field," the boy explained with a wince. "Am I in trouble?"

"No," Natalie said. "But I'm going to hang on to this."

"Can we go now?" India pleaded, a warm breeze raking her long hair in ribbons and waves.

Natalie checked through the most recent calls on Riley's phone. "According to his call logs, he phoned you five times yesterday, India. And it looks like you called him back twice."

India grew defiant. "Is this an interrogation? Because we have our rights, you know. You can't keep asking us questions without our parents' permission."

It was true. These children were minors. They weren't obligated to co-operate with the police, even if they'd witnessed a crime. You could only push things so far, and India's father was an attorney. Timothy Cochran,

Esquire, was known as Burning Lake's super-lawyer, a diminutive man who planted his intellectual weight into every step.

"We heard Riley came up here to the cabin yesterday," Natalie said. "Do you know anything about that?"

"No," India said. "I told you. We haven't done anything wrong. We aren't doing drugs. You can't detain us for holding a séance in the woods. It's not against the law. And you can't keep asking us questions without our parents' permission."

Luke took this as his cue to intervene. "Step away from the cabin and go stand over there, please." He pointed at a swath of Douglas firs growing shoulder-to-shoulder on the north side of the cabin. "All of you. Pick up your belongings and go wait in front of those trees. We need to look inside the cabin, and then we may have a few more questions. Okay?"

The six of them grudgingly collected their belongings and went to stand on a bed of needles in front of the fir trees. Natalie activated her flashlight. The interior of the cabin contained a post-apocalyptic feel. There was the dilapidated sofa where Frederick Moth had allegedly taken his own life. The walls were covered with superimposed layers of graffiti. Decades of wind had swirled the trash deep into the crevices.

She aimed her beam at the Ouija board in the middle of the cabin, five lit candles placed around it. The planchette hovered above the word "No." A foot or two away, on the pine-needled floor, was a rumpled black T-shirt. Natalie squatted down to blow out the candles, while beams of dying sunlight shot through the broken windows. The wooden floor smelled of piss.

"I don't see any joints or blister packets, do you?" Luke said, kicking an empty cartridge box across the debris-strewn floor.

"Here's a drug pipe." She scooped the glass pipe off the floor. "But it looks old. The residue is hardened, and the bowl's broken."

Luke nudged an empty liquor bottle with the toe of his shoe. "If Riley was here yesterday, then we'll need to find out who he met with and for how long."

India came to the door just then, interrupting them. "My father says we don't have to talk to you. He told me to leave. He said we haven't done anything wrong."

Luke sighed. "All right, you can go."

"Thanks." She flashed them both a resentful smile before scurrying away.

Natalie picked up the rumpled black T-shirt from the floor and unfurled it. "Wait, you forgot your—" Out dropped Ellie's missing scarab-link bracelet.

Little pools of fear flared inside her.

She sat motionless as she cradled the delicate bracelet in her palm. Braided throughout the interlocking scarabs was a piece of knotted red twine.

"Ellie lost this bracelet at school today," Natalie told him. "And look, this is knot magic. A piece of twine, knotted nine times, binds the spell. Only when the knots are untied will the spell be broken."

"So who were they casting a spell on? Ellie?"

Fright spread across her scalp. "Let's go ask them," she said.

But the kids had scattered. They were gone.

19

Finding answers would have to wait. Natalie and Luke spent the next thirty minutes processing the cabin, searching for proof that Riley had been there recently supplying controlled substances to buyers. After sorting through the rubbish, they collected three marijuana stubs, four empty liquor bottles, two pink pills, an old sock with traces of what looked like marijuana inside of it, and a receipt from a supermarket for a packet of beef jerky and a box of plastic sandwich bags, purchased at 3:22 P.M. on the Wednesday afternoon in question.

Around twilight, they headed down the trail toward their vehicles, while the setting sun cast dying shadows on the pine-needled ground. Luke's flashlight illuminated the path ahead, laced with faded brown leaves and twigs from last autumn. Natalie stepped on a branch and it crackled loudly. Funny, she'd lived in these woods her entire life, but they still managed to overpower her at times.

They put away their equipment and got in their separate vehicles. "Meet you back at the station," Luke told her, and took off.

Thirty yards down Drummond Lane, Natalie spotted a homeless woman pushing her shopping cart by the side of the road and pulled over.

Thirty-six-year-old Bunny Jackson wore mismatched layers of clothes she got from local charities. She and Grace had once been close in high school—together with Daisy and Lindsey Wozniak, they'd formed their own coven—but Bunny had subsequently suffered a schizophrenic break in college and was never the same again. Everyone in town cared about Bunny's well-being, but none of these well-meaning people could convince her to get the help she needed.

Bunny wasn't looking particularly well today. She had a cold and was thin and jaundiced. Her short hair had gone prematurely white, creating a fine mist around her head. Natalie rolled down her window and said, "Bunny? Can I give you a lift?"

"No, thanks, I'm fine," she muttered, eyes downcast. She wore that smelly old army jacket year-round. It was her favorite item of clothing. Written on back in gaudy pink and purple sequins was the message: I'VE GOT THIS. Some of the sequins had fallen off, but Bunny never went anywhere without her beloved jacket—winter, spring, summer, or fall.

"You're a long way from home," Natalie said, opening her wallet. She took out a twenty-dollar bill and handed it to the disoriented woman through the rolled-down window. "Remember me? Natalie?"

Bunny's face lit up. "Yeah, of course I remember you. You're Grace's sister. Sure do. Thanks, Natalie. You're so kind."

"When was the last time you ate? Hop in. I'll take you to the women's shelter. It's supposed to get pretty cold tonight."

"No, I'm okay." She tucked the money into her jacket pocket.

"Bunny, you're shivering," Natalie coaxed. "Let me buy you a cup of coffee."

"No, thanks," she said grumpily.

Bunny rarely ventured this far out of town. The A&P was her favorite haunt. Goodwill came next, then the food banks and the women's shelter. She refused to stay in one place for very long, because she believed that malevolent forces were chasing her.

Natalie unbuckled her seat belt and stepped out of the car as a ghostly fog rolled in and night descended. "What are you doing way out here?" she tried again. "Collecting cans?"

Bunny's mouth drew taut. "Those kids are up to no good."

"Kids?" Natalie repeated quizzically. "What kids?"

"They asked me for a cigarette," she said, rolling her eyes. "I don't smoke."

"Who asked you that?"

"Those damn kids. I've seen them out here before."

"In these woods?" Natalie took a stab. "Heading for the Mummy's Cabin?"

Bunny shivered and rubbed her arms. "Temperature's supposed to drop tonight."

"It'll be warmer at the women's shelter." Natalie made a gesture of reassurance, but she drew abruptly back.

"Don't."

"I'm sorry. I'm just concerned, is all."

Bunny's eyes lit up. "Guess what, Natalie? I'm getting married."

"You are?" Natalie had dealt with Bunny's delusions before, and over time she'd discovered it was best to humor her. Anything less could set her off. "Congratulations."

"The Devil and me are getting married. See?" She held up a dirty wad of rolled-up newspapers about the size of a baseball. "Here's my wedding ring." She unwrapped the sheets of butcher paper and newsprint, letting them flutter to the ground. She peeled off the last stained sheet and displayed a small round rock. She backed away slowly. "He's watching us now. The Devil."

"Maybe you should come with me," Natalie suggested.

Bunny grabbed the greasy handle of her shopping cart and tried to push it away, but the rattling front wheels got stuck in a rut. "The Devil gets inside us. Each and every one of us."

"Bunny, please . . ." She snagged her by the army jacket sleeve, not wanting her to run away again—not while she was off her meds and hallucinating about the devil.

"Leave me alone!" The homeless woman tugged herself free and, panicking now, picked up a heavy broken branch from the ground. She brandished it threateningly. "Don't you come near me! I'm warning you!"

"It's okay." Natalie was forced to step back. "I just want you to be safe."

Stark fear flooded the poor woman's face. She hurled the dead limb at Natalie's head, missing by inches, then abandoned her cart and fled into the woods.

"Bunny, wait!" Natalie headed after her, but Bunny was surprisingly nimble, scrambling swiftly through the undergrowth, impervious to the brambles that eventually prevented Natalie from moving forward. "Bunny, hold up!"

Soon she'd vanished into the woods, and Natalie couldn't help feeling like shit—it was her own stupid fault. She'd practically chased the poor woman into the state park. She thought briefly about calling her contact at the Department of Wetlands and Woodlands, Jimmy Marconi. The New York DWW Forest Rangers were stationed throughout the state, and Natalie had known Jimmy since she was in grade school. She remembered laughing at his bow legs. Forest rangers served as first responders. They protected visitors to the state forests and parks. Their duties were varied, but they were often called upon to assist with search-and-rescue efforts. They'd been trained to administer first aid and CPR. Some of them specialized in climbing and dive rescues. Jimmy and his crew had even searched for some of the Missing Nine.

But that would've been an overreaction. You only called the DWW when you'd exhausted all your options. Besides, the social workers and civil rights lawyers had made it clear that not even family members could force the homeless to do what was good for them without violating their autonomy—it was a fine line, legally and socially, and it burned a hole in Natalie's gut. In short: She could only protect Bunny if Bunny allowed it.

She decided to wait for her anyway. Ten minutes later, just as Natalie was about to give up, she heard a rustling sound in the woods. Bunny returned, shoulders hunched, disheveled and bleeding from scratches to her hands and face. Her eyes in the headlights' glare were round and drained. She walked up to the driver's side window and said in a contrite voice, "Can you give me a lift back to town?"

"Yes, of course," Natalie said, getting out of the car.

"What about my cart?"

"We'll put it in back."

20

Night had fallen, bleak and sodden. By the time Natalie had settled Bunny into a shelter and driven across town to the Buckner residence, the media vans had departed and yellow police tape cordoned off the property. She preferred to be alone at a crime scene, where she could think without disruption. She wiped her shoes on the welcome mat and went inside.

Brandon, who was staying with his parents across town, had given the BLPD permission to search the entire property on the night of the murder, but since Luke didn't want there to be any gray areas, Natalie had filed affidavits and secured an extensive warrant for the Buckner residence. Now they could come and go as they pleased.

The living room was modern and understated. Nothing too garish or bold. No stripes, plaids, or primary colors. The stairs creaked under her light steps. The banister felt sturdy in her hand. At the top of the landing, she slipped on a pair of disposable gloves and headed for the master bedroom at the end of the hall.

Cherry modern bedroom set. King-size bed. Egyptian cotton linens. Neat as a pin. On the nightstand was a pair of women's designer glasses and a stack of books.

Natalie picked up a volume of nineteenth-century poetry. The pages were faded and worn from repeated readings. She examined the other titles. *Dead Souls* by Nikolai Gogol, *Lady Chatterley's Lover* by D. H. Lawrence, Virginia Woolf's *To the Lighthouse,* Tolstoy's *War and Peace.* The baby books were at the bottom of the stack.

No wonder Brandon thought Daisy was bored by him.

Next, Natalie activated Daisy's Kindle Fire. The two breakup ebooks she'd purchased were there at the top of the list on the home page. Unread.

Natalie walked over to Daisy's brass-handled bureau and sifted through her underthings—plain cotton panties, sports bras, socks, hose. Very practical. The second drawer contained the more sensual stuff—silky camisoles, mesh-back panties, lacy thongs, push-up bras, delicate teddies. Everything was lightweight and airy, made of the softest fabric imaginable. Next came the pajama drawer, then a sweater drawer.

Natalie crossed the room and entered the walk-in closet. She flicked on the overhead light. There were two distinct sides—one for Brandon, the other for Daisy. She inhaled the acerbic scent of cedar and rifled through Daisy's outfits on their wooden hangers. Skirts and dresses, all colors of the rainbow. Silk and cashmere, cocktail attire and dressy casual. A camel-hair winter coat and a goose-down parka. Silky kimonos and chiffon robes. Little black dresses and formal wear. Daisy had built herself a serious wardrobe, one to match all occasions and moods.

Downstairs, she took a seat behind Daisy's desk and powered up her laptop. She combed through Daisy's emails and found an exchange between Principal Truitt and Daisy regarding Riley's status. No new information surfaced. There were faculty emails discussing the prom committee and other school events. Also, Daisy had contacted her minister, the Reverend Thomas Grimsby, trying to set up an appointment for next week. She wanted to meet with him—urgently, it seemed—on a private matter. Natalie made a mental note to follow this up.

Daisy's text messages to Brandon were brief and mostly revolved around domestic issues—*the car needs oil, call the roofing contractor for an estimate.*

Natalie rummaged through the desk drawers and found Daisy's daily planner. She rifled through the pages until she'd reached the calendar section. There were plenty of obstetrician appointments, dental appointments, and beauty appointments. Also, oddly, scrawled throughout the calendar on random dates, going back seven or eight months, were the initials, "T&I." Natalie puzzled over what this could possibly mean. Teaching and instruction?

She did an online search for "T&I" and came up with a list of acronyms that didn't seem to fit. Transportation and Infrastructure. Trade and Industry. Technology and Innovation. Team and Individual. Testing and Inspection. Teachers and Interpreters. Toledo and Indiana Railroad.

She sighed and set the issue aside.

There were other appointments jotted on Daisy's calendar, various committee meetings, faculty meetings, student activities, and other school events—along with her many beauty treatments. Haircuts at the Cutting Edge, mani-pedi's at Zoey's Salon, bikini waxes at the Palace Spa—scheduled at regular intervals, six to eight weeks apart, beginning approximately nine months ago.

Natalie put down the planner and checked her watch. Luke was waiting for her back at the station—he'd requested a debrief about today's findings. As she shifted in her seat, ready to give up, she felt the bump with her right foot. She pushed Daisy's roller chair back and peered underneath the desk. Shoved into a corner, behind the woven wastebasket, was a brown leather briefcase.

Natalie retrieved it, then propped the heavy briefcase on her lap and unzipped it. She scooped out a heavy handful of paperwork—student essays, test papers, lesson plans, faculty meeting schedules, curriculum notes. There was more paperwork inside, straining the briefcase. She took it all out and sorted through the mess, but nothing stood out.

She dug around in the inner hidden compartments, unzipping and probing them all. Finally, she found a sealed manila envelope and slit it open with a letter opener.

Inside was a paperback book titled *Tristan und Isolde*, by Richard Wagner.

Natalie recalled the classic tragedy from her college days, a medieval love story about star-crossed lovers, retold in countless manuscripts. Isolde, the daughter of the King of Ireland, was betrothed to British King Mark, who sent his nephew, Tristan, to escort her back to England. The couple fell in love en route.

Tristan and Isolde. *T&I*.

But there was more. Pressed between the pages of the book, folded in half, were several lined sheets of paper. She took them out and spread them across the desk. The love sonnets had been copied by hand, and all were signed, "Love, Tristan."

21

It was midnight by the time Natalie popped her head inside Luke's office.

"Yeah. Okay." He waved her in. He was seated at his desk, talking on the phone. His shoulders sagged under the weight of the unit's caseload. "Have a seat," he told her, still on the phone, and she closed the door behind her.

Tonight, Natalie had to sit on her hands to keep from fidgeting. She was dead tired but wide awake, a strange mental state to be in.

Luke hung up. "That was the chief. The media's way up his ass right now. News outlets have picked up on the story. It's going national. Did you know there were satellite vans camped out on the village green? Each time I leave the station, some reporter will shove a microphone in my face and try not to look too excited about it. Phones have been ringing off the hook. Now the mayor's concerned we don't look like such a warm-and-fuzzy vacation destination anymore. . . ."

"What does he expect us to do about it?" Natalie asked.

"Nothing. I told him, nobody's pressuring my people. We don't take shortcuts. We don't have the manpower to work the case any faster."

"So . . . just continue with the investigation?"

"Right. I told the chief we're working as hard as we can." He sipped his bottled water. "What do you have for me?"

She handed him the evidence bag with the love sonnets tucked inside.

"What's this?"

"I found it hidden away in Daisy's briefcase. Those are love sonnets, as far as I can tell . . . one looks like it was copied from Shakespeare, I don't know, I'm not an expert. A couple of originals. All signed 'Tristan.' A reference to Tristan and Isolde."

Luke gave her a blank look.

"It's a medieval love triangle. Tristan and Isolde fell in love while traveling from Ireland to England, where she was supposed to marry the king."

He put down the evidence bag. "So Daisy was having an affair. Is that what this means?"

"Either that, or she had a secret admirer. But then, why keep it hidden from her husband?"

"Who the hell is Tristan?"

"That's the million-dollar question." She handed him two other evidence bags. "The handwriting doesn't match these two samples I found at the Buckner residence. I'm no expert, but see for yourself . . . there's no comparison between Tristan's handwriting and Brandon's or Riley's."

Luke lined the three evidence bags side by side on his desk. "Nope," he said. "Not a match. But we'll need a handwriting expert to do the comparisons for us." He handed everything back. "What happened to Tristan and Isolde?"

"It doesn't end well. They died of broken hearts."

Luke nodded. "Don't most love stories end that way?"

"Which way—crying yourself to sleep at night with a pint of cookie dough ice cream?" she said with a smirk.

"Or you could take the low road and drink yourself into oblivion."

"You tried that, huh?"

"Oblivion is overrated," he said with a smirk. "After the divorce, I got so drunk once, I shaved off an eyebrow. True story."

Natalie smiled. "I'm numb to your confessions by now."

He held her eye a beat too long, and she felt the delicate tension between them. He'd kissed her once, on the day of her high school graduation—kissed her on the cheek, and it felt like a bee sting. She hadn't wanted to wash her face for weeks.

"Anyway," Luke said. "What does your gut tell you about this Tristan guy?"

"First of all, Daisy's the last person I'd ever suspect of having an affair. And Grace reinforced that—she said Daisy loved Brandon and couldn't wait to be a mom."

He watched her carefully. "But?"

"But it's confusing. I mean, she was in the middle of cooking when this happened. Looking up baby things online. Very domestic. But she also bought *The Breakup Bible*, and she owns some pretty sexy lingerie from Victoria's Secret. And for approximately the past year, she's been following a strict beauty and grooming routine . . . manicures, pedicures, leg waxes, a Brazilian. You live with someone for twelve years, my sense is you'd feel comfortable enough letting your legs go unshaved for a few days."

"Until *Tristan and Isolde*," Luke said.

"Right."

"But wouldn't Brandon notice the sudden uptick in grooming?"

"You said so yourself . . . if they were on a sex schedule while she was ovulating, sex can become pretty routine. Maybe she told him she got a Brazilian to keep things interesting? Anyway, let's assume she was having an affair," Natalie went on. "Let's assume it started nine months ago, and this affair was so unexpected . . . so out of character for her . . . she couldn't even tell her best friend about it. She was deeply conflicted. She was struggling with it. But then, once she discovered she was pregnant, let's say a month or two ago, she had to break off the affair to save her marriage."

"Which would explain *The Breakup Bible*."

"To help her cope with her choice."

"She loved him?"

"Maybe she loved them both," Natalie speculated.

"A love triangle? You think?"

"Hiding it from her best friend. Hiding it from Brandon." She shrugged. "Still waters run deep."

"Because this strengthens two new possibilities," Luke said, folding his hands on his desk. "Either Daisy's lover killed her, or else Brandon found out about the affair and lashed out in a fit of rage."

She tugged on her lower lip. She hadn't wanted to go there. But you had to be objective. "I'm not so sure about that," she said hesitantly. "Brandon seemed so knocked off his axis when we found her lying in the kitchen. I doubt he's that good an actor."

"I don't want to believe it, either," Luke said. "But you never know. Plenty of people lie. Some are lousy liars. Others are very good liars."

She couldn't dispute that. It was a chilling thought. What if Brandon had killed Daisy? But there was no proof. It was just wild speculation at this point.

"Shit," she said quietly. "We have to talk about this, Luke."

"Talk about what?"

"This is our *friend*. A few days ago, we were all kidding around, and now his life is ruined. And the possibility that he might've done something . . ." She shuddered.

"Look. We all like Brandon. Love the guy. But we have to go where the facts lead us. Period."

They sat there dully, watching the potential train wreck unfold before them.

"This is your first homicide," Luke reminded her. "You're still feeling your way through. But it'll come. Trust me. The answers will come eventually."

Natalie cringed. "Eventually?"

"Be patient. Put your blinders on and trust the process."

"Use the fork, Luke," she quipped, an old childhood joke.

He smiled. "Enough of your clever words."

Then a worn-out lethargy filled them both. The mood tonight was grim.

"So, again," he said, "who's Tristan?"

"Getting the baby's DNA results should help us narrow it down."

"Right. Barry says it's going to take a few weeks, though. Okay." Luke sat forward. "Let's continue interviewing Daisy's friends and colleagues tomorrow, see if they know anything about this guy, Tristan. Let's track down the sonuvabitch."

"Okay."

"Anything else?"

"Yeah," she said. "About the markings on Teresa's grave? It's called hypergraphia. I looked it up. Some people have an obsessive need to write things down. It's like being a hoarder, only instead of hoarding belongings, they hoard words."

"Hypergraphia?" Luke repeated.

"It's been tenuously linked to epilepsy, bipolar disorder, head injuries, or other mental illnesses. Also certain medical conditions. Basically anything that spurs activity in the frontal lobe, which controls speech. It's a rare condition. They don't know much about it yet, but antidepressants have been known to help."

"Which means whoever did this could've been treated for a psychiatric disorder or a medical condition in the past," he said. "We should make a list of all the psychiatrists in the area who specialize in hypergraphia."

"It's so rare, I doubt we'll find any in the immediate vicinity. But there are a couple of experts . . . one in Massachusetts, one at Johns Hopkins. I'll contact them and see if they can provide us with any information," Natalie said. "In the meantime, I've asked Lenny to digitize the photographs I took of Teresa's headstone and see if he can decipher any other words or messages. If somebody's leaving us messages, then we need to know what he's trying to say."

"Our priority's the Buckner case."

"Of course." She noticed her fingers were trembling. She'd had too much coffee today. No way was she going to sleep tonight.

"Did you eat yet?" he asked.

"Eat?" She cracked a smile. "What does that mean? You mean food? Because I haven't seen any of that in a while."

He laughed. "Right." He opened a paper bag on his desk, and she accepted half a Reuben sandwich from him.

"Thanks." She took a bite and said, "Mmm. Tastes good."

"Feel better?"

There was an awkward moment when they looked at each other with feelings of warmth that came from shared loyalties and confidences. His confessions had taken place over the years in hushed whispers, as if they were inside a confessional booth instead of a bar or a party at work.

"First homicide I ever caught," Luke said. "The victim was six years old. Curly brown hair. Big brown eyes. I think about it every year on the date she went missing. We searched the town and surrounding area. We dragged the lake. We zeroed in on the mother's boyfriend and found the girl's body in an abandoned building. Purple bruises around her neck in the shape of a man's hands. We tracked him down, but he saved us a lot of trouble by shooting himself point-blank. Easier that way. Less paperwork."

She watched him simmer over the memory of it.

"That case put me in touch with myself. It changed my life. I became attuned to the ugliness that surrounds us," Luke said. "I finally realized it's part of human nature to want to destroy, and that I'm never going to defeat all the bad guys in the world. But I can try to beat them in my little corner of the world."

She studied his face. She knew that look. It was a look that said he was about to reveal something even more personal. Whenever he got these urges, Luke's professional demeanor would slip away and his vulnerable side would reveal itself.

"My relationship with Audrey died a slow, agonizing death. During our last year together, we were both on autopilot, but I couldn't bring myself to admit it. We kept trying to reignite the old flame, but by then it was snuffed out for good. In the end, we decided to put our marriage out of its misery. Just kill it quick. Before it grew back."

Natalie smiled sympathetically.

"One day, when Skye was a toddler, she crawled up on my chest while I was lying down and sat there gazing down at me, her sweet face hovering above mine like an angelic moon . . . and I knew she was onto me. Onto my falseness. Onto my hypocrisy. She could read through all the bullshit. She knew that I'd totally fallen out of love with her mom. She had that toddler's piercing gaze, like a hawk staring down its prey. And the big lie came tumbling down, and I couldn't hide it anymore. Because my own kid had ferreted out the truth. And so I moved out the following week, and then a few months later . . . Audrey took Skye to Los Angeles with her." He sat rubbing the nape of his neck. "The hardest part was picking up the pieces. Booze helped for a while. You get used to that smoky flavor. The burn going down the throat—that's addictive. After my wife took my daughter away, I became disgusted with myself. I was divorced and alone. I couldn't be a significant part of Skye's life anymore, so I used to hang out at the Barkin' Dawg, where I wouldn't feel so isolated. But it's a paradox, because booze tastes like loneliness."

"But you pulled your shit together eventually, didn't you?" she reminded him. "After the eyebrow incident?"

He smiled ironically at her. "I had to prove to myself that I was a better man than my father. I was five when he lost his job. Lost his mind. Lost us. One day, he stopped coming home from work. My mother watched his dinners going cold, night after night. When she finally got up the courage to ask him where he'd been, he became abusive. He never hit her, but he yelled and kicked things. A month before he walked out on us, I asked him, 'Do you love me?' You know what he said?"

She shook her head. "What?"

"'Get your out-of-touch ass the fuck out of here.'" He laughed. "It was funny, but not in a ha-ha way. Anyway, it took me a long time to realize . . . if you're alive, then it's going to hurt. If you don't feel pain, then you must be drunk. The saddest part about being a cop? You find out death isn't sacred. It's commonplace. Pain and grief are all around us. There's no way to avoid it. You have to embrace it."

"Embrace the suck."

He grinned crookedly at her. "Yeah, like Joey used to say, embrace the suck. I tested my resolve and learned I'm a better man than my father was. Stronger. If I can stand up to an ice-cold beer, then I can stand up to anything."

She remembered riding with her father to the funeral parlor late at night, and gazing at the starry darkness outside her car window. They drove past neighbors' lit-up houses, yellow squares of warmth where families huddled together, intact. Natalie was jealous of those cozy homes where girls her age hadn't lost their big sisters. Where families hadn't fallen apart and scattered, each to his or her own linty corner of agony and grief. As Joey drove his wife and daughters over to the funeral parlor, he gripped the wheel, grim-faced. Grace was silent in back. The potholes were plentiful, and Natalie could feel her entire lumbar region reacting to the bumps, as if God wanted to punish them some more. As if losing Willow hadn't been enough. The car vents sending soft currents of air across her face, like Willow's last sigh of farewell.

Now she lowered her head and asked, "Why did you promote me over Ronnie Petrowski? Since we're being completely honest here."

He frowned. "You have to ask?" He ticked off the reasons on his fingers. "A degree in criminal justice, graduated summa cum laude. A yearlong stint at the police academy, followed by three years on patrol. Volunteering for overtime constantly. Taking every shit detail nobody wanted. Up for promotion—competitive exam. Top marks for your work, and then your commanding officer puts in a request for you to join homicide. Sounds obvious to me."

"I'm serious," she told him stubbornly. "Ronnie has more years on me."

"This wasn't about seniority."

"What, then? I really want to know."

"Kimberly Gleesing."

She remembered—a teenage runaway who fell in with the wrong crowd. She fell for a boy who didn't reciprocate, got into drugs, and it was downhill from there.

"I know how important that case was to you," Luke said. "Things like that can give you an ulcer. Such a nice girl. Nothing in her background to indicate why. Her parents doted on her. All those childhood toys in her bedroom, the pink walls and a canopy bed. You worked that case hard, Natalie, door-to-dooring morning, noon, and night. Volunteering after hours. That first day we searched for her, after the sun set . . . when midnight rolled around, I had a gut feeling something terrible had happened. But you refused to give up. You persisted. You kept looking. You tracked down every lead. Answered phones. Talked to maybe a hundred witnesses. And when we found her, forty-two hours later, hiding inside a hay shed, she was fine, a little dehydrated, a little bruised, but okay . . . only then did you let your guard down."

She remembered bursting into tears when Kimberly stood up and walked out of the shadows into the light of day.

"You passed the test," Luke said. "My stubborn-as-shit test."

"You have a stubborn-as-shit test?"

"Hell, yeah. For all my hires." He smiled warmly at her. "You've got a wicked stubborn streak, and guess what? You've had it all your life. Remember when my dog disappeared? Charlie? Just a raggedy old mutt, but I loved him like crazy. One day, I couldn't find him anywhere. Mom figured the coyotes must've got him. But you wouldn't let it go. You refused to give up so easily. You dragged me around the neighborhood, calling out his name. 'Charlie? Charlie?' You figured he was kidnapped by the Meekers, remember them? Way up in the woods. That creepy old trailer on cement blocks. Those folks nobody ever saw. Just a rusty bent mailbox that said 'Meekers.' You dragged me up that hill every day for two weeks, and we hollered Charlie's name, and once we even heard him barking in the distance, remember? You never gave up. Maybe he's down by the stream, you said, or in one of the caves out by Devil's Point. Or trapped in the junkyard, remember? We even went to the gravel pits. I had my driver's license, and you'd hop in the car and always have a new suggestion. I'd pretty much given up by the end of week two, but then, miraculously, Charlie came dragging his sorry ass home, looking beat-to-shit. That's when I realized . . . by us going out there every damn day, by never giving up, we gave Charlie hope, and he found his own way home." He rested his hands on the desktop and said, "You're stubborn as shit, Lockhart."

She cracked a bashful smile. "I'll put that on my résumé."

Her feelings for Luke always surprised her, because she was forever tucking them away. She remembered their old ritual. Thumb squeeze. Offered instead of a hug. Six-year-old Natalie would hold out her thumb and adolescent Luke would squeeze it. A sign of loyalty and forever-friendship between two mismatched kids.

He blinked, and the moment was gone. He picked up an old file from his desk and handed it to her. "Anyway," he said, getting back to business. "You wanted to take a look at this."

She read the label. HANNAH DAUGHERTY: RAPE.

22

By the time Natalie pulled into the driveway, the sky was inky black. She turned off the ignition and pushed her pain to another place. She rubbed her forehead as if she wanted to bury her fingers in her skull. Sometimes her mind burned furious and white-hot, a thousand thoughts cramming into her head all at once—but then, in a flash, they'd be gone, leaving her gasping for air.

The house was quiet and dark, except for a strip of light running underneath the front door. She let herself in and walked through the empty rooms. The curtains billowed in the wind. The few pieces of furniture she'd purchased over the years were economical and functional. Comfort was more important than style—big sturdy armchairs, plenty of reading lamps, blocky side tables stacked with stuff. Those fugly curtains had been there forever and she hadn't bothered to replace them. There was no telling how old the kitchen appliances were. The gas stove and humming refrigerator had guest-starred in some of her earliest memories. Behind the counters in those hard-to-reach places was an intimidating amount of encrusted grease and grime. A cockroach's dream home.

Inside her father's old den—now hers—Natalie removed her shoulder holster and pressed her service revolver into the foam padding of her gun case. The oak bookcase held a motley collection of police manuals and forensic pathology books from her days at the academy. On the top shelf was a gift from her niece—a teddy bear wearing a "My Hero" baseball cap. She ran her fingers over the spines of old textbooks collecting dust and couldn't recall the last time she'd opened one. As a child, Natalie had memorized all the BLPD rules and regulations, and when Joey used to test her at the dinner table, she could spit them back with pinpoint accuracy.

She recalled a time when her father took her to a pub with some of his cop buddies. They were all smoking cigars and drinking a thick dark ale, which tasted horrible (he let her have a sip), and there was a young man sitting with them at the bar, and they kept slapping him on the back. Her father explained, "This is the guy who saved my life." A robbery, five years earlier, in a convenience store on Mountain Laurel Road, two robbers, and the first robber took aim at Joey, but the second robber stopped him from firing, and both got busted and put away. But now, five years later, the second robber was out of prison, and the cops were treating him like a hero, buying him drinks and slapping him on the back, offering him part-time work through a friend of a friend, because he'd saved Joey's life, and they owed him. What Natalie learned that night was that, rarely, but occasionally, cops and robbers could be friends.

Joey liked to share stories about his adventures with his wife and children, but there were some things he couldn't reveal. Secrets. One night, Natalie found him shredding documents in his den. He glanced up, pale and drawn, and told her to go back upstairs. He shut the door, and Natalie could hear him shredding paperwork behind the closed door.

Now she scooped out her old St. Jude's medallion on its long silver chain, the one she used to wear close to her heart. St. Jude, the patron saint of lost causes. Joey had given it to her on her eighth birthday. It was their private joke. He called her a lost cause, but he meant that in the very best way—he meant she was stubborn and headstrong. That she wouldn't give up. That she refused to listen to the status quo and didn't let anything stop her. He was proud of her achievements at school, but even prouder that she relied on her conscience.

He taught her everything he knew about being a cop, but as the years passed, Joey became afraid for Natalie. After a lifetime of encouraging her to follow in his footsteps, Joey pleaded with her not to. It was too dangerous, he said. He didn't want her risking her life for a paycheck and a pension.

"Dad, it's okay," she told him. "I have your St. Jude's medallion to protect me."

"But that's not real, kid."

Her fingers closed around the medallion, and she told him of course it wasn't real . . . she knew that this pendant couldn't protect her. How could it? It was supposed to have magical powers, and that was bullshit. "But everything you drummed into my head all those years . . . *that's* going to protect me," she said. "You're my St. Jude's medallion, Dad."

He wasn't convinced, but Natalie's mind was made up.

Now she tucked the pendant away, took a seat behind her father's desk, and unlocked the bottom drawer. She kept her Threat Level II protective vest in here, along with a pair of handcuffs and her off-duty revolver wrapped in muslin. The vest was scheduled for replacement next year, since they wore out every five years or so, but Natalie really liked this one. She'd worn it on a drug raid three years ago, and it had caught a bullet at point-blank range. She kept the deformed slug in a jar on top of her computer. It was her lucky vest. It had stopped a bullet from entering her heart. Sometimes you got lucky. Sometimes you walked away with your life intact.

Now she unclipped her shield and studied it. Natalie had taken one oath in her lifetime. She'd sworn to uphold the law and protect the community. She'd made this solemn vow to the entire town. She wondered if any human being was capable of living up to such a task. Protecting a whole town from evil.

The same evil that had taken Willow's life.

The same evil that took Daisy's life.

Like her father used to say, *Grief fades. And that bothers me.*

Grief may fade, but memories didn't. Natalie's heart pulsed with emotion. Every day during Justin Fowler's trial, inside the courtroom, Deborah would clutch Willow's favorite purple silk scarf in one hand, occasionally pressing it to her nose and inhaling the peachy scent of Willow's perfume. Natalie's mother had cried so much during the trial, she'd had to wear amber-tinted sunglasses to hide her anguish from the press. Toward the end of her life, Deborah stopped eating, and her skeletal frame became a hanger for her flowery clothes.

Joey used to call his daughters "triple trouble" because he loved them so much. He never shouted. He hardly ever raised his voice. Toward the end of his life, gravity dragged his face down, but he was the same old Joey, still strong and in charge. He used to say, "Life is long. It just feels short." Death must feel longer.

After four years of college and travel abroad, Natalie was compelled to return home when her father became seriously injured after his car slammed into a tree. Natalie was twenty-two when she got the bad news. She came home to find Joey in the hospital. She was there one week later when he passed away.

Grief doesn't come with instructions.

Her mother died a few years later. After the funeral, Natalie stayed on to help Grace with the estate, but then something kept her here—deep roots, a need for healing, unfinished business. She'd never been able to explain it to her more adventurous friends. A strange sense of belonging, or fate.

Upstairs, Natalie took a long hot shower, brushed her teeth, and changed into her nightclothes—her extra-large BLPD T-shirt, athletic socks, and a pair of pink boxers.

Downstairs, she grabbed a bottled water from the fridge, plopped down on the living-room sofa, and opened Hannah Daugherty's file.

Hannah Daugherty was seventeen years old when she was raped by an ex-boyfriend in the foundation of the old Shell station. Afterward, while the police were doing a grid search, Luke and his team came across a peculiar message written in chalk on the cement wall of the foundation, which was open to the elements. New York State's unpredictable upstate weather should've erased it within a week or two, at the most.

Now Natalie pawed through the pages until she found a photograph of the chalk message. Then she cross-referenced Minnie Walker's case file to verify that it was located in the same corner of the foundation where Minnie was last seen giving head to one of her johns before she disappeared. Check.

Next, she did a side-by-side comparison of the pictures she'd taken of Teresa McCarthy's gravestone, and the police photo taken at the scene of Hannah Daugherty's rape. The handwriting looked eerily similar. She could only make out a few words, though. *Delicate, your sins, pussy.*

Okay. The police had discovered this bizarre message at the time of Hannah's rape, which occurred two years *after* Minnie Walker's disappearance. Natalie activated her laptop and checked her notes. Minnie was reported missing on March 17, four years ago. Hannah Daugherty was raped on March 23, two years ago. The incidents had occurred two years and six days apart. Was it possible that the vandal had returned to the scene of the crime on the anniversary of Minnie's abduction, March 17, and left his message—just as he'd left a message on Teresa McCarthy's grave? Natalie checked with the online historical weather database and discovered that two years ago, it hadn't snowed or rained for ten days after March 17, which was well within the bounds of March 23, the day the police found the chalk message.

Next, she skim-read the police reports for any other clues she could find. Like a typical teenager, Hannah was an amalgam of conflicting emotions. She was both fascinated and terrified by horror movies. She collected My Little Pony figurines and soft-core romance novels. Her long blond hair was dazzling, like sunlight bouncing off a waterfall. She loved to sing "Milkshake" by Kelis. She was a happy child who was afraid to be alone at home. Nothing connected Hannah to Minnie, except for the coincidental location of the rape and the disappearance.

Perhaps this was an "anniversary" thing? Natalie wrote down Teresa's disappearance date, April 4. There hadn't been any precipitation over the following two weeks, not until Wednesday evening, when Natalie discovered the message on Teresa's grave, but she wanted to be sure, so she checked the historical weather database again—zero precipitation between April 4 and Willow's deathiversary. Which meant that the vandal could've left the chalk message on Teresa's grave on April 4, the anniversary date of her disappearance.

She realized she'd been sitting in the same position for more than an hour and was beyond worn-out. She felt molded to the sofa, virtually part of it. Her phone rang, and she checked the number. It was Luke.

"Can't sleep?" he asked tiredly.

"No. My mind's going a mile a minute," she admitted. "You?"

"I'm still at the office."

She glanced at the clock. "It's two in the morning. You're aware of that, right?"

"I've been talking to Murph," he said. "He's got the night shift, so I'm standing in front of your desk. I think your plant is dead."

"Um. No. You can't actually kill an ivy plant."

"Does your plant know this?"

She smiled. "You're funny tonight. But you're right, I am deadly to plants. It's genetic. I inherited my father's gangrene thumb."

He laughed softly. Then he said, "What do you think of Hannah's file?"

"I think whoever did this acted deliberately and calculatedly. He revisited the scene of Minnie Walker's disappearance on the date she went missing, two years later, and left us a message. Just like the message he left on Teresa McCarthy's headstone on April fourth, the date she went missing. Both messages were written in chalk, and there was no precipitation to eliminate them before they were discovered."

"What kind of a message is he sending us?"

"I don't know, but I suspect it might be connected to the dead crows."

"You think?" Luke sounded surprised.

"It's a stretch, I know. But somebody out there is trying to get our attention."

"Not trying hard enough if it's taken us this long to detect it," he said. "Do you think it's related to witchcraft?"

"Could be." Natalie closed her eyes.

There was a brief pause before Luke asked, "What is it with teenage girls and witchcraft?"

She opened her eyes and made a face. "What do you mean?"

"Murphy told me that, statistically speaking, it's mostly girls who get involved with witchcraft. Why's that? Do you know? What's the attraction?"

She considered it for a moment. "It starts with an unfulfilled wish, in my experience. You have a crush on a boy who doesn't even know you exist. Somebody brooding and unreachable, like Neo from *Matrix* in his floor-length trench coat. Or the lead vampire in *Twilight*, with his sultry eyes and black eyeliner. Whatever—he's your dreamboat. But then, at some point, you get tired of writing his name in your notebook with a Sharpie, so you join a coven and cast love spells on his oblivious ass."

Luke chuckled. "Are you serious?"

"Yeah, absolutely. You try to hex him into loving you. Or maybe it's more academic than that. Maybe you want to ace your midterms. Or you'd like the other kids at school to stop picking on you and mocking your outfits. I suppose there are plenty of reasons. And then one day, a friend invites you to join her coven, and it's such an alluring proposition. You'll be part of an exclusive club. It's a chance to control your own destiny. So you join the sisterhood and learn about rites and divination. You cast your first love spell, conjure up straight As, and before you know it, you're hooked . . . and now you're spending all of your hard-earned babysitting cash on spell kits and Ouija boards and malediction books. Eventually, though, you realize things haven't been working out the way you'd hoped. And so, when you don't get your way, when the cute boy still ignores you, and you get a B-minus on your midterm, and the mean girls are still picking on you, well then . . . things can take a darker turn."

"How dark?" he asked.

"It all depends. When you find yourself kneeling before a handmade altar, chanting to invisible forces . . . that kind of wakes you up. At some point, most kids quit the craft and move on."

"What was your wish?" he asked her.

"My wish?"

"You just said it always starts with an unfulfilled wish."

"Oh." The moment stretched until it became painful. She wanted to confess her deepest secret to him, to tell Luke—it was you. The boy she cast a love spell on. The reason she'd gotten into witchcraft in the first place. Simple, really. Nothing complicated about it. Natalie hesitated, then said the only thing that popped into her head. "I had a lot of pain and shame whirling around inside, and so it was tempting to do something radical. To not let the world overwhelm me."

"I get that," he said softly.

That night, she fell into a merciless slumber full of black voids and swirling emptiness. She woke up the following morning to the sound of her blaring alarm clock. She thumbed the OFF button. The darkness gradually washed away and an odd drumming sound grew louder. Rain on the roof.

She took a shower, got dressed, and drank her coffee inside the drafty, outdated kitchen. The jerry-rigged plumbing should've been upgraded ages ago. The farmer's sink wouldn't drain properly. The stove light was always on, because that corner of the kitchen was so dark. She'd spent her entire youth inside this house, imagining herself elsewhere. Now she couldn't picture herself anywhere else. It was a paradox.

After graduating from the police academy, Natalie applied for the position of a rookie patrol officer with the BLPD. When she was twenty-five, her mother died of breast cancer. Deborah spent the last few weeks of her life in the hospital. In the will, Natalie's parents had bequeathed everything to her, which wasn't much—but it meant the world to her. An old house on two overgrown acres. A collection of boxy rooms. The windows were drafty as tissue paper. The fireplace was unusable. Large flies buzzed around the ceiling in the summertime. Maybe it was time to claim the place as her own, tear everything down and start over again.

Joey loved telling stories—or more accurately, he told one long, rambling story his entire life, constantly interrupted, a story without end and punctuated by the phrase, "But the point is . . ." All those years later, he never managed to come to the point.

Toward the end of his life, during one of Natalie's last visits to the hospital, after Joey had coughed up half a lung, she asked him, "Dad? Were we enough?" He didn't seem to understand the question, so she repeated it. "Were we enough for you? Mom, Willow, Grace, and me. Were we enough?"

After a beat, he cracked a smile and said, "You were the whole fucking point."

Now her phone buzzed.

"Natalie?" said a husky male voice. A little desperate sounding.

"Brandon?" she responded.

"Can you meet me in twenty minutes?"

"Where? Your lawyer's office?"

"Fuck that Ivy League gorilla. Meet me at the old farm in Chippaway. Remember the place I showed you last year?"

"Yes, I remember."

"Thirty-six Crying Lane. Come alone." He hung up.

23

Natalie sat inside her idling Honda Pilot, staring at the barn through the pouring rain. Last year, Brandon had lured her out to this fringe-of-nowhere place, this eighty-acre plot of ruination, to show her the one thing in the world that created a kind of magic inside his head.

She didn't see it. The magic.

She kept her keys in the ignition and the headlights on. She stepped out of the vehicle, stamped her feet and shivered in the rain, her breath smoking before her. Thunder. Lightning. Rain pissed down on her head. With all the fancy equipment she'd remembered to stash inside her SUV, how could she have forgotten an umbrella? She grabbed a slicker out of the back and put it on.

The barn formed a monstrous face in the dark. The Honda's headlights illuminated the tangled burdock lapping against the crumbling foundation. She glanced around at the various outbuildings and tumbledown sheds composing the abandoned farmstead. The village of Chippaway was twenty miles west of Burning Lake, two towns over in the back of beyond. Chippaway was a hardscrabble burg, appropriately named because it had been chipped down to nothing by the modern world. It was little more than erosion and rust now. Lots of boarded-up buildings. Lots of foreclosures. A synergy of misery and abandonment.

Brandon's grandparents used to own this farm, but at some point they'd sold it off for pennies on the dollar. Now Brandon wanted to buy it back from its current owner, who'd left it to rot. Natalie sensed he might already be there, waiting for her. She shielded her eyes and searched the misty fields around the barn and the watercolor woods beyond. She studied the deserted road, then spotted his 1955 Porsche Speedster Replica zipping along Crying Lane—scarlet with a black top, a tremendous eye-catcher. Hard to miss. Because of the threats to his life from the Skinner clan, who'd been spreading false rumors that he'd punched Riley into a coma, Brandon should've ditched the Speedster for something less flashy, like a Japanese import, but he couldn't let go of his toys that easily. They were inextricably woven into his rich kid identity. The Buckners had made their fortune harvesting timber, and Brandon and his father were always butting heads about his career choice. Being a police officer was simply beneath Kenneth Buckner, II.

Now the Porsche swung into the driveway, chirped to a halt, and Brandon got out. "Thanks for coming, Natalie," he said moodily, heading toward the barn and motioning her inside. "Let's talk in here."

The interior of the old barn was musty and dank. She choked back the cloying smell of pickled hay and took a seat on a questionable wooden crate, while a wet-leaf chill clung to her skin.

In this confined space, Brandon said softly, "I swear to God, I didn't touch that kid. Dominic is running around saying I acted like a thug, not a law officer, which is complete bullshit. You know I didn't hurt him, right?"

"That's what the internal investigation's going to clear up," she said evenly.

"It's bad enough I had to lose my wife and baby, now I have to deal with this crap."

"I'm sorry, Brandon."

He looked bloated and puffy-eyed, as if he'd been up all night. His cheeks sagged, and the veins in his neck pulsed dully. His father, a vastly wealthy man, had hired the best criminal attorney available for his son's defense.

Frank Moorecraft, Esquire, was one tough son of a bitch—assertive, irascible, impatient. He had forked hair and dead eyes, and he looked like Satan, if Satan dressed in Brooks Brothers and owned a Cartier watch.

"I'll admit it was dumb of me," Brandon said, brushing his fingers through his hair, "to go chasing after him like that. But I was in shock. My wife was *dead*. Jesus Christ, it still doesn't register." He rubbed his nose and scowled. "My blood alcohol content was only slightly over the legal limit— and those tests have been proven wrong before. And I've never received so much as a warning about my behavior, Natalie. I've never been suspended or disciplined. No verbal or written warnings. I have an outstanding record."

"I know," she said sympathetically.

"The minute Riley fled the scene, my training kicked in, and I followed standard procedure . . . I gave chase, but as I approached the suspect, he swung at me and started spouting gibberish. Then he collapsed." He sighed and looked at her. "They say he might never come out of this."

"Nobody knows what's going to happen."

"Do I have any regrets? Yes. I wish I could take it all back," Brandon admitted, crossing his arms protectively. "But the truth is, I did nothing wrong. They're looking for a scapegoat. Dominic's attorney keeps hounding Internal Affairs, asking them to charge me with abusing the suspect's civil rights. Believe that? My attorney says the hospital staff couldn't find any evidence of assault or bodily injuries that weren't caused by Riley's own seizures or CPR performed in the ambulance. Hopefully the toxicology results will clear things up."

"You've got yourself a great lawyer," she said.

He rubbed his forehead worriedly. "My attorney tells me the union will stand by me, because that's their assigned role."

Rain pounded against the roof of the barn like thundering horse hooves.

"Where were you on Wednesday between four and six P.M.?" Natalie asked, and his face grew clouded with shock.

"The hell? Am I a suspect now?"

"You know how it is, Brandon. We have to eliminate all of those closest to the victim—spouses, lovers, relatives," she told him. "What's your alibi for Wednesday between four and six P.M.?"

He rocked gently back and forth. "My shift ended at four. I stopped by the gym after work. Then I headed for the Barkin' Dawg at six."

"So you were at the gym for two hours? Can that be verified?"

He studied his hands. "Well, not the entire time."

She frowned. "What do you mean?"

"Christ," he said, his mood toggling between frustration and anger. "I went for a drive after work, and *then* I headed for the gym, okay?"

"How long of a drive?"

He shrugged. "I don't know. About an hour."

"An hour? Where'd you go?"

"I came up here. To the farm."

"Did anyone else see you?"

"I don't know," he said defensively. "I'd been thinking about buying the place, you know? I figured we'd need more room for the kids." His eyes glazed over. "I was hoping there'd be more children. . . ."

She nodded sympathetically. "No witnesses, though? You didn't stop for gas?"

He stared at her without blinking. "No."

"So you came up here. Looked around. Drove back. And went to the gym?"

He nodded. "Around five o'clock, I guess."

"Okay. Now, listen." She swallowed hard. She didn't want to go there, but she had to. "You've indicated there were problems with your marriage, Brandon. Do you think it's possible Daisy may have been having an affair?"

He looked about as stunned as she'd ever seen him. "What are you talking about?"

On the surface, Brandon and Daisy had led the perfect life. She was a popular teacher, and he had a prominent position in law enforcement. They were both involved in local charities, like the women's shelter and the Special Olympics. They were exceptionally good-looking and well-to-do, a power couple in this town.

Brandon grew agitated. He stood up and started pacing back and forth across the sagging floorboards. "An affair? Hell, no."

"But you told me the other day you two were having sexual issues."

"I said my marriage wasn't perfect, okay? I know I brag a lot, but I can't help myself. My dad's a jerk. I inherited his jerk genes. They're hardwired into my DNA. Anyway, what kind of questions are these, Natalie?"

"Well, look," she said, "we found something inside the house. Sonnets. Love sonnets to Daisy. Signed 'Tristan.' Would you know anything about that?"

He reacted as if he'd been stabbed in the chest. He drew his hand to his heart and muttered, "God."

"I'm sorry, Brandon. But I'm trying to get to the bottom of things."

He shook his head, bewildered.

"Because if you two were having marital problems, then maybe she was cheating on you?" Natalie suggested. "And if she was cheating on you, then maybe it was her lover who killed her? If you could give us a name, anything, any little detail . . . we can investigate further."

He plopped down on a nearby hay bale and said, "If Riley didn't do it, then I don't have a fucking clue."

"Think a minute. Take your time."

Brandon cradled his head in his hands. Then he took one fierce, shuddering breath and lifted his head. "It's true Daisy and I were having problems but, listen . . . we were committed to making it work for the baby's sake. We were really looking forward to being parents. And it kills me that you think . . ."

"I'm sorry."

He shifted his weight on the soggy hay bale. "We've been trying to get pregnant forever, it seems. Two miscarriages. She was so damn nervous about this one. She didn't want to jinx it again."

"Regarding the sonnets, though, do you have any suspicions?"

"No."

"At the autopsy . . ."

"Christ." He lowered his head into his hands again and groaned.

"I apologize, Brandon. But at the autopsy, we found scars on Daisy's wrists. Old slash marks. Barry Fishbeck called them hesitation scars from an old suicide attempt."

He nodded slowly and said, "I had a crush on her forever. But we fell in love for real our senior year of high school. We fooled around. She got pregnant. She had an abortion, but it messed with her head. She fell into a depression. At one point, she cut her wrists, but they were superficial . . . more like a cry for help."

"Then what happened?"

"We put it behind us. We went away to college. Look," he said, "we were both so young. It was a tough decision, but neither of us was ready to raise a baby. Are you kidding me? We went away to different colleges. How was that supposed to work? But then I think that over the years, Daisy came to regret her decision, because of the miscarriages . . ."

"So she thought the abortion may have made it more difficult to stay pregnant?"

Brandon scrubbed his head hard with his fingers. "You know what I think, Natalie? I think Riley Skinner had a thing for my wife. And I think she was trying to help him, but he took it the wrong way. Maybe he's the one who wrote those sonnets? Maybe he's Tristan?"

Natalie nodded. "That's a possibility. But the handwriting doesn't match."

He gave an angry shake of his head. "There's no way this baby isn't mine. Daisy would *never* cheat on me. I loved her and she loved me. We were committed to this baby. God, I mean . . ." he said in a sinking voice. He looked at her. "Do you think she was cheating on me? Really, Natalie? Do you think it's possible?"

"I don't know."

"But with who?"

Natalie shook her head.

"Fuck."

She took out her phone and scrolled through images of Daisy's messy desk. "Can you tell me something else, Brandon?" She handed him the phone. "Is there anything missing from Daisy's desk?"

He stared at the phone screen for several minutes, swiping through the images of Daisy's desktop and open drawers full of clutter. "Well, yeah . . . I don't see her diary."

"She kept a diary? What did it look like?"

"Leather-bound. Pink, with yellow daisies on the front—daisies for Daisy—and a little brass clasp. It was from her childhood. One of those vintage-looking things. She kept it in the top drawer. It had a tiny key for the lock."

"I kept all my childhood diaries," Natalie said. "Just the one?"

Brandon nodded absently. "I think so. I'm not sure."

"And she stashed it in her top desk drawer? You're positive?" Natalie would have to search the house again, since they hadn't found any diaries— no leather-bound pink diaries with yellow daisies on front. "Where did she keep the key?"

Brandon shrugged. "In her jewelry box, I guess. I'm not sure."

"Did she let you read it? Her diary?" Natalie asked.

He studied her blankly. "No. Why would she?"

"I don't know. Was there stuff written in there about you?"

"About me?" He looked as if he'd never considered the possibility.

"Do you have any idea what was in her diary?"

"No."

"Are you sure, Brandon?"

"What are you implying?"

"Nothing. It's just that . . . if she had a diary, I would've thought you might be curious to see what was in it. Right?"

"Natalie." He drew a sharp breath, on the verge of losing it. "It wasn't like that between us. I didn't care. That was girl stuff. Besides, I trusted her. . . ." His voice faltered. He looked at her with tears in his eyes. He wiped his sweaty face with his hands, then straightened up and said, "Listen, I wasn't supposed to meet you against the advice of my attorney . . . but I wanted to help with the investigation."

"Help us how?"

"I have this snitch who knows everybody on the west side. He's plugged into the drug culture—Jules, you know him?"

"No."

"Anyway, he's an expert in Wicca and has knowledge of occult activity in the area. He's reliable, he's credible. We've done a dozen drug busts together—Jules, Jacob, and me—and I trust the guy. He just might know where Riley was that day. Here's his contact information." Brandon opened his wallet and handed her a slip of paper. "Jules Pastor. You should ask him what Riley was up to during the TOD. He can at least steer you in the right direction."

She recognized the last name—Pastor. A prominent family in this town.

"Natalie."

She looked up. "Yes?"

"Please find out who killed my wife."

24

Natalie was on her way back to the station when she got the call from Dispatch about a reported drowning in the lake. It was all hands on deck. She turned her car around and headed east.

It wasn't a call you wanted to get. It was never easy, emotionally, to recover a body. Occasionally, some misguided soul would take a dare and swim out to the island, thinking it wasn't so far away. Often the water was choppier than expected. The cold could paralyze you. Hypothermia was a real killer. So was exhaustion.

During the summer months, motorboats and water-skiers buzzed across the lake and didn't always notice the lone swimmer making his solitary way out to the tiny island. There were sudden drop-offs into deep water, where logs and other debris could snag you. Currents in the lake were powerful and unexpected. Drownings happened quickly—less than three minutes.

A common saying in these parts was, "You can't legislate common sense." Upstate New York had approximately six million visitors a year, and every year, a couple of people died in Burning Lake. Media campaigns and safety task forces weren't enough. Warning signs and barbed wire fences were easily broached. Poison ivy wasn't a deterrent. Park rangers writing tickets and public service announcements couldn't prevent the next tragedy from happening.

By far, the most dangerous part of the lake was Devil's Point on the eastern shore, where cliff jumping had been a tradition for generations. Here, the rocky outcroppings rose fifty to eighty feet above the water and attracted thrill seekers of all ages. It was a rite of passage for some of the locals to dive off the cliffs, even though such acts were forbidden.

The BLPD didn't have the authority or the resources to patrol Devil's Point, which was part of the state park. Jurisdictions needed to be respected. Park rangers were constantly issuing citations for alcohol-related offenses and trespassing, but it was an ongoing problem. The rangers were exclusively in charge, except in an emergency, when local law enforcement agencies got involved.

Now the waterfront came into view with its docked boats, food shacks, and designated swim area. A County Fire Rescue vehicle came tearing up the road toward Natalie and zoomed past her, grit from the blacktop swirling up. She let it go, then waited a beat before pulling into the public parking lot, where she found a spot and got out. The lakefront consisted of a manicured park with an information kiosk, several restaurants, three lifeguard towers, public restrooms, and a boardwalk nestled on the western shore of the lake. People took their kids swimming here in the summertime, where they were monitored by a team of lifeguards. Water-safety tips were posted on the menus of all the lakefront restaurants. SWIMMERS SHOULD ALWAYS WEAR A PERSONAL FLOTATION DEVICE. USE THE BUDDY SYSTEM. CLIFF DIVING AT DEVIL'S POINT IS STRICTLY FORBIDDEN.

A large group of people had already gathered on the sandy shore to watch the rescue efforts this morning. Members of the BLPD were out in force. Firemen from the surrounding townships had come to assist, along with an ambulance crew, a volunteer search-and-rescue organization, and a handful of forest rangers. Natalie wondered who could've been crazy enough to go swimming this early in the season, before the spring sun had warmed the region's lakes. But it was also inevitable. It had been a thing for decades—proving your manhood.

Natalie crossed the waterfront and approached her old friend, Jimmy

Marconi, and his elite cliff-and-dive-rescue team of rangers. They were packing up their gear. Nobody was suited up. They all wore their vinyl jackets with the DWW logo on back.

"What's going on, Jimmy?" she asked.

"False alarm," he explained, stashing an oxygen tank into his emergency bag. Slim and pallid, in his late thirties, Jimmy looked more like a computer nerd than a forest ranger, whereas the six men he supervised were athletic looking and deeply tanned. "Some jerk took his kids up to Devil's Point, and after he jumped in the water, the kids couldn't see any bubbles, so they called 911. Turns out the bastard was trying to scare them, just for laughs. He resurfaced in a reedy area and hid there where his kids couldn't see him."

"Just for laughs?" Natalie said, disgusted. "He did it deliberately?"

"Yeah. The idiot."

"Imagine doing that to your kids," one of the team members, Samuel Winston, interjected. Natalie and Samuel had gone on an embarrassing date once, many years ago, while he'd been attending a firefighting seminar at the Massachusetts Firefighting Academy and she was a sophomore in college. She'd been so relieved to find another upstate New Yorker who missed the same things she did—Stewart's ice cream, Duff's wings, cider donuts, Saranac beer—that she gave Samuel her phone number. But then, during their date, they completely ran out of things to say as soon as they'd exhausted their nostalgia for back home. After an awkward farewell, they moved on. Now Samuel was married with kids, working for the DWW, and always happy to see her.

"It's patently dumb," Jimmy said. "You don't take chances like that when your kids are watching."

"It's hubris," Samuel said, stashing more gear into a duffel bag. "What if he died right in front of them? I have two little ones at home, and I can't imagine doing anything like that to them."

"You can't fix stupid," Jimmy said with a shrug.

"So the idiot's okay?" Natalie asked them.

"Yeah, he waded ashore, unharmed," Jimmy said. "Surprised by all the commotion—or so he claims."

"Are any charges being brought against him for this stunt?" she asked.

"No. He received a severe talking-to by the fire chief, though," Jimmy joked.

"A severe talking-to?" Samuel repeated. "They should fine his ass."

"I'll kick his ass," muttered one of the other rangers on Jimmy's squad.

Natalie counted at least fifty officers, firemen, and volunteers gathered on the waterfront, along with the dive team. False alarms cost money. "At least nobody died this time," she said, looking on the bright side.

"Silver lining," Jimmy said. "We got lucky."

She remembered teasing Jimmy mercilessly about the mustache he was attempting to grow. She remembered laughing at his knobby knees. He'd been in Grace's class, and he used to hang out with her and Daisy. He was an easygoing guy who used to butcher the lyrics of all his favorite songs. He'd attended the prayer vigil with her family. He was there during the days and weeks that followed, while Natalie and Grace dragged themselves to school in a grief-stricken stupor. He'd been part of the background her entire life, like wallpaper. Like elevator music. Bland but comforting. A nice guy with a poorly developed personality. He was oatmeal. He was vanilla.

Now Jimmy pinned her with his sincere gaze. "How're you holding up, Natalie?"

She expelled a long breath. "Okay. Thanks for asking."

"You never think it'll happen here," he said sadly. "I remember when Daisy and I had to dissect a frog for biology, and she was so squeamish about it I told her just think of it as plastic, you know? Not real. She did okay after that."

"How much money did we waste today?" Samuel said indignantly, packing up the last of his gear. "This is the second time this year, right? How are we supposed to recoup our costs?"

"The taxpayers will have to eat this one," Jimmy said with a shake of his head.

"Better misled than dead," Natalie said, and they all laughed at that.

Dark humor was a comfort in the worst of times.

25

Natalie drove to downtown Burning Lake in record time, found a parking space, killed the engine, and stepped out of her Honda Pilot. The rain had blown away, the sun was making dramatic exits and entrances behind the swiftly moving clouds, and the maples and oaks swayed in the cool breeze. The weather changed quickly in the spring. Upstate New York was bipolar.

Sweat Central was a popular health-and-fitness club. Her heels splashed in and out of puddles as she headed for the low flat building. The large open space was full of fitness enthusiasts gazing into the mirror-paneled walls, serious-looking runners and lifters in colorful spandex. The banner above the reception desk announced, GYM RATS WELCOME—EXTERMINATORS NOT ALLOWED. The glossy brochure beckoned: ARE YOU A WORKOUT-AHOLIC? JOIN THE SWEAT CENTRAL REVOLUTION!

She caught the attention of one of the staff, a ripped, tanned man in his midthirties who came over and said, "Hi, can I help you?"

"Detective Lockhart." She glanced at his name tag. "I need to ask you a few questions, Anthony."

"Sure. How can I help?" He leaned one sweaty arm on the reception counter.

"Is Brandon Buckner a member of this gym?"

He nodded. "Sure, I know Detective Buckner."

"Was he here on Wednesday evening?"

"As far as I recall. I mean, it gets pretty busy on weekday evenings. Our peak hours are between five and eight P.M., but yeah . . . he was here."

"What time did he arrive?"

"Let's see. He came in around five thirty to do some squats and lifts."

"Five thirty? Are you sure?"

"Well, I'm a trainer, and I have a lot of clients. It was pretty busy that night, like I said. But yeah, he was here . . . lifting and resting between sets. He wanted to use the squat rack, but we only have two racks, and there's always a power struggle over who gets to use them. Most of the beefs between gym bros are over the racks."

"Was there a confrontation that night?" she asked.

"Oh, no. Don't get me wrong. Brandon plays by the rules."

"Are you his trainer?"

"No, Brandon doesn't need one. We're gym buddies. Whenever I'm not working, I'll spot him on the rack or something like that."

"Did you spot him this past Wednesday?"

He shook his head. "I was jammed, like I said."

"Where's his locker?"

Anthony furrowed his brow. "Don't you need a search warrant for that?"

"Just a quick look around," Natalie suggested. "Will that be okay?"

"Sure, I guess." He shrugged. "It's this way."

They passed a fresh stack of towels, water bottles, yoga mats, and a group of intensively peddling women who were using their phone apps to monitor their heart rates on the exercycles. Anthony led Natalie toward the back of the club, where the lockers and showers for customers were located. He pointed out Brandon's locker, and she went over to inspect it. No blood smears. Nothing out of the ordinary. The door was locked.

"When you've spotted him in the past," she said, "what do you two talk about?"

He shrugged. "We don't spend a lot of time on banalities. We're here to work out. A gym is a place to get things done."

"So—no small talk between reps and sets?"

"Nothing memorable. Sports, NBA finals. Clean and jerk. Quads and traps."

"Did anything unusual occur that evening?" she asked.

"I don't think so." He frowned and combed his hand through his short-cropped, highlighted hair. "Just busy. Like I said, peak hours."

"What did Detective Buckner look like when he entered the building?"

"A little disheveled, wearing sweats. Why? What's this about?"

"Just routine. Thanks for your help," she said and left.

Natalie drove eight blocks north to the police station, where she parked around back and went inside. Right away, she noticed the low body count—half the staff was out in the field today. She poured herself a cup of coffee and took an elevator up to the third floor, where she bumped into Luke in the hallway.

"My office," he said.

She followed him down the hallway and took a seat, while he closed the door.

"Where've you been?" he asked. "It's like World War Three around here."

"Why? What's going on?"

"I spent half the morning putting out fires." He took a seat behind his desk, which was stacked with paperwork. "From now on, whatever you say about this case, the press is going to run with it, so act accordingly." He took a breath. "Where were you, Natalie?"

"Talking to Brandon."

His eyebrows lifted with surprise. "How did that happen?"

"He called this morning and asked me to meet him in Chippaway. You know the old farm he wants to buy? He told me to come alone."

"Does his attorney know about it?"

"No."

Luke nodded thoughtfully. "What did you two talk about?"

"He had a lead for me," Natalie said. "A guy named Jules Pastor."

"Yeah, I know Jules. That's Jacob's and Brandon's snitch."

"He thinks Jules might know what Riley was up to on Wednesday."

"Okay. Pursue it. What else?"

"I asked him where he was on Wednesday, and he gave some bullshit response. First he said he was at the gym between four and six o'clock. Then he changed his story and told me he went to the gym around five. But when I spoke to one of the trainers at Sweat Central, he said Brandon showed up at five thirty. Only he couldn't be sure, because it was a busy night."

"Don't they have membership verification? A mobile check-in app?"

"We'd need a warrant."

"Okay, let's initiate one." Luke leaned back. "So where was Brandon between four and five thirty?"

"He says he drove up to Chippaway to check out the farm."

Luke rubbed his lined forehead, trying to rub away all the nuisance paperwork in his mental in-box. "Did anybody see him? Did he stop for gas?"

"No. And he could've mentioned that right away, but he fudged the truth. He didn't help himself today."

"Why would he lie about it? Do you think he could've killed her?"

Natalie lightly touched her cheek. She experienced deep discomfort at the thought. On the surface at least, everything had come so easily for Brandon. Rich parents, classic American good looks, a sports car at sixteen, married to his high school sweetheart. He got into Cornell, where he'd majored in pre-law and finance and could've landed a job anywhere—the UN, Wall Street, the tech industry. His decision to become a cop had cost him dearly, creating a deep rift between him and his father, and the other recruits used to complain about Brandon's penchant for noogies and other frat boy nonsense. But he had a solid record and a good heart. "Honestly? It raises a lot of questions, but I just don't see him for the murder. And I'm being as objective as I know how."

Luke rubbed his chin distractedly. "Did you tell him about the sonnets?"

"Brandon admitted their marriage was less than perfect, but he was extremely upset at the thought of Daisy's infidelity. He seemed genuinely shocked. And if Daisy was having an affair, I doubt he knew anything about it. He also suspects Riley could've written those sonnets."

"Riley was hot for teacher? What do you think?"

"It doesn't make sense. If Riley wrote them, why would she keep them hidden in a sealed envelope? Why not show them to Seth Truitt? Why mark her calendar *T* and *I* for Tristan and Isolde?"

They sat for a moment in contemplative silence.

"Maybe Riley and Daisy were having an affair." Luke said.

"You're playing devil's advocate again."

"I'm just saying . . ." He shrugged and let the words sit there.

She rolled her eyes. "Anything's possible, but I can't imagine Daisy doing such a creepy thing. Besides, the sonnets aren't Riley's style. He's into rap and hip-hop. He would've recorded a song in her honor, not copied from Shakespeare."

"Maybe he did, and we don't know about it yet."

"I'll talk to Kermit again. See if he has any other videos."

"In the meantime," Luke said, "we need to find out who Tristan is."

"I'll ask my sister. See if she has a clue."

"Good. What about the traffic light cams?"

"I'm still waiting on DOT, but Lenny's got a stack of videos from the city cams and gas stations along the route. He's compiling a list of DMV plates and unidentifieds. Since the murder happened during rush hour, he figures we're going to end up with hundreds of vehicles, maybe as much as a thousand."

"Anything so far?"

"After reviewing the videos from three of the surveillance cameras within a two-mile radius of the Buckners' residence . . . zero sightings of Riley's vehicle, or the other two on our list. But we're still in the early stages of the process."

"How's the canvassing going? Neighbors? Witnesses?"

She shook her head. "Nothing new to report."

"Okay," he said. "Go talk to Brandon's snitch. See if he's got anything for us."

She got up to leave.

"And Natalie?"

She paused with her hands on the back of the chair. There was a long line of single ladies in Burning Lake who were anxious to try their luck with Luke. He stood tall, with broad shoulders, and had an intimidating look that rubbed some people the wrong way. He could be abrasive and a bit too honest, and he could bust your balls if he thought you deserved it. But in unguarded moments, whenever he smiled at Natalie like that, the warmth of his generous nature shone through.

"Keep up the good work," he said.

26

Although Burning Lake was not as famous as Salem, Massachusetts, it occupied a unique place in history for a brief period of madness at the beginning of the eighteenth century, when three innocent women were executed for witchcraft on Abby's Hex Peninsula, a slender piece of land jutting into the lake like an accusing finger. More than three hundred years ago, onlookers had gathered at the water's edge to celebrate their deaths, while flames flickered across the lake. Now the shops along Sarah Hutchins Drive sold casting kits and tarot cards, and the waterfront was a popular tourist destination.

Natalie parked in front of Pioneer Memorial Park and got out. Historic homes lay snug against this upscale cemetery. She felt a shiver of wind kiss her skin. TRUST JESUS read the scarred monument at the ornate cemetery gates. The park encompassed twenty acres of conflicted history and boasted such esteemed family names as Buckner, Clemmons, Grimsby, Pastor, and Deckhart. There were a couple of Lockharts buried there as well, but Natalie's loved ones resided in one of God's more modest burial grounds across town.

She waited near a towering limestone angel with chiseled wings that watched over the well-manicured grounds and adorned postcards advertising the town's historic charms. Among the gray graves, a lone trash bag fluttered in the wind. There were depressions in the cobblestones from centuries of foot traffic.

Natalie checked her watch. She was early, so she decided to call Teresa McCarthy's parents, Violet and Hamm. She'd interviewed the couple last fall, shortly after she'd been assigned the Missing Nine. Violet was quiet and small; Hamm was large and loud.

"Hello?" a timid-sounding woman answered.

"Ms. McCarthy? This is Detective Lockhart. I'm sorry to bother you like this, but I need to ask you a few questions."

"Of course. Please call me Violet."

"Thank you, Violet. Did you and your husband visit Teresa's grave recently?"

"Yes, on the fourth of April. The day she went missing."

"Around what time?"

"Ten in the morning."

"Was there anything written on the headstone?"

"What's that?"

"Any graffiti? Something in chalk?"

"No."

"Did you notice anything unusual at all that morning?"

"Just a man standing on the far hill."

Natalie gripped the phone tighter. "A man?"

"I thought it was a little strange," Violet said hesitantly. "The way he kept staring at us from afar. But grief can make you do strange things."

"That's all he did? Stare at you?"

"Yes. We both noticed. And finally, he turned and walked away."

"What did he look like?"

"I don't know," Violet said. "He was too far away."

"You can't tell me anything about his appearance? Hair color? Fat or skinny? Short? Tall?"

"He was just a silhouette on the hillside," Violet said. "The sun was behind him. He was just a shadow."

Jules Pastor came slinking out of the shade trees toward her.

"And you didn't notice anything else unusual?"

"No, I'm sorry."

"Thank you, Violet. You've been very helpful," Natalie said and hung up.

"Detective Lockhart?" Jules Pastor was a pale, thin twentysomething with a deep, gravelly voice, a leathery face, and eyes the color of dirt. "I'm Jules."

"Hello." They shook hands, and she noticed the needle tracks on his arms, along with an intricate circus of colorful tats crisscrossing his exposed skin. "Thanks for seeing me on such short notice," she told him.

"Hell, if Brandon says I should to talk to you, then I'll talk to you." He sprayed a little when he spoke.

The Pastors had deep roots in Burning Lake. Jules was distantly related to Jeremiah Pastor, the town elder who'd sentenced Abigail Stuart to death. But karma was a bitch, and life had a way of balancing things out. Jules's father once owned five hundred acres of fertile farmland, and Jules would've been a wealthy man today if his parents hadn't invested poorly and lost everything in the 2008 recession.

Now he was a confidential informant, or CI, for the Burning Lake police. The violent-crime rate had risen by five percent on the west side of town over the past couple of years. The drug problem was getting worse. It seemed almost impossible to Natalie, who'd grown up peddling her bike around town without a care in the world, but nowadays drugs and violence festered on the west side. Sometimes they bubbled over. Men like Jules helped the police prevent the worst of the worst from wreaking havoc.

"What's this all about?" Jules asked. "Want me to wear a wire?"

She shook her head. "Do you know the Skinners?"

"Yeah. Paranoid motherfuckers."

"I need to know what Riley was doing on the day Daisy Buckner was murdered. His family says he went MIA for a couple of hours that afternoon. I need to know where he was."

"Sure, I can sniff around for you," Jules said.

"What else could you tell me about Riley?"

"Okay, so . . . you're talking about a talented kid who's throwing his life away, right? He's tormented. He broods a lot. He's a brooder. It's all an act, though. That kid knows what he's doing. Stoking the flames of sympathy— like performance art."

She frowned. "You think it's an act?"

"Well, look. He's a James Dean disciple, know what I'm sayin'? Not too many people realize what a scam artist James Dean was. For instance, he was so nearsighted, he could barely see straight without his glasses. So he'd take them off and squint at people, and it drove the girls crazy. They fell in love with that James Dean squint, you know? Riley likes to twist his life all out of shape and then rap about it, yeah. He thinks it's his route to fame and fortune."

"What's his relationship with India Cochran?" she asked.

Jules shrugged. "Those two are tight as ticks. They have a weird love-hate thing."

"Really? They still hang out together?"

He scratched his head and looked around. "I wasn't sure if I should open this can of worms, but . . . I was invited to a party in the woods about a month ago, my first underage contact. They've been meeting every couple months for about a year now. Anyway, these are smart kids. They know how to cover their tracks. It's by invitation only, in alternating locations, and they only announce it at the last minute. So you won't find it on any of their social media. It's by print-out invitation only. Strictly hush-hush."

"What's that got to do with Riley?"

"Long story short?" Jules glanced around the graveyard. "Five years ago, I was attending community college, minding my own business, and I needed money for tuition and textbooks, so I decided to start dealing on a casual basis, right? I got pretty good at it, too, until one of my so-called friends ratted me out. I remember thinking, 'I am so fucked.' I couldn't believe that eighteen grams of pot was enough to put you in prison. Anyway, that's when I became Brandon's CI. So here I am."

Natalie nodded patiently.

"My last bust was three months ago, and I'm always on the prowl for my next score. So I figured the next underage party, I'm gonna bust Riley. But in light of what just happened, I'm going to have to pick another target."

"And Riley attended these parties?"

"Yeah, he's a hustler. He can flip anything. Weed, Special K, spice, booze. He'll show up like King Party."

"How many kids are we talking about?"

He scratched his head. "Not a whole lot. Twenty or so."

"And this was by print invitation only?" she clarified. "Nothing on social media?"

"Once you arrive, you toss your paper invite onto the bonfire, very *Mission: Impossible*–style. Like *Burn After Reading*. Just your typical hellacious bullshit. Kids getting fried and holding séances . . ."

A trickle of sweat curled down her neck. She took out her notepad. "Do you have any names for me?"

"Just the usual suspects." He cleared his throat. "Riley, of course. Kermit Hughes, Benjamin Lowell, Owen Kottler, Sadie Myers, Berkley Auberdine, Angela Sandhill, India Cochran . . ." His lips were stuck in a smile. "Ellie Guzman."

A syrupy wave of nausea passed through her as she struggled to maintain her composure. "My *niece* was at this party?"

"I wasn't sure I should mention it, but yeah . . . she was there." He nodded.

It took her strength away.

"Riley was selling weed. Lots of kids were buying . . . not your niece, though."

"What about India?"

He rocked his head forward. "Oh yeah, she gets all her killer bud from Riley."

"Riley's her dealer?"

"You bet."

Natalie put away her notepad. "What went on at this party?"

"Oh, you know," he said with a shrug. "Glow sticks, Molly, brews, ganja. India and her crew were holding a séance." He crossed his arms and tilted his head. "Now you know. I hope I did the right thing."

"Did you tell Brandon about this yet?" Natalie asked. "Did you talk to Jacob or anyone down at the station about my niece being involved?"

"No. I was still scoping it out. Figuring out my next move."

"Where were they being held? These parties?"

"Different places, like I said. The last one was at the Hadleys' old farm."

Another shock rippled through her—Willow had died on that property, behind the old barn. She'd bled to death in the grass.

"Just to warn you," Jules added, and she could detect a faint animal-like odor as he inched closer. "I've been busting low-level drug runners for marijuana mostly . . . small-fries. I'd never rat out a friend. I always set up nobodies, which is to say . . . I won't involve your niece in any of my busts. You have my word."

She nodded numbly.

"Brandon and Jacob told me to pick a new target, but my sources keep drying up. Word gets around. People look at you funny, so I'm constantly casting a wider net. But I swear, if a deal is about to go down . . . I'll warn your niece beforehand. I'll give her a heads-up, so she can get her under-age booty out of there."

Natalie gave a soft exhalation that wasn't quite a breath.

"In the meantime, I'll find out what Riley was up to last Wednesday."

"That'd be helpful."

"Would you do me a favor, Detective? Will you put in a good word for me down at the station? I'd appreciate it. Let the chief know I'm on top of things."

"Sure."

"Excellent. I'll get back to you." He slipped into the shadows and vanished.

27

Natalie struggled to keep her emotions in check as she navigated her way through the school corridors, while a barrage of metal lockers banged open and shut. *Pop, pop, pop.* It sounded like gunshots.

She pushed through the heavy exit doors and crossed the athletic field toward the field house, where the ball courts and pool house were located. Natalie remembered coming here with Willow to watch Grace compete for the state championship in the butterfly stroke, which Grace specialized in. There was no utilitarian purpose for the butterfly stroke—it was hard to learn and quickly exhausting—but Grace had mastered the powerful, dolphin-like movements through the water, and she was devastated when she'd earned only second place. But Willow had told her, "A winner is just a former loser who never gives up."

Outside, the midafternoon sun filtered down through the canopy of newly green leaves. Inside, the gymnasium's high-gloss hardwood floors squeaked beneath a barrage of reversals and assists from the girls' sophomore basketball team. They rammed their skinny, aggressive bodies into one another, trying to steal the ball. Two teams of feisty young athletes, darting back and forth. Jumping and scoring.

About a dozen more girls sat on the collapsible bleachers, cheering their teammates on. Now the coach blew her whistle and said, "Nice job, ladies. Next time we'll focus on jump shots. Okay, everyone to the showers."

They spilled out of the gym like a basketful of apples.

Natalie waved at Ellie, who came running over, her heart-shaped face beaded with sweat. "Aunt Natalie, what are you doing here?"

She handed Ellie the scarab bracelet. "I think this belongs to you."

"Oh my gosh!" She laughed excitedly and put it on. She admired it for a moment, and then said, "Thanks so much! Where'd you find it?"

"India had it."

The girl's mouth dropped open.

"She was conducting a séance in the woods yesterday."

Ellie squinted at her aunt as if she were trying to read between the lines. "She was?" she asked in a small voice.

"You, India, Berkley, and Sadie—is that the coven you were talking about?"

She nodded.

"Then why was Angela Sandhill there yesterday, instead of you?"

"Because," she said softly, "I quit."

"You quit the coven?" Natalie drew back. "Since when?"

Ellie glanced across the echoey gymnasium toward the locker room door. They could hear distant, mocking laughter. Teenage girls never changed, Natalie thought. Only the target of their revolving-door cruelty did.

"Why did you quit the coven, Ellie?"

Her face fell. She seemed to recognize the depth of Natalie's concern and hardened herself against it. "I really don't want to be late for my next class."

"Ellie, I'm trying to figure out what's going on. Can you help me out here?"

She bowed her head. "I can't," she mumbled.

Ellie used to love watching *Gilmore Girls, Friends, I Love Lucy* reruns, Nick at Nite. She used to daydream about owning a pony. She'd loved each and every one of her stuffed animals. None of that was true anymore.

"I'm not judging you, okay?" Natalie assured her. "I'm sure your mother has told you about some of the crazy stunts she pulled off in her youth. We've all done it."

Ellie took a deep breath and said, "I quit right after I heard about Ms. Buckner."

"Why didn't you tell me?"

"I don't know." The girl's shoulders slumped. She looked around for an exit. "I seriously can't be late for my next class, Aunt Natalie."

Looking down at that perky face, she suddenly pictured her niece lying dead, and it sent shivers racing across her flesh. Silence enveloped them. The evasions were piling up. Natalie felt a nauseating sense of disorientation, as if the room were shaking furiously. "Tell me about these underage parties you've been going to," she said.

"You mean, the party last month?" Ellie winkled her nose. "Because I only went to one."

"Does your mother know you were at an underage party?"

Her eyes widened with alarm. "Please don't tell her, Aunt Natalie."

"Then explain it to me. What's going on?"

"All my friends were going," she said. "So I wanted to go, too. But I didn't do drugs or get drunk or anything like that, I swear. I just wanted to hang out with them."

Natalie couldn't help herself. The incipient lecture leaked out. "Right, you've never gotten stoned with your friends or tried alcohol or anything like that."

"I'm not stupid," Ellie whispered fiercely. "I'll take a sip of beer once in a while to fool people, so they won't think I'm a narc or a total loser. But I'm not dumb. Some of my friends will get stoned and post it on Instagram, and it's totally humiliating. I don't want to end up like them. I'll pour a little beer in a cup and carry it around with me. But then, at the end of the night, I'll dump the rest out."

"Why even pretend? What happens if one of your friends takes a video of you pretending to be drunk and posts it online?"

"They wouldn't do that," she said stubbornly.

"Why not?"

"Because they're my friends."

"Right." Natalie shook her head, recalling her own self-indulgences in high school. Getting stoned, getting wasted—Friday nights you didn't want to be alone. Boys came and went. Nameless crushes. She experimented with drugs in order to find herself, but instead got lost inside her woolly mind. She snuck drinks with her friends in order to numb the pain but ended up racked with grief.

Across the gymnasium, the locker room door opened and girls' raucous laughter rang across the basketball court. Natalie saw India and Berkley watching them from behind the cracked-open door before it slammed shut again.

"I didn't realize India and Berkley were like this," Natalie said. "You can't be involved in these parties anymore. I'm worried about you. You have to tell your mom—"

"No, please!" Tears sprang to Ellie's eyes.

"You're only fifteen," Natalie said. "You have your whole life ahead of you."

"I should've known you wouldn't get it," she said fretfully.

"Oh, believe me. I've been there. Look, I understand you're under a lot of pressure. Too much pressure, maybe. SATs, ACTs, thinking about college, I get that. It's tempting to do something crazy, something that doesn't have the approval of the entire adult world. But you're going to have to tell Grace about this."

"I can't," she whimpered.

"Why not? She needs to know."

The bell rang.

"Great, now I'm really late," Ellie fumed.

"Tell your mother tonight. Otherwise, I'm going to have to do it."

"No, please . . . I'll tell her, Aunt Natalie. I promise," Ellie pleaded. "Tonight. But I have to go. Seriously. I'm late for next period. . . ."

Natalie nodded.

"Thanks," she said, looking vastly relieved that the conversation was over and hurrying away.

28

Natalie found Grace's biology class on the third floor. Grace was grading papers at her desk. Beams of sunlight wove through the dusty, old-fashioned windowpanes. Natalie knocked, and Grace looked up and smiled.

"Come on in, Nat."

"How are you feeling?"

She put down her pen. "Like a safe just dropped on my head."

"Been a lousy couple of days," Natalie sympathized.

Grace leaned back and folded her arms. "I thought coming to work might take my mind off things, but my students have been so sweet and considerate, it breaks my heart all over again."

Natalie nodded solicitously, then glanced at the diagrams hanging on the wall, full-scale renderings of the Invisible Man and Invisible Woman, their anatomy exposed. Natalie wasn't the only sibling who'd been affected by their father's profession. When your father was a cop, you learned not to fear the human body. He used to leave crime-scene photos lying around, and Natalie and Grace would sneak a peek, fascinated at an early age. As a family, they used to watch *Law & Order, NYPD Blue,* and *Hill Street*

Blues together, and afterward Joey would interrogate the girls about the shows' procedural accuracy. He wanted to make sure they understood which stories were factual and which ones were false.

"Have a seat," Grace said. "You look like the cat that ate the canary, Natalie. What's up?"

"Did you know that Daisy was having an affair?"

Grace brushed it aside. "That's complete BS."

"But there are rumors . . ."

"Oh God." She rubbed her forehead with her fingers. "There's a group of teachers here at the school who're a bunch of gossiping magpies. Whatever happened to girl power? Anyway, Daisy and I just ignored them."

"But not everything was perfect between Brandon and Daisy, right?"

"Who has the perfect relationship, Natalie? Tell me. I really want to know."

"So there was trouble in paradise?"

Grace wiped the weariness from her eyes. "Daisy told me they'd been arguing about the farm in Chippaway . . . Brandon wanted to move up there, but it's so isolated and desolate. Daisy didn't want to have to commute to work. Plus, he wants more kids, but she'd just reached her first trimester. She wasn't ready to think about it yet. So yes, there was some tension between them. But isn't that perfectly normal?"

Natalie folded her hands together. "I found a few love sonnets in Daisy's possession. They're all handwritten and signed 'Tristan.' Any guesses as to who that might be?"

"Love sonnets?" Grace repeated skeptically. "Well, I don't know. She was popular with the students, and some of the boys had crushes on her. Girls, too. And Shakespearean sonnets are de riguer for the upper grades. We like to emphasize the classics."

"What about Riley? Could he have written them?"

"I don't think so." Her teeth dug into her lower lip. "Well, it's possible, I suppose. Daisy was trying to submit some of his rap songs in place of the required essays. She talked to Seth about it. It makes sense, since scholars have compared the Bard's work to hip-hop—you know, rhyme schemes, alliteration, meter, form, iambic pentameter."

"What happened? Was she able to substitute the rap songs?"

"No. Seth's hands were tied. The tests are pretty standardized now."

Two female students knocked on Grace's door.

"Sorry. My study group."

"One more thing, Grace. What were the magpies saying about Daisy?"

"The rumors?" She brushed it away. "You hear things in the faculty lounge. Marriages get rocky sometimes. I hate gossip. I won't participate in spreading lies."

"So you figured they weren't even remotely true?"

"Oh please. Teachers are worse than the students. You have to ignore it." Grace held up a hand, signaling to her students to wait a minute. "Anyway, she was my best friend in the world. I would've known if she was cheating on her man, right?"

"These rumors about Daisy. Give me a name."

A soft silence pressed between them.

"Grace, this is important. I'm not interested in spreading gossip. But if she was having an affair with somebody here at the school, then I need to find out."

"Ethan Hathaway."

"The English lit teacher?"

She nodded. "Isn't that ridiculous? For a handsome guy, he's such a stuffed shirt. I feel guilty for even bringing it up. It's complete nonsense. But . . ."

"But what?" Natalie pressed.

"I don't know," Grace said uneasily. "I'm only thinking about this in retrospect. Because after the rumors started, they always made a point of completely ignoring each other. . . . For instance, if one of them entered the faculty lounge, the other would leave immediately . . . and that was like . . . methinks thou doth protest too much. It only fueled the rumor mill."

Another knock at the door. Half a dozen students were peering through the glass.

"Sorry, I can't keep them waiting any longer."

"Thanks, Grace. This helps."

"I really hope it isn't true, for Brandon's sake," she said.

The door swung open, and the bright-eyed students swept into the room, brushing past Natalie on their way to their seats, bringing in the wisteria-soaked smell of spring.

29

Fifty minutes later, Hathaway's English class was over. The bell rang, the door flew open, and a flurry of shoes landed on the sparkling waxed floor. Natalie waited until the classroom was empty before she ventured inside. Ethan Hathaway looked as if he hadn't slept in weeks—dark circles, pasty complexion, veiny eyes.

"I'm here to talk about Daisy," she told him.

"Of course. Whatever I can do to help." He began to erase the blackboard.

Natalie closed the door behind her. "Have a seat."

He put down the eraser and clapped the chalk off his hands. "The whole town's in shock," he said. "She was a special person . . . kind, generous, talented. An inspiration to these kids."

Natalie showed him photocopies of the love sonnets. "We found these at Daisy's house. Do you happen to know anything about them?"

He stared down at the pages while sunlight filtered in through the blinds. He sat heavily behind his desk and dropped his head in his hands. "Oh God."

"Ethan . . . may I call you Ethan?"

He nodded, looking up.

"Did you write these love sonnets to Daisy? Are you Tristan?"

"Yes," he admitted.

That was easy. Natalie felt a rubbing numbness travel through her nerve endings. It was one thing to speculate about love triangles, but quite another to validate the truth. If Daisy had been lying about her marriage, what else was she lying about?

"I appreciate your honesty," Natalie told him. "So what happened?"

He held the pages in his caffeine-shaky hands. "She was a force of nature. I fell in love with her. I couldn't help myself."

"Did Brandon know you were writing love letters to his wife?"

"No."

Natalie handed him the paperback, *Tristan and Isolde.* "How did she get this?"

Ethan put down the photocopies and cradled the book in his hands. "I gave it to her," he admitted.

"So, in your eyes, you saw yourself as Tristan, and Daisy was Isolde."

"That's right." He took a shaky breath. "It happened so gradually, we hardly noticed. It started in the faculty lounge. We're both avid readers, and we were just chatting about books. I loaned her *Cathedral* by Raymond Carver. I wasn't sure she'd like it, but she did." He rubbed his face hard. "The next thing you know, we were meeting for coffee after hours, sort of an informal book club. We used to joke about it. The binary book club. Then one thing led to another."

"Led to what?" Natalie asked.

"This unspoken whatever-the-hell-it-was. Whatever-the-heaven." He smiled, then winced. "God, that was corny. But Daisy didn't mind my sentimental side. She thought it was cute."

"When did you both realize you were in love?"

"At a student dance. Brandon was working late. We were chaperones."

"And after that, it was no longer platonic?"

Tears brimmed in his eyes, and he brushed them away. "We were careful to keep it hidden from everyone else. Not even Grace knew about us. It was a dilemma, because we never intended to hurt anyone. Daisy struggled with it. She wanted to do the right thing. We tried ending the relationship a few months ago, but . . . we couldn't help ourselves."

"And Brandon knew nothing about it? You're positive?"

Drained of all feeling, his voice had become mechanical. "Like I said, we were discreet. We ignored each other at school functions. No phone calls, no emails—except for Daisy's hidden account."

"What hidden account?"

He looked up and flinched. "Tristan dash Isolde seven nine two at-Yandex dot com. Password blackink."

Natalie jotted it down in her notepad. "Blackink?"

"A line from Shakespeare. 'That in black ink my love may still shine bright.'"

Natalie couldn't help feeling sorry for him. By every measure, it looked like he was telling the truth. But looks could be deceptive. "Where were you this past Wednesday between four and six P.M.?" she asked.

He stiffened. "Why do you need to know that?"

"If you two were having an affair, then you automatically become a person of interest. We need to verify your alibi before we can cross your name off the list."

"God, I didn't kill her," he said with alarm. "I loved her. Living through this . . . it's like a bad dream you can never wake up from." His eyes grew dull with pain. "It's terrible. Just terrible."

She nodded sympathetically. During an interview, sometimes it was best to kick back and relax. Breathe. If you kept yourself perfectly still, the subject of the interrogation might keep talking, just to break the silence.

"What was your question?" he asked. "Where was I on Wednesday between four and six? Well, let's see. There was an after-hours meeting for the student newspaper. I stayed until four fifteen, and then I went home."

She jotted it down. "Do you live alone?"

"Yes."

"Did you make any phone calls? Emails? Order a pizza?"

"No, I make my own meals," Ethan explained. "I'm a pretty good cook. I spent the evening correcting papers. But listen, we'd split up by then."

She paused with her pen hovering over her pad. Finally, an explanation for the books Daisy had ordered online. *The Breakup Bible* and *Getting Past Your Breakup.*

"Daisy ended it about a month ago." He exhaled. "Less than a month ago. After she knew for certain she was pregnant. She decided to recommit to her marriage."

"So she broke it off with you . . . just like that?"

"Yes."

"How did that make you feel?" Natalie asked.

"Awful. But I accepted it."

"You did?"

He nodded. He was sweaty and pale. He didn't look so accepting. He wiped his mouth and licked his dry lips.

"Did you and Daisy keep in touch after she broke up with you?"

"I emailed her a few times." He folded his trembling hands on his desk.

"And how did she respond?"

"She never answered back. She avoided me at work. When she finally closed her Yandex mail account, that's when I knew it was truly over."

"And you were okay with that?"

"No," he quietly admitted. "I felt deeply saddened by it."

"Saddened or betrayed?"

He gave her a pained look. His body made no movement.

"How did you cope?" Natalie went on. "After the breakup? Long jogs in the morning? Booze? One-night stands? Weight lifting? More books?"

"Well, look," he said, angry now. "This was exactly *not* what I wanted to happen. Emotionally I was torn apart. But I'm not into self-pity."

"So you pulled yourself up by the bootstraps?"

"Why do I detect sarcasm, Detective Lockhart?" he asked her sharply.

"I'm simply trying to figure out how you coped with such a loss."

"Good grief. How did you cope with your own breakup?"

Something stirred inside Natalie—a fresh awareness that Grace and perhaps even Daisy had spoken to other people about her relationship with Zack. But this was Burning Lake, and people talked. She decided to try a different tack. "Ethan, let me ask you, did you ever witness any of Riley's threatening behavior toward Daisy?"

He took a steadying breath. "No, but we discussed it. I was concerned for her safety. Adolescent boys can be pretty aggressive. I told her to report him, but she insisted she could handle it. Nobody was expecting this. Least of all me. It's horrible what happened," he said. "Makes me physically ill."

She paused—there was no delicate way to put this. "When you found out about the baby . . . did you think it might be yours?"

The anguish showed on his face. "I knew it was a possibility."

"So Daisy didn't know who the father was?"

"No."

"Just to clarify—she had sex with you and with Brandon around the same time?"

"I don't know. I didn't ask." He wiped his sweaty upper lip. "But around the time when she might've gotten pregnant . . . three months ago . . . Daisy and I had a falling-out. She was torn with guilt. She didn't want to destroy her marriage. We . . . For lack of a better term, we split up. She never told Brandon about me. She just wanted things to go back to the way they were before. This was three months ago, for a few weeks, but . . . it didn't stick."

"So—around three months ago—she recommitted to her marriage? Meaning she broke up with you, and presumably slept with Brandon . . . only Brandon didn't know about the affair or any of this?"

"I believe so."

"Do you think she was sleeping with Brandon the whole time? Regardless of whether you'd 'split up' or not?"

He shrugged and said coldly, "I have no idea."

"You two never discussed it?"

"No."

"She couldn't make up her mind? Between the two of you?"

"Not until last month—when we split for good." His jaw muscles clenched. "She said it was final."

"Did you try talking her out of it?"

"We had a few heated discussions."

"How heated?"

"Arguments. I was upset. I was in love with her."

"Did you drive over to her house on Wednesday afternoon?"

"No," he said, eyes widening. "I told you. I was at home grading papers."

"And it didn't bother you that she could've been carrying your baby?"

"Of course, it bothered me."

"Did you ask for a paternity test?" Natalie asked.

"No."

"Why not?"

Ethan shrugged. "Because it's her body."

"But it could've been your baby. Didn't that kill you—not knowing?"

His face grew red. "She wanted to believe it was hers and Brandon's."

"And you accepted that?"

He balled his left hand into a fist and looked away.

"Ethan, I'm sorry to ask such blunt questions. But it's vital to the investigation."

He gave her a defeated look. "Ultimately, it was her decision."

Natalie frowned. "Is there anything else you can tell me about Daisy? Were there any other problems at school? Any other issues with her marriage?"

"Only . . ." He hesitated. "I noticed an abrupt change when Brandon hired Lindsey Wozniak to do their landscaping. Daisy became depressed and circumspect. It was odd, seeing this change in her. I couldn't figure it out at first. But then . . ." He shifted uncomfortably in his chair, eyes darting.

"What?" she asked.

"Did you know Brandon and Lindsey hooked up in high school? Daisy told me about it once. Apparently the two of them had a fling years ago, and now here was Lindsey, working with Brandon on an extensive landscaping project. It upset Daisy quite a bit."

"Why would Brandon do that? Hire Lindsey, if it upset Daisy?"

"I've asked myself the same question." Ethan fingered one of the folders on his desk. "To be fair, Lindsey is the top-rated landscape designer in town. And this happened more than two decades ago. But Daisy told me the whole story once. . . . Were you aware that Brandon impregnated Daisy in high school? She decided to get an abortion without consulting Brandon.

She only informed him about it after the fact, when it was too late. She said she'd never seen him so angry."

"How angry?"

"Emotional abuse, she called it."

"Did he hurt her physically?"

"No, but he came close." He ran his finger along his lower lip. "In retaliation, Brandon slept with Lindsey. God, it sounds like a soap opera, when you say it out loud. Anyway, Daisy took it hard. That's when she attempted suicide."

"Right, I noticed the scars on her wrist."

Ethan sighed. "Anyway, Brandon ended his affair with Lindsey, they all went away to college in the fall and, then, a few years later . . . Brandon and Daisy got married."

"Given this history, why do you think Brandon hired Lindsey?"

"I don't know. I thought it was pretty manipulative and controlling of him."

Natalie wondered if Brandon was punishing Daisy for not wanting to move to the farm in Chippaway. Or perhaps there was some other reason. "Did you know about the farm in Chippaway?"

Ethan shook his head. "What farm?"

"Brandon wanted to move his family to Chippaway."

"No, she never mentioned it."

"Did Daisy ever complain about Brandon being abusive?"

"Physically, no. He had two switches, according to Daisy—happy and not happy," Ethan explained. "When Brandon was happy, everything was fine. But when he was unhappy, he drank. He became a loudmouth jerk who passed out on the sofa. That's what she told me."

"How did that make you feel?"

"I'll always wonder why she picked him over me."

There was an impatient knock on the glass-paneled door. A handful of students.

"My next class," he apologized.

"I'd like you to come down to the station for an official interview and a polygraph, if that's okay," Natalie said. "Since you don't have an alibi, this is the only way we'll be able to clear you."

He swallowed like a drowning man. "Sure, but I can't this afternoon. I've got commitments for the rest of the day. We're rehearsing the school play and . . ."

"How about five o'clock? Are you free then?"

He nodded. "For an hour."

"Good. Just the interview then," Natalie said. "We'll schedule the polygraph for some other time." She stood up. "See you at five."

30

Natalie took a right onto Harvest Lane where Lindsey Wozniak lived, pulled into the long driveway, parked behind Lindsey's BMW hybrid, and cut the engine. The sign out front read WOZNIAK LANDSCAPE AND INTERIORSCAPE DESIGN—WE WORK WONDERS. The residence had major curb appeal—ornamental pots, a marble fountain, fruit trees around the perimeter. The elegant Victorian was built in the late 1800s with a spacious front porch and a turret. Lindsey was constantly changing the look of the place. Last year, she'd painted the exterior smoke gray with winter-flannel trim. This year, it was pewter with bone-china trim.

Lindsey answered the door looking elegantly professional in a suede pantsuit, a tailored white blouse, and Italian flats. Her sharp features contributed to her predatory corporate look. "Natalie," she said with a bright smile. "Long time, no see."

"Hello, Lindsey."

"What do you think of the new color?"

"It's very pretty."

"I was aiming for a mountains-in-the-mist type of thing. C'mon inside."

Like her closest childhood friends—Daisy, Grace, and Bunny—Lindsey

Wozniak was thirty-six years old. The four of them used to watch *The Parent Trap* and *Freaky Friday* together. They used to party together. They'd once formed a coven together—Lindsey had been the leader. Now Lindsey was a successful landscape designer and flower stylist who did weddings, parties, and formal occasions. She maintained half the gardens on the north side and gave flower-arranging workshops at the community college. Lindsey was a big deal in this town.

"Thanks for seeing me on such short notice."

"Sure, Natalie. Anything to help. I'm heartsick over this. The whole town's reeling. Grace and I talked for two hours last night. Come into my office."

The house was full of stunning period detail—original hardwood floors, stained-glass windows, pocket doors, and a domed skylight. The home office was a welcoming space full of period armchairs, floor-to-ceiling drapes, and all the trappings of a small business—steel file cabinets, top-of-the-line equipment, excellent lighting.

Natalie paused to admire the glossy promotional photos on the walls—airbrushed images of elaborately manicured courtyards and gardens full of expensive stone statuary, interspersed with professionally framed garden design awards and certifications.

"Impressive," she said.

"I'm lucky to have such a strong client base. Espresso?"

"No, thanks."

"Have a seat," Lindsey said, reaching for her iPhone.

"Brandon mentioned that he hired you to do some landscaping?" Natalie began.

"That's right. Initially, he wasn't sure what he wanted. We went over his options, and I got him to focus on his main concern, which was the holiday season. So I told him about winter landscaping, and he dug it. He got involved with the design and execution."

"Is that typical? For homeowners to get involved in the landscaping design?"

"Depends. Some do. Some don't. I'm flexible. That's one reason why I'm doing so well." She smiled.

"When did you start working for the Buckners?"

"About two months ago."

"And when was the last time you were over there?"

"On Monday. With my maintenance crew."

"Since you've been working for them, have you noticed anything unusual?"

"Unusual how?" Lindsey asked. "What do you mean?"

"Let me put it this way. Is there anything you can tell me about Brandon and Daisy's relationship, since you've been spending so much time over there? Were they happy? Unhappy? Any disagreements? Fights?"

"Well, there was tension, for sure."

"What kind of tension?"

"Little things," Lindsey said. "Normal couple things, I suppose."

"Like what?"

"Well, I was the first to suspect that Daisy was pregnant. I asked her about it, point-blank. She pleaded with me not to tell a soul, so of course I kept my mouth shut."

"Anything else?"

"Yeah, about a month ago, I walked into the living room while she was on the phone, and she freaked out a little. You know how sensitive her skin is, right? Redheads. She turned crimson and hung up immediately, then mumbled something about school. Anyway, it didn't sound job-related to me. It sounded pretty friendly. So I wondered—why the secrecy? What's the big deal? I don't know." Lindsey waved it away.

"Any guesses as to who it could've been?" she asked Lindsey.

"Not even. But she was acting so flustered and distracted—something was up."

"Do you remember Daisy's suicide attempt?" Natalie asked.

"Wow, yes," she said, taken aback. "That was a long time ago, Natalie. It's kind of embarrassing, isn't it? You grow up in a small town, and people will inevitably throw your past in your face. Look, it wasn't serious. She scratched herself with a knife. Created a little drama."

"I remember how upset she was," Natalie said carefully. "But I don't recall any other details. There are conflicting accounts about what happened. For instance, somebody told me that you and Brandon had a fling back then—this must've been your senior year in high school—and that's why Daisy attempted suicide, even though the cuts were superficial."

Lindsey sighed hard, suddenly looking thin and drawn. "Oh God, Natalie. It's all water under the bridge."

"I also heard she became distraught when Brandon hired you."

"Seriously?" She shifted in her seat and crossed her legs. "I doubt that's true. We came to terms with it a long time ago." She heaved an impatient sigh. "Affairs are messy."

"But you and Daisy were so close back in high school. What happened? How could you betray her like that?"

"Betray her?" Lindsey rolled her eyes. "Are you judging me now? Do you want to see a grown woman break down and sob buckets over her dead friend?"

A heavy discomfort settled between them.

"I'm sorry. Let me rephrase that," Natalie said. "Tell me what happened between you and Brandon during your senior year of high school. How did it transpire?"

"We had a fling, okay?" Lindsey said flippantly. "It was dumb. But once Daisy found out about it, that put the kibosh on everything, because Brandon went crawling back to her. And that was fine with me."

"You aren't still attracted to him?"

"Brandon? Are you kidding me? He's a goofball. No. We're friends. He can be funny as hell, though. He makes me laugh. Bottom line, he pays his bills on time. That's all that matters to me."

"So you and Daisy . . ."

"Daisy and I were good friends in high school, but after the whole Brandon drama, we sort of drifted apart. We became . . . less-intense friends. Look, she was a sweet kid who could be a real drama queen, overreacting and getting intensely emotional about everything. But in this town, you have to let it go. Eventually we put it behind us. I mean, look, the three of us still got together for drinks occasionally—Grace, Daisy, and me. The Witches of Eastwick, we called ourselves. We laugh about it now. Maybe cast a few spells, for yucks. White magic only." Lindsey exhaled. "You want the truth? There was a point when I was jealous of Daisy way back when. I'm not afraid to admit that. She had such gorgeous green eyes and gawd . . . such perfect teeth. Me? I had an overbite and no-color hair, and my eyes have always been too close together." Her phone buzzed. "Sorry." Lindsey paused to check the message. "God, this is my worst habit. I have to check, like, a million times a day." She quickly texted back. Her phone buzzed again. "Sorry, it's like a tic."

"Lindsey, please . . . put that thing away and talk to me."

She set the phone aside. "Apologies. Go on."

"When was the last time you spoke to either one of them? Brandon or Daisy?"

"Monday, like I said."

"No phone calls since?"

"I don't think so. I'd have to check my logs."

"Where were you on Wednesday?"

"Working. I'm always working, Natalie. Constantly on the go. My day starts at five and doesn't let up until midnight. No weekends off. Everything blurs together after a while," she said with a strained smile. "But it's all good. Business is booming. I have deadlines up the wazoo. Consulting with clients, maintenance, talking to suppliers, marketing, the list goes on. I pride myself on my attention to detail, but it keeps me running around like a crazy person, twenty-four/seven."

"You sound busy."

"Ha. Busy ain't the word. By the way, I'm also in charge of the flower arrangements for Daisy's funeral. I want everything to look stunning." She brushed a sheen of sweat off her brow. "Anyway, you asked if I'd seen anything unusual lately at Brandon's house? I just remembered something. Last week, my work crew was digging up the backyard, and they found an old poppet doll buried in one of the flower beds. I didn't think anything of it at the time. You know, things like that are a dime a dozen in this town. I told the guys to toss it out, but it still might be in one of the leaf container bags."

Natalie furrowed her brow. Poppet dolls were used for magic, supposedly for healing and love, but they could also be used for darker purposes. Revenge curses, bad luck, ill health, even death spells.

Lindsey's phone buzzed. "Sorry, I have to take this." She stood up. "Do you mind, Natalie? I hate to cut it short, but . . ."

"Sure. Thanks for your time."

Lindsey escorted her to the door. She had a warm handshake. "You should try one of my flower-arranging workshops, Natalie. You know what's exciting? When you push yourself out of your comfort zone."

"Yeah, right." Natalie rolled her eyes. "If I had any extra time, Lindsey, I wouldn't spend it rearranging flowers in a vase."

Lindsey laughed. "Same old Natalie."

They paused on the threshold.

"You never answered my question, though. Where were you last Wednesday?"

"The Applewhites, I think," Lindsey responded. "I'll check my datebook and get back to you." She gently shut the door in Natalie's face.

31

Natalie parked in the Buckners' driveway and got out of the car. The fluffy clouds had blown away, and the air was crystal clear. A few of last autumn's brittle leaves blew across the asphalt, making a dry ticking sound.

She took out the house keys and entered through the Buckners' garage. Brandon's top-of-the-line gardening tools were stored in here, along with the lawn mower, a custom-made Zektor men's bike, and various lawn care products—bags of fertilizer and bottles of herbicides. Natalie couldn't find any leaf container bags inside the garage, so she locked up and went around back, where a dozen newly tagged bushes lined the cedar fence. Beyond the tall fence were the conservancy lands—white spruce, red pine, bear oak, balsam fir. The distracting smell of pine sap blew across the landscape.

Spring was a time for weeding and fertilizing. The flower beds had been recently mulched, and the grass was several inches high. Seedlings had started pushing up through the ground, straining to catch the sun. The wheelbarrow held a precarious pile of polished river stones. Natalie found the leaf collection bags leaning against the back of the house. Four heavy-duty natural-fiber bags with Lindsey's company logo printed on the front—a green and white design with the annoying tagline, WE WORK WONDERS!

Natalie unsealed the first bag and rolled down the top. Using her phone's flashlight, she peered inside at a messy collection of pinecones, twigs, nettles, leaves, and weeds. She worked her hands through the lawn debris and poked her flashlight beam down into crevices, but couldn't find any poppet dolls. Bag two—same thing. Bag three—she spotted something farther down, scooped out a few handfuls of grass and lawn debris, pushed aside more foliage—and there it was.

She scratched her finger on something sharp, then reached down and took out the dirt-stained doll. Most people had never heard of poppet dolls, but everybody knew about voodoo dolls—those creepy little forces for evil. Unlike their voodoo counterparts, poppets could be used for harm or for good.

Many years ago, Natalie and her friends had made a poppet doll. It was easy. First, you drew two identical "gingerbread man" outlines on a piece of fabric, then you stitched them together around the edges, leaving a small enough opening to stuff the doll with cotton. Then you tucked a few "magical" items inside, such as herbs, crystals, talismanic objects, and a personal item or two you'd swiped from your intended target. Finally, you sewed up the opening, added buttons for the eyes, yarn for the hair, and anything else that created a magical link to your victim.

According to local Wiccan lore, poppets were meant for "sympathetic" magic only. Love spells, friendship spells, healing spells, good luck spells—all were encouraged. Anything negative was discouraged. Because whatever you did to the poppet doll allegedly affected the person it was meant to represent.

The soggy poppet in Natalie's hands was made of a dirt-stained pink felt material, with two green buttons for the eyes and short red yarn for the hair. It was about a foot tall, stitched together with black thread. Red stitches formed a ghoulish mouth. It was unmistakably meant to represent Daisy Buckner.

Even more troublesome, the doll was bent backward and bound with a heavy piece of black cord, then stuck with straight pins—one of which had pricked Natalie's finger. Natalie examined the pins. Witches stuck straight pins into poppet dolls in order to cause pain. This was a negative curse, for sure. And the target was Daisy.

This doll had been underground for an unknown period of time and was coming apart at the seams. Some of the cotton balls were popping out. They smelled of herbs and earth. She carefully ripped one of the seams loose and found unidentified herbs among the cotton balls, along with two personal items—a red Bic ballpoint pen like the kind she'd seen on Daisy's desk, and a torn piece of paper, folded in half. Natalie opened the two-inch square, just the corner of a page. Written in red ink on lined white paper, it read: *Good job, B-*. There was nothing else written on the torn piece of paper. Also tucked inside the doll was a twelve-inch-long length of heavy red twine, knotted nine times.

32

Natalie waited in her car with the engine running. As soon as the bell rang, the school's exit doors flew open and hundreds of students came streaming out, chatting excitedly now that their boring-ass day was over.

She spotted Ellie heading across the lot with India, Berkley, and Sadie. Angela wasn't with them. The four girls looked as if they'd waltzed straight out of the *Teen Rebel Handbook*—black T-shirts, black skirts, black jackets, black leggings, black shoes. They reminded Natalie of any other group of teenage girls, though, tilting their heads together and whispering conspiratorially among themselves.

Now Grace's Mini Cooper pulled up to the curb and Ellie bid farewell to her friends and hurried off. Natalie watched her get in the car and ride away.

Meanwhile, India and her crew continued on their way past the school buses and across the parking lot. They moved like ballerinas, their heads positioned elegantly over the midline of their bodies. They paused to chat with a boy in a fleece hoodie. He had an appealing smile. The girls crowded around him, laughing and talking.

Natalie rolled down her window to catch the conversation.

"Don't look at me, Caleb," India said. "Quit staring."

"I wasn't looking at you," the boy objected, his voice cracking.

"Holy shit, dude, you're making me uncomfortable."

"But I wasn't—"

"Seriously, dude. If you don't stop staring, I'm going to report you."

Caleb's face collapsed. He gave up, turned, and hurried away.

"Snowflake!" India called after him, and she and her friends burst out laughing. They continued on their way across the lot, until they came to India's silver Lexus. The girls piled in and drove off.

Natalie snapped on her directionals and followed the Lexus through downtown Burning Lake, past boutiques, barbershops, bistros, and bed-and-breakfasts. She kept a safe distance between herself and the car as it detoured onto Lakeview Drive, where birch trees loomed across the road like Roman centurions. It was a nasty, bumpy ride. The asphalt was all chewed up here. Last summer had been especially loud and splashy, with too many tourists and lots of bumper-to-bumper traffic. Now that it was spring, the work crews would be filling in the potholes and causing rush-hour bottlenecks.

Ten minutes later, they drove past the lakefront with its four-star restaurants and boat-rental businesses. A broad swath of marsh grass gave way to a sandy beach dotted with lifeguard towers. In early June, white sand was trucked in by the ton. Orange buoys delineated the swim area. Today the water was calm, but that could be deceptive.

Natalie followed India's Lexus toward Abby's Hex Peninsula on the south side of the lake. The vehicle took a right down a deserted two-lane road and drove for another three hundred yards or so before pulling into a gravel parking area. The girls spilled out of the car and headed for the trailhead, while Natalie hung back and watched them slip like sprites into the woods.

Once the girls were out of sight, she swung into the parking area, fetched two evidence bags from the trunk, and took the trailhead onto the wooded peninsula. The trail was long and winding. A bed of shiny dark needles and fall leaves muted her footsteps. The peninsula was two hundred and fifty yards long, and the hiking trails looped around the perimeter. It was a beautiful April afternoon. Birds swooped down from the treetops to scoop up the seeds on the forest floor.

Natalie had lost sight of the girls through the trees but could hear them faintly up ahead, their reedy laughter light and frothy. She followed their musical voices along the winding aromatic path through a dense growth of coniferous and deciduous trees, until she came to a fork in the trail. She paused to listen, then took a left. After another fifty yards or so, the thinning woods gave way to a clearing at the tip of the peninsula, where gentle blue waves lapped against the rocky shore. Several rustic benches were provided for park visitors, offering an unobstructed view of the lake. The three girls sat huddled together on one bench, speaking in hushed tones— confident India, multiply-pierced Sadie, and snooty Berkley.

Natalie held back for a moment, catching a few random phrases. *She said. That's like. Beyond bad.* The rest of their conversation blew away in the breeze.

This was one of the most popular places where tourists congregated in the fall to photograph the changing foliage and catch the annual Halloween festivities. A large, mounted bronze plaque commemorated the execution area—an engraving of three terrorized young women in shackles being led to their fate. The spot where they'd died was marked by a historically inaccurate depiction of three large wooden stakes, erected inside a replica of the original fire pit, which was ringed with blackened stones. The witches had originally been hanged, but it was an annual tradition in Burning Lake to build a bonfire on Halloween night in honor of the victims' memories. Revelers gathered to watch the flames billow and dance across the lake. Some of the townsfolk wanted to put an end to the tradition, which they called barbaric, but they were overruled by the town council every year.

The day before Halloween, three large stakes were pounded into the ground inside the functioning fire pit; then a pyre of wood was stacked around it; finally, three shabby mannequins representing the accused were placed on stakes. The "witches" wore cotton dresses, aprons, and old straw hats.

According to legend, the children of the village were put in charge of building the pyre, while the accused were manacled and trussed to the stakes. The colonists waited until nightfall, when the flames could be seen from far away, reflecting hellishly off the surface of the water.

Sarah Hutchins was twenty-eight years old when she died. Abigail Stuart was thirty-four. Victoriana Forsyth was seventeen. According to those who believed they were burned, you could hear their screams for miles around, and they died of shock and smoke inhalation before the flames finally engulfed them. It was certain they died agonizing deaths, as fiery cinders rose in the air and singed their lungs. The executions had taken place at the peak of autumn, when the woods were ablaze and the landscape turned into a conflagration of orange, crimson, and gold leaves.

Nowadays, on Halloween, hundreds of locals and tourists alike gathered on the peninsula to build a traditional bonfire and hold competitions—the most authentic-looking mannequins won. Some of the revelers would toss pointy paper witch's hats onto the blazing pyre. When Natalie was a child, she thought it was scary fun. But the weathered mannequins looked so sad, with their wigs askew beneath their cheap straw hats and their plain cotton frocks blowing in the breeze, revealing their plastic legs. They were bound with rope to the wooden stakes, and their manufactured smiles betrayed the genuine terror the real victims must've felt.

Now Natalie took a deep breath and approached the girls, who were talking with a rapid-fire energy. They looked up, startled by her intrusion into their world.

"Aunt Natalie? What're you doing here?" India asked, exuding the delicate haughtiness that came from having so much luck—wealthy parents and good genes.

"Ellie's bracelet," Natalie said. "How did you end up with it?"

India was sucking on a lozenge. "Oh, that. She must've dropped it in gym class. We were going to give it back."

"Why bring it to the cabin yesterday? And what's this?" She held up the evidence bag with the knotted piece of red twine inside.

All three girls exchanged nervous glances.

"It's called knot magic," India explained with a condescending smile.

"I know what it is. Why were you girls doing knot magic with Ellie's bracelet?"

Without missing a beat, India said, "We wanted to cast a healing spell for Riley. And the scarabs represent immortality, so . . ."

"So you were using Ellie's bracelet to cast a healing spell for Riley Skinner?"

"Yes," she said, wiping a bead of sweat off her brow, while the sun's reflection flashed across the lake. The sun was like an unmoving heart—bright, powerful, indifferent.

"Why not tell Ellie about it?" Natalie countered, trying to remain neutral. "She thought it was lost. Why put her through that?"

"Because, she quit the coven," India explained. "She doesn't want to hang with us anymore. I didn't think she'd approve."

"So you just took it?"

"We didn't take it. She must've dropped it. We found it," India insisted. "We were going to give it back."

"And you did this for Riley?" Natalie said skeptically. "I thought you didn't like him, India? I thought he was your stalker?"

Her eyes narrowed with indignation. "I feel sorry for him, okay? He's in a coma."

Natalie pocketed the piece of twine. "What were you doing at Berkley's house this past Wednesday between four and six P.M.?"

There was a small commotion on the bench, a ruffling of feathers.

"Girl stuff," India responded with the emotionless demeanor of a practiced liar, or a child who'd never had to suffer the consequences of her own actions.

"Watching Netflix and doing our nails," Sadie added, coming to her friend's defense.

"And Riley didn't drop by to see you that day?" Natalie pressed. "Are you sure?"

"We already told you," Berkley said with an unflattering scowl.

Natalie showed them the evidence bag with the poppet doll inside. "Do you recognize this? It was buried in Ms. Buckner's backyard. Do you have any idea how it might've gotten there?"

The three of them grew still as dust, their faces flat and affectless.

"I've never seen that before in my life," India finally said.

"Me, neither," Sadie added.

"Ditto," Berkley said.

"This is dark magic. Straight pins, knot magic." Natalie held India's eye. "Come on, India. I've known you all your life. We used to bake cookies together and play hide-and-seek at Ellie's birthday parties. I've been to your piano recitals. You called me Aunty the other day. I'm not trying to entrap you. I just want the truth."

The other girls' eyes burned with conflict, but India looked away, shutting down the conversation.

"Can you help me out here, Sadie? Berkley?" Natalie noticed something poking out of Sadie's unzipped JanSport backpack, which had fallen over on its side. Natalie's heart raced. It looked exactly like Willow's purple silk batik scarf, the one Deborah had taken to the trial with her. "Sadie? Where'd you get that?"

"Get what?"

"That scarf." Natalie pointed.

"This?" She reached down and snatched it. Something flickered in her eyes, and she quickly stuffed it inside her backpack.

"Can I see the scarf, please?" Natalie insisted.

"No. It's mine. I bought it."

"Just show me the scarf, Sadie," Natalie told her.

"I found it at the Goodwill."

India took out her phone. "My father said to call him the next time this happened."

"Okay. I'm leaving."

Back in her car, Natalie willed her hands to stop shaking. Was it true? Had Grace donated Willow's old scarf to the Goodwill? She tried to reach her sister at home, but the machine picked up.

"Hey, it's me. Call me back as soon as you get this. We need to talk."

Then she turned the car around and headed back to town.

33

Natalie parked behind the Burning Lake Police Department and glanced around at the cruisers with their two-digit numbers on the trunks—Cruiser 01, Cruiser 02, Cruiser 03, et cetera. A row of identical midnight-blue Ford sedans with TO PROTECT AND SERVE stenciled on the doors. They used to have a witch on a broomstick painted on the trunks until the chief put the kibosh on that little experiment. He thought it was tasteless, capitalizing on an ancient tragedy.

Now Natalie sat for a moment, rubbing her exhausted eyes. She felt like a tightrope walker balanced on a tautly strung wire. Here she was, knee-deep in the case, and yet the frustration was hard to describe. It hurt inside her head, it hurt in her heart, it hurt in the roots of her hair. As a rookie detective, she'd been given full access to Willow's archived file. The crime scene photos were particularly earth-shattering, all those chilling details. But it was Willow's unseeing eyes that got to her the most—fixed on the overcast sky. You could see miniature clouds swirling on the lenses. It had rained that day, and Willow's long, dirty blond hair swirled wetly into the grass and tangled around her porcelain fingers, making paisley patterns.

Willow had always been a protective big sister with a mischievous streak.

She taught Natalie how to spit down a well, how to pirouette, how to sing with a hairbrush, and how to sneak cookies when their mother wasn't looking. Willow owned hightops in every color—pink, green, purple, red—and wrote messages in black Magic Marker on the white rubber fronts. She'd write *There's No Place* on one shoe, and *Like Home* on the other. *E.T.* on one shoe, and *Phone Home* on the other. *Bond, James Bond.* Funny, how life gave you all these little moments, then pulled the rug out from under you. Natalie gathered her reserve energy and got out of the car.

The police station was a hive of activity this afternoon. The assignment board was full of new cases—burglaries, shopliftings, bicycle thieves, drug ODs, fugitive farm animals, you name it. Just like any other midrange town, their department ran twenty-four/seven. They were often stretched thin, and the detectives didn't partner up like they did on TV. Natalie worked alone most of the time, and her caseload was straining at the seams. She didn't need another drop-everything case.

She checked the board. Luckily her name wasn't on it. She walked down the hallway and found Luke in his office. "Got a minute?"

He leaned back. "Yeah. Come on in." The sound of his voice soothed her brain.

She sank into the only chair in his office that wasn't stacked with paperwork.

"How're you holding up, Natalie?"

"Terrified I might've missed something. Otherwise . . . overwhelmed, but things aren't spinning out of control yet."

"Welcome to my world." He picked up a bag of pretzels from his desk and said, "There's bottled water in the fridge. Help yourself. Pretzel?"

She fetched a bottled water out of Luke's minifridge, unscrewed the cap, and scooped a couple of pretzels out of the bag, more out of politeness than hunger.

"What do you have for me?"

"Besides a killer headache?" She placed the poppet doll on his desk. "I found this buried in Brandon's backyard. Lindsey Wozniak's landscaping crew dug it up. Whoever put it there was hoping to cause major pain."

"A voodoo doll?"

"They're called poppets. This one is bound with twine and bent backwards, stuck with a dozen or more pins—which means it's serious black magic. I'm pretty sure it's a revenge curse. All that negative energy supposedly transfers to the target. You bury it somewhere on the property to maximize its power."

"The target, meaning Daisy?"

"Looks like it," she said. "Sewn up inside the doll was a red ballpoint pen and a torn piece of paper, just the corner. I'm assuming it was Daisy who was doing the grading, and she gave the student a B-minus. Whoever did this, whoever went to all the trouble of making a poppet and burying it in the backyard, was most likely the recipient of that B-minus."

"So this was a revenge curse?"

"Or a death curse, depending on the incantation."

"And most likely, whoever made the poppet was an A student."

"Who else would get so upset over a B-minus? Riley sure wouldn't."

"No, he'd be happy with a B-minus."

"But a B-minus could pull down a high achiever's grade average." She handed him the smaller evidence bag. "This is cord magic. Also known as knot magic. I found it tangled up in Ellie's bracelet, and it's identical to the one that was hidden inside the poppet doll. Same length and color of twine. Both knotted nine times. The knots are supposed to bind the spell to the target."

Luke nodded solemnly. "Lenny can verify if the two pieces of twine match."

"It would be significant. It would link the doll to India. She's an honor student. A B-minus could've affected her grade point average. I followed India and her friends to Abby's Hex today, but before I could ask her about it, she pulled the dad card."

Luke handed everything back to Natalie. "Have Lenny do a comparison test for the twine, and then process the rest for DNA, prints, and age. See what we can find."

She nodded. "Meanwhile, I'll start a search of Daisy's grade rolls for the current year and extrapolate which students received a B-minus from her. We'll focus on India and her friends."

"Good."

She shuddered. "It's a chilling thought. I've known these girls since they were toddlers."

He studied her closely. "Is this going to be a problem? The fact that Ellie and her friends might be involved?"

"No," she protested, feeling a swell of emotion in her throat. "Ellie knows I'm a cop, first and foremost." But she was going to have nightmares about this.

"Then you need to interview your niece as soon as possible."

"Tomorrow," she said. "Meanwhile, India told me she used Ellie's bracelet to perform a healing spell on Riley, but that's complete bullshit. They wouldn't need Ellie's bracelet for that—they'd need something of Riley's."

"So she's lying."

Natalie nodded. "I think it has something to do with Ellie quitting the coven. Looks like they're replacing her with a new recruit. Angela Sandhill."

He sipped his bottled water and asked, "When did that happen?"

"When did Ellie quit the coven? The day after Daisy was killed."

"So there's some connection, but I don't see it," Luke said. "Help me out."

"India's been lying about her relationship with Riley. She claims he's been stalking her, ever since they split up. But according to Jules, Riley is her dealer."

"Ah. And he was dealing on Wednesday afternoon."

"I think it's possible he went over to Berkley's house to sell India some weed." She handed Luke another evidence bag. "This is Riley's Samsung, as you know. I searched the digital pix stored in memory and found a bunch of selfies taken of Riley and India together, as recently as last week, and she doesn't look the least bit intimidated or uncomfortable."

Luke swiped through the digital images. "So she's been lying about it to cover up her drug habit?"

"Maybe. I'll have to have a heart-to-heart with my niece tomorrow, see if I can get to the bottom of things."

He pulled on his knuckles. "What was your impression of Ethan Hathaway?"

"He was very cooperative, for the most part. Daisy ended the affair about a month ago. He doesn't know if the baby was his. Daisy wasn't sure, apparently. He didn't seem fazed when I asked him to take a polygraph." She glanced at her watch. It was 4:55 P.M. "He's coming in for an interview at five."

"Do you think he killed her?"

"He doesn't have a solid alibi, and some of his answers were a little hinky—for instance, he accepted the fact that the baby could be his but didn't ask for a paternity test. According to Grace, some of the women Hathaway's dated found him to be antisocial and bookish. But Daisy loves to read, she loves books, and Brandon suspected she was bored with him, so . . . to each her own." It sounded flippant, but she hadn't meant it to sound that way.

"Bookish people aren't all they're cracked up to be," Luke said.

"Tell me about it."

He eyed her curiously. "You're over that guy, right?"

"Who, Zack?" She made a face, then let the seconds slip past. Their first night together felt like ages ago. In the middle of the night, she'd crawled out of bed with a craving for ice cream. They tiptoed into the starlit kitchen, giggling like children. Zack fetched them two mismatched spoons and they leaned against the counter, watching the moon rise and eating Hood's chocolate chip ice cream straight out of the carton. "Yeah," she said. "It's relationship roadkill."

He held up his hands. "Not that it's any of my business."

"Jesus, you're weird." She laughed.

"Why?"

"'Are you over him?' 'None of my business,'" she teased.

"Are you mocking me?"

"Not at all."

"Because affectionate mocking is not allowed." Luke had never liked Zack, which should've been her first clue, since Luke was an excellent judge of character. Now he took a swig of bottled water and loosened his tie. The world came alive and sparked inside his eyes. "I think we're sharing a moment. Are we sharing a moment?"

"God, you're impossible."

When Luke was a scrawny kid, every single one of his T-shirts had holes or rips in them. His sneakers were threadbare. He couldn't wait to get his driver's license, and as soon as he did, he bought a beat-up Buick Skylark for $500 and got lost on the back roads of Burning Lake while blasting the B-52s' "Dirty Back Road" on his crummy Radio Shack speakers. He was proud. He was vengeful. He kept score. He was a misunderstood superhero. He was Deadpool. He was Wolverine.

"Anyway, I've kind of given up on love." Natalie shrugged. "If that helps."

"No, it doesn't help at all," he said.

She could feel the blood thundering in her ears.

He was about to say something else when the phone rang. He picked up. "Hello? Okay." He hung up. "Hathaway's waiting for you."

34

Natalie escorted **Ethan Hathaway** into the interview room and offered him something to drink. "Coke, Pepsi, Dr Pepper . . . ?"

He declined them all.

"Have a seat." She turned on the video recorder. The interrogation room was windowless and sparsely furnished, with a table, two chairs, and a camera on a tripod. Some of her fellow detectives were content to talk for hours about nothing in an attempt to relax the suspect and catch him off guard, but Natalie preferred a more direct approach.

"You've known Daisy for how long now?" she asked.

"Three years."

"Only three?"

"Well, I'm four years older than Daisy," he said, "so our paths never crossed until I started teaching at JFK, which was about three years ago."

"Where did you work before JFK?"

"I got my teaching degree in English from Syracuse and my master's from NYU. After that, I taught creative writing at a boarding school in Albany. The Gilchrest School. About five years ago, my mother became seriously ill, and as her illness progressed, I decided to apply for a teaching gig closer to home. Fortunately, something opened up."

She nodded. "Tell me about your relationship with Daisy."

He stared down at his hands. "First of all, she's a terrific person. An inspired teacher and a caring human being. We were on the same wavelength, I guess you could say."

"When did you realize you were attracted to her?"

"We started out as colleagues. Friends. We had a lot in common . . . just two teachers jawboning about our crazy profession. Daisy's pretty much an open book—very honest and plainspoken. Whatever she wants in her life, it's plastered all over her face, like a billboard. To tell you the truth, I felt an instant attraction to her, but then I noticed the wedding ring. As the years progressed, however, so did we."

"Tell me again . . . when did it begin specifically?" Natalie asked.

"June of last year."

"And you've never been married?"

Ethan shook his head. "Never found the right person, I guess." He drummed his fingers on the tabletop and looked around. There was no place to rest your eyes, except on the detective seated opposite you. "I'm a writer, so that makes me . . . I won't say antisocial exactly. But solitary. Some people can't stand to be alone with their thoughts, but I can. Daisy was drawn to that private side of me."

"And Brandon had no idea about the affair? You're sure about that?"

Ethan shook his head. "We were very discreet."

"But there were rumors among the faculty members . . ."

"There are always rumors flying around school." He shrugged. "People talk. Grace and Daisy squelched those rumors pretty quickly. Grace gave it legitimacy."

"And Daisy was okay with that? Lying to her best friend?"

"Not okay with it," he said. "Out of necessity."

Natalie noted his bloodshot eyes. He'd been grieving, possibly self-medicating, not getting much sleep. His shirt wasn't tucked in, and there was a smudge on his collar. "How did it make you feel when Daisy broke up with you?" she asked.

"Terrible."

"Did you try talking her out of it?"

"Of course. We discussed it for hours. But in the end, I accepted her decision."

"But the two of you had temporarily split up once before. Why did you accept her decision this time?"

"She was never pregnant before."

"But she could've been pregnant with your child."

"It also could've been Brandon's."

"That didn't *bother* you?" Natalie pressed.

"I wanted to be . . . respectful of her decision."

"What would you have done if Brandon had found out about you and Daisy before she got pregnant? Would you have fought for her then?"

"I'm not a fighter."

"So then—you just gave up?" she said.

"I don't understand the question. That's not what happened."

"Maybe the thought of confronting Brandon influenced your decision to respect Daisy's wishes? Maybe it didn't have anything to do with her decision, as much as it had to do with avoiding a showdown with her husband?"

Ethan heaved a frustrated sigh. He took a throat lozenge out of his pocket. It was covered in lint, but he popped it in his mouth anyway. "I'm not naïve, Detective. I understand when someone's calling me a coward. Like I told you, I'm not a fighter."

"Those love sonnets are full of bravado," Natalie said, egging him on. "And I could've sworn that the person who wrote them would've fought for Daisy's hand to the death."

He looked at her with utter contempt. "Then you read them wrong."

"Oh? Explain it to me."

"Shakespeare was known for turning the traditional sonnet on its head. He often wrote about unrequited love, more specifically . . . between a poet and the lady he worshipped who was above his station and who, in the end, abandoned him. In many of his sonnets, the poet ends up blaming himself for the loss of her affection."

"So you blamed yourself?" she asked.

He nodded. "Brandon's an imposing presence. He's loud and annoying, but he lives life fully in the present. He's a kind of eat-drink-and-be-merry type of guy. Whereas I have a tendency to dwell inside my head. I think that's why Daisy ultimately chose him over me."

"That's very chivalrous of you."

"Chivalry means courtesy, generosity, and valor."

"So you consider yourself a generous man. Not an angry, jealous man?"

"What you feel and how you behave are two different things," he said.

"But you were confused that she chose Brandon over you?"

"I was angry, jealous, confused, sad, bitter, and heartbroken."

"Okay," she said. "That's a lot of emotional baggage."

"And I carry it well. With a heavy heart."

Natalie nodded. He was a little arrogant and standoffish, and he liked to play word games. He came across as humorless, but the dry wit was there. "Tell me about last Wednesday," she said. "Walk me through it."

"Like I said, there was an after-school meeting—fairly boring procedural stuff. I went home around four fifteen and started grading papers. Not the best way to spend your evenings, but hey, it's a living."

She smiled. "Did anyone contact you during that time? Between four fifteen and let's say, six thirty?"

"No. I turn off all my devices when I'm grading papers. Better concentration."

"All?"

"You should try it."

"Are you right-handed or left-handed?"

"Right," he responded.

"What kind of soft drink do you prefer?"

"Soft drink?" He shrugged. "I prefer bottled water."

"And if you had to pick between Coke, Seven-Up, Dr Pepper, Pepsi, Fanta . . . ?"

"Coke or Pepsi, I suppose."

Natalie nodded. "Did you kill Daisy Buckner?"

"No." He winced.

"Ever hit or strike her?"

The corners of his mouth drew down. "No. Never."

Lies took effort and concentration. Hathaway seemed too worn-out to be lying, but the extraction of truth was a tough business. Even well-intentioned adults lied about some things. Joey had taught her to look for clues. Defensive posture. Furtive glances. Sweaty foreheads. Shallow breathing. Everything was a tell.

"Did you and Daisy argue a lot?"

"We disagreed on occasion. Just like any other couple."

"But you weren't like any other couple."

"No," he agreed.

"Did you ever lose your temper with her?" Natalie asked.

"I'm pretty even-tempered."

"Ever yell? Shove? Maybe an argument that got physical?"

"No."

She observed him carefully. "Are you willing to take a polygraph?"

"Yes," he said, his face drawing into a blade of pain. "Jesus. Why would I hurt her? I was deeply in love with her."

"I don't know," she said. "Maybe because she broke your heart? Maybe because you couldn't stand the idea of another man raising your child? These are just a few of the possibilities that pop into my head."

"Look, I'll take a polygraph test," Ethan said in a stressed tone. "But you have to believe me. I loved her. I never would've hurt her. I don't know who killed her. I don't know whose baby it was." He pinched the bridge of his nose. "All I know is . . . Daisy wasn't happy in her marriage, Brandon's a loudmouth drunk, Riley Skinner was behaving in a threatening manner, and Daisy insisted she could handle it."

"Handle what?"

"Everything. Riley, her marriage, the baby. She wanted to do the right thing. She told me that getting pregnant changed *everything* for her."

"Meaning what?"

"I don't know. But she was unyielding, once she'd made up her mind."

"Did Riley ever show signs of hostility or aggression toward Daisy that you witnessed personally?"

"No. I only heard about it secondhand from her."

"About Riley. Any outward signs of pathology? Any interest in witchcraft, Satanism, animal mutilation?"

"Animal mutilation?" he repeated with disgust. "No, not that I recall. Although he was into rap, death metal, Goth, and horror flicks. He wrote violent rap lyrics instead of poetry and drew disturbing pictures in the margins of his test papers, but that isn't unique for a teenage boy."

She could feel her phone buzzing in her pocket. "I'll introduce you to Detective Labruzzo, our polygraph expert," she said. "He can schedule an appointment for you. Excuse me a minute, I have to take this."

She took the call outside. "Brandon?"

"Natalie," he said breathlessly, "we need to talk."

35

Darnell's Motor-Inn boasted nine "log cabins," each with its own vibrating bed and color TV with hard-core pay-per-view. Brandon was staying in cabin five. The red sports car was gone. A black Jeep Cherokee was parked out front. Natalie knocked on the door and Brandon answered looking strung-out in gray sweats and blue athletic shoes.

"Come on in. Quick." He closed the door behind them.

"What are you doing way out here?" Natalie asked.

"The media's camped out at my dad's house. I couldn't stand it anymore. I had to get some fresh air."

"There's nothing fresh about this air," Natalie said.

Inside, it was dark and nasty-smelling. She took a seat in one of the matching tangerine vinyl armchairs angled in front of the TV. These places were all the same—bed, bureau, minifridge. The curtains were faded. The carpet was the color of lumpy mashed potatoes

In this confined space, she could feel the heat crawling up her neck—she was glad to see Brandon, but more than a little concerned. The queen-size bed was covered in survivalist gear—a bulging backpack, his off-duty revolver with extra ammo, his handcuffs, a Taser.

"What the hell is this?" she asked, pointing at the cache of weap-onry.

"Dominic wants me dead. I gotta be careful." Brandon opened the mini-fridge and took out two Coronas. "Want a beer, Nat?"

"I'll pass. Couldn't you find a safer hideaway?"

"Nobody knows I'm here. The owner's a buddy of mine. Coke? That's all I got."

She studied him closely—he was a sweaty mess with bloodshot eyes and knots on his forehead. She shook her head and felt an inexplicable weight on her shoulders.

He sat down and cracked his beer. "Maybe this is karma. Maybe life is just one big cosmic joke."

"Karma for what?"

He shrugged. "I'm a fuckup. Straight up."

"Look," Natalie said, "if Dominic breaks parole, we'll be on his ass in a heartbeat, okay? Meanwhile, you've got yourself a killer lawyer. You need to listen to him. You can't keep running around like some backwoods vigilante—"

"Did they get the tox screen results yet?" Brandon interrupted.

She took a frayed breath. "You need to back off and let us do our job. Listen to your attorney. Avoid Dominic."

His eyes widened. "You think that's all I care about? Dominic spread-ing lies to protect his punk-ass son? Fuck him. Nothing shocks me anymore, Natalie. Nothing rocks me. I'm just looking for the thread running through all these questions. . . ."

Natalie folded her arms. "Can I be honest?"

"Go ahead."

"I watched you self-destruct before my eyes. And that was a horrible feeling."

He gave a sullen nod.

"Right here in my gut," she said. "Like you put a bullet through me. Like you chewed a hole through our ranks. And I hated you for that. Because I really care what happens to you, Brandon. We all do."

His eyes glazed over. "I made some poor choices. But how can you not see this, Natalie? My wife was *dead on the floor*, and I'm supposed to make rational decisions? How is that in any way fair?" He was silent for a moment as he gazed out the motel windows at the evening sky, sprinkled with stars and dominated by the planet Venus. He looked down at his hands. "What did Jules say?"

"You know I can't talk about that."

He scowled at her. "Give me something, Natalie."

"We're working around the clock. That's all I can say."

He gave her a look of utter despair. "How'd we get here? Huh?"

She'd intended to hammer him with questions, but now she could feel herself softening and sympathizing. Brandon had lost his wife and their entire future together in one blow. He'd lost his whole world. How would she have coped? How would anyone? These thoughts were stuck like burrs in her mind. "Brandon, this is the second time we've met against the advice of your counsel," she said. "So what's up?"

He gave her a pleading look. "Can I trust you?"

"Are you kidding me? I'm your most trusted ally. I'm the only one who's going to tell you the truth, even if you don't like me very much. And so, yes, Brandon, you can trust me."

The muscles of his back tensed as he released a sigh. "Okay, fine. Ask me anything. I'm an open book."

"Are you sure?"

"Fuck my lawyer . . . go ahead. I want justice for my wife and baby."

She leaned forward and said, "I know about your fling with Lindsey back in high school. I know you weren't consulted about the abortion, and I was told you reacted with anger. So what happened, in your own words?"

He smoothed his greasy hair behind his ears and said, "Of course, I was pissed off. Who wouldn't be? I wanted that baby. I wanted to marry her. But Daisy never let me know what was going on until it was too late. And that hurt like hell. She thought we were too young, and . . . you know what? She was right. Still, at the time, that didn't make it suck any less."

"Did you ever hit her? Lose your temper?"

"Christ, *these* are your questions?"

"You said I could ask you anything, Brandon. Why did you hire Lindsey to do your landscaping, when you knew how much it might hurt Daisy?"

"Lindsey's the best in town."

"Bullshit."

"I don't know what else to say. I guess I wasn't thinking."

"You weren't thinking about Daisy's feelings?"

"Our marriage wasn't doing so great," he said heatedly. "We were struggling to get back to a place of intimacy, real intimacy. Maybe there was a side of me that wanted to make her jealous," he admitted. "Reignite those old feelings."

"Old feelings of jealousy?"

"Passion," he said, looking at her. "Love. Lust. Fun."

She nodded.

"We don't always act rationally when it comes to love, do we?"

"No, we don't," she admitted.

His face had grown tense and expressionless. "I wasn't paying attention, okay? I was thinking about our future together. What does it matter? I loved her, you know that. We were going to have a baby. Sure we argued. Things weren't perfect. But I've been in love with Daisy since the fifth grade, and everybody fuckin' knows it."

"I know you love her, Brandon. That's not in dispute here."

"And now, come to find out . . . my wife's been cheating on me." He took a swallow of beer. "All this time, it turns out she was screwing around behind my back." Brandon gazed blankly out the window. "With Ethan Hathaway."

The hairs on her arms bristled. "How do you know it was him?"

"Are you kidding me? You think anyone can keep a secret in this town?"

"We have a leaker? Who told you?"

"Relax, Natalie. I saw it on the news. All those cameras in front of the police station. I spotted him walking up the steps behind the talking heads. One plus one equals a threesome. Besides, it was you who planted the idea in my head in the first place."

"Jesus, Brandon."

"Love sonnets, you said. Ever since you told me about those sonnets, it's been eating a hole in me. Bottom line, some egghead was bonking my wife while I was agonizing about her and the baby. That's the takeaway from this." He wiped the sweat off his face.

Natalie steepled her fingers together and said, "Just tell me one thing. Why did you lie to me? You didn't get to the gym until five thirty, according to the staff."

"Who cares?"

"I do. Because it speaks to the timeline. You know exactly what I mean."

Brandon stood up and balled his hands into fists. "I wasn't lying to you, Natalie. I honestly don't remember. My head's been fuzzy for days. D'you realize what this feels like? It feels like a Valium-induced waking dream. It's down to brain-dead levels now. My wife is *dead*. Do you have any idea what I did today? I had to go pick out the casket." He ran his hands through his messy hair. "I had to fetch a copy of the death certificate. And you wonder why I can't pin down the exact time I went to the gym?"

"It's significant. You changed your story twice. First, you said you went to the gym at four, then at five, now it's five thirty. So, fine. Now we know you drove to Chippaway at four—no witnesses, no stops for gas, no receipts. And that presents a problem for me. Because basically, there's an hour and a half unaccounted for."

"I picked out her *casket* today," he cried, the sound of his pain reverberating. "I made funeral arrangements for my dead wife and baby. Where's the justice? How am I supposed to deal with this? Nobody told me I'd feel this way."

"You need to get your head on straight," she said firmly, afraid for him.

He looked at her and broke down crying. He plopped down on the edge of the bed and cupped his wet face in his hands, shoulders shaking in agony. He took a deep breath and said, "She wanted to take the train to New York . . . she wanted to go check out the art galleries or the theater, but I never had time. Now I can't stop thinking about all the things I should've done. I can't switch off my mind," he said, tears clinging to his eyelashes. "I feel so fucking alone."

"You aren't alone." Her nerves were raw. Natalie was afraid to leave him here with his weapons and paranoia. She tamped down her anxiety and said, "Is there anybody I can call? A family member or a friend?"

He shook his head.

"I can't leave you alone like this. Who can I call?"

A small silence passed between them.

"My minister."

She took out her phone and called Reverend Grimsby, whom she'd met at one of the Buckners' parties. The reverend promised to head over to the motel right away, and Natalie waited with Brandon until he arrived. An exhausted silence settled between them. Her stomach felt queasy. Moonlight glowed through the cabin windows.

Brandon looked at his hands. "Thanks, Natalie."

"Stay out of trouble. Do what your attorney says, okay?"

He glanced up. "I used to think she was as good as gold."

Natalie nodded.

"Whenever I got suspicious, Daisy was always proving me wrong. Like for instance, just a few weeks ago, she was moody and quiet all afternoon . . . and then out of the blue, she tells me we're out of milk and scoops up her car keys and takes off. But I noticed there was milk in the fridge. So I followed her across town, wondering what she was up to, you know? She drove to that bakery across town . . . Sweetie's. You know the one? I parked down the street and observed her. She came out of Sweetie's with a pink bakery box in her hands. I thought—this is odd. I had no idea what was going on. Long story short, she drove over to the Hadleys' old farm, pulled into the driveway, and Bunny came out of the barn, and Daisy gave her the box. It was cupcakes. Bunny ate one while I watched them talking for a while. And I thought, my God, Daisy's as good as gold."

Natalie frowned. "But why would she lie to you about that?"

"I have no idea." He shook his head. "I was just relieved she wasn't cheating on me. What a clueless jerk I was, huh?"

36

Natalie hadn't been out this way in quite some time. The Hadleys' abandoned farmstead was located two miles past the Citgo station on Little Falls Road, just beyond the covered bridge. She pulled into the rutted driveway and parked next to the dilapidated barn. Ever since Caleb Hadley died of a heart attack twenty-five years ago, the farm had fallen into disrepair. After the widow moved in with her butcher son across town, she insisted on keeping the porch lights burning all night long, just as her husband had done for forty years. Her son grudgingly obliged, paying each month's electric bill, while the widow claimed it kept the coyotes away. When she passed away eight years later, the lights were finally turned off for good.

Now Natalie sat in her car, staring at the barn. The weather changed swiftly in the spring. Another rainstorm was kicking up, and scattered raindrops shimmered through the air. The barn's great doors were padlocked shut, thick chains fused together with crusted orange rust. Once upon a time, a herd of cattle was housed inside but after Caleb died the widow sold them off. Somewhere out back, behind the weathered barn, was the spot where Willow had bled to death in the grass twenty years ago.

According to the prosecution, Justin Fowler had lured Willow to the abandoned farm with the intention of killing her. His footprints were found at the scene, along with tire marks from his car. Police also found items of bloody clothing tossed in a dumpster two blocks away from Justin's house. Willow's blood was found on the pants and T-shirt that were positively identified as belonging to Justin. The murder weapon was never found—a steak knife, according to experts.

Since his arrest, Justin maintained his innocence despite the mountain of evidence against him, but the jury wasn't buying it. He had no alibi for the time of death, and even more damning, Grace had verified at the trial that Willow had broken up with him on the day of the murder. Justin Fowler was sentenced to life in prison.

Now Natalie grabbed her flashlight from the glove compartment and got out of the car. A stinging rain hit her in the face and streaked down her cheeks. The knee-high grass was wet. Soon her pant legs were soaked. The rain made pitter-patter sounds against her unprotected head, and the accompanying lightning strikes brought the landscape eerily to life, before plunging everything into murky darkness again.

During the next intense lightning flash, she saw the old pentagram carved into the side of the barn—six feet across, an inverted five-pointed star inside a circle. A symbol of black magic. It had been there for as long as she could remember.

Surrounding the barn was a muddy yard with a grain bin and a rusty wheelbarrow. The hay shed, where cattle had once found shelter from the rain, formed a bovine face in the gloom. Natalie's flesh crawled as she trudged around the side of the building, which was propped up with long boards. The peeling paint revealed the weathered wood underneath, and she shuddered to think that the whole structure could come crashing down any second now.

The relentless downpour flattened the wild grass as Natalie slogged past a broken-down tractor, dismantled for parts. Beyond the foggy overgrown fields were the ever-encroaching woods.

She came to the back door of the barn and shone her flashlight inside. The milking room was divided into dozens of stanchions and rotting mangers where the cows used to feed. The metal stalls had gone to rust. The walls were covered in graffiti and the cement manure gutters were full of trash—fast-food containers, liquor bottles, condoms, rolling papers, just the usual party detritus.

She walked into the main part of the barn and stood for a moment inhaling the pungent aroma of ancient hay bales and silage. She shone her light toward the thirty-foot ceiling. It was as quiet as feathers in here. The floor bowed dangerously. The rain was coming down hard, water seeping from the leaky ceiling and hitting stagnant puddles on the floor, every drop echoing. *Drip, drip, drip.*

The place was full of a surreal trapped energy. She searched the clammy walls for her sister's old pentagram—the one Natalie had seen years ago. Layers of curses, jealousies, and insults obscured the older graffiti. Generations of teenagers had made a pilgrimage to this barn to act out their aggressions and obsessions. *Sext Madison for a good time. Caden is a skeevy fuckbud.*

She stood motionless with her chin raised.

Life will fling everything it can at you, kiddo. Good or bad. You have to deal with it. You have to accept your losses.

Truth was elusive. Love was fickle.

All her questions had questions.

The mystery circled in on itself, like a snake devouring its own tail.

Natalie aimed her light against the weathered wall, then swung the beam slowly sideways—there. There it was. Prickles rose up on her body. She took a few steps forward and studied the old pentagram, half-hidden beneath decades of spray paint. Twenty-one years ago, Grace and her three best friends had added their names inside the points of the pentagram— Grace, Daisy, Lindsey, Bunny. Now Natalie studied the orderly penmanship, the uniform *e*'s and *y*'s.

The skin of her temples pulsed with emotion as she traced the five-pointed star. She hadn't seen it in years. *How naïve we all were back then,* she thought.

Behind the barn was an overgrown field. It took Natalie a few minutes to locate the wooden stake that marked the site where her sister had died. There was a pile of ancient offerings nearby—a soggy heap of withered bouquets, prayer cards, melted candles, and faded handmade signs. Many séances had taken place here. The local ghost hunters deemed it a portal into the spirit world.

The site had an otherworldly feel, both solemn and surreal. Willow had been such a sweet, funny, and marvelously flawed human being—their mother's favorite. Whereas Natalie's father had showered all three girls with love and guidance, Deborah struggled to love them equally. She'd never planned on having more than one, and it was obvious she loved Willow the best. Willow knew how to make her happy, helping out with the chores and spending time with Deborah, gossiping and giggling while they made dinner together. Underlings Grace and Natalie couldn't wait to get away from Deborah's grasp and go play instead.

Willow had a wild side, to be sure, but around their mother, her demeanor became reserved and polite. She clasped her hands in her lap and smiled warmly as she listened to Deborah's stories and asked for motherly advice. Willow used to wear the most colorful outfits—beaded jackets, pleated skirts, Nordic sweaters, Adidas track pants, Mary Janes, rhinestone earrings—that were outdated by the time Grace and Natalie inherited them. For a while, Willow's palette had been monochromatic—black on black, with bloodred lips. She'd dabbled in witchcraft for a short time, but Deborah hated it. She'd done everything in her power to stop Willow from going down that road, and it worked. Willow's flirtation with witchcraft hadn't lasted a hair's breadth of time, and soon she was back to her colorful outfits and carefree ways.

Natalie had always assumed that Grace joined a coven to spite their mother. One day, during her sophomore year in high school, she changed her tidy purple bedroom into a Goth nightmare, painting the roller shades black and hanging up posters of *The Craft, The Crow,* and *The Texas Chainsaw Massacre.* Grace caught hell that day. She was grounded for a week. No allowance for a month. She and Deborah screamed at each other in shrill, misunderstood voices, then withdrew to separate corners of the house and slammed the doors. In instances like this, Joey advised Natalie to give them a wide berth, and eventually all would be forgiven. But the rift between them never completely healed.

Deborah Lockhart had once been formidable, a bastion of strength, a domestic warrior with boundless energy. Hurtling herself from one errand to the next—cooking, cleaning, marching the girls through their homework, doing the laundry, shopping for food, her grocery cart rattling noisily up and down the aisles. It was in Deborah's nature to hurry things along—setting the table, clattering plates, banging cupboard doors. She would bump her elbows on the doorframes while rushing from room to room. She would whisk the teakettle off the back burner before it'd had a chance to whistle. She scooped the silverware out of its designated drawer and dropped it on the table, as if she were at war with the world for failing to provide her with the life she *really* wanted—not this domestic hellscape. But then, after Willow died, Deborah's grief calcified in her bones and she became as brittle as a twig. Natalie and Grace had to move delicately around her after that, understanding that too much activity or emotional input could snap her in half. Deborah's former strength was a mirage. Toward the end of her life, she became as faded as the pages of an old phone book.

Thunder rumbled. A thick mist boiled across the fields like something out of a 1950s sci-fi flick, bleak and sodden. Natalie thought she saw something in the miasma. What was that? She headed across the overgrown field into the mist. Cattle used to graze here in the back pasture, but now everything was lush, green, tangled, and dense. Nature was reclaiming the land.

In the next flash of lightning, she noticed something strange on the barbed wire fence that ran around the periphery of the pasture. She shined her light on one of the old fence posts—a dead crow tangled up in twine and fishing line, tortuously bound to the wooden post. A crow. Natalie felt as lifeless as a puppet.

Her flashlight sputtered for a moment, and she shook it until it blinked on again, illuminating the ryegrass at her feet. She raised the beam and swung it down along the fence line. Nine dead crows in a row, bound to nine fence posts. Everything ground to an ugly halt. What had once been beautiful was dead. The birds had been here for quite a while. Nothing but feathers, beaks, and skulls.

37

Twenty minutes later, Luke was leaning against one of the department cars, a two-door hardtop, talking on his phone. Natalie watched him briefly as if he were a stranger—such a brooding, handsome guy in a gray suit. He hung up and smiled, then walked up to her like a waiter in a posh hotel and handed her a coffee.

"Hey, thanks." She took a sip and secured the lid.

"You're welcome." They had their own shorthand. "Show me."

They moved across the field and stood in the wet weeds, studying the nine dead birds twisted up in twine and fishing line—a truly gruesome sight. Each crow had been bound tightly to its post—their heads pointing skyward, beaks open, fan-shaped tails pointing downward, iridescent black wings spread. It reminded Natalie of a crucifixion scene, played out in miniature, all the way down the fence line. These birds had been deliberately killed and posed in a shocking display for anyone to stumble across and wonder. There were no easy answers here. Only infinite shades of madness.

Now Natalie had to push through a membrane of surprise and shock in order to get to the other side, where she could assess the scene professionally. She stood studying the raw details, little beads of sweat trickling down her neck. Each of these poor, intelligent creatures had died an agonizing death—so tangled up in synthetic fishing line, zip ties, and heavy-duty twine that any attempts to free themselves would've made the situation worse. It was chilling.

Crows were highly intelligent animals. They belonged to the Corvidae family of birds that included ravens and magpies. Some biologists referred to them as "feathered primates" because they were able to perform difficult tasks and make strategic decisions. They had remarkable memories.

Natalie examined one of the bird carcasses with latex-gloved fingers—the glossy blue-black plumage, the reptilian eyes ringed with violet, the strong legs, and shiny black beak. A mature male crow.

"How did he catch them?" Luke asked. "Did he shoot them?"

"I don't think so. I'm not finding any buckshot wounds. Probably snares or spring traps. That way, he could keep them alive for a while before deciding what to do with them."

Luke shuddered. "A disturbing thought."

"They've been dead for quite a while," she went on. "And there are markings on these birds that don't match their current bindings, which indicates he killed them somewhere else, then transported them here and staged the carcasses."

"Which would explain why nobody else reported them until now."

Natalie nodded. "He killed them someplace private, and then brought them here recently, posing them in a intentional pattern. He enjoys the theatricality of it."

"There's a method to this sick fuck's madness," Luke muttered.

Natalie could feel her heart hammering in her chest. She decided to throw it out there. "It's obvious, right? Nine dead birds for the Missing Nine."

He rubbed the back of his neck and nodded. "Maybe he's sick of not reading about himself in the papers."

"So he's boasting? Flaunting his achievement?"

"It's been out of the news for a couple of years now."

"Well, he's got our attention now."

"Yes, he does."

She nodded. "This is definitely the work of a sociopath. Too elaborate for a teenager, I think."

"I agree."

"An adult sociopathic loner. This was methodically planned, which makes him an organized offender. Sadistic. Premeditated." Her flashlight sputtered off again, and the darkness was unsettling. She shook it, and it blinked on, illuminating the dead crow in front of her, its beak frozen in midshriek. She lowered the light and shuddered.

"Aren't crows supposed to symbolize death?" Luke asked.

"Death, catastrophe."

"So we can assume he's into witchcraft?"

Natalie shook her head. "Any true Wiccan would never sacrifice animals like this. They have a reverence for nature."

"Maybe he's not a true Wiccan? Or maybe he's a Satanist?"

"Every time we look into rumors of satanic cults, we come up empty."

"Right. Because nobody's going to admit to being a Satanist."

"Not to the police anyway."

Rumors of devil worship had been floating around for years. Just last May, there was talk of a satanic cult sacrificing people's pets due to a three-month spate of animal disappearances. Missing cat and dog posters had popped up all over town. But a representative from the U.S. Fish and Wildlife Service issued a statement clarifying that the local coyote population was responsible for killing people's pets. He held a news conference and showed reporters definitive proof—a bag of coyote scat.

"We can't blame this one on coyotes," Natalie mumbled.

Luke shook his head. "No, we can't."

"It feels like a warning. Like a threat to the entire town."

"Maybe he's about to strike again?"

The thought was too alarming to contemplate. She caught an erratic movement out of the corner of her eye, a convulsion of particles. *Thwick, thwick, thwick.* Bats traveling through the foggy air. More than a dozen police officers had been called to the scene, and now they were scouring the Hadley property, including the abandoned house and barn.

"Hold on a second," Natalie said, beaming her flashlight directly into the bird's mouth. "I need some tweezers." She rummaged around in her evidence kit, then leaned over the crow and used the tweezers to pull out a tiny scroll of paper that had been lodged in the bird's throat. She carefully unfurled the scroll, while Luke held the flashlight steady for her.

Covering the narrow band of torn paper, in the tiniest handwriting she'd ever seen, were the words, *What the hawk eats, What the hawk eats, What the hawk eats* . . . Over and over again.

"'What the hawk eats'?" Luke repeated. "What the fuck is that supposed to mean?" He looked at her significantly. "What *do* hawks eat?"

"Rodents, squirrels, roadkill, and . . . other birds."

"What?"

"They eat crows."

"Birds eat birds?" He shook his head, repulsed.

"I witnessed it a couple of times at my grandfather's farm." The wind stirred through Natalie's hair. "We used to visit him every summer up in Kripplebush. A flock of crows would follow Grandpa's plow and devour all the earthworms that were churned up in the soil. The red-tailed hawks would hide in the trees and wait until the crows started pecking at the ground, searching for worms. Then they'd glide through the air, swoop down into the final run, and grab a crow in their claws and beak."

"So maybe the Crow Killer grew up on a farm?" Luke surmised.

"He knows how to snare birds, that's for sure."

Over the years, Natalie had encountered bird snares in the woods made of simple materials. Poachers and hunters used a few wooden poles tied together with twine, a fist-size rock, and a cord. Once a bird had perched on the trap, the stick would be displaced, the rock would drop, and the cord would loop over the bird's legs, trapping it. Simple materials, but it took skill and practice to construct such a trap.

"My grandfather told me that crows have two sides to them—good and bad," she said. "On the one hand, they ate his corn, which was why there'd sometimes be a dead crow hanging around the scarecrow's neck. He claimed it got rid of them for months at a time. On the other hand, he liked that they ate the weevils, grasshoppers, and June bugs that infested his crops. It was a mixed blessing."

"What did your grandfather say about hawks?"

She shrugged, trying to remember. "They're solitary hunters. Birds of prey. They prefer to kill shortly before nightfall, when the nocturnal animals emerge and hawks have a visual advantage."

"Is that how the Crow Killer thinks of himself?" Luke posited. "As a bird of prey?"

"Could be," she said, thick braids of discomfort knitting into her muscles.

A pair of turkey vultures glided in ever-widening circles above their heads. The rain was beginning to dissipate. They heard a shout from across the field. In the tall grass beyond the barn, a police officer was waving his arms.

Her heart made slow wing beats as they headed across the field.

Officer Keegan was holding up an army jacket—very familiar-looking, with pink and purple sequins on the back spelling out, I'VE GOT THIS. There were drops of blood on the denim fabric.

38

In this cynical modern day and age, there was something almost sub-versive about Natalie's desire to be good in a bad world, to hunt down the bad guys and expose their deeds to the light of day. To admire men like her dad and the gritty heroes of old TV westerns. The simplicity and moral certainty of it all, the lines drawn in the sand. White hats and black hats. Good was good, and bad was bad. It felt naïve to want to save the world. But with Daisy's case, and now the Crow Killer, Natalie knew she had touched real evil. Evil felt like something slipping into you—as deceptive and sleek as a scalpel blade. Like a rustling sound deep in the woods, when everything else grew quiet and the wind stirred your hair with a ghostly hand.

She fought off these ropy, feverish thoughts. Bunny Jackson was miss-ing. Natalie had to find her. She sped past the old brick warehouses with their busted-out windows and chained-shut doors. Road surface noises whistled through her wheel wells as she drove farther north beyond the posh, high-end estates and entered the vast tracks of farmland—meadows, orchards, nature preserves. Beyond the nature preserves were the retail outlets, which skirted the highway—Walmart, Rite Aid, Pep Boys, Kohl's, Costco.

Natalie took the nearest exit off the highway and passed several big-box stores before she came to the A&P supermarket, one of Bunny's favorite haunts. She pulled into the lot and drove around back, where the parking field was sprinkled with idling delivery trucks. She braked in front of a cement loading dock, spotted a homeless man digging around in a dumpster, and stepped out of her SUV. "Hello, Marvin," she said, approaching the dumpster.

The homeless man squinted down at her. Marvin Brooner's hair was shaggy, as if he'd cut it himself. He wore new-looking sweats from a clothing giveaway. "What's up, Detective?" he said with a toothless grin.

"I'm looking for Bunny Jackson. Have you seen her?"

Marvin half climbed, half fell out of the dumpster.

"Careful. Watch your step."

He righted himself. "Bunny? Not since last week. Why?"

"We found her army jacket behind the Hadleys' barn, and I'm worried she may have gone missing. Any word on the street?"

He scratched his head. "Bunny never goes anywhere without that jacket."

"I know," she said apprehensively. "If you see her, would you tell her I'm looking for her? And please ask someone at the shelter to contact me. It's very important."

"Sure thing."

"And get yourself a hot meal, Marvin," she said, handing him some cash for his trouble.

He took it and said, "Bunny always shows up eventually, though, doesn't she?"

"Let's hope so. Take care of yourself."

Natalie spent the next several hours searching for her friend. The Goodwill was closed. The Fitzgerald overpass was abandoned. Panhandlers in front of the Rockaway Café hadn't seen Bunny lately. The dank alleyway behind the art house movie theater where *The Last Picture Show* was playing was vacant. She wasn't in any of the local shelters, churches, or food

banks. She wasn't camped out on the village green or asleep in the courtyard behind the town library, where transients sometimes occupied the
benches.

Natalie took comfort in the fact that everybody down at the BLPD was
searching for the missing homeless woman tonight. A BOLO had gone out.
Bunny was loved. People cared. Hopefully, one of the night-shift officers
would find her and transport her to the women's shelter. That was Natalie's best hope.

Her palms grew sweaty on the wheel. Throughout the years, every once
in a while, some ambitious rookie would pick up Bunny on charges of loitering or panhandling, and Luke would have to set them straight. Natalie
had personally escorted her friend to homeless shelters dozens of times
this past winter, in order to prevent her from freezing to death. Once in a
while, Bunny went missing, but she always showed up a day or two later.
It was a fine line between help and harassment.

This time was different.

This time was terrifying.

Blood on the jacket. Nine dead crows.

Natalie squeaked through a yellow light, then took the next exit, eased
her foot off the gas, and came to a stop in the roadside weeds next to a stand
of birch trees, their slim white trunks making a spooky contrast against
the dark woods. A few yards away, a crumbling stone wall encircled a large
meadow full of wildflowers, like a golden sheath of velvet in the moonlight.

Natalie's flashlight created liquid shadows as she headed toward the
centuries-old ruins of a colonial house covered in wild grapevines. She
walked past the old stone foundation and came to a carved-stone sundial
that'd fallen on its side. "Bunny?" she called out, parting the Queen Anne's
lace and sidestepping a broken terra-cotta pot. Sweet ferns and gentians
grew on the bank of a small pond, bordered by skunk cabbage and picker-
elweed. She found the cast-iron chair where Bunny sometimes sat in the
sun, next to a fallen statue whose limestone face had been chipped off.

The air smelled marshy sweet. Natalie's flashlight beam settled on a
small swarm of insects, their elliptical dance mesmerizing. Flitting and
darting in acrobatic loops. She watched their veined, gossamer wings

reflecting iridescent spikes from her flashlight beam and imagined Bunny trying to catch one in her hands.

Her ringing phone startled her. She checked the caller ID.

"Luke? Anything so far?" she asked anxiously.

"Nothing. You?"

"Nothing to report, but I'm still looking. I'm not giving up."

"She's done this before," Luke reassured her. "She always shows up eventually. At least it's not the middle of March."

"But she never goes anywhere without that jacket. I'm scared for her."

"Me, too," he admitted. "In the meantime, we found her abandoned shopping cart. I'm at the impound lot now, and there's something you should see."

"Be right there," she said and hung up.

39

Luke greeted her in the front office. "Murphy's coordinating with all local search-and-rescue organizations, along with department personnel and the police academy," he said. "We're putting together a team of volunteers and cadets tomorrow morning at dawn. In the meantime, we've issued a countywide BOLO, and the night shift will be canvassing for information on Bunny's whereabouts. Everyone is aware. Everyone is concerned."

He led the way through a maze of hallways toward the impound lot's suite of storage rooms on the ground level, past the entrance to the multi-level parking garage. He unlocked the storage suite, flicking on the lights as they walked into a windowless room, where the contents of Bunny's shopping cart were spread across the cement floor, fluorescent lights buzzing distractedly above their heads.

"Technically," Luke explained, "this cart is stolen property, so it's legal for us to search it without a warrant."

The room smelled bad. Natalie studied the items of soiled clothing, crumpled aluminum cans, several rolls of toilet paper, a broken MP3 player, moldy food in wrappers, receipts for coffee and snacks, a few battered paperbacks, a tattered blanket, old shoes, and more.

"We found the shopping cart inside the barn," Luke explained. "No sign of a struggle. The cart was upright. Bunny had lined dozens of water bottles and empties against the wall next to her sleeping bag, and nothing had been disturbed. We're having the blood on the army jacket tested. I've made it a priority. Also, we found this in the cart." He bent down and picked up an evidence bag with a dead crow inside.

Natalie's heart began to race. "Another one?" She took the bag and studied the dead bird. Its neck had been broken and twisted around several times so the head flopped over to one side. The tattered wings were pinned against the bird's body with a length of heavy-duty twine. "This looks like an initiation binding," she said, a sick awareness curdling inside her.

"What's that?" Luke asked.

"During Wiccan initiation rites, you stand with both arms behind your back, and the priest or priestess will loop a red cord over your left wrist, tie it with a square knot, then loop it over the right wrist, and up around your neck. It's called a binding, and it forms an inverted triangle."

"That's creepy."

"Joey used to say 'Treat every crime scene like a psychiatric examination, and you'll get closer to the heart of the matter,'" Natalie said. "What if the Crow Killer is initiating his victims? Maybe he has his own private version of Wicca?"

"A delusional version."

Something passed through her. A blurry awareness. She noticed the pink corner of a box sticking out from underneath a pile of clothes. "What's that?"

"Just an empty bakery box."

She pawed through the smelly clothing, shirtsleeves and pant legs braided together. Printed on the lid in red cursive was Sweetie's Bakery. She opened it. There was nothing inside but crumbs and smears of chocolate icing. "Daisy snuck out of the house a few weeks ago and bought these cupcakes for Bunny, according to Brandon."

"What do you mean—snuck out of the house?"

"She made up some excuse about needing more milk, but Brandon said they had some in the fridge. So he got suspicious and followed her across town to Sweetie's Bakery, then to the Hadleys' farm, where she gave Bunny the cupcakes."

"Why would Daisy lie about something as innocent as that?"

"I don't know." She dug through the rest of the trash, pulling things out and hoping to find other clues, but there was nothing of significance.

She sat back on her heels, peeled off her latex gloves, and said, "When I ran into her the other day, Bunny told me the Devil was watching her. So now I'm wondering . . . what if the Crow Killer's been to the Hadleys' farm, staking it out. Maybe he figured Bunny was an easy target?"

"Why leave so many clues behind? Nine dead crows. The markings on Teresa's grave. And now this crow in the shopping cart."

She repeated her theory. "He wants us to see him."

"Catch him, you mean?"

"No. *See* him. He feels invisible. He wants to tell his story."

"Or else it's a game," Luke said cynically. "Like walking up to the edge of a cliff without falling off. Maybe he thinks he's impervious."

"Or else he figures we aren't all that bright."

"He's right," Luke admitted. "All these years later, we're fucking clueless."

"Not anymore," she said.

"No. Not anymore."

She stood up and dusted off her hands. "I hope this is all a misunderstanding. I hope he doesn't have Bunny. God, I hope not. No way this turns into the Missing Ten. Not on my watch."

He shook his head, then said, "If he wants our attention, he'll like the name we've given him. The Crow Killer."

"Maybe if we put it out there, he'll contact us?"

"I'll give it a shot. In the meantime, we need a picture of Bunny for the missing-person poster."

She felt a spike of self-consciousness, as if someone were maliciously singling her out. "I know where to find one."

40

Around ten P.M., Natalie headed for the neighborhoods where Burning Lake's upwardly mobile professionals lived, full of historic homes designed by nineteenth-century architect Stanford White. Grace's Mini Cooper was parked in the driveway. The house was all lit up—porch lights, outdoor floods and spots, an interior yellow warmth. Natalie could see Grace and Ellie through the bay windows, having a heart-to-heart on the living-room sofa. She watched them for a moment, and then Ellie hugged her mother and went upstairs.

Natalie got out of her car, crossed the yard, and rang the doorbell.

Grace greeted her at the door. "Hey, Nat." She wore tight low-riding jeans and a red T-shirt with pink sequins on front that read LIFE IS A SEXUALLY TRANSMITTED DISEASE. Her skinny jeans hugged her slender hips and gave her a shot of youthful vigor.

"They let you run around like that?" Natalie teased.

"Hey, free speech. I can wear whatever I want inside my own home, can't I?"

"Don't let the PTA sluts see you."

"Ha. PTA sluts. That's a good one." Grace smiled weakly.

"How are you doing?"

"Better, thanks. I'm hate-watching some stupid reality show. Come on in." She drew Natalie inside with a warm maternal gesture.

"I know it's late, Grace, but I need to ask you a favor. We think Bunny's gone missing. Do you have any recent pictures of her?"

"Bunny? She's done this before, hasn't she?" she asked anxiously. "Gone missing? She always shows up a day or two later."

"We think it's different this time. I can't explain why."

"Hold on." Grace hurried upstairs with quick footsteps, and Natalie could hear her moving around directly overhead.

A few minutes later, Grace came bounding downstairs and handed her a framed photograph of the four of them—Grace, Bunny, Daisy, and Lindsey—taken at the women's shelter. You could tell it was Christmas from the decorations. "This was taken a few years ago. Daisy had copies framed for each of us. She was trying to get social services to move Bunny into her own apartment, maybe get her a part-time job, but it didn't pan out. You know Bunny. She won't stay on her meds for very long. This was the last time the four of us got together."

"Thanks, this is perfect," Natalie said.

"Did you check the A and P yet? What about the Goodwill? Sometimes she hangs out behind the library. . . ."

Natalie nodded. "I've been to all those places. We've got a BOLO out. All the guys will be looking for her tonight."

"What happened? Did she find out about Daisy and freak out?"

"I don't know," Natalie hedged, unwilling to fill her sister in on the details, which were much more grim.

"Because she loved Daisy. Daisy was the one who made sure we all stayed in touch." Grace rested her hand on Natalie's arm. "Why haven't you arrested him yet? Riley Skinner?"

"You know I can't discuss the case with anyone," she said gently, concerned about her sister's pallor, the miserable tension around her eyes.

"I keep getting questions from friends, students, other faculty members. The grocery clerk. The freaking gas station attendant. What's going on? When are the police going to make an arrest? What if the killer's still out there? We could all be in danger. They think I have access to the informa-tion, since you're my sister. I tell them I have no idea what's going on, but listen, everybody's scared. What happened was so horrifying. . . ."

"I know," Natalie said. "But we have to power through it."

She took a deep, uneasy breath. "That's it? You can't share anything else?"

"Can I sit down, Grace? I'd love a cup of coffee."

"Oh, sure. Of course."

Natalie took a seat in the living room while Grace went into the kitchen and started the coffeemaker. She got a couple of mugs down from the cup-board.

"Anyway, I'm glad you're here," Grace said, looking over at her. "Ellie and I had a long talk. She told me everything. She said you advised her to open up to me—and, by the way, thanks for that. The truth is . . . I knew she was experimenting," Grace said, coming back into the living room and folding her legs underneath her on the sofa while the coffee brewed in the kitchen. "God, I don't want her to grow up."

"Did she mention the parties, too?"

Grace blinked. "One party. Just the one."

"Right," Natalie said, tilting her head slightly.

"Anyway, I convinced her not to do it again. And I'm relieved she quit the coven. She's making the right decisions. The right choices. We talked about everything. She was very candid with me." Grace's eyes filled with tears. "Best conversation we've had in a while."

"Girl witches are just like anybody else. Searching for answers."

Grace cracked a smile. "Yeah, right. The first time I walked into Broom-stick Books, I was hooked. I remember those creaky old floors and the cramped little aisles dotted with melted candle wax. As soon as you walked through the door, you were hit with all these delicious lemony smells and the tinkle of wind chimes. Not to mention the free herbal tea. It was so otherworldly. So enchanting."

Natalie nodded, recalling her own experience. It had started with an intense friendship, a bond. Natalie and Bella wanted to be prettier, more popular. They wanted to be loved. Adored. So yes . . . blood-brown lipstick and faux leather jackets and combat boots. Crescent-moon jewelry and broomstick pins—why not? Menstrual cycles—blood rituals. *I wanna be a teen witch, fuck you.* You thought you could control it. You thought you could flirt with the dark side and never get hurt.

Natalie, Bella, Bobby, Max, and Adam had followed the instructions from books they'd checked out of the library. They made their own poppet doll using mud from the bank of the stream where Natalie had encountered the bogeyman. They put a curse on the boy with the birthmark. They got stoned and fooled around with the Ouija board and sought revenge. They got drunk on the expensive vodka Bobby snuck from his uncle's liquor cabinet—a yucky combination of vodka and orange soda you sipped through a straw. They sat in the ruins of the old theme park on the outskirts of town, the one place they loved to meet because it was so cut off from the rest of the world, and so hilariously weird—big goofy cement figurines of giants and elves and twisted old crones covered in crawling vines and out-of-control ivy. They got stoned on the Bridge to the Future and giggled as they conjured up spirits with the Ouija board. *Cross my heart, and hope you die.* The first night of her initiation into Wicca, Natalie had lost her virginity to Bobby Deckhart. For real.

"Natalie?"

She blinked. Her sister was handing her a cup of coffee.

"Oh. Thanks."

Grace sat down on the sofa again and took a careful sip.

"Do you still have Willow's old scarf?" Natalie asked.

"The purple one? Yeah, of course. Why?"

"This may sound strange, but I need to make sure you have it."

Heavy sigh. "Right now?"

"Humor me, okay?"

"Fine." Grace put down her coffee and went upstairs to the master bedroom. Bureau drawers slid open and shut. Wooden hangers coasted across the metal rod in the walk-in closet. Objects were moved around with small thuds.

She came downstairs empty-handed. "Hmm, that's odd. It's not up there. Which is weird, because I always keep it in the bottom bureau drawer." She heaved a frustrated sigh. "Well, sheesh . . . it's got to be around here someplace. It didn't just get up and walk away." She tilted her head. "Why? What do you need it for?"

"When was the last time Sadie Myers came to visit Ellie?" Natalie asked.

Grace furrowed her brow. "Ellie had a sleepover last week with the whole gang. India, Berkley, and Sadie. Why?"

"I think Sadie may have taken Willow's scarf. I saw her with it earlier."

Grace gave a precise little shiver. She stood up and called out, "Ellie?"

The girl shouted back, "What?"

"Can you come downstairs please?"

With feather-light steps, Ellie traipsed down the stairs into the living room, where she watched them anxiously. "What's up, Mom?" She looked like a child in her penguin pajamas.

"Did Sadie go into my room last week during your sleepover?" Grace asked.

Ellie's face flushed. "No, Mom. What are you talking about?"

"Well, someone took Aunt Willow's scarf."

"The purple one?" Ellie asked.

"Yes. Do you know where it is?"

"No, Mom." She shook her head, confused. She cringed as she landed in the armchair farthest away from them. "Sadie wouldn't do that."

"But Aunt Natalie just *saw* her with Willow's scarf."

"That can't be true," Ellie protested. "Maybe it just looks like it?"

"That scarf is batik. One of a kind. I couldn't find it in my bottom bureau drawer, where I always keep it. Suddenly it's gone." Grace sipped her black, sugary coffee in silence, then said, "You can't keep hiding things from me, Ellie. That's not how this works."

"But, Mom, I'm not hiding anything!"

"I want the truth."

Ellie sighed with deep frustration. There was a chilly space between mother and daughter that hadn't existed a few seconds ago.

Grace turned helplessly to Natalie. "Why would Sadie take it?"

"Personal belongings from powerful people or negative sources can make the curses much stronger," Natalie reminded her.

"Great. Now you're really freaking me out." Grace rubbed her forehead with her fingers, trying to wipe it smooth. "I've known these girls since they were in Pampers. Why would they do such a thing? Sneak into my room and steal that scarf?"

"Nobody stole it, Mom."

"Ellie, why did you quit the coven?" Natalie asked.

The girl's mouth drew taut. "I didn't like it."

"Why not? What happened to make you change your mind?"

The answer was obvious, right there in front of them, but Ellie didn't respond. She rubbed her anguished face, and Natalie had a flash memory of her as a baby, cradled in her mother's arms, wrapped in a mint-colored blanket—a marvelous bundle of needs, smelling of baby powder.

"Last Wednesday after school," Natalie said, "did Riley stop by Berkley's house? Did he visit the four of you there? It's really important, Ellie."

"No," she said with glaring self-righteousness.

"Are you sure?"

Eyes wandering. Lips quivering. She was hiding something.

Natalie took out her phone and scrolled through the images. She stood up and handed Ellie the phone. "Do you recognize this poppet doll?"

The girl sucked in her breath. "I don't think so," she hedged.

"Are you sure you've never seen it before?"

"I don't know." She handed the phone back.

"Can I see that?" Grace asked, and Natalie showed her the screen. "A poppet?"

"It was buried in Daisy's backyard," Natalie told her.

Grace gave Ellie a mortified look. "What the hell . . . do you know about this?"

"I wouldn't know anything about it," Ellie said, deeply offended.

"Don't lie to me, Ellie," Grace snapped.

"Mom, please," the girl pleaded. "Don't be mad at me."

"Ellie," Natalie said solemnly, taking a seat beside her. "Do you have any idea who could've buried this poppet in Daisy's backyard?"

"I don't know anything about it," she insisted. Eyes blazing with defiance.

"Is anyone going to explain what's going on?" Grace said.

"Ellie . . ."

The girl leapt to her feet. "I don't know!" she shouted, hurrying up the stairs and slamming her bedroom door. The house reverberated with an angry tension. It was as if a hurricane had blown through.

After a tense moment, Grace said, "God, what's going on? I thought we'd sorted everything out, and now this?"

Natalie glanced around at the comfy armchairs and river stone fireplace, the recessed lighting and hardwood floors, the sleek hardcovers from Barnes & Noble and glossy magazines piled everywhere, while a solemn stillness closed in around them.

"Are you going to tell me what all of this is supposed to mean?" Grace pleaded, looking haggard and defeated.

"I don't know for sure yet. I'm still trying to fit the pieces together."

"She stopped confiding in me months ago," Grace admitted. "I should've known something was up. It's like she stepped into another dimension where mothers aren't allowed."

"That's okay. Let's give her time."

Grace drew a troubled breath. "Now what?"

"I don't know. This is new territory for me, too, Grace."

"Kids are much more sophisticated than when we were growing up, Natalie." She picked up a framed photograph of herself as a teenager, posing with her swim team, and said, "Feels like forever ago, doesn't it?" She squinted at the old snapshot. "This has to be the worst haircut in recorded history."

"Nah," Natalie said with a smile. "You look pretty, as usual."

"I didn't feel so pretty. I felt ugly. But Dad suggested I take up swimming, and I lost all my baby fat, and everything changed after that. It was fun winning trophies for the girls' swim team, you know? For a while, Dad even thought I was Olympic material."

"Yeah. Thanks, Dad . . . no pressure."

Grace laughed. "Hey, remember Willow's hair? So swirly, like cotton candy. She looked like a doll, with a dusting of freckles over her face. 'Fairy dust,' Dad called it. But she was a fucking warrior. Remember the time she jumped off Devil's Point?"

Natalie bit her lower lip, confused. "Wasn't it you who jumped?"

"No. That was Willow."

"Funny, I don't remember it that way."

"Huh. You were probably too young to remember. Anyway, I had a huge crush on Gregg Lewis that summer. Remember him? What a loser he turned out to be." Grace laughed. "He sells condo shares in the Adirondacks now. Anyway, a bunch of us went up to Devil's Point that day, just for laughs. Willow and her friends came along, and Gregg was there . . . and all of us were fooling around, thinking we were so rad. We were the cool kids. Anyway, Willow announced she was going to jump off the cliff. Everyone became riveted, because there'd been two deaths that summer . . . two drownings . . . and we weren't supposed to even be there. But then, Willow said she would only jump if I jumped, too. Believe that?" Grace paused. Between those azure eyes, worries gathered and infiltrated. "I was scared to death of those cliffs. I knew I was an excellent swimmer but, come on, this was Devil's Point. People had died there. Kids hit the rocks and drowned. But Willow just walked over to the edge and jumped, and we all stood around in shock, staring down at the water. We didn't see her for the longest time, and I remember thinking, God, is she dead? What am I going to tell Mom and Dad? It felt as if I'd swallowed an anchor, but then, miraculously, her head bobbed out of the water, and she laughed and told me to jump. But I couldn't move. I was petrified."

"That wasn't fair of her," Natalie said, feeling protective of Grace. "You both could've drowned."

"She didn't mean anything by it," Grace hastened to explain. "She just wanted me to break the record for youngest diver ever to leap off Devil's Point, that's all. She wanted *me* to be the superstar that day. In her usual, Willowish way, she was trying to make me look good in front of Gregg. Boost my confidence. But I chickened out."

"Good for you," Natalie said. "I've pulled dead kids out of the lake, Grace. It's an ugly feeling. Just last year, a sixteen-year-old was impaled by a tree branch floating in the water. It was really wrong of Willow to put you on the spot like that."

"She didn't mean any harm by it," Grace said with a shrug. "She was hoping I'd dazzle them with my athletic prowess, because she'd seen me do triple somersaults off the diving board. Anyway, kids are dumb. They think they're immortal. And Willow was blind to reality in some ways. She didn't put any restrictions on her life, and she refused to see the negative side, only the positive. She took a lot of risks. She thought I should take risks, too, but she was special. All it did was make me feel like a loser."

"You? A loser?" Natalie scoffed. "You're the least loserish person I know."

"You have no idea what it was like for me, Natalie. First days of school were hell. All my teachers would gush about Willow. Big shoes."

"Well, guess what? You were my Willow. First day of school, all my teachers would say, 'Oh, you're Grace Lockhart's sister. Grace is fabulous! Grace is wonderful!'"

She made a funny face and laughed. "Bullshit."

"Seriously. You with your fucking academic excellence awards and your achievement awards and outstanding senior athlete trophies. Come on. Get real. Besides, you inherited Mom's magical blondness."

It was nice to see Grace laugh. "Yeah, right. I'm the crazy blond chick in the short shorts and the tube top. Me and my fabulous Crocs."

"Just be thankful you didn't get Dad's toes."

"Why? What's wrong with your toes?"

"They look like peanuts."

"I've got news for you, Natalie. Most people's toes look like peanuts. But come on. You're gorgeous, are you kidding me? Half the guys I dated couldn't keep their eyes off you. You little vixen." Grace stretched out her arms. "Besides, look at me now. I've got biceps like Jell-O and a big round face like a porridge bowl. And my ears stick out. I have to cover them with my hair."

"Quit boasting, you're making me sick."

"Hey. Once you get to know me, I can be quite humble."

They laughed about the past. It was a nice feeling.

Like the calm before the storm. A reprieve in the middle of so much evil.

41

Half an hour later, Natalie met Luke at a seedy watering hole that served the best cheeseburgers on the planet. Pour Richard's had cracked, stained linoleum tables, a low pine ceiling, and tacky floors from years of spilled beer. Don McLean's "American Pie" was playing on the jukebox. They ordered burgers and fries.

"What about your niece?" Luke asked. "Anything helpful?"

"Not really," Natalie said. "She denied knowing about Willow's scarf or the poppet doll. And she seemed genuinely shocked that one of her friends might've stolen it. But she's also aware that I found her bracelet in India's possession. I think she doesn't want to believe her friends are capable of such a betrayal. But Ellie quit the coven, and there could be animosity between them that Ellie isn't aware of yet, or that she isn't willing to admit to herself."

"Do you think she's telling the truth?" Luke asked.

Natalie put her burger down and wiped her mouth on a paper napkin. "I believe in her essential honesty, but . . ."

"But what?"

She looked down at her unfinished meal and pushed her plate aside.

"She was being evasive. I think she knows more than she's letting on. My hunch is that Riley dropped by Berkley's house sometime on Wednesday and they all got stoned. Drinking is one thing, but Ellie's never going to admit to smoking weed, not with her mother there anyway. I need to interview her without Grace being present. I'll try to arrange it."

Luke wiped his mouth on a napkin and said, "We've got a bit of good news."

"I could use some of that right now," she said hopefully.

"Riley's tox screen came back positive for synthetic marijuana," he said, "enough to do serious harm. Which supports Brandon's claim that he didn't use force. It'll help with the internal investigation. Also, Lenny found a match for Riley's prints on the receipt we found at the Mummy's Cabin. The supermarket's pulling the surveillance tapes for us."

"Which places him inside the cabin on Wednesday afternoon."

Luke nodded.

"If Riley left his house around three ten P.M.," she said, "and drove to the cabin, he would've arrived around three twenty-five. According to his buddies, he was planning on visiting India after school, which means that, at some point, he left the cabin and headed across town to Berkley's house. But we don't know how much time he spent at the cabin."

"Selling drugs isn't that time-consuming," Luke said offhandedly. "They give you a twenty, you give them a bag. It's a cash transaction, like a pizza delivery. For argument's sake, let's say the transactions in the cabin took a solid hour. And that's conservative."

"Okay, so around four thirty," she said, picking up the thread, "he drove over to Berkley's house to sell the girls some weed. So maybe he left Berkley's place at five thirty and went to talk to Daisy. That would only give him half an hour, but it's within the TOD."

"Right," Luke said.

"Still, it's a lot of unknowns." She rubbed the back of her neck, trying to get the kinks out. "Did Lenny find anything?"

Luke shook his head. "There was a lot of unidentified trace on the poppet—hairs and fibers, but no prints. Same with the pen and paper. He's focusing on separating and identifying the hairs and twine, but as for the rest, this thing has been underground for quite some time. Bad weather, degraded materials."

"Does he have an estimate for how long it was underground?"

"A few months to a year. He couldn't pin it down. But the army jacket tested positive for Bunny's blood type," he told her.

Natalie's stomach roiled, her fears swamping all other thoughts.

"It could be menstrual blood, or blood from a cut," he tried to reassure her. "At this point, anything's possible."

She clenched and unclenched her fists. "Now I'm really worried."

"It's not looking good."

Sometimes Bunny made her face as blank as possible, as if she were recharging her batteries. Back in high school, she'd been a bright, athletic kid with a cute overbite who got along with everyone. Now she lived on the streets and could possibly be the Crow Killer's next victim. It was grossly unfair. Natalie wished she'd done more to help her friend when she had the chance.

"Daisy's funeral is tomorrow," Luke told her. "Between that and the search and rescue for Bunny, we've got our hands full, so I'm assigning the task of extrapolating who could've received the B-minus from Daisy to Jacob. His caseload isn't as heavy as yours."

Natalie nodded and took out her phone. "I'll send him what I've got so far." She wanted a drink. A glass of wine. Craved it all of a sudden.

"We're coordinating tomorrow's search with the DWW. Jimmy Marconi has volunteered his time." Luke rested his elbows on the table and said, "Didn't you used to date him?"

"God, no." She laughed. "Jimmy? Shudder."

"Really? I thought you two were an item once?"

"An item? Stop. Seriously. You're thinking of Samuel Winston, and this was way back in college. It was a disaster. I was bored after five minutes, but the evening stretched on and on, like the Boston Marathon."

"Heartbreak Hill?" he said.

"Exactly."

He smirked. "I know the feeling."

"You dated Rainie Sandhill for a while, didn't you?"

Luke cringed. "She's a nice person. Always checking her text messages and talking about her kundalini. And you and Hunter Rose hooked up once, if I remember correctly."

"His Peter Pan act quickly lost its charm." She smirked.

"With that creepy salesman's smile of his," Luke added. "Too many bong hits back at the ranch. Have we dissed everyone yet?"

She laughed. "Not hardly."

"I love it when you do that," he said.

"Do what?"

"Laugh. You have this little line on your upper lip . . . like a smile above your smile." He waved his finger in the air. "Never mind. Scratch that."

"You're a hit-and-run flatterer."

"Am I? Shit." He smiled and picked up his burger.

Her face flushed as she tucked a strand of hair behind her ear.

"Anyway," he said, brushing it away, "let's not get sidetracked. God forbid."

"Speak for yourself. You've been getting sidetracked an awful lot lately."

"I know. It's not healthy." He stared at her, nakedly awake.

Her heart misfired. The warmth and pleasure of his company was overwhelming. She sensed his physical body across the table from hers. It was a distraction from the important issues, but Natalie had to acknowledge that something was happening.

She hesitated before saying, "My last relationship was such a train wreck that falling in love again feels like the kind of wild abandon I can't afford right now."

He gave her a half shrug. "I know what you mean."

"I'm over it. But it took a while."

"After my wife took our daughter away, it was like she'd ripped my heart out," he said softly. "The hardest part of my divorce was picking up the pieces. I hated that. Here I was, this tough-guy cop, struggling to control his emotions. But this job . . . this occupation where we're constantly reminded about the brutality and depravity of mankind . . . it's not easy being a law officer. It's a devouring job. You immerse yourself in the town's business. You know everybody's secrets, their shameful truths, and you somehow manage to keep it to yourself—you're like a priest that way."

The dynamic, loud, Friday night atmosphere of the bar faded around them as they huddled inside their exclusive bubble of intimacy and vulnerability.

"Remember Alma's Bar on Bearkill Road?" Luke went on. "The one with the mechanical Hawaiian lady dancing in the window? It got torn down last year. Anyway, your father used to sit in the corner by the jukebox, drinking vodka martinis and listening to Frank Sinatra. He didn't bother anyone. Two or three drinks, and then he'd head down to the lake to skim stones. I followed him one evening. I was a rookie cop at the time, and he was retired by then, but I loved the son of a gun. Anyway, after you went away to college, he missed you so much. He worried about you. We used to play golf together. Well, not exactly golf. Remember the Zambranos' dairy? They had a couple of black walnut trees growing on the property, and every September, the walnuts would drop off and litter the ground. Those husks are heavy and round as golf balls. Tony Zambrano hated it, because he couldn't mow his lawn without picking up hundreds of them first. So Joey and I would take our clubs over there, and Tony would join us, and the three of us would have a competition to see who could whack the most walnuts into the woods.

"One of those times, one of those beautiful, golden late summer days . . . Joey asked me a question. He said, 'What's the most important factor to skipping stones? What stops the stones from sinking into the lake?' And I said, 'That's easy. Angle, speed, and spin rate. If the stone hits the water too steeply, it'll sink. But if the angle's too shallow, it won't bounce.' He said, 'That's right.' He told me the perfect angle is twenty degrees. A flat stone is best, of course. The whole thing is about a transfer of energy. When you skip a stone, you're transferring energy from your arm into the stone. Just like when you swing a golf club, you're transferring energy from your body into the club." Luke shrugged. "So Joey said, 'Okay. But what's the *most* important factor?' Well, I didn't know. 'Stability,' he said. Stability is critical. Primates can't skim stones or swing golf clubs, because they have no stability. They can't balance on two legs. But human beings can. We can.

Stability is crucial to skipping stones, playing golf, and being a cop—that was his point. Police work means lots of grueling hours and follow-up interviews. All those homicides, suicides, car accidents, rapes, drug overdoses—all the evil you can see and smell and practically touch . . . what you need is a stable home life to keep you grounded. That's the secret to being a good cop, he said. Stability. That's what it's all about."

She stared at the ceiling, blinking the tears out of her eyes.

"Stability, he told me," Luke said softly. "Find it wherever you can, Natalie."

42

She drove home and put the teakettle on. Moonlight fell in icy squares on all the polished surfaces. The violet flowers on the dining-room table looked real until you touched them; they were made of fabric and coated with dust. Her mother's collection of yard-sale lamps gave the place its nostalgic glow.

Natalie took her cup of peppermint tea into the living room, sat at her desk, opened her laptop, then stared at the blank screen. Her fingers were shaking. She closed her eyes and watched vivid bursts of color painting the surfaces of her eyelids. It looked like an iridescent butterfly. She bit her lower lip and tried not to cry. Her face grew feverish. Her thoughts would not stop spinning.

The stick. The dead raccoon.

She logged on to the National Crime Information Center's database. The NCIC kept track of sex offenders, fugitives, repeat offenders, gang members, and terrorism. All across the country, the distinguishing body marks of criminals, such as tattoos, moles, birthmarks, and scars, were photographed as part of the booking process. However, as Natalie had discovered, the procedure wasn't universally enforced. Record-keeping errors were common, and older files could get lost, misplaced, or destroyed by fires. Also, the state databases weren't organized in the most efficient manner, either. There were categories for criminals and categories for victims, but it was impossible to make a positive ID if the keywords hadn't been entered properly.

You never knew how many incarcerated individuals had birthmarks until you searched through the national and state databases. Thousands upon thousands. It wasn't easy coming up with a list that fit the specific variables. Besides, nothing would help if the perp hadn't been registered in the first place. If Natalie's attacker had led a quiet life under the radar, she'd never find him in any of the databases.

Now she drew a troubled breath. She'd been searching for the bogeyman ever since she was a rookie cop. She'd tracked down a few promising candidates, but nothing had ever come of it. Not that she wanted to reopen old wounds. She kept trying to put it behind her, but this recent spate of violence brought it all screaming back. The attack in the woods had changed her on a primal level. It made her want to save the world. It made her strong. It made her believe in monsters.

Now she opened the menu, chose her selections, then keyed in the variables and cross-references, including race, sex, and age of the criminal. At the time of the attack, the boy was approximately five foot ten, a hundred and sixty pounds, eighteen or nineteen, perhaps older. Today, he would profile as a male Caucasian, thirty-five to forty-five. She left a lot of blanks: no name, no DOB, no hair or eye color. Just the distinctive birthmark—a port-wine-colored butterfly on the inner left arm.

Her last promising lead had occurred two years ago. Stewart Rawlins was a barrel-chested ex-con in a motorcycle jacket and straight-leg jeans. Late thirties. Cagey eyes. A natural-born bullshit artist. According to the NICC, he had a port-wine-colored birthmark on his arm. The description was vague enough to capture her imagination—a four-leaf clover. Four-leaf clovers were similar to butterflies in some people's eyes. Plus, he fit the general profile, so Natalie tracked him down on her off-hours. He lived in a village north of Albany, just a freckle on the map. She staked him out as if she were working undercover. She followed him into a bar one night and deliberately got him drunk.

Rawlins had distracting spaces between his teeth and comb-over hair you could see his glistening scalp through. At some point, the motorcycle jacket came off, revealing a Grateful Dead T-shirt and two fleshy arms leaning against the bar, but the geography of the birthmark wasn't the same. Rawlins was not the man she was looking for, and Natalie promptly left the bar. He followed her out the door, hollering, "Hey! Come back! Was it something I said?" She drove home feeling defeated that night, vowing never to put herself into such a bizarre situation again.

Now she couldn't resist. She hit Enter, and a list came onscreen. She selected Most Recent, but nothing new came up. She checked her watch and realized she was no longer officially on-call. Detective Augie Vickers would be taking over. She could relax. Maybe take a couple of sleeping pills tonight.

She felt ashamed of her feelings, which overwhelmed her occasionally. She hated the bogeyman, and yet he'd become such an alluring target. She couldn't stop thinking about him during her weakest moments; she wanted to catch him, fiercely; she wanted to catch the butterfly and kill it. She wanted to squash it flat, obliterating her bad dreams once and for all. The thought of it infuriated and excited her all at once.

She powered down her computer and went upstairs. She stood in the shower stall and scrubbed herself raw with a nailbrush—trying to rid herself of the last few molecules of the crime scene. Of Daisy. She closed her eyes, and a cluster of falling stars burst across her field of vision.

She toweled off, got dressed for bed, and swallowed two sleeping pills with a glass of tepid water. The house lights cast crawly shadows. She gazed out her bedroom window at the clamoring darkness across the street, where trees tossed lazily in the wind. Traffic was sparse on her dead-end road. Nothing supernatural lurked in those woods—even though, whenever the moon slipped behind the clouds, the landscape became bathed in mystery.

A heavy silence filled the house. Her thoughts grew stagnant. She went to bed and closed her eyes. Tomorrow was Daisy's funeral.

43

Natalie barely got six hours of sleep before it was time to go to work again. She took a shower, got dressed, gulped down her coffee, and drove across town to the police station. Luke had put Detective Peter Murphy in charge of the search-and-rescue mission. The more she got to know Murphy, the more she liked him. In his midforties, he had slick dark hair, a dour sense of humor, and heavy, Muppetlike eyebrows. He was insatiably curious and knew a lot of trivia.

"Sometimes they show up, Natalie," Murph said by way of a greeting. "You never know. Last year a hiker went missing in the park, and we searched for three days before discovering he was at home in Alabama with his family." He shrugged. "You have to think positive."

"How many volunteers showed up?" she asked.

"Thirty-five so far, including a retired veteran of the National Park Service and the vice president of a volunteer SAR organization from Vermont. The phones are ringing off the hook. We'll probably have a hundred more by this afternoon."

"Good," she said. "Where's the starting point for the operation?"

"The Hadleys' farm, the point last seen. We'll be increasing our range concentrically," he explained. "We've also got searchers stationed at the ten containment points—all of the places Bunny was known to frequent, like the A and P. They'll remain in those positions while the search is ongoing, in case she shows up. We're also going door-to-door, asking about potential sightings and handing out missing person posters. We've got a separate hotline for any new leads."

"What can I do?" Natalie asked.

"We're looking for volunteers to replace our guys in six to eight hours . . . we're doing rotating shifts."

"Okay, I can put in a few hours later today."

"Bunny's gonna be just fine," Murphy said.

"Those are comforting words, Murph."

"You have to learn to relax, Natalie. I'm reading this book called *Zen Anus*. It teaches you how to relax your asshole. It says that if you can relax your asshole, then everything else will fall into place."

She laughed. "Don't let this define you."

"I'll try not to. See you later."

She headed for the elevators and rode one down to the first floor. The station was crowded with volunteers and off-duty officers. On her way out the back entrance, Jimmy Marconi came strolling over.

"Natalie, how are you doing?" he asked.

"Thanks for volunteering, Jimmy."

"No problem. Samuel and the guys are here, too. We've got our people going deep into the woods, checking out clearings and creek beds that are off the main hiking trails. We've got dogs, but no helicopter—too sunny out."

Natalie nodded. Helicopters were not only expensive, they were less effective on sunny days like today, which cast too many shadows on the ground, obscuring the target.

"I hear Bunny's disappearance is connected to the Missing Nine?" Jimmy said, rubbing a red spot on his chin. "Is that true?"

"We're trying to tease out the details, but we recently found an unmistakable pattern to some of the old cases."

"What kind of pattern?" Jimmy asked.

"We need to dive further into it, but there were clues we'd managed to overlook."

"Clues connecting the nine cases? Like what?"

"Come on, Jimmy. I'm not willing to make any judgment calls yet."

He nodded, always courteous and respectful, but his face was tense with curiosity. "Sure, Natalie. I understand. But it might be helpful to the team if we knew this was the work of a serial offender, since they tend to be highly organized and forensically aware."

"All I can say is . . . it's a possibility."

"Okay." He nodded, crossing his arms. "Good to know."

"Thanks again, Jimmy. I'll be joining the search later on."

"We're doing group text messages to keep in touch with the volunteers," he said, taking out his phone. "Do we have your number?"

"I think so." She gave it to him again anyway, and they parted ways.

Natalie got in her car and drove over to St. Paul's Church, where half the town had shown up for Daisy's funeral. Every available officer who was not on the SAR mission was tasked with crowd control. It was their job to ensure that the church parking lot wasn't blocked by the army of satellite vans, and that the mourners weren't ambushed by obstinate news crews. They were also supposed to note down any suspicious-looking vehicles slowly driving past the church, or any oddly behaving funeral attendees.

An audience of 250 people was packed inside the church, with a spillover crowd of 200-plus mourners outside. Natalie's assignment was to develop a behavior profile of those in attendance—specifically Ethan Hathaway, Brandon Buckner, India Cochran, and her closest friends, along with Kermit Hughes, Owen Kottler, and Benjamin Lowell.

The mayor greeted Natalie at the church door as if he were campaigning for his next election. He wore his navy-blue Chamber of Commerce jacket and shook hands vigorously. Ms. Agatha Williamson played a moving "Amazing Grace" on the pipe organ. Brandon was surrounded by friends and family in the front row. His lawyer was in attendance, taking up valuable real estate. Natalie couldn't get anywhere near them.

Pink roses, lilies, and white orchids covered the chrome-handled oak coffin like a parade float. Daisy's parents moved with halting steps down the aisle toward their pew. Jasmine Forester wore a black dress with a white lace collar. She steadied herself by clinging to her husband's trembling arm.

Grace and Ellie were seated in one of the middle rows. Grace wore a subdued dove-gray outfit and kept a tissue pressed to her lips. Ellie had tamed her wild black hair, combing it behind her ears and securing it with a pink headband. Lindsey Wozniak sat next to Grace. She wore a Christian Dior dress and gold jewelry, unafraid to flaunt her success. Bunny hadn't shown up—a faint hope on Natalie's part.

Ethan Hathaway sat in the back row, looking shell-shocked and isolated. A few rows in front of him, India Cochran sat next to her dad, who kept checking his phone messages. Berkley and Sadie were nearby with their families. None of Riley's friends had shown up to honor their dead teacher.

Natalie stood in back and observed them all, taking mental notes.

The service was straightforward. The Reverend Thomas Grimsby gave a heartfelt eulogy. "Daisy is with God, for . . . surely, if there's a waiting room in heaven, then she'll be the first in line." There were tearful remembrances. "Today we celebrate her life."

When it was over, Brandon and five pallbearers slow-walked the coffin out of the church toward the waiting hearse. A solemn parade of mourners followed, and then everyone got in their cars and joined the funeral procession across town toward the cemetery.

Forty-five minutes later, hundreds were gathered beneath the sprawling oaks of Pioneer Memorial Park. Everything shimmered in the stained-glass sun. The burial mound was at the top of a hill. There were heavy bulldozer imprints on the grass. They stood among carved limestone markers, granite headstones, and ornate brownstone urns with Gothic and Egyptian motifs. Between two large floral arrangements was a propped easel displaying an airbrushed photograph of Daisy.

"She looks so happy," everyone agreed.

People kept their voices low and their tissues handy. There were anguished faces and lowered eyes. Carved into Daisy's brand-new marble headstone was an angel, her wings spread protectively over the hole in the ground. Natalie held back and observed relatives and family friends closest to the grave site. Brandon stood as rigid as a monolith. Grace was sobbing silently into her tissue. Lindsey and Ellie were trying to comfort her.

Daisy's students and fellow teachers were holding heart-shaped balloons, which they planned to release at the end of the ceremony. The reverend spoke at length about Daisy's accomplishments, and then others stepped forward to eulogize her.

Jasmine Forester's good breeding showed in her comportment—head held high, chin thrust forward, breathing rapidly through her nose. "Daisy used to light up a room," she said. "Why would anyone want to harm such a beautiful human being?" She ended by saying, "We've been through hell. We need closure." She glanced at Natalie. "We want to know what happened to our precious girl."

Next, the pallbearers placed the coffin on a contraption that painstakingly lowered Daisy and her unborn child into the ground. Natalie listened to the mechanical hum of the lowering device and watched the casket disappear behind the stacks of sod.

Feelings welled up, threatening to overpower her. She recalled Willow's razor-straight bangs and her long ashen hair catching the sunlight and blowing loose around her shoulders. Elegant, articulate Willow used to keep junk food in the trunk of her car, an old Chevy Nova they called the Snoozemobile because of its lousy acceleration. Joey had given it to her on her sixteenth birthday, and Willow used to love cruising around in that thing. She'd taken Natalie, Grace, and Daisy for rides in the mountains, and they'd crank the radio and sing along to Laura Nyro's "Wedding Bell Blues." Whenever they stopped to explore a hiking trail, Willow would take deliberate, delicate steps across the rocks, as if it was a decision she'd made to be graceful.

Now prayers were said. More tears were shed. Finally, the mourners took turns scooping handfuls of dirt onto the casket, and the students and teachers released their balloons. Silver hearts filled the sky.

After it was over, Natalie tracked down Reverend Grimsby. "Now's probably not the time," she apologized, "but Daisy made an appointment to see you about an urgent matter, I understand."

"Yes," he said with warm gray eyes.

"Do you know what she wanted to discuss with you?"

He pursed his lips and glanced around. "I couldn't possibly share her confidences with you, but I can say she wanted to speak about spiritual matters."

"Reverend, please. This is important."

"The good news is . . . she was coming back to the church. She admitted she'd been drifting away. But the baby was drawing her back to God. I saw it as a positive sign. Now if you'll excuse me . . ."

"Anything else you can tell me?" Natalie asked.

"No, I'm sorry. Now if you'll excuse me, Detective." He disappeared into the crowd.

There was a commotion behind them. Natalie turned to face the Revolutionary Monument, beyond which Dominic Skinner and a few friends were stepping out of their four-wheelers onto the cemetery access road. She hurried toward them. Dominic and his crew weren't dressed for a funeral—he wore camouflage pants, an Incubus T-shirt, a backward baseball cap, and a ramped attitude. The others were dressed in a similarly disrespectful fashion.

"Dominic, what are you doing here?" she said in a hushed voice.

Pent-up fury roiled behind the ex-con's eyes. "My son's still in a coma. They don't know if he'll ever come out of it. Brandon used excessive force. He acted like a thug, not a law officer. He needs to pay for what he did," he said angrily.

"Let's wait and see what the internal investigation says," she told him, a contraction of muscles pushing an acrid taste into her mouth.

"Oh, right. I'm supposed to buy that? The police investigating the police?" he spat, maintaining his menacing posture, feet firmly planted on the cracked asphalt. The three other men stood mute and immobile behind him, like a primitive diorama of alpha males.

"I'm not going to argue with you," Natalie said. "This isn't the time or the place."

"He should be locked up in jail," Dominic said in a tortured voice. "Riley was trying to get away, and Brandon went after an unarmed child, and you know it."

"Quit spreading rumors. You're only making things worse."

"Look at those reporters back there," he said through gritted teeth. "Nobody wants to talk to me about my son, who's also a victim."

Her hands were shaking. She felt a sharp, sympathetic pinch. If Riley died, then Dominic would enter another dimension, an alien world where he'd spend the rest of his life imagining what could've been. Parents of murdered children spent their entire lives with their hands pressed against a thick, impenetrable membrane, trying to see through to the other side.

Above their heads a canopy of leaves quivered in the breeze, but despite the brilliance of the sky, today felt as oppressive as a dungeon.

"You need to go home, Dominic," Natalie told him gently.

He shook his head stubbornly. "I have every right to be here."

"Think of the Foresters," she pleaded. "They're also grieving. They lost their daughter—at least your son has a chance. Let them bury her in peace."

He looked stunningly worn-out.

"Think of Daisy's mother," she pleaded. "This is her time. Please, Dominic."

After a tense moment, he gave a reluctant nod, and he and his men slowly retreated, unwinding their hostility and saving it for another day.

Natalie's limbs felt rubbery as she stood her ground, waiting for the four-wheelers to take off. She watched them drive toward the cemetery gates, past row upon row of headstones stretching off into the distance. *Harriet Truitt, Ezekiel Pastor, Clementine Leacock.* Every Halloween, Pioneer Memorial had to hire extra guards to patrol the park so the kids wouldn't vandalize the graves. The cemetery gates were locked at night, but there were gaps in the ornate, wrought-iron fence where a skinny teen could sneak through.

Her phone buzzed. It was Augie Vickers.

"The court order came through for Riley's phone service providers. I sent you the link—did you get it yet?"

She checked her emails. "Yeah, got it."

"Subscriber billing and account information, call-detail records, cell tower locations, plus all stored voice-mail messages, photographic and video images. We've been combing through the data, and the only thing of significance so far are his locations for Wednesday afternoon."

"Tell me," she said anxiously.

"Bear in mind, this is only accurate to within about three hundred feet, but it appears Riley was en route to the cabin at three fifteen P.M. when he made a pit stop at the supermarket. Looks like he left the cabin at around four oh-six and drove to the east side, where he stopped in the vicinity of Berkley Auberdine's house between four twenty-eight until five oh-two. Then he left at five thirty-five, heading north, at which time he must've turned off his phone, or else the battery ran out of juice."

"What about the rest of the evening?"

"Nothing. That's it. We're still sorting through the data. Anyway, the lieutenant wants me to reinterview Riley's buddies about Haymarket Field, exactly what they talked about that night, what was his frame of mind, et cetera."

"Okay. Thanks for the update, Augie." She hung up and sensed a shifting of the wind. Her hands were trembling from caffeine withdrawal. Above her head, the spring leaves quivered in the breeze. The burial service was over. Everyone was dispersing. She searched the crowd but couldn't find Grace and Ellie anywhere.

Then she spotted India's silver Lexus gliding along the access road toward the cemetery gates. She would have to hurry if she wanted to catch up.

44

The wind blew the litter off the sidewalks into the street sweeper's bristling maw. Natalie followed the Lexus past the quaint three-story shops of downtown, where the clubs were always packed on the weekends. The ER would be busy pumping stomachs on Sunday. Upstate New York boasted enough Dunkin' Donuts, Starbucks, and Burger Kings to satisfy anyone's weekend hangover.

Now the Lexus turned down the road leading to the peninsula, and Natalie's nerve endings hummed. The girls had flat-out lied to her—she had proof of it now. Riley's phone logs showed he'd spent about thirty minutes in the vicinity of Berkley's house that afternoon. What had transpired? What did they know?

She could see the glistening pewter surface of the lake through the tree trunks. This area teamed with lakes. During the warmer months, tourists flocked to Burning Lake to partake of the bountiful woods and waterways. For the rugged outdoorsy types, there were plenty of diversions and people were regularly getting injured or lost in the mountains. Emergency response came from a network of agencies—rangers, state police, local rescue crews, along with the county fire rescue team and the water rescue team—covering a vast geography of woodlands and wetlands, thick and rolling as a fairy-tale kingdom.

The silver car slowed as it approached the entrance to Abby's Hex. Natalie kept her distance, while the girls got out and took the trailhead into the woods. She waited, drumming her fingers on the steering wheel, before finally swinging into the lot and taking the sun-dappled path onto the peninsula.

Once she'd reached the tip of the peninsula, she hung back and observed them—India, Berkley, Sadie, and their new recruit, Angela Sandhill, a demure girl with a self-conscious theatricality about her movements. They'd formed a circle around the fire pit.

"It's stupid to do everything in one night," Berkley said.

"We've already decided," India insisted. "We should stick to the plan."

"Do you think it'll work?" Angela asked.

"Of course it will work," India shot back. "It's worked before."

Sadie made a disgusted sound at the back of her throat. "Will you stop already?"

"Angela, don't be dumb," Berkley said.

"Okay. Whatever." Angela shrugged.

They began to chant. Softly, at first. Building slowly. Natalie didn't recognize the divination. It had been such a long time since she'd performed any Wiccan rites herself. She noticed a burnt-rubber smell in the air before spotting a small plume of smoke in the fire pit.

She stepped out of the woods. "What are you girls up to?"

They turned at once and let out gasps of astonishment.

"Aunt Natalie?" India clasped her throat. "What are you doing here?"

"I have a few more questions," she said, stepping into the clearing. "We've subpoenaed Riley's phone service records and have him within three-hundred feet of Berkley's house between four twenty-eight and five oh-two P.M."

India shook her head numbly, while the others glanced cautiously at one another. Natalie knew not to let her personal relationships interfere with an investigation, but her instructors never told her how hard this would be. She wanted to embrace them and tell them that everything would be all right.

"Are you still saying you didn't see him Wednesday after school, India?"

"No," she responded with a shudder. "I mean, maybe he drove by the house, I suppose, but we didn't see him. Maybe he parked on the street or something? I mean, ew. Dude. Go away." She was intractable.

Natalie drew a patient breath. "Did Riley know that you put a curse on Ms. Buckner?"

"What?" she cried. "Who told you that?"

"Did you tell him about the B-minus you got in sociology? Did you tell him you wanted Ms. Buckner to suffer for it?"

She stared at Natalie with deep hostility.

"Did you talk him into harming her, or at least approach him about it?"

"Approach him? What's that supposed to mean?" India shook her head, her long hair flowing across her shoulders in raven waves. "This is ridiculous." She took out her phone. "My father told me to call him if this happened again."

"Okay, fine. Call him."

India hesitated.

"Go ahead," Natalie said, calling her bluff.

India scowled. "Maybe you should go," she suggested.

"No, you're right, India. You don't have to talk to me. You can all leave now."

"But . . ."

"You aren't supposed to be lighting fires in the state park."

India's eyes widened, while the other girls froze.

"Go. All of you."

After a moment's hesitation, they hurried past her and vanished into the woods.

Natalie stood studying the calm surface of the lake. Any time beachgoers or swimmers were reported missing, dozens of first responders and rescue vehicles would show up at the scene. The dive team, attached by ropes to the shore, would search the lake bottom, while the beach patrol linked hands with dozens of volunteers and waded into the reedy part of the lake. At some point, they may have to do that for Bunny.

The burnt smell lingered on the air. She walked up to the fire pit, where the girls had left several smoldering pieces of paper on the blackened stones. She stomped out the embers, smoke whispering from the charred pages.

She knelt to retrieve one of the pages and read a few lines. Her palms grew black with ash. Her cheeks flushed. She felt indignant and incredulous. What she read shocked her.

45

Natalie could feel the blood thundering in her ears as she left the lake behind and took a right onto Crenshaw Road, which led to the quiet neighborhood where her sister lived. She pulled into the driveway and parked behind Grace's Mini Cooper.

Once Grace and Ellie were gathered in the living room, Natalie took out the semiburnt pages she'd rescued from the fire pit and unfolded them on the coffee table, pressing them flat. "I found these today."

"What are they?" Grace leaned forward.

"Ellie," Natalie said. "Why don't you explain to your mother?"

Ellie shrank from them both. Her pale blue T-shirt read COLLEGE-BOUND.

"What's going on?" The strain showed on Grace's face. "What is this?"

"Ellie and Justin Fowler exchanged a couple of letters, Grace. These partially burnt pages are all from Justin to Ellie."

"My God, Ellie? Is this true?" Grace picked up one of the pages and read a few lines. Then she sat back with her mouth open, utterly blown away.

Ellie studied her mother with trepidation, a light sweat coating her upper lip.

"Why on earth would you do such a thing?" Grace asked, looking more fragile than Natalie had ever seen her.

"Mom, please . . ."

"You wrote letters to him *in prison*?"

Ellie glanced at the stationery and cringed. "It was for a school report."

"A report? Is this some kind of joke?"

"I didn't think he'd write me back," she protested weakly.

Grace turned to Natalie. "Where'd you get these? Why are they burnt?"

"India, Berkley, and Sadie lit them on fire," Natalie explained.

"Why?"

"I don't know. Some sort of ritual. They were chanting."

"Ellie, how did your friends get these letters?" Grace demanded. "They're addressed to you. I don't understand. I've tried my whole life to keep you safe. How could you do something like this without telling me?"

"Mom, please. It's no big deal."

"No big deal?" she repeated angrily.

Ellie's face grew ashen.

"Grace, can I talk to her?" Natalie asked.

"Go ahead," Grace said, tears glistening in her eyes.

Natalie gave her niece her undivided attention. "Ellie, tell me what happened."

The girl took a moment to catch her breath. "I was curious," she confessed, "about how Aunt Willow died. I mean, Mom already explained it to me, but I wanted to find out for myself. So I looked him up online and read everything I could about the trial, and it's pretty awful. But then I found a few articles about him being locked up in prison for a crime he didn't commit, and so—"

"Oh God." Grace dropped the letter on the coffee table.

"Mom, there's proof on his lawyer's blog . . . proof of his innocence and police corruption. You should read it sometime. At least there should be another trial, but the DA refuses to consider it. Anyway, I told India about it, and she said I should write to him. I didn't think he'd write back, but he did. So I wrote to him again. But after the third time, I freaked out a little, and so I stopped."

"When was this?" Natalie asked.

"Last October. But Justin kept sending me letters. I had to check the mailbox every day after school before Mom got home." Ellie glanced at her mother and blushed. "Mom, I'm really sorry."

"How many times did he write to you?" Natalie asked.

"Eight or nine."

"And what did you do with his letters?"

"I gave them to India," she admitted.

"Why?"

"Because . . . she said they were powerful."

"Powerful?" Grace gasped. "He stabbed your aunt Willow twenty-seven times. My God, don't you dare feel sympathy for that bastard. Nobody's going to weep for Justin Fowler when he's gone. I mean . . . how could this happen? I didn't raise you to act this way."

"At least it's out in the open," Natalie said quietly, trying to keep everyone calm.

After a choked-up moment, Grace said, "Excuse me. I'll be right back." She went upstairs. The door to the master bedroom thumped shut.

Once they were alone together, Natalie asked Ellie, "You told me you quit the coven right after Ms. Buckner died. Why did you quit at that moment?"

Ellie was looking stunned, dazed—but she sounded relieved to be unburdening herself. "Being a witch was fun for a while, but then . . ." Tears spilled down her cheeks. "After Ms. Buckner died, it stopped being fun anymore. Besides, I didn't think anything bad was going to happen to her . . . otherwise I never would've done it."

"Done what?"

Ellie whispered, "Put a death spell on her."

"A death spell?" Natalie repeated, stunned to hear these words coming from her niece's mouth. "Are you talking about the poppet doll?"

She nodded. "We all made it together. India, Berkley, Sadie, and me."

"And you buried it in Daisy's backyard? When?"

"About six months ago. We snuck over there when nobody was home."

"Why?" Natalie asked, struggling to understand.

"Because we wanted to curse her. We all hated her," Ellie admitted.

"Hated Daisy? Why?"

Ellie took a sharp breath, eyes shiny with innocence. "Because Mr. Hathaway was *in love with her*. And India said we should do something about it."

Natalie's heart pulsed with a dull ache. She was losing altitude fast. "So you put a death curse on Ms. Buckner because you were jealous of her?"

The girl's face crumpled with remorse. "It's not like we expected anything to happen. We only *wished* she was dead. And we definitely didn't kill her, Aunt Natalie, I promise. We felt horrible about it when we heard the news."

"And you did this because you had a crush on Mr. Hathaway?"

She took a swipe at her tears and nodded glumly. "We loved him."

"All of you? You all wanted Daisy to die?"

Her voice wobbled. "She was *fucking* him."

Natalie drew back. "How do you know?"

"Everybody knows. The whole school knows. You could tell by the way he looked at her. The way he talked to her." Fresh tears scaled down Ellie's cheeks, and she brushed them away.

Natalie couldn't square the circle. She felt a throbbing pain inside her head. "Ellie, promise me you didn't have anything to do with her death. Tell me the absolute truth."

"I would never do anything like that," Ellie protested.

"What about India?"

She burst into tears. She collapsed on the arm of the chair and sobbed.

Natalie was overcome with pity. She moved closer to her niece and rested her hand on the girl's trembling shoulder. "Shh. Everything's going to be all right. Please stop crying." She waited for the sobbing to subside, terribly conflicted. Afraid for Ellie, but at the same time relieved. Maybe now the truth could come out. Maybe now the case could be solved. But her niece couldn't possibly be involved. Could she?

Ellie regained her composure and gazed at Natalie through a glaze of anguish. "India threatened to put a hex on me if I didn't write to Justin. She said she'd ruin my life."

"Why?" Natalie asked.

Grace was standing at the bottom of the stairs, holding her leather bag and looking at her daughter. "India threatened you?"

Ellie hunkered into herself, curling up in the wide embrace of the armchair.

"Why did India threaten you?" Natalie pressed. "Why were Justin's letters so important to her?"

"I don't know," Ellie insisted. "But she made me do it."

Natalie suspected that all four girls, including Ellie, had wanted to see what would happen if she wrote to Justin Fowler in prison. She figured her niece was attempting to push the blame away from herself.

Grace sat down on the sofa and turned to Natalie with agonized eyes. "How can this be?"

"Ellie, do you know who killed Ms. Buckner?" Natalie asked, pressing the point.

"They're all saying Riley did it," she answered flatly.

"What about India? Could she or Berkley have had anything to do with it?"

"No." She recoiled. "None of us had anything to do with it."

"Are you sure?"

Doubt creased her brow. "Sadie and I were really sad after it happened. We were both shaking. We couldn't help thinking . . . maybe those curses worked? Sadie and I felt terrible about it, but India and Berkley . . . they were cracking jokes. Almost as if they were glad she was dead. That's why I quit the coven."

"The day after Ms. Buckner died? Last Thursday?"

"I couldn't deal with it."

"Do you think Riley killed her? Do you think he might've done it for India?"

"I don't know." She blinked as if she hadn't thought of that before.

"What's so appealing about him? Mr. Hathaway?"

Ellie brightened a little. "He's different from most of our teachers. He doesn't lecture you for fifty boring minutes. He says, 'Forget the notes. Eyes and ears, people.'" She warmed to her topic. "Once, he put up a Nerf basketball hoop in the back of class, and we shot baskets while reciting poetry. It was fun. He makes things exciting. He cares about us."

"Tell me where you were last Wednesday," Natalie said.

"Over at Berkley's."

"Doing what exactly? Tell me everything."

Ellie glanced warily at her mother.

"Could you give us a second, Grace?" Natalie asked.

Grace bit her lower lip, trying to contain her fear. She got up from the sofa, red-faced, and went into the kitchen.

Once she was gone, Ellie admitted softly, "Riley dropped by."

"He dropped by, and then what?" Natalie coaxed. "What did he do?"

"I don't know. I had to leave, because of the deathiversary. But Riley came over around four thirty, and I left a little before five. I rode my bike home."

"What happened between four thirty and five?"

She wiped her nose with the back of her hand and said, "We just talked."

"Was Riley part of the coven?"

"No." She shook her head. "Girls only."

"But he's into witchcraft?"

"I don't know. Sometimes India would let the boys hang out with us. But other times, she didn't want them around. She changes her mind a lot. Once, she put a curse on Riley because he sold her a bag with too many twigs. She said it was karma."

"So then, India does buy her drugs from him?"

Ellie cringed. "She doesn't do hard drugs."

"Weed? A couple of joints?"

"Ellie, don't tell me you smoke pot," Grace said, stepping into the living room.

"Mom, no," Ellie pleaded, emotionally fragile. "I never hold the smoke in my lungs. Same with drinking, like I told you."

"Okay, that's enough, sweetie." Grace went over to her and put a hand on her daughter's arm. "Stop talking."

"Why?" Ellie asked. "What's wrong?"

"Natalie, I'm sorry," Grace said. "You have to go."

"But, Mom . . ."

"Don't say another word, Ellie. Go upstairs. Now."

Ellie gave her aunt a hesitant look before hurrying up the stairs.

"Sorry, Natalie," Grace said, escorting her to the door. "But I can't let you continue to grill her like this."

"Grace, think about it. I'm trying to find out who killed your best friend."

"I know, but you have to understand. My daughter needs me right now," she said. "I won't always be able to protect her from all the bad things in the world, but I can protect her now. Right now, when she's the most vulnerable. Good night," she said, closing the door in Natalie's face.

46

It was half past midnight by the time Natalie pulled into her driveway. Lethargy had set in. Exhaustion claimed her. She trudged up the porch steps and went inside.

She'd spent the afternoon and evening searching for Bunny, following up on any new leads. Now she checked the Weather Channel. Another storm front was headed their way. Today's search had ended in failure. They would have to start again in the morning. Every year, thousands of missing person cases were investigated by SAR teams across the country. They used survivability statistics to determine when to call off a search. It was always a tough decision. This one would continue for ten more days—or for as long as Bunny would be able to survive in the wilderness. That window could narrow, depending on the severity of the storm.

She checked her watch. Luke was coming over in twenty minutes for a debrief. He hadn't been to her house since she and Zack had thrown a barbecue last summer, and now she looked around the place, trying to see what other people saw. Last autumn after Zack took off, Natalie had painted the kitchen green and the hallway yellow in an attempt to brighten up the place, with disastrous results. Now she stood in the living room, assessing the mismatched furniture and ugly throw pillows, her books in their rifled-through boxes, a pile of laundry on the sofa, stacks of files on the chairs. Nostalgia usually clouded her vision, but tonight everything looked cheap and embarrassing. No wonder Zack had disparaged her "crib," but the fact that he'd called it a crib in the first place should've clued her in.

There wasn't enough time in the day to do all the things Natalie wanted to do with her life, so she'd let it all drift. The house, the yard, her personal issues. She couldn't seem to change directions. She couldn't get unstuck.

Maybe she was waiting for something. A catalyst. An idea to magically beam itself inside her head, like a sci-fi movie. Like *The Day of the Triffids*. A foreign body burrowing into her and transforming her into a whole new person.

Anyway, her big excuse . . . she had her hands full.

Now she did the dishes, took out the garbage, and cleaned up as best she could.

Just as she finished, a pair of headlights flared across the ceiling, and a car engine died outside. She peeked out the living-room window. Luke stepped out of his Ford Ranger, a tall athletic-looking man washed in amber moonlight, like a sepia-tinted photograph.

She'd been expecting him but couldn't help feeling a nervous flutter in the pit of her stomach. The house was a mess. She was a mess. He rang the doorbell. "Just a minute!" She smoothed her hair behind her ears and opened the door.

He handed her a bottle of wine. "Housewarming gift."

"Hey, thanks."

"You're officially no longer on-call."

She stepped aside, and he moved into the house with a loping, predatory grace, carrying a woodsy smell in with him.

"Nice paint job," he observed.

She cringed at the yellow hallway walls. "Yeah, well, I'm quietly mortified."

"Didn't these walls used to be white?" he asked.

"A few years ago."

"Don't they sell white paint at the hardware store anymore?"

"Ha. You're funny. Two days in a row. I swear I'm going to get my act together eventually. In the meantime . . ." She showed him into the living room. "Have a seat."

He balked. "Any suggestions?"

"Create a space."

He moved a bunch of reports off a chair and sat down. "Some days it seems all I do is push paperwork from one side of my desk to the other."

"Sucks to be you."

He laughed. "You like paperwork, do you?"

She smiled.

"Seriously, though. How're you holding up?" He folded his arms and studied her carefully.

"Not great," she admitted. "I can handle the workload. It's just that there's a lot of information to process."

"So let's start with this morning. Walk me through it."

Natalie debriefed him on the day's events, and when she was done, Luke said, "They buried the poppet in Daisy's yard?"

She nodded. "Ellie admitted to everything. They were jealous of Daisy. They found out about the affair. Daisy and Hathaway weren't as discreet as they thought they'd been. Anyway, Ellie insists she and her friends had nothing to do with the murder."

"Do you believe her?"

"I believe my niece, but she could be wrong about her friends. I asked if she thought it was possible India might've persuaded Riley to harm Daisy in some way, and Ellie waffled. Apparently India and Berkley were laughing and joking on Thursday, after the news broke. Now this thing with the letters—I think it's possible that India, Berkley, and Sadie, along with Angela Sandhill, their new recruit . . . were hexing Ellie for abandoning them. Or else she knows something, and they're trying to intimidate her into silence. Grace stopped the interview as soon as Ellie admitted they were smoking pot."

He nodded slowly. "So Ellie might know something about it, but she's too scared to tell you."

"It took her a long enough time to fess up," Natalie said with a heavy heart. "Meanwhile, Grace has gone into protective mode. I'll give her a call tomorrow, after she's calmed down. Maybe I can persuade her to bring Ellie into the station for a formal interview. I'll tell Grace we need to eliminate Ellie as a suspect, that might motivate her."

"Look," Luke said, leaning forward. "I don't believe Ellie's guilty of anything, either. I've known her since she was a kid. But the question is . . . did she witness a murder? Did any of these girls witness the murder? Or was it worse than that? Did they participate?"

Natalie shuddered at the thought. "Ellie left Berkley's house shortly before five o'clock and rode her bike home. If we can verify that, then she's got an alibi."

"Okay, that leaves the three of them, plus Riley."

"We can't forget about Hathaway," Natalie reminded him. "No alibi. He didn't want to break up with Daisy. She could've been carrying his child."

"When's the polygraph scheduled for?"

"Tomorrow afternoon."

"How did Hathaway act at the funeral?"

"He stayed in the background and left early. I was surprised he showed up at all, considering the affair's out in the open now, but he clearly had deep feelings for her."

"Or else he's a Machiavellian sociopath."

Natalie nodded. "Let's see what the polygraph tells us. Meanwhile, I got your message about the supermax facility. Thanks for setting up an appointment with the warden."

"Tomorrow morning, nine o'clock sharp." He rubbed his chin thoughtfully. "Are you ready for this? Would you like some company?"

"No, I'll be fine."

Outside, a strong breeze stirred the fir trees.

"Anything else?"

"Not that I can think of." She thumbed the numbness out of her eyes.

"Running on fumes?"

"Pretty much."

"Get some sleep." Luke's phone rang, and he picked up. "Hello? Yes, sir." He cupped his hand over the receiver. "It's the chief. You all set here?"

"Yeah, thanks for the wine."

"Don't drink it all tonight." He smiled at her, then headed out the door.

Natalie got a bottled water from the fridge and took a couple of Ambiens, wanting the fog of sleep to roll across her brain and snuff her out like a candle. She wondered if she could handle the demands of the task ahead, but, like Joey used to say, "If you can't handle it, just pretend."

47

Merryville Correctional Facility was situated in one of the most beautiful places on earth, twenty miles south of the Canadian border. The morning sunlight sharpened every lime-green bud on every tree for miles around, and in the distance you could see the mountains with their toothy spires and ragged fissures.

The supermax prison sat on eighty acres of pristine wilderness and housed some of the state's worst criminals. The staff was polite and professional. Natalie filled out a visitor's form and stopped at the security checkpoint for a pat down.

A beefy guard with a crew cut escorted her to the warden's office in the east wing. Warden Edward Northcutt had the look of a man who'd forfeited his soul a long time ago—weathered, rumpled, and as if he hardly ever slept. "Welcome to MCF, Detective Lockhart. Please, have a seat."

"Thank you, Warden."

"First of all, I wasn't aware of the situation until I received Lieutenant Pittman's call last night. You can rest assured, this sort of thing won't ever happen again."

"I appreciate that, but I'd like to know how it could've happened in the first place."

"I promise you, we'll be looking into it," he said gruffly. "Our policy is to examine all incoming and outgoing mail, so I assume that one of our department staffers made an error in judgment." Northcutt started typing on his keyboard. "Any contact between inmates and minors is restricted—the child would have to get her parent's permission." He opened a database on his computer. "What's the name again? Ella?"

"Ellie Guzman." She spelled it for him.

"Okay, let's see what we've got." He typed Ellie's name into the database. "Ah. I see what the problem is. The correspondences weren't flagged by our records office because your niece contacted Inmate Fowler through an outside registry."

"A what?"

"An outside registry for prison pen pals," he explained. "There are hundreds of them. Anybody can go online nowadays and communicate with our inmates. We encourage them to stay in touch with the outside world as much as possible, since it keeps them hopeful while they're doing time. We've found that, statistically speaking, those who have contact with folks on the outside are less likely to re-offend. Anyway, we have our own registry at MCF, but your niece appears to have used an outside source. There are so many of them nowadays that, unfortunately, we can't police them all."

"What outside source did she use?" Natalie asked.

"I'll print out the information for you." He typed a few commands and hit the PRINT button. "Of course, if she showed up for a visit here at MCF, we would've asked for her ID and been able to confirm her age. However, since your niece was using an outside registry, we didn't have any control over it. At any rate, we'll be reviewing our procedures going forward."

"I still don't understand, she's only fifteen. How could you not know?"

"To be blunt? Your niece fudged the guidelines." He scrolled through the directory. "Our records office has a strict protocol for assessing all correspondence, but in this case, your niece disguised her identity to get past the restrictions. She listed her age as twenty-two."

"I see," Natalie said, deeply concerned. She'd caught Ellie in numerous lies so far, pointing to potentially deeper deceptions. "How many times did she write to him?"

The warden studied the monitor. "She stopped corresponding five months ago. We only received three incoming letters from her." He leaned back in his seat. "Again, Detective Lockhart, my sincerest apologies. However, you can rest assured that Inmate Fowler has been a model prisoner. He received his correspondent's college degree—not an easy feat, and now he tutors other prisoners. He's earned his privileges. The guards have never found him to be threatening in any way. It's been nineteen years, and there's barely a blemish on his record."

"I'd like copies of all the correspondence, if that's okay," Natalie said.

"As long as the prisoner doesn't object, I don't see why not."

"Did you talk to him about my request?"

"Yes, and he's willing to meet with you."

"Can I see him now?"

Northcutt stood up and shook her hand. "I'll have a guard escort you to C block."

The inmates were monitored twenty-four/seven by armed personnel using state-of-the-art technology. Doors hissed open and shut. Justin Fowler was housed in C block—three tiers of cells made of thick concrete walls and iron bars under a cavernous forty-foot ceiling, an enormous space that echoed Natalie's footsteps back at her.

The guards were all built like linebackers, and C block was hard core—populated by killers, rapists, and assorted sociopaths. This morning, post-breakfast, the gallery stood empty and the prisoners were locked inside their cells. Some of them clutched the iron bars and stared at Natalie as she walked through the lower level on her way toward the supermax visitors' room, a windowless cinder-block cube painted life-sucking gray.

The taciturn guard didn't flinch at the clanging, metallic bang of the massive steel doors as they boomed shut behind them. This morning, the visitors' room was sterile and empty, full of government-approved plastic-molded chairs and tables, their legs screwed into the cement floor so they couldn't be used as weapons. Natalie took a seat in front of a bulletproof barrier, and several minutes later the prisoner was escorted through a back entrance into the enclosed Plexiglas booth, from which escape was not possible.

"Hello, Detective Lockhart," Justin Fowler said politely as he took his seat.

"Hello," she said, returning the greeting and choking back a cloying sense of outrage. This was going to be more difficult than she thought. He had a pensive mouth and sober eyes. Oh God, how painful—they let him have eyeglasses. They let him read books, whereas Willow was dead. "Thanks for agreeing to talk to me," she said.

"I'm glad to have the opportunity." His prisoner number was printed on the breast pocket of his beige uniform. He wasn't shackled or restrained in any way. She remembered the slender, good-looking boy he used to be; and now here he was, a middle-aged man wearing dark-framed glasses, his salt-and-pepper hair combed neatly behind his ears. He held a cup of orange liquid, a disgusting-looking brew of unfiltered tap water and powdered institutional indifference.

Back in high school, Justin had been a bad boy from the other side of the tracks with a sexy Ryan Phillippe pout and Johnny Depp hair. He was deeply in love with Willow. Nobody ever doubted that. All through the trial, he maintained his innocence, despite the mountain of evidence against him. Now he was serving a life sentence and would most likely die in this place.

It looked as if Fowler's lawyer had prepared him for Natalie's visit. "I shouldn't be here," he said emphatically. "I didn't kill your sister. I'm completely innocent. This is a gross injustice. I've been saying it for decades."

"Okay," she said cautiously, giving the devil his due.

"And even though my latest appeal for parole was denied last month, my lawyer's looking into this latest killing as a possible means for a new trial."

"Daisy Buckner's homicide?" Natalie said, taken aback.

The prisoner nodded. "Same death date."

"Yes, it's quite a coincidence. But they're entirely different cases. Different MO's. Different everything."

"He told me he was looking into it." Justin sipped his beverage. "Anyway, let me just say up front . . . I'm very sorry about your sister, Detective. I loved Willow. I never would've hurt her, not in a million years. But the media kept pressuring the police to make an arrest. My conviction was a fiasco of biblical proportions."

"I've seen the transcripts of the trial," Natalie told him. "I've read your statement. You deny everything, and yet the police found plenty of evidence—your footprints and tire tracks at the scene, Willow's blood on your clothes. You had no alibi. Why should anyone believe you?"

"I had nothing to do with her death. All I know is, I was at home when she called me after school and told me to meet her at the Hadleys' farm in half an hour, and I said okay. She had a surprise for me, she said. So I drove over to the farm and found her dead. I tried to revive her. It ruined my life. I went into shock and never recovered. A year later, I found myself locked up in this place. Guess I came across as cold and heartless to the jury, which worked against me. But I was in shock. What happened, all that blood . . . it blanked me out. Imagine finding yourself locked up in prison for something you didn't do."

"Why didn't you call the police?" she asked.

"They already had me on possession charges. I'd been to juvie my freshman year. Come on. I figured they'd assume I did it, so I panicked."

"You found her dead and fled the scene? You didn't call the cops, and instead you dumped your bloody clothing in a dumpster . . . but somehow you're innocent? Because those are the actions of a guilty man."

"Look, I've been over this a million times in my head, wondering how it could've turned out differently," he said in a low, circumspect tone. "So, okay. Maybe if I'd called the police, maybe if I'd cooperated. Maybe if I hadn't tried to get rid of my clothes? In prison, your thoughts bounce off the walls. Sometimes you can't turn them off. The gears keep turning. But you have to, for your own sanity. Like I told the judge at my trial, I was a dealer at the time—it's in the court records. I was up front about my mistakes. I came clean. I'm from the west side, with all that implies. I wasn't one of those middle-class kids, headed for Harvard. My parents couldn't afford to hire a decent attorney, and I got stuck with a public defender. Justice was lopsided."

"But why would somebody kill Willow and frame you for it?" Natalie asked.

He waved a dismissive hand. "Willow had lots of guys chasing her. She was gorgeous, she was funny, she was smart as hell. She could really put a guy in his place if she wanted to. I watched her slam a few dudes pretty hard. Maybe one of them wanted vengeance?"

"Who's your top contender?"

"You aren't going to like it."

"Why not?"

He put down his plastic cup and said, "Brandon used to call me a poseur, but he's the one who was slumming it. There he was, this swaddled upper-class kid, the trust-fund baby driving around in daddy's Prius. Only one of us was the real deal. Only one of us grew up dirt poor. Of course, I didn't have much in my life back then, but I had style. Doc Martens, motorcycle jacket, safety pins, studs and spikes. I listened to Pearl Jam and Alice in Chains, and so of course Brandon had to listen to them, too. He was a wannabe."

"Brandon Buckner?" she repeated.

"He was a head case over her."

"Willow?" She drew back—she'd never heard of this before.

"He had a thing for her, but she blew him off in a big way."

"Brandon? Everyone knows he had a lifelong crush on Daisy Forester. And I never once heard Willow talk about him."

"I'm telling you, for a period of time there, she had to shake him off plenty of times. She used to get super annoyed. The putz was two years her junior. It drove her nuts. He used to leave notes on her car," Justin insisted. "He followed her home a couple of times. He'd stare at her in the parking lot. He acted like a fucking weirdo."

"And you think he killed her because she rejected him?" Natalie pressed.

"He worshipped her," Justin said. "I'm telling you, the guy was certifiable. And now he's a fucking detective with the BLPD. And here I sit, locked up in prison. You tell me how justice was served."

Natalie recalled the crime scene photos—Willow's slender arms frozen in repose above her head, her blood-soaked blouse, twenty-seven stab wounds. A crime of passion.

Justin sighed heavily, and she could see it in his eyes—this was all he ever thought about. "You've read the court documents, right?" he said. "There were several unidentified partial footprints in the mud—not mine—that the rain hadn't completely washed away. Willow's Nokia phone logs show her in the vicinity of the Hadleys' farm up to an hour *before* she told me to meet her there. The murder weapon was never found. Willow's phone was never found."

The guard poked his head in the door. "Two minutes," he announced.

"Thanks, Jesse."

The guard nodded and disappeared.

"Look," Justin said quietly, "I've been locked up for twenty years now, and I've got nothing to do all day but stare out my window at the razor wire. I didn't do anything wrong, and yet I'm being punished every day for it. It gets tedious in here. Boredom's a real killer. The world goes on without you, and nobody seems to care. One of the few things that cheers me up is the mail. Your niece. That was nice of her. To write me like that."

"Those letters should've never gotten through," Natalie said. "She's fifteen."

"Hey, I had nothing to do with that. The warden's in charge of who gets the mail." He shook his head. "But I'm grateful, just the same. One thing you find out when you're locked up is who your friends are. Anyway. Tell her I said thanks."

48

It was late afternoon by the time Natalie pulled into Grace's driveway. Grace answered the door in cut-offs and a baggy T-shirt. "Sorry about last night, Natalie."

"That's okay, I totally understand," she said. "Can I come in?"

"Yes. Please."

As Natalie stepped inside, she could smell the booze on Grace's breath. "It's called Sex on the Beach," she said with a slack smile. "One ounce vodka. Half an ounce peach schnapps. Cranberry and orange juice. Tastes delicious. Want one?"

"No, thanks. Are you okay, Grace?"

"Hell, I'm upset." She frowned. "It feels like my life is falling apart."

"Nothing's falling apart." Natalie took away the half-finished drink. "Make us some coffee, okay?"

"Sure. Be great."

Natalie followed her into the kitchen, where Grace grabbed hold of the back of a chair, steadying herself, and Natalie dumped the drink down the sink.

"Sit down a minute, Grace."

She dragged the chair out and plopped into her seat.

Natalie took a seat next to her at the marble kitchen island. "Where's Ellie?"

"Upstairs. Grounded for life. Fifteen years old and she knows everything. Right. Give me more of your shouty wisdom."

"You know I only want the best for you both, right?"

Grace nodded listlessly. She looked depleted, her face washed with worries, little grooves of unhappiness embedded in her forehead. "It scares me," she admitted, "being alone in the middle of the night, when everything's closing in around you . . ."

"It'll be okay. She's tough," Natalie assured her. "You'll get through this."

"God, I hope so."

"Let's go into the living room, okay?"

The house was full of solid blocks of furniture with well-established boundaries—assertive dark wood tables, a sectional sofa, obstinate armchairs with tufted upholstery. The antique chest was stacked with *Vanity Fairs* and *New Yorkers*. The windows were open, and a mild breeze played with the drapes. The earthy smell of cedar and pine intruded.

Natalie took out photocopies of Ellie's prison pen pal letters and spread them across the coffee table. "I visited Justin Fowler in prison today."

Grace gasped. "You did? Why?"

"These are the letters Ellie sent him. I talked to the warden, and he assured me it will never happen again. As a rule, they inspect all correspondence before forwarding it to the inmates, but Ellie was using a third-party website for prison pen pals, and she lied about her age on the guidelines. As a result, the prison staff didn't red flag it. They had no idea she was fifteen."

Grace frowned. "I'd like to read them."

"Okay," Natalie said.

Grace sat mute and immobile, reading them all.

Ellie's first letter to Justin was dated seven months ago.

Hi, Justin,

I found you through a prison pen pal website that listed your name and profile. It says you killed your girlfriend, but then your lawyer explained what really happened on his blog, and I don't believe in judging people. I doubt you could've hurt someone you cared about so much. Would you like to be my pen pal? If so, please write me back. My address is on the envelope.

Sincerely, Ellie Guzman

The second letter was more revealing.

Hi, Justin,

Thanks for writing me back so quickly. Well, I have a confession to make. I wasn't entirely honest with you before. Willow Lockhart is my aunt. But I don't believe in judging people until all the facts are known, and after checking out your lawyer's website, I agree that you at least deserve a new trial. One of my friends thinks you were railroaded. I was wondering if you could answer a few questions for me? I'm writing a report for my creative writing class, and I could present your point of view to my class. I feel bad that you've been locked up for so many years—that seems like such a long time. I'm an open-minded person, and I really liked your last letter describing what prison life was like. If you don't mind telling me more, I could include it in my report.

Sincerely, Ellie

The third was a birthday card of an illustrated owl, saying, *Whooo's* one year older? Inside, Ellie had written,

Happy birthday, Justin!

I enjoyed your last letter. I didn't realize prison life could be so funny and awful at the same time. I hope you had a nice birthday. Did they at least give you a piece of cake?

Your friend, Ellie

Justin's letters to Ellie were detailed and friendly. In response to the birthday card, he wrote,

Dear Ellie,

Your card was my favorite birthday gift. No, I didn't get cake, but we all got an extra slice of nutraloaf today, which is a special type of prison food that's a gag-worthy combination of oatmeal, beans, raisins, applesauce, garlic, meatloaf, and spinach. Yep, it's disgusting. Nutraloaf is so terrible, in fact, that some courts have ruled it unconstitutional. But they still serve it here every Monday. Believe that? Anyway, your card came as a pleasant surprise, and I've been wondering lately, how do you measure a life? William Wordsworth once said, to paraphrase, The best portion of a good man's life are all his little, nameless, unremembered acts of kindness and love. Well, I have to say, your birthday card was certainly an act of kindness. Say a prayer for me, Ellie.

Your pal, Justin

Visibly shaken, Grace put the letters down. "Ellie and I have talked about this. She knows he killed Willow. Why would she do this?" She began to sob.

"Hey." Natalie squeezed her sister's hand, then reached for the box of tissues, and Grace plucked one out.

"Sorry," Grace sniffled. "It's been a terrible week."

"I'd like to talk to Ellie," Natalie told her gently.

"Why?" Grace asked with a nervous gulp.

"No one's in trouble here. I just need to talk to her." When her sister hesitated, she said, "You have to trust me."

"Okay." She blew her nose and wiped her eyes, then went to stand at the bottom of the stairs. "Ellie?" she called out. "Aunt Natalie's here. She wants to talk to you."

After a moment, the girl came traipsing down the stairs.

Grace pointed at the letters on the coffee table and said, "I read what you wrote to Justin Fowler. We've been over this before, Ellie. You know he killed your aunt. The police evidence was irrefutable. He was tried and convicted by a jury of his peers."

"Grace," Natalie said.

"Tell me you aren't this naïve," Grace went on. "All prisoners claim to be innocent. How could you fall for such a scam?"

"Grace, please," Natalie said firmly.

Ellie sat down on the sofa and curled herself into a wounded ball. The living room smelled of vanilla incense. Late afternoon light shone through the gilded windows. "Mom, I told you, it was part of my school assignment."

"That's bullshit," Grace said.

"Ellie," Natalie interrupted. "I need to ask you a few more questions."

The girl crossed her arms and nodded sullenly.

"Tell me again why you wrote to Justin."

"It was India's idea," she admitted in a trembling voice. "We were going to use his letters in our rituals, because he's evil, and his letters are super-powerful."

Grace sat heavily in the nearest chair.

"And did you use them? As part of your revenge curses on Ms. Buckner?"

"Yes." She glanced at her mother. "I know he killed Aunt Willow. I know that."

"And it was all India's idea?" Natalie repeated.

"Are you kidding me?" Ellie drew a sharp breath. "India wants to be a high priestess someday. She took over the coven completely, even though it was my idea. I don't know why I went along with her, I really don't," she said, on the verge of tears. "Ms. Buckner's always been good to me. I've known her ever since I was a kid. She used to pencil in my eyebrows, remember, Mom? She bought me Little Debbie's cupcakes all the time. Why would I hurt her? I'd never hurt her. Ever."

"Do you have any idea who killed her?" Natalie pressed. "Besides Riley. Did you see anything? Hear anything?"

Her face changed; something penetrated her psyche, a buried but fiercely held emotion. "Well, I mean . . . when Riley came over Berkley's on Wednesday, I took off because I didn't feel comfortable. They were talking about her . . ."

"About Daisy?"

"Yes. India and Berkley were calling her Ms. Fuckner. And the next day, when I heard about what happened . . . I was, like . . . really scared. I told India I didn't want to be in the coven anymore. And now they're after me."

"Who is?"

"India and Berkley. They were mad at me for leaving, but I told them I couldn't be part of it anymore. India said they were going to hex me—put a death spell on me. They called me a bitch. They said karma is real. I'm scared, Aunt Natalie. Those curses really work."

"Why would they come after you, Ellie?" Natalie pressed. "The four of you have been inseparable since birth. India's your best friend. What changed?"

"Maybe I know too much," she said, eyes wide with trepidation. "I know about the death spells and the poppet and where India gets her drugs. Plus, she's jealous of me, because I always get straight As. Mr. Hathaway keeps praising my writing, even though India thinks she's a better writer than me. And because I don't cheat. I won't let her crib off my test papers. India had a fit when Ms. Buckner gave her a B-minus . . ."

There it was, the missing puzzle piece. "Was that her B-minus inside the poppet?"

"Yes."

"What about Sadie and Berkley? Are they mad at you, too?"

Ellie shook her head. "Berkley is, but Sadie feels the same way I do, only she's too scared to confront them or quit the coven. She's afraid they'll go after her, too. Sadie's only pretending to get along."

"And India and Berkley both threatened to put a death spell on you, Ellie?"

"Yes," she said with a shivery gasp. "That's why they stole my bracelet, Aunt Natalie. It's why they stole Aunt Willow's scarf. And I'm really scared right now, because . . . what if black magic is real?" Ellie wept.

In a flood of love for her daughter, Grace folded the girl in her arms. "Black magic isn't real, honey," she whispered. "Trust me on this."

"How do you know, Mom?"

"It just isn't."

Ellie took a painful breath. "I know I've been acting really stupid lately."

"Shh. It's okay. We'll figure it out." Grace turned to Natalie and said,

"Can you make them stop terrorizing my daughter? Could you arrest them or something?"

"We'll get in contact with their parents," Natalie said. "I'll make sure the harassment stops."

"You can cast a death spell from anywhere," Ellie said anxiously. "Mom, I tried to ignore them at school, but India said if I told a single soul, I'm dead."

"Shh." Grace held her, trying to smother the girl in a mother's protective embrace, which was half wishful thinking, half illusion. "It's okay, sweetie. Nobody's going to hurt you. I won't let them." Then she looked at Natalie, her face furrowed with distress.

"That's right," Natalie assured them. "We won't."

49

The Cochrans, the Auberdines, and the Myerses all stonewalled Natalie's request for an interview. Brandon wasn't reachable. Having hit a wall, frustrated and full of concern for her niece, Natalie decided to strategize with Luke about her next move and was on her way to his office when her phone buzzed. It was Lenny.

"Ethan Hathaway's here for the polygraph," he told her.

"Be right there." She hung up.

Natalie had always relished the challenge of finding the bad guy, pinning him like a bug to a board and dissecting him. To shred him; to ruin and destroy him. In other words, justice. But now that she was looking into the possibility of children as homicide suspects, her mind swam with confusion. She found herself floating in a toxic sludge of self-doubt, her thoughts slowly twisting and untwisting. In the smoky play of light, a bundle of worries nagged at her. As a detective, you had to tease the truth out of good and bad information. Right now, Natalie had only incomplete information. She was pecking at facts littered with false leads.

Ethan Hathaway wore a tweed jacket and an uneasy smile. "I'm a little nervous," he admitted as she led him down the hallway.

"Just answer the questions truthfully, to the best of your ability."

The polygraph room was compact and windowless, with a table, two chairs, and the polygraph machine. Intimidating, for sure.

"Have a seat," Natalie said. "Lenny will be joining us shortly."

Ethan drummed his fingers on the table and glanced around. The lie-detector machine consisted of a suitcase-size box with wires sticking out, a blood-pressure cuff, finger electrodes, a motion-sensor pad, and several pneumograph tubes for measuring the subject's breathing. The tubes would be attached to Hathaway's chest with Velcro straps. The stark fluorescent lights emitted a faint background hum.

"Take off your jacket and roll up your shirtsleeves," Natalie said.

He proceeded to remove his jacket, which he draped over the back of his chair.

"Roll them up past the elbows, please."

He hesitated with his fingers on one of the shirt cuffs. She held her breath and waited with something akin to lust—a wild yearning to know. Despite her determination not to, Natalie always looked at the arms of any male suspect who fit the profile. As Hathaway slowly rolled up his shirtsleeves past the elbows, she had a good line of sight, but there weren't any birthmarks on his inner forearms. She'd checked out a lot of exposed hairy arms in this town, looking for the bogeyman. It was an automatic response. A reflex action from a scarred psyche.

Ethan dropped his arms by his sides and surprised her by suddenly opening up. "You know, Detective Lockhart, I've been thinking about our conversation the other day, and I'd like to be completely honest with you. The first thing I thought of when I heard the news about Daisy was that Brandon had done it. I thought he may have found out about us. That was my initial impression."

She crossed her arms. "Why do you say that?"

"Some of the things Daisy told me about him, about their marriage."

"Such as?"

"He comes from wealth. He's used to having his own way. He's an imposing guy, a big guy. Whenever he drank, he became belligerent."

"Was there physical abuse? Yelling? Hitting?"

"I have no direct knowledge of that, it's just . . ."

"You have a suspicion based on what then?" she pressed.

"Like I said, it's just an impression."

Lenny came strolling into the room just then. "Ethan Hathaway?"

"Hello, sir."

The two men shook hands.

"I'm Detective Labruzzo," Lenny said, touching his laminated ID card, which he wore on a long chain around his neck. He sat down in a chair that squealed as it rolled across the depressing carpet. "I'm going to attach some stuff to you now. Lean forward, please." It took several minutes for Lenny to hook up Hathaway to the polygraph and establish a baseline. The control questions were easy—What is your name?

After every question, Hathaway glanced away for a second. Eye direction. Eye flutter. Touching the face. Deep breathing. Shallow breathing. Everything was a tell. The eye glance could be from nerves. Or force of habit. Or it could mean he was lying. That was what the machine was for.

"Have you ever lied to anyone who trusted you?" Lenny asked.

"Probably," Hathaway said.

"Have you ever stolen anything?"

"Pens and pencils."

"Have you ever lied to anyone to keep from getting into trouble?"

"My mom."

"Did you kill Daisy Buckner?"

"No," he said, his chiseled face flushing with emotion. "Absolutely not."

Lenny waited a beat, then put a pencil mark on the printout. "Where were you between four and six P.M. last Wednesday?"

"I spent the evening grading papers. What can I say? My life's a thrill a minute."

"Have you ever been inside the Buckner household?"

"For a Halloween party last year."

"Did you go into the kitchen?"

"Probably."

"Did you see a medium-size skillet hanging from the pot rack on the ceiling?"

"No."

"Do you drink Coke?"

"I prefer bottled water."

They were measuring for physiological distress. The tubes around his chest measured his breathing; the arm cuff monitored his heart rate; the electrodes attached to his fingers measured perspiration. Polygraphs weren't a hundred percent reliable. A guilty man could game the machine by learning how to control his breathing and body movements, and by altering his reaction to the control questions. An innocent man might come across as nervous. But to law enforcement, the polygraph was another weapon in their arsenal. Sometimes they got a confession.

"Did you see anyone on Wednesday afternoon between four and six P.M.?" Lenny asked.

"No," Ethan said. "I was home alone. All evening."

"Did you order a pizza? Make a phone call? Talk to the neighbors?"

"No."

"When was the last time you spoke to Daisy Buckner?"

Ethan hesitated for a second. "At school, two weeks ago. We found ourselves alone in the faculty room. It was a little awkward. I asked her how she was doing. She said she'd found peace."

"Peace?"

"Yes, that's right. I told her I was happy for her. She got up and left."

Natalie was watching him closely. "What did she mean by 'peace'?" she asked.

Ethan steepled his fingers together. "I took it to mean that she'd found peace in her marriage. That she'd made the right decision. But . . ."

"But what?" Natalie asked.

He shook his head. "I didn't press the issue. That's the last time we spoke."

Natalie had gone off script. She nodded at Lenny to proceed.

"Would you describe your relationship with the deceased as emotionally fraught?" Lenny asked, reading from the list of questions.

"No," Ethan answered. "During the times we were together, we were just like any other couple. We had our disagreements, but we were passionately in love."

Lenny marked the printout with his pencil. "Did you ever hit Daisy Buckner?"

"No. Never."

"Have you ever used physical violence against anyone?"

Ethan stroked the nape of his neck. "No."

"Ever struck anyone?"

"Not since I was a kid."

"What happened when you were a kid?"

"I got into a few tussles with boys at school. Normal stuff."

"Anything since? High school? College?"

"No."

"Have you ever been arrested?"

"No."

"Did you have anything to do with the murder of Daisy Buckner?"

A shadow crossed Ethan's face. Pain silenced his eyes. "I already told you, no."

"Did you ever fantasize about killing her?"

"What?"

"Did you ever fantasize about killing Daisy Buckner?"

"Hold on."

Tension surrounded them.

"Ethan?" Natalie said. "Is there a problem?"

He met her concerned gaze. "I didn't sign up for this."

"What's that?"

"I was willing to come down here and take a polygraph test, because I sincerely hoped it would help with the investigation, but I didn't realize you were going to probe my subconscious." He tugged the electrodes off his fingers. He ripped off the arm cuff. He tore off the pneumograph tubes around his chest and rolled down his shirtsleeves.

"Ethan, calm down . . ."

"Fantasize?"

"These are standard questions . . ."

"Did I ever *fantasize* about killing her? No, Detective Lockhart. I'm sorry I trusted you. Now I realize I probably should've hired an attorney." He put on his jacket. "Did you polygraph Brandon yet? Did you ask him if he ever *fantasized* about killing his wife? No? I didn't think so. You police protect your own." He walked out of the room.

Lenny glanced at Natalie and shrugged. "That struck a nerve," he said.

"I wouldn't answer it, either," she admitted.

Together, they leaned over the graph paper and studied the responses.

"What do you think?" she asked.

"I'll need more time to extrapolate, but I'd say the results were inconclusive."

"How's that?"

"He was nervous all the way through. Even with the control questions. Sometimes their emotions get the better of them, and they generate a lot of false positives. They get jittery, whether or not they're guilty. It's a type of performance anxiety." Lenny circled the results with his pencil. "I want to go over the results more thoroughly before making an official determination. I'll let you know tomorrow."

"Thanks." She left the room.

50

Lindsey Wozniak wasn't kidding about her crazy hours. It was half past six by the time Natalie caught up with her at the Kirkpatricks' estate, where she was supervising a landscaping project on Lazy Bend Road. A tumbledown stone wall enclosed the dead garden. A yellow forklift was in the process of digging up the yard.

"Sorry, I can't talk," Lindsey said breathlessly. "I'm facing a tight dead-line."

"Just a few quick questions," Natalie said.

Lindsey heaved a sigh and tugged off her garden gloves. "Okay, but I'm seriously pressed for time, Natalie. Let's talk over there."

They went to stand in the driveway, away from the noisy equipment.

"I need to know more about your relationship with Brandon," Natalie began.

Lindsey brushed the sweat off her brow, leaving a streak of dirt. "Our relationship? When? Now, or back then?"

"Tell me about your fling in high school."

"He was a sad little boy, okay? He had a lifelong crush on Daisy, and she didn't return his interest until . . . I don't know, the eleventh or twelfth grade. But he and I were good friends all along. And yes, at one point, he *really, really liked me.*" She shook her head mockingly. "Let me tell you something, Natalie. Being the librarian's daughter was no picnic."

Natalie smiled. "Being a cop's daughter wasn't much better. All the boys were terrified of Joey."

"Right. So you get it. I was this pasty-faced egghead, always with her nose in a book. Even my best friends thought I was a pointy-headed little nerd. But once I discovered *Practical Magic* and *The Witches of Eastwick* and *Teen Witch,* I realized—hey, I can change all this. So we formed our own coven—me, Grace, Daisy, and Bunny. This whole concept of sinners . . . *pfft.* Who defines what's sinful? That's only to keep you in line. Sometimes 'sinning' can be fun. Anyway, I loved everything about it—full moon rites, the witches' cradle, spiral dancing, all of that stuff . . . and who in this town hasn't tried it? You dipped your toe in the cone of power once yourself, didn't you, Natalie?"

"So let me get this straight," she clarified. "Brandon had a crush on Daisy, but she didn't return his amorous feelings until at least their junior year of high school? And during their senior year, Brandon got Daisy pregnant, but she decided to have an abortion without consulting him. So in retaliation, he hooked up with you. And Daisy became so distraught, she attempted suicide. Is that pretty much the gist of it?"

The blunt recap didn't faze Lindsey in the slightest. "Like I said, Daisy could be quite the drama queen. Their relationship was very bumpy. I was collateral damage."

"Bumpy how?"

"They had crushes on other people all the time. Jealousy, screaming matches, a long history of emotional turmoil."

"I heard Brandon had a crush on Willow?"

She nodded. "Oh, yeah."

"When was this?"

"In the tenth grade, I think. Brandon started dogging after Willow. But now I suspect he did it to make Daisy jealous."

"Why?"

"Because Daisy had a crush on Justin," Lindsey explained.

"Justin Fowler? I don't remember any of this."

"You were too young to get sucked into the histrionics, lucky you."

"So Daisy had a crush on Justin Fowler?"

Lindsey laughed. "Oh God. We used to call her Justin's shadow."

Natalie paused for a moment to collect her thoughts. "I just visited Justin in prison," she said. "He believes Brandon killed Willow."

"Brandon?" Lindsey gave Natalie a tight-lipped smile. "What a lying sack of shit. No. Willow broke up with Justin, so he killed her. End of story."

"But you and Brandon have always been close. Did you ever suspect anything at the time? That he might've been involved somehow?"

Lindsey put her gardening gloves back on. "No, Natalie. That's absurd."

"What about Ethan Hathaway? Did you know Daisy was having an affair with him?"

"Really?" She shrugged. "Well, as you know, I suspected something was up, but I figured it was none of my business. I didn't realize it was him." She glanced over at the forklift, which was making a loud, annoying beeping sound. "I run my own business, okay? I love my job, Natalie. And I'm too busy to worry about other people's shady romances, okay?"

"But you suspected as much. Why didn't you mention it to Brandon?"

She shrugged it off. "Like I said, none of my business. Anyway, I've got a long list of things to do. Have I answered all your questions? Please, sweetie? I'm swamped." Her phone chimed. "Can I take this?"

"Almost done. You never told me where you were between four and six P.M. last Wednesday."

Lindsey took a sharp breath, then reorganized her face into an expression of wounded dignity. "Are you kidding me?"

"Nothing personal."

"Not personal?" Lindsey balled her fists. "God, this is ridiculously upsetting."

"You told me you'd look it up."

Lindsey clasped her hands in front of her. "I'm always working, Natalie. How many times have I pitched you about cleaning up your yard?" She smiled tensely. "Seriously, your crabgrass is out of control. I could give you a discount. Heck, I'd do it for free, just to beautify the neighborhood." She laughed. "I hate to brag, but I can work wonders."

"Would you mind checking your schedule for last Wednesday?"

"God, you're persistent. Four to six?" She glanced at the horizon, where the setting sun had turned the sky pink. "Probably at home, going over my accounts."

"Did you take any calls that afternoon? Have any visitors?"

She squirmed a little. "Why does it feel like I'm being accused of something?"

"I'm trying to pin down your timeline."

"My timeline? Am I a suspect? I told you, Natalie, I take advantage of any quiet moment I can get." She crossed her arms. "When I was growing up, I didn't think I'd end up here, you know? In my old hometown. I had big plans for myself. But such is life. It can be humiliating, living in the same place where everybody remembers your bad-hair days, your mistakes, and your most embarrassing moments . . ."

Natalie made a helpless gesture with her hands. "Do you think Brandon found out about Daisy and Hathaway? Do you think he might've killed her?"

Lindsey's face flushed. Her nostrils flared. "God, no. He was so excited about becoming a father. A little apprehensive, maybe. But I've never seen him happier. Why would he kill his own baby? Anyway, listen." She tucked her hands in her pockets. "About last Wednesday? I was probably on the phone with a hundred people, as usual. I'll dig up my phone records, and then maybe you can stop with the third degree."

"Can you do it now, please?"

"No, I have to finish here. But I'll email you later on, okay?" She walked away.

51

It was eight o'clock by the time Natalie pulled into Grace's driveway again and parked behind the Mini Cooper. The air smelled earthy sweet. The stars were out. She felt a chill as she took the flagstone walkway up to the front door and rang the bell.

The door popped open with a familiar *ker-plunk*. Grace stood in a golden light, looking sleepy-eyed and fuzzy-headed. "Hey, Nat."

"Can I come in?"

"Sure." She stepped aside.

Natalie followed her sister into the living room, where Grace crawled underneath an old patchwork quilt on the sofa. She'd been drinking. There was a near-empty wine bottle and a long-stemmed wineglass on the coffee table. Natalie took a seat. "Grace, are you okay? Talk to me."

"I've been looking through our old high school yearbooks," she said, smoothing her hands over the pages. "Most likely to succeed, most likely to end up in jail. God, what idiots we were." She closed the yearbook and sighed. "Just having a lot of regrets."

"Where's Ellie?" Natalie asked.

"Upstairs. I told her I've had it with her. God, that phrase just rolled off my lips, and I thought, dear Lord, I'm becoming my mother. The dreaded Deborah. Remember how angry she used to get? She'd blow a fuse, and her face would turn all shades of purple. Then she'd kick us out of the house. We could've been kidnapped. Now I find myself muttering the same obscene phrase. And it sucks, because I've always wanted to be the cool mom."

"News flash. You are the cool mom."

She shook her bleary head. "When it comes to Ellie, I can't do anything right. If I bake brownies, she's on a diet. If I'm too busy working, she'll complain that I'm never around. If I take a week off, she gets bored with my company. I told her, 'Go ahead. Slam your door. Insult me. Just remember, the more you push me away, the more I'll stick like glue.'" Grace smiled. "Boy, she hated that."

"She's confined to her room?"

"Yeah, that's her so-called punishment, right? I send her up there with all her toys and gadgets and devices . . . ha. Some punishment."

"That's okay," Natalie said. "I wanted to talk to you alone."

She nodded nervously. "Look, Natalie . . . I'm beat. This week has been so hard on me, I can't do anything involving mental effort right now."

"It's about Willow," Natalie said. "We're considering reopening her case."

The tense lines around Grace's mouth showed that she was both repulsed and fascinated by this idea. She rummaged around in her large leather bag for her cigarettes and moved the ashtray closer on the coffee table. "What the hell for?"

"A couple of new things have come to light. What can you tell me about the day Willow died? Think about it. Take your time."

She drew her legs to her chest and rested her chin on her knees, like a child, like the pensive older sister Natalie remembered. "It was a normal school day. We heard the news that evening, and I just . . . fell apart. It was raining, and I was sitting in my room, watching the rain outside. The police pulled up out front, Dad answered the door, and they told him what happened, and he just . . . collapsed. Mom began wailing like an animal. I felt so drained, I hardly had any feelings left in my body. It was as if a razor had cut me in half, dividing today from yesterday." She rubbed her forehead. "God, it still hurts."

"You were in a coven with Daisy, Lindsey, and Bunny at the time. They were your closest friends. Can you think of anything they might've said or done around the time Willow was killed? Anything unusual?"

"No. We were all upset. It was a difficult time."

"Any gossip or rumors you might've overheard?"

"I can't think of anything." Grace shook her head, confused.

"Did anybody say anything to you after Willow died? Did the four of you ever talk about what might've happened to her?"

Grace rolled her eyes. "No. After Willow died, I completely fell apart. I was so messed up, I left the coven. You know, dark magic. It didn't sit right with me anymore." She rubbed her nose. "Well, I mean, Lindsey was . . . I mean, she always came across as quiet and reserved, but there was a hidden side to her that could be very domineering. She wanted us to keep it going, but I couldn't stand it anymore. Neither could Bunny."

"So, in the coven . . . you were doing dark magic? Black magic?"

Grace tamped out her cigarette and rubbed the base of her throat. "Okay, look. Lindsey's the one who wanted to try it. I've blocked some of it out because, frankly . . . look at my life now. I've got a terrific kid, and I love my teaching gig. But truthfully? Back then? We might've done a few things in a group that we'd never do on our own. I don't know. All the charms and fortune-telling games were fun. Keeping secrets. Testing our loyalty. Truth or dare. We pushed and pulled. It was exciting for a while. But then, eventually, it began to take on a life of its own and . . . How can I say this? Lindsey wanted to go darker. She encouraged the rest of us to cast negative spells on some of the girls at school. You know, just the ones who deserved it. There was a group of popular kids who used to pick on Lindsey a lot, and she wanted revenge. You know, make-our-enemies-cower-before-us type of thing. She was pretty persuasive, and she convinced the rest of us to try black magic, and at first it felt powerful. We were going through such intense emotions at that time, it felt like a rush . . . as if we were superhuman. But it was all playacting, Natalie. Because, after Willow died, it all fell apart. What happened was a horror. A hole. I can't even talk about it. Life goes on, but there's a big part of me that's still frozen in time."

"And so it ended?"

Grace nodded. "For me it did."

"What kind of black magic?"

"Oh, come on. We were into some heavy shit back then. Things got pretty negative, but it wasn't the end of the world."

"How negative?" Natalie asked.

Grace eyed her skeptically. "Didn't you test those waters yourself?"

"Not really. It scared the hell out of me."

"Secret rituals, invocations, sleeping naked in a graveyard. Willow was into black magic herself once, but she disavowed it pretty quick, especially after Mom got to her. But, hey, none of us stayed witches forever, right? We didn't become Wiccan priestesses. It was just a blip on our radar. We all went on to do other things. We outgrew it. We grew up. I'm not the same person I was six months ago, Natalie. Are you? We wanted to be in control of our lives, that's all. Or maybe we wanted freaky powers, because the world can be pretty overwhelming at times. But, come on, Natalie . . . you get that, don't you?"

"I get it. Definitely."

"Anyway. That's why I'm so upset about Ellie. The same thing just happened to her. I didn't expect her to go down the same rabbit hole." Grace looked at her hands. "When I signed the divorce papers, Burke told me he never understood what I wanted. How the hell could he not know? I wanted romance, I wanted flowers, I wanted to travel to Tibet and parachute out of an airplane . . . anything but this boring, repetitive life with its worries and domestic issues to be resolved, and him commuting to Manhattan every week doing God knows what." Grace made a sour face. "I don't know why I married him in the first place. But I fell for the whole crummy package. He can be charming when he wants to be. He's a good bullshitter, and he had me convinced . . . this was the one. But it was all fakery. He hid Asshole Burke really well." Grace smoothed the loose hair off her neck and said, "Anyway, my daughter is all I care about now. We had a fight. I feel bad about it, but it's for her own good." She worriedly rubbed her forehead. "Sorry. Do you mind? I have to go check on Ellie."

"Go ahead."

"I hope she isn't listening to any of this." Grace stood up. "Be right back."

Wiccans were not Satanists or Goths, although there could be plenty of overlap. Wicca was a crazy brew. You could shape it any way you liked—there weren't very many specific rules. Invoke the devil. Tattoos and piercings. An obsession with death rites, coffins, and hearses. Magical words repeated for protection. It drew misfits, socially awkward kids, shy types, loners—but also it attracted plenty of unsuspecting, naïve, well-rounded teenage girls.

Natalie could hear Grace's footsteps in the upstairs hallway, then she knocked on Ellie's door. "Sweetie? You awake?" There was a pause. "Honey? You in there?"

No response.

The door creaked open.

Silence.

And then, Grace called out, *"Ellie?"*

Natalie went to stand at the bottom of the stairs. "What's wrong?"

Grace leaned over the banister. "She's not in her room." She disappeared again, and Natalie could hear all the bedroom and bathroom doors swinging open and shut. "Ellie? Where are you? This isn't funny."

Moments later, Grace hurried down the stairs, looking deeply shaken. "Her wallet and phone are gone. *Ellie?*" she called out.

"Try her number," Natalie suggested.

Grace picked up the landline and dialed Ellie's number. She shook her head. "No answer." She left a frantic message. "Where are you? It's Mom. Call me!"

Then Grace put on her jacket and scooped up her leather bag.

Natalie stopped her. "Whoa. Where are you going?"

"To look for my daughter."

"No way. You've been drinking," Natalie told her. "You can't drive now. You need to sober up first."

"What am I supposed to do? Sit here and hope for the best?"

"Call everyone you can think of. Friends, classmates, parents, teachers. In the meantime, I'll go looking for her. If she's on foot, she can't have gotten very far."

"She's never done this before," Grace said, breathless and scared.

"Give me your keys."

Grace clutched them in her hand.

"Grace, what if Ellie comes back? She'll need you to be here, waiting for her."

She bit her lip and nodded.

"Start dialing," Natalie told her. "I'll put out a BOLO. All the guys in the department will be looking for her, okay? Don't worry. We'll find her. This is what I do."

52

Momentarily overwhelmed, Natalie sat in the car and could feel her face throbbing with exhaustion. The neighborhood was ghostly at night. The wind howled cinematically, as if piped in through speakers hanging in the trees. Grace's front yard sloped down toward the street, where the garbage cans were lined up for tomorrow morning's pickup.

Okay. What was the best strategy? If Natalie searched Twitter or Instagram or Facebook long enough, she'd eventually find out where Ellie had gone tonight. Most teenagers wanted to be famous and posted pictures of themselves on their social media sites, especially at parties or events. If you combed through the comments section long enough, you might discover a secret social media account where teens posted pictures they didn't want their mothers to see. But that would take time.

She decided to try a more direct route. Natalie had previously stored the girls' numbers on her contact list, and now she tapped one of the names.

Sadie Myers picked up. "Hello?"

"This is Detective Lockhart, Ellie's aunt. Please don't hang up."

"Aunt Natalie?" she whispered nervously.

"Where's Ellie?"

"I don't know."

"Listen, Sadie, you aren't in any trouble, okay? Do you understand?"

"Uh-huh," she whispered.

Natalie could hear party noises in the background. "Where are you?"

"Um, with some friends."

"Where?"

"At an old farm."

"Have you heard from Ellie tonight?" she asked.

"No, I mean . . . yes, she was here. But she's not anymore."

Natalie's heart rate spiked. "Where did she go?"

"They took off, the three of them . . . Ellie, India, and Berkley."

"Where are you right now? What's the address?"

Sadie gave her the information.

"Okay. Now listen very carefully. Don't tell a soul that I'm coming," Natalie said sternly. "Understand?"

Sadie was compliant. "I won't. I promise."

"Wait for me there," she said and hung up.

Natalie sped across town and took a series of back roads through the woods until she came to a run-down farmstead on the west side of town, where dozens of cars were parked out front. Several rusty signs warned PRIVATE PROPERTY—KEEP OUT.

She got out of her car and scanned the abandoned farm. Nothing had changed in years. The weathered Gothic sat at the end of a weedy driveway. The barbed-wire fence was choked with nettles. The azaleas were in bloom. A tattered American flag waved in the damp breeze.

Natalie could hear booming music coming from behind the old Dutch barn. There weren't any nearby neighbors to get alarmed at the noise, which made it the perfect place for an underage party. She headed across the field, while moonlight fell on the decrepit outbuildings and boarded-up sheds. The orchard had reverted to its natural state—wild fruit trees draped with climbing vines. By midsummer, the crab apples would ripen and fall to the ground, making a pulpy feast for the bees.

Natalie waded through the knee-high ryegrass while the moon disappeared behind the slate-gray clouds. She aimed her flashlight at the salvage cars in the yard, pieces of rust-eaten machinery and miscellaneous farm equipment. The party was in full swing out back. She could see the glow of the bonfire before she turned the corner of the barn.

The area was clogged with at least fifty kids. Earsplitting music throbbed in the air. Beer bottles and crumpled bags of leftovers from the Cheesecake Factory and Taco Bell were scattered around the bonfire.

Underage parties could be dangerous. Overdoses were common. When Natalie was a rookie on the night shift, she had been occasionally called to scenes like this one, where teenagers were "skittling," taking random pills and falling unconscious. A girl had died while participating in the Strangulation Game—said to increase euphoria.

Now a bra winged through the air. There were puke stains in the grass. A group of girls were holding hands and swaying to the pounding bass line, lost in a trance of mesmerizing repetition. A group of boys tossed their beer bottles into the woods, shouting as the glass shattered.

Natalie didn't want to cause a panic. If she flashed her badge, there could be a stampede, and someone might get hurt. She'd been trained to use discretion. Tonight, she would have to find Ellie first, and then she'd call Dispatch.

She passed a group of teenagers who were wandering around in the meadow, thumbing through their phones. Natalie scrutinized a dozen wasted faces, but couldn't find Ellie's face among them. A leggy girl in a black denim outfit was standing over by the sprawling Japanese maples, staring down at her phone with a disturbed look on her face.

"Sadie?"

She turned with stunned-raccoon eyes. "Hi, Aunt Natalie. I waited, just like you said."

"Where is she?"

"They ghosted about fifteen minutes ago," Sadie lisped.

"Do you have any idea where they went?"

"India said she wanted to teach Ellie a lesson."

Natalie tried not to panic. "What lesson?"

Sadie's eyes were glazed; she had a difficult time staying focused. "They were laughing at us," she said defensively, "because we made the mistake of looking at cute puppies on YouTube. I guess that's a crime now. Anyway, they got angry and said we needed to grow up. They were mad at Ellie for quitting the coven." She shivered and hugged herself. "Ellie tried to reason with them, but they wouldn't listen."

Natalie clutched Sadie's arm. "Where did they take her?"

The girl's eyes widened with fear. "They told me not to tell. They said they'd get me next."

Natalie softened her grip. "It's okay. I'll protect you. Where did they take her?"

After a moment's hesitation, she confessed, "Abby's Hex."

53

Natalie called Dispatch as she hurried back to her car. "We've got an underage party going on. Fifty or so minors. Drinking, possible drug usage." She gave Dennis the address, then got in her car and headed for the lake, flying past all-night gas stations and convenience stores. She took the curving two-lane road that led to Abby's Hex Peninsula and swerved into the near-empty parking area, braking hard, gravel kicking into her wheel wells.

India's Lexus was parked close to the trailhead. Natalie grabbed her flashlight out of the glove compartment and stepped out of the car. She could smell a faint trace of marijuana in the air. Above her head, a canopy of leaves sparkled in the moonlight.

She took the trail into the woods, and for several heart-pounding minutes all she could hear were old leaves crinkling underfoot. Something darted in front of her, two devilish eyes caught in the flashlight's glare. She froze while the raccoon lumbered into the thickets, leaving a rustle of air behind.

She hurried along the trail, her flashlight probing the underbrush. She could hear several girls talking in the distance, their voices high and burbling. Clouds drifted overhead and darkness enveloped her for a moment. The lake beyond the trees was a yawning hole, without any reflection.

Soon, the voices grew louder. The girls were having an argument.

A scream.

Fear ripped through her.

Natalie broke into a run, all self-control gone. Wild-eyed. *Do something.* She raced through the thinning woods, swatting the branches aside and bounding toward the end of the peninsula, where she could see the three girls through the trees. Ellie was struggling to free herself from India and Berkley, her shrieks carrying across the lake.

What happened next felt like slow motion. India and Berkley shoved Ellie into the fire pit, squirted lighter fluid on her, and tossed in a lit match.

Whoosh. Ellie went up in a ball of flames.

"Get down!" Natalie screamed, punching her way out of the brush and stumbling into the clearing. "Get down on the ground!"

Ellie was flailing around in the fire pit, screaming, while India and Berkley stood transfixed, their eyes sparkling with malevolence, their mouths twisted with insane glee.

"Help!" Ellie shrieked—her jacket on fire. Hair on fire.

"Drop and roll!" Natalie barreled toward the fire pit and tackled her niece around the middle, knocking them both to the ground. She ate a mouthful of dirt and banged her head against one of the blackened stones. She flung herself on top of Ellie and rolled her around in the dirt. She didn't stop until she'd beaten every last flickering flame out with her fists.

Ellie lay dazed, in shock. Smoke wafting up from her jacket.

Filled with incoherent rage, Natalie stood up and drew her weapon. "You're under arrest. Both of you. Don't move!"

India dropped the lighter fluid on the ground. Berkley dropped the matches.

"Put your hands up where I can see them."

They raised their shaky, skinny arms.

"Please don't hurt us!" India begged.

"Get down on the ground. Now!"

They looked at each other feverishly before finally complying.

Natalie got on her radio and called for backup and an ambulance. Then she tucked her weapon into its holster and knelt on the ground next to Ellie, who was moaning and rocking her head back and forth. There were pine needles in her hair.

"Don't leave me . . ." she said, gasping in agonizing pain.

"It's okay," Natalie whispered, terrified for her. "You're going to be okay."

Ellie's pupils were dilated. She was panting rapidly.

Natalie allowed herself to take a sharp breath, and the smell of burnt flesh scorched her nose. "Stay awake, Ellie. Come on." *Clammy skin. Shallow breathing. Going into shock. Oh God, please be okay.*

Ellie struggled to sit up, but it hurt so much to move that she grimaced.

"It's okay. Lie still. Help is on the way," Natalie promised.

There was a shuffling sound behind her as India and Berkley got to their feet. Instinctively sensing Natalie wouldn't chase them, not while Ellie's life was in danger, the girls fled into the woods, shrills of drunken laughter trailing after them.

Natalie leapt to her feet, reaching for her gun, a stark fury animating her limbs. "Come back!" she shouted, but it was pointless. What was she going to do—shoot them? Her father used to take her down to the firing range and teach her how to cock the hammer and pull the trigger. They'd spent many afternoons together, taking out targets. *Bam.* Rule number one—never fire your weapon unless your life is in danger. Restraint was necessary. Never use brute force. *Don't make it harder for the next man in blue.* So far, Natalie had been lucky. She hadn't fired a single shot in the field—not even the time she had caught a bullet in her vest during a SWAT response to a botched robbery. She'd always managed to deescalate the situation through dialogue but, realistically, at some point it would become necessary. She secretly dreaded that moment.

Now she holstered her weapon and put out a BOLO with a description of the two girls, then attended to Ellie. "It's okay. You're safe now," she promised.

The girl burst into tears. "Why did they do this to me?" she sobbed.

Natalie hated to see her niece cry. It broke her heart. "Shh. It's okay," she said. "I'm right here."

Ellie groaned in pain. Part of her jacket had melted into her flesh, revealing patches of charred and smoking skin on her injured arm. "Aunt Natalie, don't leave me," she pleaded through gritted teeth.

"I'm not going anywhere."

"I can't stop shivering."

Natalie could feel her own heartbeat at the base of her throat. Wind in the trees. Sirens across the lake. "Hang in there, sweetie. The ambulance is on the way."

"I was trying to make things better between us," Ellie said with slowly unwinding focus. "I was trying to do the right thing. . . ."

"Everything's going to be okay, I promise," Natalie assured her, letting the sadness wash over her.

54

Ellie was rushed to acute care at Langston Memorial, her left arm swathed in seeping bandages. She had suffered second- and third-degree burns from the top of her left shoulder all the way down to her left wrist. Miraculously, the rest of her body, along with her left hand, had been spared.

The emergency personnel gave her drugs to blunt the pain, and now Ellie was so loaded up on painkillers she barely recognized her mother. Grace sat next to the hospital bed in the ICU, stroking her daughter's cheek.

Ellie opened her blood-riddled eyes. "Mom?"

"You're going to be okay," Grace said a little too quickly, trying to absorb all of Ellie's pain at once.

"Aunt Natalie?" Ellie said hoarsely. "Thanks for saving my life."

Natalie smiled back, all torn up inside—if only she'd arrived a few seconds earlier. "You're welcome," she said, brushing away a tear. She had a flash memory of two-year-old Ellie smiling happily in her crib, tiny hands clasping her tiny feet. First smile, first step, first word. First tragedy.

Way off in the distance, a TV set droned. Natalie took a moment to check her messages. A patrol car had stopped the girls heading out of town on Route 87. They were being booked and charged with assault and battery.

Soon the attending ER physician was back. Their time was almost up. They were going to prep Ellie for transportation to the burn unit in Albany. "How's the patient?" Dr. Mendez asked, securing a cotton cuff around her right arm.

"Better," Ellie said bravely.

Natalie listened to the dull pump of the inflation bulb and the snake-like hiss of the air-release valve as the doctor pressed his stethoscope to Ellie's chest to assess her heartbeats, in sync with the heart monitor's rhythmic blips.

"Is she going to be okay?" Grace asked.

"She's in guarded but stable condition," he answered, tearing off the Velcro strap and jotting a few notes on the clipboard. "Her left arm sustained most of the damage. Albany has a great burn unit. They can fix this. She was lucky. It could've been much worse."

"Mom?" Ellie whispered. "I'm sorry. For everything."

Grace shook her head. "There's nothing to be sorry about, sweetie."

"You're crying. Why are you crying?"

"Shh. Doesn't matter." Grace traced a finger down her daughter's velvety cheek and watched her fondly, the worry lines on her forehead beginning to soften. "Listen to me, Ellie. I love you so much."

"Love you, too, Mom."

"You make me proud every day." Grace brushed a veil of hair off Ellie's face. "Now get some rest."

The girl's eyes dragged shut.

Grace turned to Natalie and said, "We need to talk."

"Buy you a cup of coffee?"

"Sure."

They took an elevator car down to the hospital cafeteria. Tears rolled freely down Grace's face as the elevator descended.

"Hey, hey. Everything's going to be okay," Natalie reassured her. "You heard what the doctor said. They can fix this."

Her sister's teeth chattered involuntarily. She had a lost, terrified look—sweaty forehead, shallow breathing.

Natalie grew worried. "Grace?"

"I'm okay," she said, giving into waves of involuntary shuddering.

"What's wrong?"

She shook her head stubbornly. "Like you said, everything's going to be fine."

Downstairs in the brightly lit cafeteria, Natalie fetched herself a cup of coffee, while Grace grabbed a can of Coke.

"My one guilty pleasure lately," Grace muttered. "Sugar and caffeine in one brilliant package."

Natalie didn't respond. There was no click. No ah-ha moment. Just the dull thrumming of blood inside her skull.

"I've got this, Natalie." Grace rummaged through her big leather bag. "Oh, shit . . . did I forget my wallet at home?" She dumped everything out on a nearby table—lip balms, ballpoint pens, her phone charger, a tube of sunscreen, hand wipes, loose tampons, Tic Tacs, her car keys. Grace found her wallet, but among the spillage was something that made Natalie's heart go glacially still.

A vintage leather-bound pink diary with yellow daisies on the front cover.

Daisy's missing diary.

Grace suddenly went rigid, her stunned eyes acknowledging that something vital had passed between them. She set the Coke down on the countertop, grabbed her keys and took off, leaving the entire mess on the table.

"Grace? Where are you going? *Grace?*"

When Natalie realized she wasn't coming back, she shoved everything back in the leather bag and ran after her sister, her heart going supernova.

55

Natalie's hand grasped the railing as she circled down the concrete-and-steel stairwell, until she'd reached sublevel one of the hospital's enormous underground parking garage. She pushed open the metal door and shouted, "Grace! Wait up!"

She jogged past row after row of parked cars in search of her sister's Mini Cooper, but couldn't find it anywhere. She heard the screech of tires echoing throughout the cavernous space, and it took her a moment to realize Grace was gone.

She went bounding back up the stairs to level two and got in her Honda SUV, chucking Grace's leather bag in the backseat. She fumbled for her keys, gunned the engine, and backed out of the parking space, fear galvanizing her as she turned the wheel sharply through the descending levels. Something damp touched her psyche as she punched her ticket, paid the fare, and shot out of the garage.

Now where to?

Natalie dug her iPhone out of her bag and dialed Grace's number, but of course the ringtone began playing inside her own car. "Beautiful Day" by U2.

"Fuck!" She spotted a distant set of taillights taking a right onto Garland Drive—Grace's Mini Cooper. She followed the car along a series of back roads until she finally caught up with her sister, who was driving erratically through a residential neighborhood, red taillights dancing on the road ahead like a pair of drunken, blood-soaked eyes.

The night felt colossal and immense as she followed her through the countryside, snaking around corners and hitting potholes. They were heading for the eastern end of the lake, where the granite cliffs rose eighty feet or more. Natalie stubbornly dogged her sister's taillights down one pitch-dark meandering road after another. She caught her breath every time Grace swerved across the center line.

The Mini Cooper surged over the next hill, and Natalie floored the gas pedal, speeding after it and grinding up the incline. As soon as she'd crested the hill, she could see the accident down below. Grace had crashed into a tree.

Natalie roared downhill toward the scene, feeling her pulse in her neck, then hit the brakes and swerved onto the soft shoulder. She switched on her high beams, threw her elbow into the door panel, and got out. All she could hear was the muffled thundering of her own heart.

The Mini Cooper was wedged against a tree, hissing steam. The front end was crumpled. The back windshield was cracked. The doors were blown open, and things that'd once been inside the vehicle were strewn across the road.

"Grace?" She ran toward the wreckage and looked inside. It was empty. The interior smelled of burnt rubber. There was an old parking sticker on the windshield. The keys were in the ignition. She straightened up and looked around.

"Grace, where are you?" she called out.

Her sister was nowhere to be found. Stars glittered overhead. A throbbing pain began at the back of Natalie's head, like two fists hammering against her eyeballs.

"Grace?"

The wind caressed the moonlit trees. In front of her was the steeply wooded hillside that led up to Devil's Point. She heard a rush in the thickets midway up the hill—twigs cracking and popping. She stood very still, craning her neck toward the noise. Her sister was taking one of the hiking trails to the top of the cliffs.

"Grace?" she hollered. "Whatever's going on, we can deal with this."

No response.

"Grace? Answer me!"

Natalie stepped back and looked around for the trailhead. She spotted a road sign for Devil's Point ten yards away, grabbed her flashlight from the glove compartment, and jogged down the road. She took the overgrown trail into the woods, anguish gripping her. Willow had once humiliated Grace up there, many years ago—egging her on, pushing her into a dangerous situation. Now they were both in danger. Natalie dug her heels into the steep grade and it felt like running underwater.

Clouds were gathering overhead. Another storm was moving in. Natalie's legs burned on the rugged ascent. The trail wound treacherously through thick woods, past huge boulders, thorny thickets, and clusters of poison ivy. She shouldered her way up the hillside trail, adrenaline coursing through her veins, and braced herself for confrontation. Near tears, she shouted, "Grace, wait for me, okay? I'm coming!"

She kept her flashlight aimed at the undergrowth, avoiding pitfalls, while sweat poured down her face. She stepped gingerly over gnarled roots that grew across her path. As the wind picked up, blowing through the pitch pines with an eerie wail, she took a series of crude steps carved into the rock face all the way to the top, where the trail leveled off. Natalie stepped out onto an exposed granite ridge.

Grace was standing on the rocky overhang with a panoramic view of the lake. She was weeping silently, hugging her fleece jacket close.

Natalie's world froze. "Grace?" she whispered so as not to alarm her.

Her sister was balanced on the precarious overhang, just a few feet beyond which was a deadly plunge off the cliff. Grace's back was to the woods and her gaze was pinned on the lake—silently debating what to do next.

Natalie's stomach cramped. "I'm right behind you," she said. "Be careful."

Grace spun around.

"Be careful!"

Her sister looked like a specter—glassy eyes, a halo of golden, punked-out hair.

"Whatever happened," Natalie said, "we can figure it out together. Okay? But first, I need you to step away from the ledge, Grace. You're scaring me."

Her sister swayed a little. "You don't understand." Eyes pinwheeling. Labored breathing. "Bunny will talk. Lindsey will talk. They'll all talk."

Natalie struggled to comfort her, but words failed her. On the far side of the lake, trees feathered toward a darkening sky.

Grace shook her head. "It's so freaking ironic."

"What's ironic, Grace?" Natalie asked with a helpless look.

She brushed away the tears. "Nobody can keep a secret in this town. And yet, the four of us did. For years."

Everything thundered to a halt. "Grace. Step away from the ledge, okay?"

"And here's the weird part . . ."

"Grace, I'm serious. Take my hand."

"We all agreed . . . we had to stick together . . . we told ourselves we had a pact. A coven. A sisterhood."

"Stop talking," Natalie said heatedly. "Do you understand? Not another word."

Grace shook her head fiercely. She looked at Natalie as if she were already dead inside. "None of us said we should stop. Not a single one of us questioned what we were doing. Isn't that disgusting?"

"Grace, listen to me," Natalie pleaded. "Whatever you say can and will be used against you."

Grace shook her head violently. "Yeah, I get it. You want to protect me."

"It doesn't matter that I'm your sister . . . do you understand? Please stop talking. I'm advising you . . . you don't want to incriminate yourself."

Grace rested her fingers delicately on her forehead. "It felt like a dream. Lindsey went first . . . then we all took turns, while Willow screamed and tried to get away."

Natalie's arms flew up, trying to push away the words. Trying to find a way out of this nightmare. So tangled up in the revelation that any attempt to free herself would only make it worse, like a crow caught in a snare.

"I couldn't believe it was happening," Grace confessed. "Willow was lying on the ground, crying and trying to defend herself, and then . . . Lindsey handed me the knife and told me to do it. But I just couldn't. Do you believe me, Natalie? I couldn't do it. But Lindsey threatened me and said that if I didn't do it, they'd have to kill me, too. They'd stab us both. Me and Willow. So I did it. A fog came over me, and I thought, Oh God, is this really happening? I was stabbing my own sister. I was totally freaking out, and I stabbed her again and again. We were all screaming and yelling . . . We went ballistic."

Tears sprang to Natalie's eyes. "Shut the fuck up."

"We had it all planned. We tricked her into it. I begged and pleaded with Willow to drive me over to the farm that day. I made up some bullshit excuse . . . so we drove over there, and Lindsey, Daisy, and Bunny were all waiting. We surrounded her, and Lindsey hit her over the head with a log, and Willow went down. At the time, I remember thinking—why should she get everything, when I get nothing? That was stuck in my head. I hated her. But I wasn't alone, you see. We all hated her, because she was so fucking perfect and everybody loved her . . . all the guys wanted to fuck her. Gregg, Brandon, Justin, all of them. We couldn't compete. It made us sick. And so we hatched a plot. I didn't think I could cross that line, but it's much easier than you think. I'm not a bad person, Natalie—you know that. I don't know what happened to me that day . . . something cracked inside my head, and for the rest of my life I didn't want to believe it. I'd almost convinced myself Justin killed her. I can even picture it in my head. I told myself it was just a bad dream, you know? That we didn't really do it . . ."

Natalie's veins had filled with ice. "Grace . . . please. Say it isn't true. Tell me you're mixing things up in your head."

She hugged herself and gazed across the lake. "I've ruined everything, and I have no idea how it happened, because I've always followed the rules. But I must be bad, right? There must be something wrong with me, Natalie. Because look at all the grief I've caused. You don't know how many times I wished I could take it all back. But we went a little crazy that day. A little insane. I can't explain it. I've had to live with it for years now, and I just can't face it anymore. I've never been so scared in my life."

"That's okay," Natalie whispered. "I'm here."

"When it was over, we stood there with blood on our hands, blood on our raincoats," Grace said tonelessly. "We had to blame someone, so we made up a story about Willow breaking up with Justin—we chose him. I called him from Willow's phone and pretended to be her. I could mimic her voice perfectly. I told him to meet me at the farm in half an hour. Then we covered our tracks as best we could, and it was raining really hard by the time we left. We got rid of Willow's phone and threw the knife in the lake. Then we drove to Lindsey's house, since her mom wasn't home, and washed the blood off our raincoats and used bleach for the bottoms of our shoes. I'd learned a lot from Dad about covering up a crime. It wasn't just you who was listening."

Natalie stood in stunned silence.

"It feels like I've been living inside a nightmare for twenty years," Grace said. "It drove Bunny crazy—literally. It drew me closer to Daisy than ever. So close, she trusted me a thousand percent. Completely. Absolutely. This was our deepest, darkest secret. Our sisterhood. But then, everything fell apart when she got pregnant . . . because, fuck, it was horrible. She totally fell apart once she realized the baby was coming. She blamed herself for her previous miscarriages—she thought it was punishment for what we did to Willow. But this time, she told me, she couldn't live with the lies. She wasn't going to keep our secret anymore. She said . . . and this was her reasoning . . . she couldn't bring a child into the world without a clear conscience in front of God." Grace made a face. "Can you believe that? She was never a religious person. She and Brandon barely went to church. But now, all of a sudden, she wants to confess everything. She was going to tell her minister about it . . . to confess her sins to him."

"Grace, listen to me. We can figure this out. Come back to the car and let's talk."

"No, baby girl," Grace said sadly.

Tears sprang to Natalie's eyes. "Just come back with me . . . please."

"I tried talking her out of it—Daisy. I told her to let it go, but she wouldn't listen to reason," Grace went on, needing to unburden herself. "I couldn't believe my best friend was about to ruin everything. It had taken the four of us forever to get over it and put it behind us and build up our lives. But now, Daisy was going to destroy everything in a heartbeat and take the rest of us down with her. She was going to ruin everything, and I couldn't let that happen. I just couldn't. She told me her minster was a good guy, that he'd keep it confidential, but that wasn't her decision to make. It was supposed to be the four of us deciding together. This wasn't about me, it was about Ellie and Ellie's future. It was about our children and everything we'd built for ourselves in this town. I couldn't let her guilt-trip me into destroying my daughter's life. I had to stop her."

Natalie didn't dare move, fearing that the fragility of Grace's emotional state would disintegrate if she reacted in any way.

"It happened so fast," Grace whispered, deep lines of stress forming on her lovely face. "I didn't plan it that way. I went over to Daisy's house after school to talk her out of this crazy notion that somehow the truth was going to save her. I was convinced I could change her mind. I was on a mission. I was determined to save us all, no matter what . . . but then, before I knew it, she was dead." Grace gasped for breath, her hands balled into fists. "I'm so sorry, Natalie. I haven't slept in days, and my head's all messed up . . . but I'm not a cold-blooded monster. You know that, right?"

Natalie didn't know how to respond to any of this. She could barely remember who Grace was or what she used to represent—all the best parts of her. "You're my sister, and I love you," she said mechanically. "I'm here to help." Desperate now. "Please, Grace, step away from the ledge."

Grace shook her head. "I'm an average person. A normal, everyday teacher and mother, for God's sake. But now people are going to think I'm a terrible human being, and I can't live with that. I tried making up for it, Natalie. We all did—we tried to make amends. But with Daisy, I had no choice. She was going to ruin our lives. And that was something I couldn't allow."

Police sirens wailed in the distance, and Grace turned her head.

"Careful," Natalie said, trying to focus on getting them down off the cliff. The second she had the opportunity, Natalie would grab her and not let go.

"I did it for Ellie," Grace admitted. "I did it to protect her."

Natalie's insides hurt, a horrible sinking feeling. "Let's go sit in my car and talk things over. Next steps," she said gently. "I promise you, everything's going to be all right. I'll make sure of that."

Grace shook her head stubbornly.

"Please, just . . . take my hand."

"Listen to me. I love you, and you're going to be fine. Better than fine, Natalie. You're going to have an amazing life."

She saw the crazed determination in her sister's eyes and realized what she was up against. "No . . ."

"Promise me you'll take good care of her?"

Natalie inched forward. "I'm going to protect you both. Understand? I'm going to do what's best for you and Ellie. Trust me." She sprang into action, all hope vanishing. She lunged forward, but Grace fought back, fiercely lashing out and slamming her fist into Natalie's nose.

Despite the throbbing pain, Natalie grabbed her sister by the wrists, and the crumbling rock face gave out, and Grace went over the side of the cliff with a scream.

Natalie landed on her stomach, clinging to her sister's sweaty wrists and slowly sliding toward the edge. "Hang on! I've got you!"

"Let go!" Grace shrieked, freeing one of her hands and batting at Natalie's arms, then digging her nails into her sister's flesh. "Let me go!"

"Please," Natalie sobbed. "Don't give up!"

Grace fought ferociously to free herself with more strength than Natalie could've anticipated, swinging her body wildly against the side of the cliff and digging her nails so deep into the backs of Natalie's hands that they drew blood.

Natalie clung to her sister with every last ounce of willpower, stars exploding inside her skull, but the pull of gravity and the slipperiness of their combined sweat was too much. Terror burned through Natalie as she lost control, and Grace slipped out of her grasp. Natalie screamed and clutched at nothing, fingers grabbing air. She could sense her entire body fighting the pitch of the ledge as a stampede of gravel followed her sister over the edge, skipping and zinging out into the night.

Natalie lay flat on her stomach on the granite ledge, breathing hard and listening to the dull echoey sound of a body impacting rocks, then a splash, and then nothing.

"Grace? Grace?"

She could smell dirt up her nose. It burned whenever she inhaled. Her arms felt like stretched-out socks, pawing at nothing, molecules slipping through her fingers.

"Grace?"

She felt a searing pain and numbness bloom inside her chest as she leaned over the edge and stared down into the abyss. The lake at night, so cold and indifferent, was pitch-black, with just a dribble of moonlight splashed across its surface.

She strained to hear her sister's voice above the booming of her own heart. But there was nothing. No screams. No gasping for breath. No cries for help.

The slow withdrawal of all feeling. Shock.

Trembling. Struggling.

Everything thundered to a halt.

Natalie wanted a do-over.

Let's hit Replay. Let's rewind the tape.

But that was impossible.

Make the call. Call for help.

She got on her phone and said, "Send rescue units to Devil's Point. Get everybody down here. There's a body in the water."

She pushed back her fear and tried to figure out her next move. Dead silence below. No one could have survived a fall like that. It was time to act. Do something. Go back down the hillside and help coordinate the search-and-rescue teams. Talk to backup. Debrief Luke. Act like a professional. Behave like a cop.

But Natalie simply couldn't abandon the spot where her sister had once stood.

56

Natalie gazed at the starry sky and tried to remember who she was. She had lost her moorings. It was almost midnight, and the temperature had dropped in Burning Lake, New York. She felt a chill as she stooped to pick up a rock, but it crumbled in her hand. The child's game, Rock Paper Scissors, should have been called Water Rock Scissors. Water transformed rock over geologic time, breaking it down into tiny fragments and washing it away.

The lake was now grainy in the moonlight, so hauntingly beautiful it broke her mind. Nothing made sense. There were no answers. The water had taken something precious from her. Natalie stood on the crumbling limestone edge of the cliff, with the woods behind her, trees swaying in a cool breeze. Everything in Burning Lake was shaped by the relentless winds and the rippling water. Natalie felt so small by comparison.

If you dove from a great height, the water didn't soften the landing. It was like hitting a concrete wall. At Devil's Point, within seconds of being airborne, you might be speeding along at sixty miles per hour, and then, if you weren't perfectly aligned, your bones could fracture as you hit the surface of the lake. It didn't matter if you were a good swimmer or not. Cliff diving required great skill and a fearless attitude—feet first, arms by your sides, in a pencil-dive position. Even the slightest angle could kill you.

It was ridiculously dangerous.

It was disorienting.

If you survived the initial plunge into the dark water, you might sink deep into the murk and not know where you were. If the lake was cold, as it often was in April, you might feel an urge to gasp underwater. If you panicked, you could drown. If you got injured, you could drown, since it was impossible to swim with broken bones. The rocks could kill you.

Natalie made her way down the gently sloping cliffside and crouched on the bluffs overlooking the lake, searching for her sister's body below and waiting for the rescue teams to arrive. The night was filled with chaos and colored lights. Firefighters and rescue personnel had to cross the lake by boat to get to such a remote area, and that took precious time. Most of the emergency assistance came from the waterfront, not the bluffs, since a cliff rescue was too dangerous at night.

Rescue efforts included a helicopter with sweeping spotlights, noisy Zodiac boats, and a dive team in scuba gear. Red and blue beacons from the police vehicles strobed against the trees across the lake, creating freakish silhouettes. It was nearly three A.M. by the time Grace's body was pulled from the lake.

Natalie met Luke down on the waterfront, where he'd been supervising the rescue efforts. He put his arms around her for a moment, trying to reassure her, but she felt nothing, no emotion, not a flicker. A strobing red light hit the side of his concerned face. She could hear urgent voices, could sense frantic activity going on around her. A group of rescue workers were waiting patiently for her in the water.

She went over to the Zodiac boat that held her sister's body and dipped her hand into the water. It was shockingly cold. She withdrew her shivering fingers.

There were spirals of black in the olive-green water of the lake. A thin mist clung to the surface. It rolled over Grace's lifeless eyes and settled into her shock-white mouth, like a cup ready to receive the fading stars. She was so pale, you could count the veins on her delicate eyelids. Her nails were painted raspberry pink, and her pretty blond hair made paisley swirls over her bloodless cheeks.

The shock of it—the cold, sharp shock—jabbed at Natalie repeatedly, like a bone knife. The terror was hard to describe. She held Grace's freezing cold hand for as long as the rescue team would let her. She tried to undo what had happened. She tried to unpack and reassemble it. She willed her teeth to stop chattering while her mind spun around in circles, thinking it could reverse time.

You're police, her father once told her. *You can't afford self-pity.*

She released a choked sob, and then buttoned up tight.

Two portable klieg lights onshore lit the entire scene. This side of the lake was a designated swim area, with lifeguard towers, restrooms, and a boardwalk. The snack bar had been converted into a temporary command post. Members of the BLPD were out in force. Firemen from the surrounding towns, an ambulance crew, volunteer search-and-rescue organizations, and the New York DWW Forest Rangers had all come to help. The DWW had set up the dive rescue effort—Jimmy Marconi, Samuel, and the rest. They had pulled Grace's body out of the water, and now they waited patiently for her to release Grace's hand.

"You ready?" Jimmy asked softly, and Natalie nodded.

She could feel a growing weakness in her knees as she waded away from the boat, away from Grace. She caught her reflection in the rippling water.

One of the rescue workers was rinsing the mud off his hands. He had peeled down the top of his wet suit, revealing his muscular torso. His arms were bare, and she could see them reflected in the ruffling water. She blinked, unsure of what she was looking at. Two bare arms in the water's undulating surface. The man's left arm had a birthmark nestled in the fleshy inner elbow. A port-wine startled butterfly.

She looked up, up, up . . . all the way up. It was Samuel Winston. She'd never seen him out of his long-sleeved wet suit or his DWW vinyl jacket before. She'd never seen his bare arms. Back in college, during their one boring date, he'd worn a flannel shirt and peacoat, since it was early winter. Natalie hadn't bumped into him again until years later, when she was a rookie cop and he was a seasoned ranger.

Now Samuel gave her a genuinely sympathetic look and said, "I'm sorry for your loss, Natalie."

She stared at him. She'd known him for years, and yet, now that she looked at him, she realized what a complete stranger he was—medium-length brown hair, hazel eyes, approximately five eleven, athletic and fit, a good-looking married guy in his late thirties. His blue baseball cap bore the DWW logo.

Words floated through her tangled brain but she couldn't capture them quickly enough. Her thoughts were all twisted up inside her head. Her tongue felt dead. Her nostrils flared from the stench of a raccoon carcass, twenty-one years ago. Samuel's eyes were like a brilliant mist coalescing into two piercing points.

Some of the rangers were gathering up their gear—portable oxygen tanks, first aid kits, respiratory kits—while others slowly dragged the boat ashore. Now Samuel walked away from Natalie and headed for the water-front parking lot, while she stared after him. Like Joey used to say, *When all possibilities are eliminated, whatever remains is the answer.*

57

Natalie's mind turned into a murmuring creek as she followed the DWW ranger across the beachfront, keeping a safe distance between them. She passed several emergency crew members on the scene, as well as a handful of reporters talking into their microphones. Stray voices threaded through the air: "A number of drownings have taken place at Devil's Point over the years . . . could not be reached for comment . . . another unfortunate accident this year . . . the drowning victim was a local woman."

Samuel paused at the snack bar, and then glanced over his shoulder at Natalie, his eyes resting briefly on her face. He nodded respectfully. After speaking to someone inside the command post, he continued on his way up the beachfront toward the parking lot. His wet brown hair was the color of baking chocolate. He had a cocky swagger.

A tear slid down Natalie's expressionless face as she hurried past Luke.

"Natalie?" he said, stopping her. "Where are you going?"

"Home," she lied.

"Let's get a cup of coffee," he suggested gently.

She shook her head. "I've got to go." She strode past him up the beach, across the boardwalk, and toward the public parking lot.

Shock meant not enough oxygenated blood was circulating through the body. Symptoms included sweaty skin, a weak pulse, irregular breathing. Psychogenic shock was caused by emotional trauma, where the blood pooled away from the brain, causing dizziness and confusion. Natalie knew she was in psychogenic shock.

Fortunately, she'd parked her car in a poorly lit corner of the lot. She made sure Samuel didn't see her as she unlocked the door and got inside. She sat for a minute, cradling her head. No tears. All thoughts gone. She was on autopilot. She inserted the key in the ignition and started the engine. She waited in a mental fog.

Samuel was loading his equipment into a weathered white pickup truck. He got in and started the engine. The mud-spattered pickup shuddered and died. "Damn. Come on." He tried again.

Natalie could hear tinny voices coming from his sputtering radio.

He peeled away in a spurt of gravel.

She could feel her irregular pulse at the base of her throat as she stepped on the gas and cautiously followed. How you began a moving surveillance was crucial. You were supposed to keep a fair distance between yourself and the subject, but you couldn't fall too far behind, or else you might lose him. Surveillance by automobile was tough in any city, but way out here in the boonies, only an idiot wouldn't notice another car following them on such sparsely traveled country roads. Natalie would have to stay sharp. She'd have to keep several hundred yards between herself and the pickup at all times if she wanted to remain undetected.

The white pickup kept rolling through the stop signs. She tried to keep one or two vehicles between them whenever she could. The roads were familiar, but the woods always looked different at night. Dark clouds were beginning to congregate overhead, creating welts and bruises in the moonlit sky.

Now the ranger took a left. Natalie took a left.

He turned onto I-87. She turned onto I-87.

She'd taken this road out of town how many times? She shuddered. She understood what she was doing—pursuing a deeply disturbed individual while she was in shock. There was nothing chaining her to reality anymore. She had no center. Her father once told her, "That's what being a detective is all about. You search for a grain of sand in the Sahara Desert. As the facts pile up, it's only a matter of time before the case collapses inward and the truth is revealed."

Natalie radioed Dispatch. "I need a license ID."

"Okay, shoot."

She rattled it off.

Five minutes later, the BLPD dispatcher came on and said, "Belongs to Samuel H. Winston, New York DWW Forest Ranger." He gave her a home address.

"What's the middle initial stand for?" she asked.

A short pause. "Hawke with an *e*."

"Thanks." She planted the mike.

Samuel Hawke Winston. *What the hawk eats.*

A strange feeling of disorientation and nausea came over her, fueled by sheer naked terror. She saw Grace's unseeing eyes. She saw the boy crouched on the bank of the stream, poking the dead raccoon's swollen belly, and the pus-filled intestines gushing out. She saw Daisy dead in a pool of blood. The smooth oblong bones of her sister's legs, kicking as she swam in the high school pool. Grace drowning in a swirl of bubbles, unable to breathe. Natalie saw her entire life in a flash of stunning emotion, but then it faded just as quickly, an ember winking out.

The pickup's taillights shimmered distantly in the smothering darkness as Samuel Hawke Winston turned north. The Adirondack Mountains were a protected area, consisting of six million acres, which included two thousand miles of hiking trails, three thousand lakes, and more than a thousand rivers. People got lost hiking in these mountains all the time. There were boating accidents in the rivers and lakes. The Adirondack Park, which was larger than Yellowstone and the Grand Canyon combined, was maintained by the New York State Department of Wetlands and Woodlands. The Division of Forest Protection had approximately 134 forest rangers, most patrolling in the Adirondacks and Catskills. They drilled for all types of missions. They responded to hundreds of missing-persons incidents in the parks and forests each year. On average, three hundred individuals were lost or injured on state lands and required an emergency response. The DWW utilized thermal-imaging equipment, search dogs, patrol vessels, all-terrain vehicles, snowmobiles, and a helicopter to augment their rescue efforts. Each ranger had a geographic territory he was responsible for.

Being a ranger was a 24-7, 365-days-a-year job. You were on-call for fires, missing persons, injured or trapped visitors, wounded animals, and any other emergency situation that fell within the park's jurisdiction. Samuel was one of many brave men she'd known for years, exchanging platitudes in the most dire of circumstances. He would've had extensive training in wilderness first aid, law enforcement, emergency medicine, and other specialized fields. He was required to maintain his Emergency Medical Responders certification and participate in high-angle rescue, swift-water rescue, and dive rescues. Because of the frequency of campfires in the parklands, he was also trained in wildland firefighting, as well as structural firefighting. Rangers at the DWW were jacks-of-all-trades. She'd once considered joining their ranks herself.

The roads were narrow and curving. Natalie drove along in silence, but there was a rush-roar sound in her ears. They were twisting through the foothills now, moonlight seeping through the heavy cloud cover. Up. Down. Gliding through the turns.

They passed the exit to Thaddeus Falls—Samuel's hometown, according to the dispatcher. But he ignored the exit. When they passed the next exit, Natalie realized he wasn't going home.

There were more lakes farther north. It was chillier up here. The farther north you went, the longer winter dragged on. Many of the rustic cottages were empty. There were lots of arts-and-crafts-style lodges and vacancy signs. After several more miles, the white pickup took a one-way street, and Natalie had to find a parallel road so Samuel wouldn't suspect he was being followed.

After a few minutes she panicked, thinking she'd lost him. She drove around in circles before spotting the white pickup again at a gas station.

Natalie kept on driving another fifty yards or so, then pulled over to the side of the road, where she picked up her phone and did an online search for the DWW website, but there was no employee information available. Next she found Samuel Winston's Facebook page. He was certified in EMT, underwater recovery, high-angle rescue, and public-safety diving by Dive Rescue International. He'd been awarded for his rescue efforts, involving everything from boating accidents and plane crashes to accidental drownings. He was married with two children. The pictures of him posing with his lovely family were Instagramworthy.

Her heart fluttered as she made an illegal U-turn and doubled back. Her fury and outrage were stuck in her throat like a handful of sand. She didn't want to lose him. As she approached the gas station, Samuel did her a favor by pulling out well in front of her and heading in the same direction she was going. She followed him for half a dozen blocks before he took a right onto Mountain Pass Avenue, the town's main artery. She kept a good amount of space between them, while he continued his ascent through the foothills. When the white pickup truck turned north onto a little traveled road, she switched off her headlights and followed him for many more miles into the woods.

58

Drizzle. **Gray country** roads.
Houses. Kids' tricycles.
Cornfields. Dilapidated silos. Rolling hills.

Rain scrabbling against her windshield. The storm had swooped in swiftly. Natalie turned her wipers on. There was static on the radio.

She listened to the rain pounding on the roof of the car. A hollow sound. Too much rain. The rivers would flood. The lakes would rise.

Exhaustion had taken hold. She was lost. Buried alive under layers of grief—some old, some new. Now the white pickup turned down an unmarked road, and Natalie couldn't spot any street signs. She didn't know where they were. Her senses grew heightened. There was barely any traffic at this hour: 3:45 A.M.

The hardest part of any surveillance was remaining invisible. Natalie pulled over to the side of the road and parked. It was dark out, a good thing. The darker the better. She hunkered down and waited, until she was sure it was okay to proceed.

She sat trembling with inner tension, idling on the soft shoulder while she watched the truck heading down the two-lane road and turning left onto a driveway between two stone gateposts, KEEP OUT signs posted on either side of the entrance.

She let another minute or two pass before she drove toward the stone gateposts, lights off, and paused in front of the driveway. It went up a steep hill into pitch blackness. No house lights up there, with thick woods all around. She drove for twenty more yards before pulling over to the side of the road and parking. The car squeaked to a jerky stop.

She phoned Luke.

"Hello?" he answered groggily.

"Hey, it's me."

She could sense the tension in his voice. "Natalie, what's up?"

"I found him."

"What's that?"

"I found the man with the birthmark on his arm. The butterfly."

Long pause. She could hear him breathing into the receiver.

"Where are you?" Luke asked.

"Up north."

"Where up north, Natalie?"

"I'm not sure," she said. "But I found him."

"Turn around and come home, okay? We can follow up in the morning."

"Luke?" she said. "I know I'm in shock. Emotional shock. I understand I may not be acting in my own best interests right now. That I'm all over the place. But I have to see what he's up to. Because I know it's him, beyond a shadow of a doubt. No one else has that birthmark. It's Samuel Winston. His full name is Samuel Hawke Winston, as in 'What the hawk eats.' He has a wife and kids in Thaddeus Falls . . . but for some reason, he didn't go home tonight. He drove farther north, and that's where I am now."

"Natalie . . ."

She hung up.

A few moments later, her phone buzzed. It was Luke again. She redirected the call to voice mail and sat in her car, trying to muster up the courage to act. She listened to the hum of the engine. The woods used to make her feel protected. But that was an illusion. Nobody was safe. Not really.

Natalie's father used to say *A secret is like a magic mirror, with endless layers of illusion. What you assume to be fact isn't always real.*

What was real? She didn't have any answers. The world was a thousand shades of gray. She knew what she'd been trained to do. She'd been trained to set aside her emotions in the heat of the moment and follow procedure. But the heat of this moment was burning her insides.

Natalie could feel her fright at the base of her throat. *Boom, boom, boom.* "Reactance" was a psychological term used for children who did the opposite of whatever they were told. Psychiatrists would try to break a child's reactance by using reverse psychology. *Go ahead and do it. You have my permission.*

Natalie told herself that. *Go ahead and do it.*

She hoped it would have the opposite effect.

But it didn't.

She turned off her ticking engine, got out of the car, and looked at the sky. The rain was coming down in a steady downpour. The moon had vanished behind the roiling clouds. The higher you looked, the more frenetic the air became—a swirling, frenzied fury. She heard a few high-pitched cries—a squall of birds swooping underneath the storm clouds.

Thunder rumbled. She pulled up the hood of her jacket and shivered all over, eyes going wide in the dark. Fear flickering in her heart. She headed for the old stone gateposts, cracked and in disrepair. She stood at the entryway and gazed up the driveway into a charred nothingness. A wet wind blew through trees. The rusty old mailbox had a name on it—HAWKE. Listening to her own panicky breathing, she started up the driveway on foot, fright bubbling up her spine.

59

At the top of the hill was a ramshackle Victorian, eerie as a dream. Lots of gables and chimneys, with a whimsical roofline, like something out of a demented fairy tale. The porch light was on. There were shade trees on the front lawn, and the gutters were clogged with leaves. Half the shingles needed replacing. She noticed the dry rot above the window frames, where the paint was wrinkled and alligatored. A trickle of sweat zigzagged down her neck and between her breasts.

Inside the house, a woman screamed.

One piercing shriek.

It stopped abruptly, like a faucet shutting off. Natalie's heart stopped with it.

She unstrapped her holster and drew her weapon. Wind chimes dangled on the front porch, creating a twinkly, carnival-like sound. The front yard was an obstacle course of Havahart traps. The night grew suffocatingly close. She glanced back down the driveway, where Samuel had parked his white pickup truck, leaving crisscrossing tracks in the dirt. Ferns grew deep on either side of the road, and all around the property were the towering, impenetrable woods.

All of a sudden, the woman screamed again. It was terrifying. A succession of tortured shrieks tunneled through Natalie, and she gripped her gun and approached the house.

Lightning flashed—so bright, it dazzled her eyes—and the clouds released a stinging rain. She took the walkway toward the porch, hurried up the steps, and tested the front door. Locked.

She followed the sagging wraparound porch around the side of the house and lingered in the shadows. The screaming stopped. The backyard was cluttered with junk—broken appliances and spring traps made of netting. Natalie had seen these traps before. They were meant for larger species of birds. *What the hawk eats.* Samuel Hawke. Serial killer.

She gripped her gun while beads of rain trickled into her eyes. Twenty yards or so away, in the backyard, was a small barn. The double doors were open. She could see a figure moving around inside, rummaging through an older-model truck, dinged and spattered with mud.

Natalie considered her options. The screen door at the back of the house stood open. Should she take a chance? She peered into the depths of the barn, where Samuel was poking around in the flatbed, hunting for something. He pushed a spine board aside and dug deeper into the flatbed. He picked up a cervical collar and tossed it aside.

She tried to gauge the distance between where she stood on the porch and the back door, primed to make a run for it, when all of a sudden, Samuel abandoned the search and, with a frustrated grunt, walked out of the barn. He unzipped his pants and peed in the weeds. Piss, shake, tuck, zip.

She ducked down behind the wooden railing while he tilted his face toward the sky and basked in a chill blast of downpour. He was dressed in jeans, white athletic shoes, and a blue vinyl windbreaker. His chest was bare. His ears were small and as curved as seashells.

Natalie fought off a burning sense of outrage as she withdrew into the shadows. Samuel turned and hurried up the back steps into the house, moving with energy and purpose. The screen door bumped shut behind him, but didn't close completely. He'd left it unlocked. Maybe he was coming back soon?

She could smell the animal life in the folds and hollows. The dull green bayberry bushes rustled in the wind. Somewhere in all that lightning-dappled darkness, she could hear a woman whimpering and moaning.

Natalie took a chance and approached the back door. Another lightning strike outlined the bones of the house, good bones, fallen to ruin . . . and then came silence, one Mississippi, two Mississippi, three Mississippi . . . and *kaboom*. Another terrible clap of thunder. She looked up at the second story, and a light at the end of the hallway blinked on.

The rain sounds on the gabled roof were sublime—a sustained orchestral unraveling, accompanied by a flutelike rattling through the gutters, funnels of rainwater pouring through the spouts and soaking into the yard, eroding the soil and exposing the wet round rocks and wriggling earthworms. She hurried up the cracked walkway, slate slabs broken or missing. The splintery wooden steps sighed underneath her weight. She stood on the worn welcome mat and nudged the door open. She could smell the dry rot in the back hallway.

Natalie entered the kitchen, where the breakfast table was cluttered with dirty dishes and empty wine bottles. The room smelled of wet insulation and moldy leftovers. There were stacks of old photo albums, corroded kitchen appliances, eight-track tapes, and a pile of raw meat on a chipped white plate—tiny bloody hearts, livers, and intestines, a rodent's or bird's innards. She suppressed her gag reflex, steadied her gun, and moved on.

Natalie brushed past the chalky wall, turned the corner, and pushed through a door. Inside the laundry room was a bucket and mop on the floor, next to a container of bleach. There were greasy tools on top of the washing machine—an old wrench, a rusty screwdriver, a dark-stained hammer.

She moved into the living room, where pale blocks of color dotted the walls where family pictures used to hang. It was chilly in here. The carpet's padding was rotten beneath the old weave. A dusty red paper lantern dangled from the center of the ceiling, and the warped wooden shelves held an accumulation of mementos from long-ago family trips to the seashore.

Natalie could hear movement upstairs. The floorboards creaked, and she stood very still, fighting an exquisite urge to flee. Let someone else handle it. Let somebody else be a hero. Like Joey used to say, *Things start out easy, but they always get hard.*

But Natalie knew—it was time to push through the hardness.

The place was so void of life, she felt like a ghost.

The clang of old pipes. The clicking of the radiators.

A china cabinet. A credenza. A musty old sofa. Quaint, prissy choices.

The house was so old, it had baked for more than a hundred summers; it had frozen for a hundred winters; now it smelled of moldering husks and dead insects.

A grandmotherly house. Outdated and creepy as hell.

A pile of papers. She leafed through them. The handwriting was illegible. It looked like some sort of bizarre, rambling confession. On every page were hundreds of tiny, inscrutable words, along with drawings of birds, drawings of maps, hieroglyphics. Signs of hypergraphia.

A loud burst of music came from upstairs, and Natalie shuddered. Everything slowed way down. Her feet became lead weights. Bass, drums, guitars, synthesizer. Edgy, mesmerizing music.

The floorboards cracked overhead, and Natalie glanced up, her stomach contracting powerfully. A lone fly buzzed around her ears, and she brushed it away, then readjusted her grip on her gun. Her father once said, *You have to look underneath. Sometimes worms crawl out.* She sucked in her gut and dug deeper. She immersed herself in her father's bravery and kept going.

The parlor was the worst. Melting candlewax. Ceramic figurines flaked with dust. Elderberry-wine-stained doilies. Graffiti on the walls—satanic horns, 666, pentagrams. A fussiness to the décor. A fastidiousness combined with psychosis.

An old sewing machine clutched an accordion of blue fabric, and the windowsills displayed a variety of dead insects. And then—the birds. Dead crows crudely preserved. Whoever the taxidermist was, he'd arranged the beady-eyed creatures into bizarre poses—crucifixions, mummifications, birds stuck with pins, wrapped in barbed wire, soaking in huge vats of liquid.

Rain hammered the roof and bled down the windowpanes.

Inside the bathroom, just off the front hall—an explosion of peach tiles. A square, utilitarian room. Natalie reached for the floral shower curtain and swept it aside.

A bathtub ringed with rust or worse. A foul smell. Quicklime. The stench of acid attacking flesh. The coppery smell of blood.

Now the footsteps thumped across the ceiling, and she looked up. Wooden drawers opened and closed. More footsteps. And then . . .

Upstairs, a door creaked like the opening of a tomb.

60

Natalie waited at the bottom of the stairs and listened. Samuel hurried down the hallway. He opened a door. She could hear two voices now—one male, one female. The female was pleading. Samuel was gruff. A short discussion.

Then silence.

A wave of despair crashed over Natalie. The corners of everything were beginning to blur. She waited until Samuel had gone back to his room at the end of the hall and closed the door.

The wooden stairs were narrow and slippery. The treads were worn to a dangerous smoothness. She was desperate not to make a sound. Every creak, every squeak, gave her pause.

She finally made it to the top and faltered on the landing. There were four closed doors to chose from. Samuel's room was down at the other end of the hall, loud music pounding behind the door.

Natalie had three choices left. She reached for the nearest one. The metal knob had a ding in it. She swung the door open and stepped inside, aiming her gun at the shadows.

The lights were off. The blinds were drawn. She let her eyes adjust to the darkness. A narrow bed. A recliner chair. Faded tulips on the wallpaper. A chipped rocking horse. Everything thick with dust.

Wrong room. She gently closed the door behind her and faced the room across the hall. Her heart had parked itself in her throat. She opened the door and stepped inside.

The lights were on. Bed, bureau, desk. A lamp in one corner cast a pale glow. Natalie shook her head, disgusted by the fetid, cloying odor of the room.

Behind the bed, something stirred on the floor. She moved cautiously into the room. The poor woman was collared to the wall, her head wrapped entirely in duct tape. Mummified, except for a slit for her eyes and a slit for her mouth. She struggled to sit up. She wore a lavender track suit with white geometric patterns. Her bare feet had superficial cuts and sores on them. The wounds didn't penetrate deeply. The bleeding had slowed, and the blood loss was not enough to cause shock.

"I'm here to help," Natalie whispered. "You're going to be okay."

The victim's bloodstained hands were splayed across the floor. Her swollen fingers looked like jointed sausages. The leather collar around her neck had left blisters on her skin. There were spots of dried blood on her tracksuit.

The room was chilly. Natalie's breath steamed ahead of her.

Now the lights flickered. The music was so loud, the floorboards were vibrating to the bass line. *Thud, thud, thud.*

Natalie knelt down beside the woman and made a quick assessment: She was dehydrated, had a rapid pulse and respirations, but otherwise appeared to be okay. She could survive this. Just as long as Natalie could get them out quickly and safely.

"My name is Natalie," she said. "I'm going to get you out of here, okay?"

The woman struggled to speak. She attempted to sit up again, but collapsed in pain and muscle weakness. She curled up on the floor and looked at Natalie through the eye slits in the duct tape. Natalie could see her glinting terror and sat on her rising panic. Fear was contagious. Fear could be paralyzing.

"Shh. He's listening," the woman hissed. "The Devil can hear you!"

"Bunny?" Natalie breathed. "Is that you?"

61

Something stirred in the room down the hall. A rustle. A thump. Now a door cracked open, the music grew louder, and heavy footsteps pounded down the hallway.

"Shh. Don't move," Natalie whispered to Bunny.

She stood up and braced herself, aiming her gun at the door.

The footsteps stopped just outside the door.

Natalie tapped the base of her magazine with the heel of her hand to make sure it was fully seated before raising the gun to eye level. She placed her finger on the trigger and focused on the front sight.

The doorknob turned slowly.

"Go away!" Bunny shouted.

The doorknob stopped turning.

Natalie felt a numbness like sand trickling through her body as she steadied her aim and aligned the intended target in her front and rear sights.

"Go away, or she'll shoot you in the head!" Bunny cried.

Natalie cringed and took a step forward, reaching for the door before Samuel could get away, but right at that instant, the door shot open as if a bulldozer had knocked it down, and Samuel burst into the room swinging a baseball bat. He knocked the weapon out of her hands, and her right wrist snapped as the gun misfired. He slammed the bat into her left shoulder, and the pain registered on her optic nerves. Cascades of white flashes. She cried out as she flew backward, gun skidding across the room and sliding under the night table. She landed hard on the floor, all the wind knocked out of her lungs.

Samuel was naked from the waist up. He wore jeans, no shoes, and a mask made out of a knotted pair of women's pantyhose—the old-fashioned, polyester kind. You could see his eyes through a slit in the mask. His toes gripped the warped floorboards and a sheen of perspiration clung to his torso.

Natalie cringed at the sight of his birthmark—a butterfly in midflight.

"*You?* What are you doing here?" Samuel asked, his strange gaze flitting across her face.

He seemed very far away, hovering somewhere on the edge of the universe. A hawk, circling high in the sky, looking down at her . . . waiting to snatch her life away.

Natalie's eyes burned. Her left shoulder throbbed. Her right hand felt broken. A gasp sprang from her solar plexus as she withstood the gravitational pull of fear.

"Don't hurt me!" The air became electrified with Bunny's screams as she strained against her chains, trying to break free.

Samuel turned toward his captive and raised the bat threateningly. "I asked you politely to stop screaming. Didn't I?"

Bunny cowered with animal fright.

Natalie scrambled for her gun, clawing across the floor and scooping it up, ignoring the pain in her right hand. She used her left hand to sight down the barrel, aiming her weapon center-mass. It took every ounce of strength she had left not to blow him away. "Drop the bat, Samuel," she said, steadying her nerves. "Raise your hands where I can see them. Slowly."

He turned in silhouette, his head backlit by the corner lamp.

"Raise your hands in the air," she commanded. "Nice and easy."

He studied her through the eerie eyeholes of the pantyhose mask.

"Drop the bat," she demanded. "I don't want to shoot you." *What a good liar.* "Drop the bat and raise your hands—slowly."

He clutched the bat in both hands and shook his head. "You followed me here?"

"Put it down," she repeated. "Now."

His head swayed ever so slightly on his muscular neck. Breathing calmly, he told her, "You followed me here from the lake, and I'd like to know why."

She stuck to the script. "Put your hands in the air—now!"

"How did you find out about this place? About me?"

She swallowed hard and said, "Your birthmark."

He glanced at his arm.

"You attacked me a long time ago in the woods. You had your T-shirt wrapped around your head so I couldn't see your face. But I noticed the birthmark."

"Oh. Okay. I understand now," he said in a measured way.

She could detect her own rapid pulse in the slight pendulum of her aim.

"I remember our date when you were in college. But I don't remember attacking you in the woods. When was this? There've been so many," he confessed. "It's hard to keep track."

She felt the muscles of her hands twitching from the strain. She recalled what her father had told her about firing her weapon in the line of duty. *It's not bragging rights. It's deeply troubling. Avoid it if at all possible.* She blinked the sweat out of her eyes.

"You shouldn't have come here," Samuel said. "This is not going to end well."

"Drop the bat," she insisted.

His eyes were raked with sadness—or a perfect imitation of human emotion. "I was the one who pulled your sister out of the lake tonight. Did you know that? She was stuck in the weeds. I had to tug her legs out of the eelgrass, but then she popped up, and I had her. I looked into her eyes," he said. "Have you ever done that, Natalie? Looked into their eyes?"

Her trembling lips betrayed her revulsion and fright.

"But you deal with dead bodies all the time in your line of work, don't you? What are you afraid of?"

"Get your hands in the air!" she shouted hoarsely.

"We all think we're going to live forever. Secretly, we all believe it." His outline was beginning to waver. "But then, once you realize you're going to die . . . once you accept your own mortality, that's the instant you become your true self."

Natalie's head filled with a crackling sound. Bright spots danced before her eyes. She was beginning to lose focus, his image snapping and shivering before her.

"Should I tell you what happens? When I look in their eyes?"

She felt like a bug you could flick away with your fingers.

"Their expression begins to change," Samuel said in a low, mesmerizing voice. "From dreaming to awake. From awake to terror. From terror to surrender. And as they take their last breath . . . they become who they truly are. The moment of transformation . . . is unimaginable."

Her sweaty finger twitched on the trigger. Her left hand was weaker than her right hand. Her aim was unsteady. She was afraid of him. It was obvious to both of them.

"Your sister was alive when I pulled her out of the lake," Samuel said in a trancelike cadence. "Her name was Grace, right? That's an elegant name. She barely had a pulse when I pulled her out of the reeds, but she was still breathing . . . I cradled her in my arms and helped her move on. I've helped a lot of people move on. She said she wanted to die. Some people believe that, right before you die, the last thing you see remains on your retina. And so, I'm sure, the last thing your sister ever saw was me."

Shoot him now.

"I helped her move on. I can help you move on, too, Natalie."

Shoot him now.

"The last thing you'll ever see," he said, taking a step forward, "will be me."

She jerked the trigger. Once. Twice.

Two startling flashes. Two explosive cracks.

Samuel took both rounds in the chest. His eyes bulged with disbelief, like a boy on a roller-coaster ride. The bat dropped out of his hands and clattered to the floor.

It took time for gravity to tug a one-hundred-and-ninety-pound human being to the ground. Samuel dropped to one knee, and then to the other. There was a terrible *thud* as he landed on his face, blood pooling from his chest and soaking into the threadbare rug.

Bunny screamed and tried to get away, the heavy chain clanking.

Natalie rolled the body over and felt for a pulse.

Samuel was staring at her, guzzling for air. The bullets had pierced his vital organs. Soon, his body would no longer be able to regulate the flow of blood to his brain. It would pool inside his sick and evil mind, starved for oxygen.

She rested her fingers on his throat.

A weak pulse.

He blinked the blood out of his eyelashes and said, "Look at me."

She drew back, repulsed beyond belief, her body shaking with resistance.

Samuel sucked in a breath. "Look into my eyes, Natalie."

A shudder ran through her. She shook her head and fought off a current of fear.

But he was relentless. "Look into my eyes. Go on. I dare you."

The temptation created a dull ache in her heart. She peered into his eyes, feeling something instant and powerful. His irises twisted like flies caught in a spiderweb. What she saw was nothing. A chilly force. A swirling emptiness. Whatever stared back at her wasn't human. It spun slowly on the edge of the known universe like a lone, barren planet.

Tears sprang to her eyes. She drew back.

Words formed bloody bubbles on his lips. "What did you see?" he asked.

"Nothing."

He stared at her like a possessed man. *The raccoon. The stick. The boy with the butterfly birthmark.* The memory was as organic as a jellyfish, alive and breathing liquidly, filling all the crevices of her consciousness with its poisonous tentacles.

He took his last breath without making a sound, shoulders jerking spasmodically, as if he had the hiccups. Then his body sagged and went perfectly still.

She touched his throat. No pulse.

Finally, it was over.

Dead. He was dead.

His blood pooled onto the floor and soaked into the rug.

Time slowed to a stop. Reality crumbled away.

Fury gripped her. She tried to shake him awake. "I saw nothing!" She dropped his head on the floor and could barely breathe, she was so full of outrage. She wanted to kill him all over again. She wanted to smash him to bits.

A horrible stillness descended.

The last thing he ever saw was her image carved on his retina.

She tried to find a path back to sanity.

The air grew dense and cold inside the room.

Sirens. A snap back to reality. Luke must've tracked her phone.

She stood up, grabbed a blanket off the bed, and wrapped it around Bunny's quivering shoulders.

Bunny reeled away. "He was gonna feed me to the crows!"

Through the window, Natalie saw red and blue lights strobing across the surrounding woods. Two officers got out of their cruiser and approached the house, signaling silently to each other. Luke had found her. She tried rearranging her thoughts in order, but it was useless.

Natalie felt like someone else. Crossing the line could do that to a person. She'd helped countless victims of car accidents, fires, rapes, and robberies. She'd seen how shock could rob people of their senses. Psychological trauma could cripple you.

She turned to face the dead body on the floor. Samuel's eyes were open, glazed and untroubled. Everything was broken inside her. She took a deep breath and began to cry.

EPILOGUE

By June, the TV crews were gone. The media circus had left town, and life had returned to normal.

Every night, Natalie secured the doors and windows before heading upstairs to bed. She checked to make sure her off-duty .45 was locked and loaded before slipping it into the creaky top drawer of her colonial nightstand. As soon as her head hit the pillow, she would relive those last few painful moments over again. In her dreams, she stretched out her arms and grabbed hold of her sister, trying to prevent the horrific from happening. In her dreams, Grace always jumped, no matter what, diving headlong into the silky water and swimming away like a fish, her golden hair coiling around her head. Scissor kicks and then long smooth strokes.

Ellie spent the next few months undergoing multiple operations to treat her injuries at the Albany burn unit, but her long-term prognosis was excellent. In July, she went to live with her father in Manhattan, and Natalie kept in touch with her daily. Whenever they spoke on the phone, Ellie's voice would rise, excitable and soft, as she relayed her new life with Dad. All was well. She was loved and in therapy. They rarely spoke about Grace, but when they did they did so in confused, hurt whispers.

Natalie couldn't stop thinking that she had failed them. It disturbed and vexed her. She understood that even if she'd managed to rescue Grace that night, she couldn't have saved her. Grace had carried a monstrous deformity inside her for years, and Natalie doubted she would ever come to terms with it. Grace had been an anchor in her life, the one person she could always depend on. Now that was completely torn away.

Lindsey and Bunny faced no official day of reckoning for what they'd done. Grace's confession was not admissible in a court of law. Bunny was declared incompetent to stand trial. Lindsey had friends in high places. She denied everything. Grace, Daisy, Lindsey, and Bunny were all minors at the time. Ultimately, the prosecutor declined to press charges.

Riley Skinner miraculously came out of his coma. There was no lasting damage, except for being held back a grade in school.

At the arbitration hearing, Brandon got to tell his side of the story, and the union stood firmly behind him. Brandon was disciplined and put on unpaid leave as punishment for his alcohol level being over the legal limit. It was determined, however, that the complaints filed against him were unfounded. After a slap on the wrist, he was given his old job back through arbitration. He was reinstated as detective, second grade. Some folks saw this as an injustice. In the end, Brandon was a free man—but a marked man. Dominic knew how to nurse a grudge.

Justin Fowler's attorney began compiling new evidence to present to the Board of Pardons and Paroles, convinced his client would be a free man by next year.

India Cochran and Berkley Auberdine were tried as juveniles and convicted of aggravated assault, since causing serious bodily harm was not enough to prove attempted murder. With credit for time served and good behavior, they could be out before their twenty-first birthdays.

Now the healing process was supposed to begin.

The parents of Burning Lake shook their heads and said, "I never thought it could happen here." Some blamed satanic cults, others blamed drugs and Hollywood violence. They gave their children curfews and drove them everywhere after school. They snooped around in their social media accounts and interrogated them about their friends.

Oddly enough, dogs still barked. The mail somehow got delivered. Kids still played in their front yards. Farmers went out to plow their fields. The shops were open for business. But nobody would ever forget the day when tragedy struck and normalcy was shattered. Somehow the town felt ruined.

As August gave way to September, the frost came early. Sooner than expected, the leaves turned and blazed. Flocks of migrating Canadian geese flew overhead, casting their trails of echoes.

By mid-September, the fiery trees ignited the lake, and the hills erupted with an unearthly array of crimson, orange, and gold. Wood smoke unraveled from the chimneys like gray yarn in skilled old hands. One day, Ellie and her father, Burke Guzman, came up from Manhattan and, together with Natalie, they rented a boat.

Burke was a diminutive, overgroomed man with exquisitely coifed hair and a rich baritone voice. Ellie adored him. She stood in the prow of the boat with Natalie, while the leading edge parted the water, creating everwidening ripples in its wake. It was a beautiful morning without any wind. The sun was about to rise over Devil's Point.

Natalie loved this time of day, when the landscape took on a special glow, sunlight reflecting off the hills and triggering memories of her nostalgia-soaked childhood. But an emotional disconnect kept her from remembering too hard.

The boat came to a slow stop in the middle of the lake, and the unexpected stillness made Natalie shiver. As the sun burned off the morning fog, steam rose from the lake, which reflected the flaming red woods all around them. This was the moment.

"Ready?" Natalie asked Ellie, who was silhouetted by the golden sun.

Ellie sang Grace's favorite song, "Beautiful Day" by U2. After she hit the final, quavering note, they opened the urn together and scooped out a handful of ashes, gritty as sand.

They released fistfuls into the lake. Down they went, into the murky depths.

Ellie reached into the urn again to scoop out more ashes, and a puff of wind blew some into her face, a fine dusting settling on her skin.

"Oh no," Natalie said, tears welling in her eyes, but Ellie brushed her concerns away.

"A kiss good-bye," she said with a sad smile.

Natalie wanted to hold on to this moment. She wanted to say something wise. Her eyes were full of dust and regret. Maybe silence was better. Forget the balloons. Forget the prayers and pictures. She couldn't outrun her memories, even though she was quick and strong. She couldn't outrun the shadows in the woods. Her recent journey had increased her craving for answers that were beyond her grasp.

One day, a long time ago, Natalie, Grace, and Willow had twirled wildly around to Alanis Morissette's "You Oughta Know," singing at the top of their lungs.

What should they know?

What did any of us know?

Death was like a secret. You could bury it deep underground, but it wouldn't stay buried for long. Eventually, our secrets—like old bones—had a way of knuckling out of the earth and into the sunlight. You had to make your peace with fate.

Ellie had brought fresh flowers with her, and now she dropped the de-stemmed white roses one by one into the water and said her final farewell.

White roses floated on the blazing red surface of the lake, as gentle waves lapped them away from the boat.

"You're free," Ellie whispered. "Like the wind and the water . . ."

Natalie joined in. "By air and earth and fire and rain, we will remember you."

These words were like tiny scarlet letters stitched onto Natalie's heart.

ACKNOWLEDGMENTS

Special thanks to:

My agent, Jill Marr, for her wise counsel, unwavering belief, and fearless guidance.

My brilliant editor, Alexandra Sehulster, for her razor-sharp perceptions, impassioned enthusiasm, and invigorating inspirations.

My rights manager, Andrea Cavallaro, for her drive and determination.

The impressive team at Minotaur Books, headed by publisher Andy Martin and associate publisher Kelley Ragland, including marketing manager Joe Brosnan, publicists Sarah Melnyk and Kayla Janas, team leader of marketing and publicity Paul Hochman, production editor John Morrone, cover designer David Rotstein, copy editor Sabrina Soares Roberts, and editorial assistant Mara Delgado-Sanchez.

The great Sandra Dijkstra, and the formidable crew at Sandra Dijkstra Literary Agency.

All my readers—without your support I wouldn't be able to do this.

My brother, Carter, for his profound advice and heartfelt encouragement.

My gifted husband, Doug, who has my back.